MAID FOR SUCCESS

THE MACBAINS BOOK 1

NAN DIXON

Kate MacBain, dubbed "the women who will never have kids," is focused on her future. She plans to be her father's successor in the family company despite her three brothers. She'll do whatever her parents ask, but cleaning houses in the Murphy's Maids subsidiary when she has her MBA? That's a punishment not a reward.

Composer **Alex Adamski's** creative well is dust dry. Since his divorce, he hasn't been able to finish his overdue sonata. Then a fiery housecleaner named Kate tells him he's a slob and jars him out of his slump.

Their chemistry is off the charts, but while Alex is thinking family and forever, Kate doesn't want anything to derail her climb to top — not even Alex.

Can he convince her there's more to life than being CEO?

PRAISE FOR NAN DIXON

CONNECTIONS

WOW! is the word that continually popped into my head while reading this story.

DISCOVERY

I am going to have a hard time finding another book as good as this one! I would have to say this was the best book I have read so far this year! If you like reading books that draw you in and don't let you go until it is finished with you then this book is for you!

HOW WE STARTED (novella)

Nan has given us characters that we can care about., with a story that pulls you in and never let's go.

EDGE OF FRIENDSHIP

A solid 5 star read (really more than that if I could!!!) … I was completely enchanted with this story. It had wonderful highs, while dropping into a dark and agony filled lows. I would find myself reading and re-reading many scenes as they were such so good that I was savoring each word. I was desperate to see how it would end but at the same time dreading for it to be over.

MAID FOR SUCCESS

Loved it. Thrilled to see this is a start of of a new series. I am eager to see what happens next in the family. The story flowed and kept me turning pages.

DANCE WITH ME
DANCE WITH ME by Nan Dixon is a heartfelt, emotional and well-written story that truly fits the description in the book —a journey of healing, hope and love.

STAINED GLASS HEARTS
STAINED GLASS HEARTS by Nan Dixon is simply absolutely incredible. It's one everyone MUST READ.

INVEST IN ME
I fell in love from the beginning and didn't want it to end. It has an excellent and spellbinding wonderful plot and in-depth characters.

SOUTHERN COMFORTS
…is a book about learning how to give and receive without any strings attached. It's about caring and trust and loyalty; and relying on those you love to help make your dreams come true. **RT TIMES - Page Turner**

THE OTHER TWIN
Nan Dixon will become a favorite author. Part of series but can read as a stand alone. Fun story that's hard to put down. "One more page...just another chapter…" until soon you've reached the end.
A complicated story that reflects the many threads of real life that so often includes knots of problems in addition to the gradual unraveling of past hurts when placed in the light of love and real caring. A story I couldn't put down.

UNDERCOVER WITH THE HEIRESS

So much more than a romance novel.
This was definitely a book I was not able to put down! I took the tablet with me everywhere! **Fabulous Brunette Reviews**

THROUGH A MAGNOLIA FILTER
…a heartwarming story that showcased the importance of family, following your dreams, and true love. I thoroughly enjoyed this tender heartwarming story. **LAS Reviewer**

A SAVANNAH CHRISTMAS WISH
FRESH PICK
…is a book that has you frolicking in gardens, battling storms and falling in love…A book of warmth and love. It will leave you smiling.

TO CATCH A THIEF
Not your everyday Contemporary genre, a little suspense, a little love and definitely entertaining… **Our Town Book Reviews**

A SAVANNAH CHRISTMAS WEDDING (novella)
Another winner. Love this series

For my Family

COPYRIGHT

Grinning Frog Press - APRIL 2022

Editor: Victoria Curran. Copy Editor: Judy Roth. Cover Design: Covers by Dana Lamothe of Designs by Dana

ONE

THE BELL ON THE DOOR CLANGED AS ALEX PULLED IT OPEN AND stepped inside. He took a deep breath and scanned the coffee shop. *Good.* Frederick wasn't here yet.

He ordered and took his coffee to a minuscule table, wedging his legs into the small space. He took his first sip and winced. Even the milk he'd added didn't soften the bitter taste. The only positive to his drink—it was hot.

The shop must have changed their supplier since he and Frederick had met here last. Back when he'd made music. Back when life had been easy.

Before.

The bell on the door clanged again, a dissonant grating sound. Frederick came in, saw Alex and waved as he headed to the counter.

Alex traced patterns in the tabletop. He didn't want to disappoint his friend. He didn't want to live through the next thirty minutes of confession time. Only priests should hear confessions.

"Alex." Frederick smiled, holding out his hand.

"Frederick." Alex stood, banging his thighs into the table. "Good to see you," he lied.

"How are you? It's been ages since we talked." Frederick took off his suit jacket and pulled a packet of papers from the inside pocket.

Alex swallowed. It was the contract he'd signed with the Saint Paul Chamber Orchestra almost eighteen months ago. Frederick let it drop to the table, and it thumped down like a big fat elephant.

"I'm fine." *Not really.* "Let's skip the small talk. It's not done."

His friend tasted his coffee and closed his eyes. "This is the best coffee in town."

Alex took a sip, forcing himself to swallow. Nope. Still bitter. "I don't know if the sonata will ever be done."

Sympathy filled Frederick's eyes. "What I've heard is wonderful."

"Yeah." He'd completed one movement before the magic had died. "I keep trying. It's just …"

All he'd written lately were commercial jingles. At least he tried. He hadn't finished any.

"How long has it been since your divorce was final?" Frederick asked.

"About a year." Fourteen months, twenty days, two hours and a handful of minutes.

A small smile creased his friend's face. "That long."

Frederick's smile evaporated. Able to control a full orchestra with a searing glare, his expression turned serious. "The orchestra took a risk when they commissioned the sonata."

"I know." Alex's jaw ached from clenching his teeth.

"You need to work. You're too brilliant to let a failed marriage ruin your career."

"I'm trying." Alex's ex-wife had not only destroyed their

marriage and the life they'd created, but her actions had sucked out every note and ounce of his creativity.

"I can buy you three more months, but that's it. I'm sorry." Compassion filled Frederick's voice. "That's as long as I can keep the board of directors off your back."

Alex clenched his mug. He'd never let anyone down before, not when it came to his music.

When he'd taken the grant, ideas had poured out of him. He'd barely slept, needing to get the notes written. His music had been joy-filled.

After his world imploded, he'd had trouble writing meaningless dribble.

"Thanks for getting me the extra time." Alex looked into his friend's eyes.

"I'll send the contract update to Aubrey," Frederick said.

"Sure." Maybe his business manager would stop leaving reminder messages about the deadline for a month or two.

"I'll get it done." The lie was as bitter in his mouth as the cold coffee he swallowed.

"YOU WANT ME TO CLEAN ... be a maid?" Kate cringed at the slight screech in her voice. She pushed down the panic trying to burst out.

Her mother's eyes flashed, a clear warning Kate was on a tightrope without a net. "Is cleaning beneath you?"

"I didn't mean it that way." She would never insult the company her mother had started. "But ... I have an MBA." Kate pressed her palms against the conference table that dominated a corner of Dad's office. "My salary is four times what we pay the cleaning crew. Our profit margin will take a hit."

"Katie." Her father leaned a hip against the granite top of his desk. "All your brothers did the same."

She was twenty-nine. When would her family call her Kate, not *Katie*? "My brothers *never* cleaned houses. Hell, they never picked up their rooms."

"Language," her mother said sharply.

Her oldest brother, Michael, snorted and slumped deeper in his chair. She wanted to wipe the smug expression off his face. Why was Michael even in this meeting? Probably to witness her humiliation and report back to their two younger siblings.

Michael grinned. "I worked construction."

"In high school." She forced her lips into a neutral position, trying to keep from frowning. Why would her parents want her working as a company maid? As an account executive, she wined and dined clients. Her role didn't include cleaning their dinner plates.

"Your mother and I have already discussed this." Her father stalked over to the window, staring down on Minneapolis from his twentieth floor office. "If you expect another promotion, you need a better understanding of every branch of the company. That means not only dealing with the leasing clients, but also the Murphy's Maids clients."

"But …" Kate raised her hands in the air, pleading. "No one else cleaned. There must be another role I could perform. I don't have to scrub floors to understand what a maid does."

"Are you better than your mother?" Her father's voice boomed out.

Uh-oh. The volume of his voice might break his office windows.

"Your mother started Murphy's Maids when she was nineteen," Dad continued. "She worked nonstop *and* graduated with honors."

He moved behind Mom and rubbed her shoulders. She flashed him a grin that excluded Kate and her brother.

Her parents were exceptional. They'd built their own businesses. But shouldn't she be launching off their shoulders and not repeating their efforts?

"Are you better than your mother?" her father asked again.

"No. That's not what I'm saying, it's just …"

Mother turned and faced her. "What are you saying?"

"I want what's best for MacBain." Kate inhaled. Something was wrong with the building's HVAC. She couldn't get enough oxygen and her head was wonky. "Is my cleaning what's best for MacBain?"

"Yes," her parents said.

She would do anything for the family business, but cleaning didn't make sense. Not every potential CEO had to get their hands dirty.

She was good at her job. But she wanted more. More of everything. When her father retired, she wanted his position.

She loved her brothers, but they didn't have the training to run the family business. Every college course, article, and seminar she'd taken attended or read were part of her bigger plan. When her father retired, she wanted to lead MacBain Enterprises.

But her father still hadn't acknowledged her as his successor. Her hands clenched into fists. She might have to crawl over her brothers' bodies to get there.

What a lovely image, all three lying in a pile as she stepped over them in a new pair of Louboutin high heels. It would have to be Louboutin; the blood wouldn't show on the red soles. She'd seen the perfect pair in Saks last week. Too bad they cost $900. And they sure wouldn't be practical if her parents forced her to clean.

"I know you're tough, Katie MacBain," her father said. "But I'm not having you swing a hammer on any of Stephen or Timothy's projects."

If she did work as a laborer, she'd figure out ways to do the job more effectively. She looked at her manicure to keep from glaring at her family.

"I've brought in new tenants in a failing economy," she said. "I'm good at what I do."

"Yes, you are." Her mother's dark brown eyebrows drew together.

"Who will handle my workload?" She had to get out of this. "I'm in the middle of negotiations with both Sorenson Law and Telling Chemicals. They're asking for massive concessions. I need to concentrate so they don't ruin the profitability of the Daschle Building."

Michael stretched out his legs. "What about that assistant you *had* to have. When does she start?"

Katie's shoulders stiffened. She'd pushed for additional help over Michael's vehement objections. Was he retaliating because Mom and Dad had finally agreed to her proposal? "She starts Monday."

"Waste of money," Michael mumbled. "Typical Katie."

Why wouldn't her family call her Kate? *Katie* was a little girl with pigtails. She tucked a wayward strand of her auburn hair behind her ear. *Kate* was a professional.

God, what she wouldn't give to have been the firstborn. Instead Michael had the honor. She was the only daughter. When the two youngest had come along, she'd been stuck babysitting.

"It will only be one job," her mother said. "You should be able to work your schedule around the cleaning, especially now that you have an assistant."

"Katie, if you want to get ahead, you need a strong foundation." Her father looked pointedly at his desk.

The desk she wanted to fill.

"You've done time in marketing, sales and public relations, but we realized you haven't had any *hands-on* experience in the company." Her mother stood next to Dad and leaned against the window. A united front.

"But cleaning?"

"Yes." Her mother didn't leave any room to argue.

"You'll have a week to orient your assistant before you start working for Murphy's. You can manage your department and learn the cleaning side of the business. It's only one job a week, but he's an important client. Probably only four hours twice a week."

"You'll still handle the lease renewals," Dad added. "Plus, I remember how slowly the negotiations for Sorenson Law firm progressed five years ago. Their office manager vets everything with the partners. Besides, their lease still has six months to run."

When her father's voice took on that head-of-the-MacBain-clan tone, there was no arguing.

"How long will I have to do this?" Kate asked.

Her mother tipped her head, her brown hair swinging to her shoulder. "As long as we say you do."

Kate had one last weapon in her arsenal. "Dad, two nights ago you complained I was still working at seven-thirty. You said I couldn't focus all my energy on the company. This will make it worse."

"On top of new experience, we're hoping you'll learn balance and how to delegate," Mom said.

God, did they have to act like a tag team?

"But … cleaning?"

"Katie, this may be a family business, but you're still an employee. If you don't like my management style," her father pointed to the door, "you can always leave."

How could they do this to her? "I want what's best for the company."

If by working at Murphy's Maids she was closer to being named her father's successor, she'd suck up her resentment. "If you think cleaning is the best use of my talents, then that's what I'll do."

Her parents nodded at her. She and Michael pushed away from the table. Her brother started to walk past her. "Kiddo, you need to tame that mouth of yours."

She whipped an elbow into his abs. "Don't call me, kiddo."

KATE MANHANDLED the van's reluctant gearshift into drive. It was mortifying driving the bright green Murphy's Maid van. She missed her BMW, but the cleaning equipment wouldn't fit in her car, not without ruining the leather interior.

She'd tried to convince Lois, her Murphy's Maid supervisor, to let her clean one of their office-building complexes—at night. No go. She was working in the residential cleaning group. Housecleaning!

Well, how tough could housecleaning be? She'd endured a two-hour training video. And she'd helped Lois clean a house the day before.

She wouldn't need her strategic leadership course to figure out the best way of removing the ring around a bathtub. And she'd bet her iPad that Lois couldn't run a project probability analysis.

Kate glanced at her phone's GPS, making sure she was on the right street. Did Murphy's provide smart phones to the cleaners? It would save time and money.

If her directions were accurate, she'd found the right neighborhood. Large older homes were set back on their lots. Trees lined the quiet street, their leaves a freshly unfurled bright green. The color would deepen as spring turned to summer. *Hopefully she wouldn't still be cleaning in summer.*

Passing bright blobs of yellow forsythia, flashes of red and yellow tulips, and jonquils … or daffodils … she didn't know the difference, Kate finally pulled to the curb in front of a lovely yellow three-story house with white trim and black shutters. A wide porch held a couple of rattan chairs. Even *she*, an apartment dweller, could tell the gray porch begged for flowerpots.

Kate wrestled the cleaning equipment and supply carrier onto the sidewalk. The buckets were the same lime green as the van. So was the hideous polo shirt she'd tucked into her oldest blue jeans. The vacuum cleaner banged her leg as she dragged everything up the sidewalk.

Mr. Adamski. Kate sure hoped this client was a kindly, tidy old gentleman.

Lois had warned her. "He's not happy Martha's gone. Unfortunately it's been almost two months since Martha retired, so the place might be dirty."

Then Lois had handed her a five-page list of written instructions on how and what to clean in the Adamski house. Christ. Kate was anal retentive, but she hadn't left five pages of instructions for Elizabeth, her freshly hired employee.

Since she was thinking about her new assistant, she set the equipment down and called. "Hi Liz, how's it going?"

"Nothing I can't handle yet. I've answered most of the questions thrown at me. The one I couldn't answer, I got your brother's help."

She didn't want her brothers bugging Liz. "Which brother?"

"Michael. Doesn't smile much, does he?"

"No." Her brother was too serious. "Call if you have any questions. I can't imagine cleaning is very challenging." Kate shivered. "I'll need mental stimulation."

"Will do. But don't worry. I know your filing system and have access to all the active leases." Liz laughed. "I think I can manage on my own for the next four or five hours. I'll see you this afternoon, right?"

"Yes." Kate sighed. Four hours of scrubbing and vacuuming sounded like a lifetime.

"Don't worry. I won't sign any new leases while you're gone."

Kate laughed as she stuffed her phone into her back pocket. With a big sigh, she climbed the porch steps. Sure, her mother had started this way, but her mother had cleaned houses while attending night school. As demand grew, she'd hired other students looking for work. Then she'd expanded into cleaning office buildings. Since the college students she'd hired attended school during the day and could clean at night, it was a perfect fit. Lois said they still got fifty percent of their new hires from the nearby colleges.

Maybe Murphy's should establish a work/study program with local colleges. She set everything down again and pulled out her phone, making a note to research setting up a program.

At the door she wound her hair into a bun and wrapped a scrunchie around it. She pushed the bell and smiled when it played a tune. It reminded her of some commercial, but she couldn't recall what product.

The door opened.

She looked up, still smiling. "Hi. I'm Kate from Murphy's Maids."

The man blocking the entrance reminded her of a bear. And he wasn't old. He wasn't much older than she was.

His shoulders filled the doorway and looked twice as wide as his waist. Everything about him was dark. Dark hair, dark eyes, and a dark scowl on his face. "You're twenty minutes late."

She straightened. "I'm sorry." It wasn't like they were negotiating a multi-million-dollar lease.

He didn't move.

She chewed her lip.

His bushy eyebrows pinched together so tight it almost

looked like he had a unibrow. He was taller than her brothers, and they were all over six feet.

She stared into his brown eyes, snapping with anger. "Are you letting me in?"

"I'm thinking."

God. Her brothers would tease her endlessly if she failed this job. And Dad and Mom. Shoot. She couldn't let that happen. She couldn't disappoint them. She wanted that CEO position. She tapped her foot against the wooden floor of the porch. She had to clean this guy's house.

She touched his arm. "Please don't get me fired. This is my first day on the job." She let her gaze drop but looked up at him through her half-closed eyelashes. Let this work. Failure was not an option.

His craggy face softened. When he wasn't frowning, he was … good-looking.

"I can't be waiting for you every week. You need to be punctual. Martha was never late."

Martha must have been part saint. "It won't happen again. I promise."

"It better not."

The client was a real grump.

He stepped aside and she hauled in the cleaning supply bucket. He grabbed the vacuum. Maybe he'd help clean too.

"Martha knew how I wanted everything," he muttered, glancing over his shoulder. "And one of my first requirements of your company was punctuality. Please remember that."

They moved through the hallway. She loved the wood floors. They were probably maple, but the stain was light and kept the hallway from feeling closed in.

"Here's the kitchen." He set the vacuum down with a thump.

Judging by the white cabinets and golden brown granite counters, the space had been remodeled. Then she took in the stain rings, lumps of food stuck to the counter, and the dishes overflowing the sink. The whole room left a general impression of dustiness. She caught of whiff of something foul, but then all she smelled was coffee. Wonderful.

Adamski poured a cup from the pot. Huh. She didn't know his first name and he hadn't offered her a cup.

Of course she hadn't given him her last name. Her cheeks grew warm. She didn't want anyone knowing what she was doing.

She waited for him to offer her a cup. Nothing. She tapped her fingers against her leg.

"Did you talk to Martha?" he asked.

She pulled out the five-page list Lois had given her. She hadn't read it yet. "I have her instructions."

"Good. I'll leave you to it. I have to work." He pivoted and headed out the door, surprisingly graceful for such a tall man.

Unfolding the list, she read.

Mr. Adamski is very particular about the service he receives.

Be on time. He only wants cleaners in the house from 10 until 2 on Tuesdays and Wednesdays.

Kate planned to propose a schedule change where she would work eight hours in one day. Then she would only miss a day out of her week. And she wouldn't have to change into regular clothes after she'd done her penance.

Most important rule—Never disturb him while he's working.

Mr. Adamski and I developed a routine satisfactory to him. Clean in the following order:

Kitchen—do dishes.

Clean all surfaces.

Clean inside microwave.

Every other week, wipe down cupboards.

Once a month clean out fridge.

He's okay if you throw away dated food.

This sounded like four hours of work right there. And there

were five pages of instructions. Maybe she should expect more of her own Murphy's house cleaners.

With a deep sigh, she began with the dishes. A week's worth of pans and plates filled the sink. She swallowed at the sight of dried spaghetti sauce and gross baked-on brown goop in a pan. Snapping on Murphy's Maids green gloves, she filled the sink with steaming water. She might need a power washer to clean the place.

Kate scraped, rinsed and filled the dishwasher. She scrubbed at the countertop until her arm ached and sweat dripped into her ear. She'd only been working thirty minutes, and she already needed a shower.

Once the counters and sinks gleamed, she stretched out her sore back. She deserved a reward.

The coffee aroma lured her to the pot. She poured a cup and found sugar in the cupboard. She sipped, closing her eyes. The man made better coffee than the shop in her office building. "Great coffee," she murmured.

"It should be. I have it shipped in special."

She jumped and almost dropped the mug. Mr. Adamski stood behind her. A smile creased his face, a dimple winking out of one cheek. God, she loved dimples.

Everything on him was large … his nose, his cheekbones and even the dent in his chin. Rarely did a man tower over her five-foot-eight inches, but Adamski did. Warmth curled through her body. This guy was cute.

She shook her head; she wasn't here to flirt. She was here to prove to her parents that she could handle everything they dished out.

"I'm sorry, the coffee smelled delicious." And she believed in rewarding her efforts. Adamski should be admiring his empty sinks and clean counters.

The muscles in his face relaxed. "Don't worry about it." He poured himself another cup. "I keep the coffee going all day. If you need to make a pot, the coffee and filters are here."

He opened the cupboard above the coffeemaker. At least that was organized.

She'd always resented making coffee at the office. Mostly because she swore her brothers never bothered. They waited for a staff member to make a fresh pot, and nobody called them on their laziness. But for coffee this good, she'd make a pot.

"So, you just started with Murphy's Maids?" He leaned against the counter.

She wiped the inside of the microwave. She might need to take a chisel to the dried-on food. Hefting out the glass tray, she set it gently in the sink. "First day by myself."

She scrubbed, standing on her toes, putting muscle into scraping off what looked like more red sauce. How much spaghetti and pizza did this guy eat?

She looked at him. His eyes were the same color as his rich dark coffee.

He topped off his cup. "Are you finding everything?"

She'd only done the dishes, and it had taken half an hour. Frowning, she sniffed. Why hadn't the faint foul smell in the kitchen disappeared? "I'm good."

She tilted her head. "Cleaning would be easier if you rinsed your dishes after you ate. Then I wouldn't have to chisel and chip at the dishes and pans. I almost threw a pot away."

He took a step back. "Martha never said anything."

Maybe she'd overstepped her role, but really. Saint Martha might have wanted to get in as many hours as possible working here, but not her. She wanted to get back to her real job. She bit her lip.

His gaze zoomed in on her mouth. "I'll rinse my dishes from now on."

"Good." She wanted him to leave. Let her finish her

penance. Wow. She needed to strip off her sweatshirt. The room had gotten really warm.

"I'll let you get back to it." His hands waved around the kitchen. "Oh, I use the filtered water for the coffee." He pointed to a spigot on the sink.

"Thanks." She swallowed and watched him leave. For a big man, he had a very nice butt. Very nice.

She wished they'd met at a bar. They might have dated for a week or two. Maybe she'd have slept with him, at least until she'd gotten this attraction out of her system. She didn't date a guy for much longer than a month or two.

Until her parents admitted she was the right person to guide the future of MacBain, nothing would distract her.

So, she scrubbed. When Adamski's home sparkled like the Hope Diamond, he would rave to her parents, and they would free her from cleaning.

Because the alternative was too awful to consider. If Adamski complained about her work, her parents would write her off, and her brothers would tease her until the end of time. And Michael would be named CEO of MacBain Enterprises.

ALEX STRIPPED off his headphones and powered off his keyboard. He took a sip of coffee, grimacing as the cold liquid slid down his throat.

Crap. Now he couldn't even write jingles. What else could go wrong?

He wasn't hurting for money. His songwriting paid for a near-perfect life. Or at least half the life he'd planned. Meredith and his dreams of a family had been the other half.

Those dreams had crumbled around him. Meredith had made a fool of him and now he could barely sit at the keyboard where he'd composed so many songs—for her.

He closed his eyes and let his chest rise and fall in deep breaths. He'd jokingly promised an award-winning jingle for Gabe. Gabe had stuck by him through last year's hell. Friends stuck together.

So, he would finish this jingle. Then he would battle the sonata.

Unstructured phrases haunted his nights, but as soon as he started working on the melody and counterpoints, everything vanished. Maybe if he finished the sonata, he could move on. Tuck away his grief.

Alex tapped his fingers against the soundless keys. He needed inspiration to create this jingle for a retail lighting store. *Maybe they'd settle for "Twinkle, Twinkle Little Star."*

Slipping the headphones back on, he flipped the switch on his electric piano. The melody should be light and bright.

He pictured a little girl with Kate's auburn curls and bright green eyes, gave her a dimple. Sure, he hated his own dimples, but a little girl would look right with a dimple gracing the corner of her smile.

The notes flowed. For the first time in months, music poured from him like liquid gold. He could hear it all: the violins, the horns and the harp. He made a quick note: *add bells or xylophone.*

The words followed. He infused the music with images of light and hope. Always set against a backdrop of a bright-eyed, one-year-old girl with copper-colored curls. Touching the record button, he played the tune one more time. Then he laid down the lyrics.

His gravelly baritone growled out the words. The ad agency wouldn't use his voice, but at least Gabe's client would get an idea of what he was after.

He played it back. Added harmonies, tweaked. His hands shook as he pushed the play button.

The song sounded like he'd imagined. Like the sun rising

on a brand-new day. A day filled with hope. Alex let out a massive sigh that ruffled the composition paper on the stand.

He'd broken through. He'd finished a composition. Almost eighteen months of creative drought and all he'd needed was a new cleaner stalking through his door. A good-looking woman with fiery green eyes who told him to rinse his plates.

He tossed his headphones on the console and rolled his chair back from the keyboard.

A vacuum buzzed above his head. Kate with her full, plump lips was in his bedroom. Her lips made him think of what a mouth like hers could do to a man who hadn't had sex in … too long.

Sure, he'd checked out her ass. Hell, he wasn't dead. Over the last few months, his libido had come back to life. Ripped, torn designer jeans had encased her nicely rounded cheeks. But she was his house cleaner for God's sake.

She was tall. He was a big man, and the next time he slept with a woman, he wanted someone in his arms that wouldn't break. Meredith had been—fragile, model-thin. He'd always worried he might hurt her.

Kate. He liked her name. Her gaze crackled with intensity. He could fall for a woman like Kate.

What the hell was a bright young woman doing cleaning houses?

THE MAN WAS A PIG. Kate threw another pile of laundry into the hamper. Didn't he pick up after himself?

She stripped the sheets off his bed. He probably hadn't changed the bed since Martha retired. She wished she'd kept the rubber gloves on.

The hamper overflowed as she carted it downstairs. He must work out a lot. Most of the dirty clothes were T-shirts and sweatpants. She pushed opened the laundry room door and snapped her head back. A foul odor wafted from the space, like something had died. *God, what was it?*

It had to be the smell she'd caught while in the kitchen.

Another pile of clothes overflowed the table next to the washer. That couldn't be the source, could it?

One of her high school chores had been doing her family's laundry. Her brothers' sports clothes had been the worst, especially Stephen's hockey uniforms, but never this bad. She gulped in a breath and the smell stung the back of her throat.

Rolling her eyes, she pulled her gloves back on and sorted his clothes. There must be a thousand athletic socks.

Family sock-matching Sunday nights had been the worst. She and her brothers had to finish before they could watch TV. Most of the socks had been her brothers', but she'd been forced to match too. Life as the only girl in the MacBain family had been unfair. Who in their right mind wanted kids?

Apparently Adamski liked silk boxers. Mostly black, very nice, but she ran across a series of holiday boxers. Santa Clauses, pumpkins, four-leaf clovers and hearts, numerous heart-covered boxers. Girlfriend?

At least she hadn't found any women's underwear. And she hadn't found evidence of a woman living in the house. No clothes in the closet, no makeup in the bathroom. No condom wrappers in the garbage. Yuck.

With the clothes sorted, she opened the washer. "God!"

Kate jerked her head away, but not before her eyes watered from the stench. The lid slammed shut with a clang.

Shit. Had something died in there? She tried to breathe through her mouth, but the taste had the coffee she'd drunk threatening to come up.

Her brief glimpse into the depths of the washer had shown sheets, towels and moldy socks. Cringing, she backed out of the door and down the hallway into the kitchen.

This was the seventh level of hell!

Kate slapped her hands on the counter and pulled in deep breaths. The smell wouldn't go away. Spores of death probably filled her nose. She would end up with consumption, coughing and weak in bed. Her family would cry by her bedside, sorry for the way they'd treated her. Sorry they hadn't cherished the too few moments they'd had with her before she died.

"I want my office. My *clean* office. Where someone else removes the garbage and vacuums the floors." She wanted to work at a job that mattered. "I hate this."

She snatched her coffee mug off the counter and sniffed. Even the heady, rich aroma couldn't clear away the stink.

What she wouldn't give to pull the whole mess out of the washer, find where Adamski was hiding, and throw everything in his lap. If it had been her brothers' mess, she would have done just that.

Grabbing a garbage bag and wishing she had a facemask, she returned to the laundry. With a deep breath, she rushed in.

Throwing open the washing machine's lid, she frantically stuffed the contents of the machine into the bag. The fabric squished and slid through her gloved hands, covered with slime. Something green came up with the clothes. It looked like a piece of meat. She gagged.

Hurry. Hurry.

She leaned over and chased the last mildew-speckled sock around the inside of the machine. *The smell. Oh God.*

She stuffed the final sock in the bag and yanked the draw strings shut. She refused to breathe until she reached the kitchen.

Gasping, she rushed to the back door off the kitchen. Wrenching it open, she stuck her head out and drew in deep gulps of fresh cool air. Even with the bag closed, the stench escaped.

"What the hell?" Adamski's deep voice made the door clutched in her fingers vibrate. "What is that smell?"

She gasped in fresh air again. Would she ever get rid of the taste in her mouth?

"What's wrong?"

He was so close, her eardrums hurt from his shouting.

"I …"

"Sweet Jesus, what is that?"

Fingers bit into her arm. He pulled her into the room and the door closed.

She fought back with an elbow to his stomach. She needed fresh air. "Don't!"

She shrugged him away and bumped open the door. She gulped in air laced with the scent of flowering trees.

"Did something die?" he asked.

"Your laundry." She grabbed the bag and then heaved it onto the kitchen deck. She hoped the crawling mess didn't eat its way out of the plastic bag and through the decking. Maybe the military needed to know about this possible new chemical weapon.

"What the hell did you do?" His face looked a little gray.

"Me? What did I do?" She poked a finger into his chest. The firm muscles didn't give. "When did you throw your last load of laundry into the washer?"

Black eyebrows shadowed his chocolate eyes. "I …" His eyes flared wide open. "A while ago."

"I think there was some sort of meat in there." She shivered. "I've never seen anything so gross."

She took a deep breath through her nose. Her eyes watered. She went back to breathing through her mouth.

"I … I … I didn't look very hard for the source of the smell." He leaned out the door, his head hovering above hers. He inhaled and then hurried back into the kitchen.

Metal screeched as Adamski opened windows. She turned

as he pushed open the laundry room. He staggered as the stench washed over them.

"Do you have candles, spray, anything?" she begged.

"Living room. On the mantle."

She ran, any excuse to escape the cloying smell. In the living room she gathered matches and large candles. The candles looked like something a decorator had placed and admonished him not to light. Too bad. Sucked to be him.

Stripping off the gloves, she set the candles on the counter and struck a match. Would the whole house blow?

Adamski returned from the basement with a fan. He plugged it in and aimed it at the open laundry door.

"You don't happen to have a gas mask?" she asked, only partly kidding.

"Don't I wish." He coughed a little.

She wanted to ask what he'd been thinking. She wanted to shake him. The man needed a keeper.

With the breeze from the fan, the candles and some spray he'd squirted into the laundry, Kate could finally breathe without her eyes watering.

"Mr. Adamski," she started.

"Alex. My name is Alex."

The strong, masculine name suited him. "What in God's name was in that washing machine?"

He ran fingers through his hair, making the thick curls stand up. His face turned red. "I think I might have dropped lunch meat in while I read the manual."

"Read the manual?" Didn't he know how to run a washing machine?

He rubbed a hand on his chin. His beard rasped against his palm. "Martha did my laundry. Up until she left me."

Kate threw her hands up. "She retired."

"Well, she's been working for me since …" Alex paused.

"Ever since I moved here. I never bothered with the laundry, or the dishwasher."

Kate had grown up in a privileged environment, but this man took the prize. How could he have survived without learning basic skills for metropolitan survival?

"I'll be updating your education. But first we have to fumigate the washing machine." And she meant *we*. He needed to be held accountable.

After mixing a batch of bleach, water and soap, she found a set of large gloves under the kitchen sink and handed them to Alex with a sponge and the bucket. "Wipe out the insides of the machine with this."

"Me?" Fear filled his dark brown eyes.

"You." She pointed at him. "I pulled everything out of the machine. Your turn."

He sighed. The gloves almost ripped as he tugged them onto his hands. With a sigh, he trudged into the laundry room. "God."

He wiped out the machine while she sipped another cup of coffee.

"Done," he called, stepping out with the bucket. Tears ran down his cheeks.

"Come on." She motioned him back to the small room.

"Do I have to?"

"Yes." She took a deep breath before entering. Once she showed him how to set the machine for a large load, she threw in the rags, added detergent and slammed the lid shut before running back into the kitchen.

"I couldn't figure out where the smell was from." He shifted on his size twenty shoes. "I thought it was the fridge."

She collapsed onto a barstool. Her hands could barely hold up her head. What waited for her in the fridge?

Her phone alarm rang. Four hours had passed already? She couldn't go to the office like this. She'd have to head home and shower. She'd planned to grab a bite to eat, but after that mess, she didn't want to touch food for a month.

Kate shut off the alarm. "I have to leave. Don't open the fridge. I can't take anymore today."

She hadn't made it through half a page of Martha's task list.

He fidgeted. Those big hands barely fit into the back pockets of his jeans. Jeans that stretched against a bulge she couldn't help but notice. Was it hands or feet or a nose that was an indicator of how well-endowed a man was?

"You'll be back tomorrow? You won't bail on me like the others?"

Her mouth dropped open. "How many people have bailed?"

"Four." His deep voice was a mere whisper.

Kate's mouth dropped open. Her mother had set her up.

TWO

Kate spun her beer mug in a slow circle. "I can't believe my parents are forcing me to do this."

Meg, her best friend since college, patted her hand.

Kate adored O'Dair's Pub, although she wasn't here as often as Meg. Her friend could walk the block and half from her condo and never worry about parking or driving.

Kate could see why Meg loved the place. It attracted so many characters and her friend had probably met most of them. Lawyers, plumbers, baseball or football fans, visited the pub. If people didn't enjoy the beer brewed onsite or the food, they might stay for the Irish bands that played on the weekends.

"It can't be that bad," Meg said. "It's a … a new adventure."

"It is. I'm the fifth cleaner since Saint Martha left. Fifth. I found out from Lois that the last two didn't even make it through two hours. They refused to return. The guy is hopeless."

Her parents couldn't make her do this for more than a

week or two, could they? Not after what she'd endured this morning.

"How old is he? Retired?" asked Meg.

"He's our age, maybe a little older. I swear he doesn't know how to use any of the appliances in his house except the coffee maker." She ran a fingernail through the condensation on her mug. Damn, she'd broken a nail and didn't have time to get another manicure. She dug a file out of her purse and tidied the ragged edges. She'd need to give up on her nails until this torture was over. "He does make great coffee. I need to find out where he gets his beans."

"He's our age? What does he do?"

"I haven't a clue."

"Is he cute?"

Was he cute? "He's ... interesting. Big. Bigger than any of my brothers." She dropped the nail file into her purse. "He's got a dimple."

"As nice as ..." Meg snapped her finger. "Who was that guy you dated last year? Jeff? Jasper?"

"Jason. God he was cute." Kate sighed. "But his idea of a romantic dinner was take-out pizza."

"Oh, yeah. Too bad. I liked talking to him about astronomy."

"Then you should have dated him."

"Oh, no. No dating for me." Meg forced a laugh. "Tell me more about Mister Clueless. Maybe you two will fall in love over his unmentionables."

Kate took a long sip of her beer. She looked into her friend's bright blue eyes, wishing she could change the events that had altered Meg, the most trusting woman she knew, into a woman who wouldn't date—anyone.

"Don't get any ideas about me and Mister Clueless," Kate said. "I haven't changed my plans. No serious relationship until after I'm CEO. Maybe never."

Meg frowned. "Everyone I've set you up with has been perfect."

Kate rubbed her forehead. There'd been a headache brewing since her close encounter with Alex's laundry demons. "Well, I still plan to be the love 'em-and-leave 'em type until my parents name me heir apparent."

"What if one of your brothers decides they should be in charge?" Meg sipped her beer.

"Then they should have gotten their MBA. I'm the one who took the time to do that. While I worked full time."

Meg's gaze held hers. "Why do you think your parents are making you work at Murphy's Maids?"

"They *say* it's because they want me to understand all branches of the business." Kate shook her head, curls slapping her cheeks. "Mom says he's an important client. But he's scared all his other cleaners."

Meg folded and refolded her napkin. Her friend's nails were perfect. The law firm she worked for didn't make Meg clean bathrooms. "Maybe there's more to what your parents are doing."

"Yeah, I figured that out. Mom knows exactly what kind of a hot mess this Adamski is. They're testing me. I'm just not sure why." Kate let her head drop against the tabletop.

"Then look at this as an adventure."

"You already said that." Kate sighed.

Meg would look at it as a new experience. Her friend might be a lawyer, but it didn't stop her from being the person her dorm floor had nominated as the *girl who would try anything, just not a date*. Kate had been dubbed the *girl who would never have kids*. They'd been right, on both accounts.

Sometimes Kate had no clue what drove Meg. But she was her best friend and always would be. The sister she'd always wanted.

"How'd your first day go?" Stephen's voice blasted her ear.

Kate thwacked her brother in the shoulder. She wasn't telling anyone but Meg how awful cleaning had been. Stephen would tell the family. No way. "What dragged you out of your cave?"

Meg stared at Stephen. "You lost a bet."

Stephen blinked. "What?"

Meg's eyes narrowed. "You wouldn't come to a place like this unless you were bribed or lost a bet."

Stephen tugged Kate's hand and pulled her out of her chair. Then he pulled over another and took her spot.

"Hey!"

"This is my spot." He angled his chair so he could view the entire room.

"Since when?" Her brother was strange. He always sat in the same chair or the same spot in the family van. Getting him to change wasn't worth the effort. He ignored people when they asked. Or did what he'd just done to her.

"I come here once a …" he looked puzzled "… a week. This is my chair. I always sit here. I can watch the whole pub from here."

"No way," Meg said.

"Just because I'm not here late at night, doesn't mean I don't come here."

Kate snorted. "You're such a geek."

Stephen shot her a lopsided grin. "How was your first day of cleaning other people's shit?"

Kate glared at him.

"It was wonderful," Meg filled in for her. "Why are you here?"

Stephen caught the eye of the server, raising his voice over the clatter of the crowd. "Beth, bring me a pint of the seasonal, please."

"Will do, Stephen." Beth shot him a bright smile and hustled to the bar.

Huh? Stephen really was a regular. She thought she knew her brother. This surprised her.

"I knew you and Kate would stop here tonight." Stephen grinned.

His tan looked darker. He must be outside a lot. This spring Stephen's residential construction team had broken more ground than all of last year. It was still slow, but that side of the business was picking up.

Maybe they should advertise. Then when the economy revved up, they'd get more than their share of new construction.

She'd run that idea by Dad.

Beth brought her brother's beer and rested a hand on his back. "How you doing, handsome?"

"Ummm, good." He blushed a little. "How's married life treating you?"

"Fantastic." Beth's smile grew even bigger.

"Good." He waved his hand at the beers. "I'll take their tab."

The older woman winked. "Sure thing, handsome."

"You really do come here." Meg shook her head. "I always thought you hid in your apartment."

Stephen bopped Meg on the nose. "Nope."

"You and the rest of my worthless brothers need to get a life and stay out of mine," Kate said.

"But I heard how you happily expanded your managerial talents." Stephen grinned at her. "What kind of deals do you spin while scrubbing a floor, sis?"

"Go bother someone else."

"I'll let you wallow in your beer." He took another sip and then caught Meg's hand. "Let's see if you can keep up with me."

Kate blinked. Stephen danced?

Meg's mouth hung open. Stephen pulled her to the dance

floor, and they joined the other couples. Meg laughed at something Stephen said. They looked good together, swaying to the music.

Propping her head on her hand, Kate checked her phone for messages. Nothing.

Her fingers beat a staccato pattern on the tabletop. At least her parents weren't calling with news that Alex had complained about her. It hadn't been professional to yell at him about the washer, but Lord he was a disaster.

She rubbed the pressure points under her eyebrows. O'Dair's smelled of beer and perfume and something citrusy, but underneath, she swore she could smell that noxious aroma from the washing machine.

She forced her thoughts to the tenant concessions Sorenson had sent her that afternoon. They wanted ten bucks a square foot for remodeling, along with a reduction in their lease costs. Damn this economy. If they lost their biggest tenant, they'd have 150 thousand square feet of empty in their prime building. She couldn't let them go, but MacBain had expenses too.

Liz could do the lease research. She would get her assistant started in the morning before she headed to Adamski's.

Alex Adamski.

Alex of the curly black hair and dimple.

Alex of the disgusting laundry and surprising lack of knowledge about appliances.

She planned to teach him that sandwich meat did not go in the washing machine.

ALEX PLAYED the jingle one more time, checking the timing. Perfect. Sixty seconds. He tweaked and cleaned it up, made sure the name of the lighting store was clear and that the message was clean. Then he sent an email with the score and music file attached.

Shoving the earphones around his neck, he called Gabe.

His friend answered. "Double A, how's it going?"

"You answered your own phone. Didn't think you knew how since you made partner."

"Ha ha. I'm rolling on the floor." Alex heard Gabe's chair creak. He imagined him leaning back and stacking his long legs on the edge of his desk. "Don't ask for any more time on the Larson Lighting account. I need the jingle next week."

"I'm hurt. I never ask for more time." Alex grinned.

"I mean it, AA. This is a new account. I can't have any missteps, or they'll pull their business, and this is a chunk of change."

"Check your in-box."

Alex smiled as the chair creaked again. He liked it when he sent something to Gabe early. Of course then Gabe always expected him to outperform his deadlines.

Oh well, this time he had.

"Great!" Gabe said.

Alex heard the tune playing in the background. He winced at the sound of his voice. He wasn't a singer. Meredith had been the vocalist.

"What happened?" asked Gabe. "When we talked a couple of days ago, you were stalled."

Kate had happened.

"I may have found my inspiration. You might include a small child in the storyboards when you present it. A little girl who grows up in the ads." He tinkered with his pencil. "Just a suggestion."

"It wasn't where we were going but let me think about it."

After ending the call, Alex headed to the kitchen. He sniffed. The smell was gone. His face heated. Yeah, he'd let things go.

Hell, he'd forgotten he'd thrown a load in the washer. He'd been trying to work on a song, anything to delay working on his sonata. It must have been the second week after Martha left.

He shouldn't have ignored the smell. He shouldn't have ordered new clothes just because he didn't want to run the washer.

No wonder the other cleaners hadn't lasted more than an hour or two. He had tried to stay focused, but then a tune or lyric would pull him back to his music room. Not that he'd finished any songs. Not until this jingle.

As he poured his coffee, he checked the time on the coffeemaker. He'd made a full pot. Just for Kate.

She was late. Again. Resentment burrowed into his chest like a shot from an elbow in a vicious basketball game.

Martha had always been on time. Surely he could expect Kate to do the same. That wasn't unreasonable.

Being late didn't mean Kate was like Meredith though. His ex had always been late. She'd always kept him waiting. He clenched his teeth. That wasn't the worst of Meredith's faults. It had been the lying that had ended their marriage. Her self-ishness had destroyed their love.

The doorbell rang. Kate. His breathing quickened. Ten minutes late.

He scanned the kitchen once more before heading to the front door. Dishes were rinsed, just like she'd asked. The room didn't look too bad. Weird. He worried about cleaning up for his cleaner. What did this mean?

Course, who was he to judge? He'd left the mess in the washer. Over the last month, he'd bought new boxers and socks because he couldn't be bothered with laundry. He grinned. Maybe after today, he'd have clean clothes.

Alex opened the door. "You came back."

Kate tapped away on her phone, one just like his. He

31

frowned. She cleaned houses but had one of the most expensive phones on the market.

"How's it going?" She slid the phone in her pocket and grabbed her equipment.

He should probably give her a key. Martha had always had one. But when the cleaners kept quitting, he'd grown leery. Maybe if she stuck with him for a month. "It's going good and you?"

"Peachy." The smile plastered across her face didn't light up her eyes. She headed down the hall, and he shut the door behind her.

In the kitchen, Kate turned with her hands on her hips. "After yesterday, I hope there aren't any other land mines waiting for me."

He jammed his hands in his pockets. "I don't think so."

She wore torn jeans just like the day before. Jeans that hugged her in all the right places. He shook his head clear. *This was his cleaning lady, what was he doing?*

Kate was looking at him, and all he could think was she was tall enough he didn't feel like he would break her in two if he hugged her. Her head would fit right into the crook of his shoulder, nicely …

Clearly he'd been alone too long, he was thinking like a sleaze-boss. She pulled a wad of paper out of her pocket. "We need to review the list Martha left with Lois. I can't get through everything this week. We need to prioritize."

Prioritize. The word seemed foreign.

"Let's take a look." He pointed at the coffee pot. "Grab a cup and a stool."

He reviewed the bullet points as she poured her coffee. Holy cow. Martha had done this every week? In eight hours?

"Yesterday I got through the dishes, cleaned the master and upstairs bathrooms and started on the laundry. We know what a disaster that was." She pointed. "What is your highest priority for today?"

He scanned the list again. He probably didn't need the dusting. Jeez, Martha dusted behind every picture, not just the frames. Cleaning the blinds could wait. If he was tidier, would the list be longer or shorter?

"Laundry. I cycled the machine through again. Twice." He tapped out the syncopation of the jingle he'd sent to Gabe. "I can't smell anything, but my nose may have adjusted. Then the downstairs bathrooms. After that how about the floors?"

He didn't know anything about cleaning houses. His parents had had servants. His girlfriends in college had done a lot of his cleaning. Then he and Meredith had gotten married, and she'd hired people.

After he left Meredith, he'd used Martha and hadn't worried about the house. Hell, when needed, Martha's husband had done handy work. He'd paid the man what he'd asked. He couldn't be bothered to get bids. He wanted a quiet place to compose. A place he could work in peace.

He shifted his weight on the chair. Someone else had always picked up after him. That sounded rather elitist. Or lazy.

A quizzical look crossed Kate's face. "You're clueless about running a house, aren't you?"

He shrugged. What could he say? "Probably."

She slapped her hands on the table. "Okay. I'll get to it."

He wanted her to stay and talk. He wanted to wrap his hands around the curve of her mighty fine ass as she bent over the dishwasher.

What the hell was wrong with him? He hadn't been a monk since the divorce. Sure, he hadn't done much more than have one-night stands. Okay, two one-night stands.

He couldn't remember the last woman he'd taken to bed.

Maybe he needed to go out. Gabe had been bugging him. He should take him up on the offer.

Alex grunted.

Kate's head snapped up, almost hitting the edge of the counter.

"Do you need something?" she asked.

"No." He poured coffee into his mug and touched up hers. That was what he would do. Have a night out with Gabe. If Kate got the laundry finished. Otherwise he'd have to wear sweatpants.

He could almost feel the hangover.

THE MAN HAD four dozen pairs of boxers. Kate folded the last pair and set them in the basket, running her hand over the midnight blue silk. This was too intimate. She'd never lived with a guy and never helped a date do laundry.

Sure, she'd folded her brother's shorts, but this was a *client*, a man she found attractive, and she was smoothing the wrinkles from his underwear.

She wrangled the full basket into her arms and headed up the stairs. Her thighs complained from this latest trip. She'd been up and down the stairs a dozen times over the last twenty-four hours.

She set the clothes on the bed, organized into piles. Did he expect her to put the clothes into his drawers and closet, a closet she coveted for its wonderful shelves and storage.

She took a breath, wishing she could sink onto the big lake of a bed and curl under his dark blue comforter. Instead she headed downstairs to what she thought was Alex's office.

Tapping her knuckles on the closed door, she waited. No answer. She rapped harder. No response. Rocking back on her feet, she frowned. What did he do in his office that he couldn't even answer her knock?

Kate opened the door a crack and blinked. This wasn't an office. She elbowed the door open a little wider.

He must have torn down walls to create such a large room. A baby grand filled the right-hand corner. Shelves set into the wall held music scores. A guitar stood in a stand next to the piano bench. Instrument cases lined a wall. Alex sat behind a console and looked like he was operating a spaceship.

He hadn't answered her knock because he had badass earphones covering his ears. He was glaring at the keyboard.

She hadn't noticed his hands before. For such a large man, his fingers were long and agile. They danced across the keys.

She started to bite her nail but pulled her hand away from her mouth. She didn't have time to correct the mess she'd made of her manicure. She didn't have time to fantasize about Alex's hands. She had to get back to the office.

When he didn't look up, she walked over and leaned against the curved bank of the console, waving her hand in front of his face.

He jerked back. A scowl forced his eyebrows together.

Kate waited while he took off those awesome headphones. She bet those didn't cost nineteen ninety-five like her last pair.

"What?" he growled, his eyes turning almost black.

She raised an eyebrow. Was he upset that she'd entered the room or that she'd interrupted?

Waving a hand at the door, she said, "I knocked. You didn't hear me."

"Do you need something?" After growling, his tone was now as cool as a Popsicle.

"Do you want me to figure out where your clothes go, or will you put them away?"

"I have clean clothes? You finished the laundry?" He looked like a puppy with a bag of bones.

"Your clothes are done. I'm working on the sheets."

"I'll put them away." He sighed. "Clean clothes. Who would have guessed how simple my needs have become."

She laughed as she closed his music room door. Her phone beeped. Liz with a question. Her smile faded. How long would her parents make her do this?

KATE ALMOST RAN down the hallway to her mother's office. She clutched the message Liz had handed her. This couldn't be happening.

"I can't do this." She shook the pink paper.

Her mother pushed away from her desk. "You can't do what?"

Kate rolled her shoulders, trying to relax her sore muscles and calm down. "Lois left a message that I need to fit in another four hours a week at Alex's house. I can't."

Her mother tipped down her reading glasses and stared Kate in the eye. "He likes your work. Wouldn't you admit that more revenue is a good thing? Even if it is from the *cleaning subsidiary* of MacBain Enterprises."

"Of course." Kate plopped into one of her mother's visitor chairs. She didn't want to upset her mother by discussing the relative worth of any arm of the family corporation. "Bring in someone else. I can't spare another four hours. When you and Dad suggested this fiasco, I promised eight hours a week, not twelve." She couldn't get her work done if she was never in her office.

Mom drummed a pen against the top of her glass desk.

Kate popped out of the chair and paced the width of the office. "Let Lois find someone else."

Her mother's eyebrows shot up like they were on a springboard. "Mr. Adamski is very particular. He's a good client. If he wants you for another four hours a week, you'll adjust your schedule to accommodate him. If nothing else, maybe you'll learn customer service." Her mother's tone told her she'd overstepped herself. Again.

"Why is he so important? There's a reason he's gone through five different cleaners in as many weeks, Mom." She wanted to reel the words back after they'd erupted from her mouth.

"Mr. Adamski is important. That's what you need to know." Her mother crossed her arms. "That's probably why he needs more hours. He's flexible on when you add the hours during the week."

Wasn't that big of him.

Her mother looked at her computer screen. "Work with Lois on what hours you'll be adding. Oh, family dinner on Sunday. We'll eat early."

Kate's feet dragged on the way back to her office.

She could already picture Sunday. Her brothers would hound her about cleaning. A chill ran down her spine. Maybe she could add the hours on Sunday and avoid dinner.

As she walked past Liz's desk, her assistant asked, "I'm ready to review the information I've pulled."

"Sure." Kate pushed aside her brewing resentment. Hiring an assistant was the bright light in an otherwise very dim tunnel. Hopefully that tunnel led to her goal. Making Dad realize she was the heir apparent.

Liz walked her through the requested information.

"Great work," she told her assistant.

"I'll put everything together into a spreadsheet so it makes sense," Liz said, "but I wanted to make sure I was on the right track."

"You are." Kate leaned away from the table and looked at Liz. "I should have asked when I interviewed you. Why did you take this job? You're overqualified."

Liz brushed at her mop of blonde curls. "Can I be candid? Without having you think I'm a pariah?"

Kate frowned. Liz's no-nonsense honesty was one of the traits she most admired. "Absolutely."

Liz took a deep breath. "I want your job."

"Really?" Kate sank into her chair. Had she screwed up? The last thing she needed was a cutthroat assistant while she scrubbed floors for the Music Man.

Liz waved her hands as if she could erase the last comment. "I don't want to undermine you or anything. When you're promoted, I want your job. I'll be so good you'll trust me with everything you do."

Kate leaned back in her chair. Having someone who wanted her to succeed could be a real asset. "Okay."

"Maybe you don't remember that I asked what your plans were. You told me you wanted your father's position." Liz straightened the spreadsheets scattered on the tabletop. "I want to be your successor."

Kate grinned. "I sure hope we can make that happen."

A rap on her office doorframe had them both turning. Her brother Timothy filled the space. Not because he was big. He was over six feet tall, four or five inches taller than she was, but even standing still, he radiated energy. She'd never figured out why it seemed to her as if he crackled with pent-up vitality. Maybe it was the sparks that flashed from his eyes. Boy, she wished she'd gotten her brother's bright green eyes instead of her muddy ones.

"Can I interrupt?" Timothy entered without waiting for her answer. Nothing new there.

"We're just finishing." Kate made a point of clipping her papers together. Timothy might believe his responsibilities were more important than everyone else's, but she had a better sense of priorities than any of her brothers. "Have you met Elizabeth?"

Timothy turned to her assistant and stuck out his hand. "I don't think I've had the pleasure. Welcome to MacBain."

He held on a little too long.

Liz blushed.

"Call me Liz. Everyone does. And thank you for the welcome." She tugged her hand out of his and gathered her laptop and the work she'd shared with Kate. "I'll leave you two alone."

Timothy leaned a hip against the table and watched Liz leave. A warning tension churned in Kate's gut. She placed a hand on his arm. "Leave my assistant alone."

Her brother always had one or two women on a string. No way would she let Timothy ruin the first relief she'd had in years and she didn't want to have a harassment suit on her hands.

Timothy grinned. "She's sure easy on the eyes."

"Stop it." This time she punctuated her words with a smack on his arm. "She's off-limits to you and my other scumbag brothers."

He pulled on his brown curls. His hair skimmed the top of his blue Oxford shirt. "I'd think it would be up to Miss Elizabeth whether she'd like to have lunch or dinner or ..." his eyebrows waggled, "breakfast with me."

"Timothy—do you want your name associated with the hashtag #MeToo?"

He winced. "No."

"I mean it. Don't mess up the best thing that's happened this week."

He tugged on her hair again. "Is K-K-K-Katie having trouble cleaning houses?"

She shook his hand off. She hated that stupid song. "Why are you bothering me?"

"Got a fax from Hanson's Toys. They aren't renewing their lease."

"Why? They have nice traffic in that strip mall."

"Economy. Age. The couple wants to retire."

"Damn it. The toy and the comic stores were complementary."

"Do you have any possible tenants for the spot?"

Kate tapped her nose. "Maybe. Last year Lotus Blossom mentioned they were thinking of expanding. They want more restaurant seating."

She needed to review the other mall leases and see if anyone else had expansion rights. She smiled. Liz could do the checking.

"That would work," Timothy said. "I'll have Stephen check the blueprints so we're ready to talk to them." He slapped his hands on his thighs. Meetings with Timothy were always short and to the point. "I'll get the For Lease signs up, but I hope Lotus takes the space. I love their steamed dumplings."

"I'll call the owner." She made a note in her planner.

To Timothy's departing back she called, "Stay away from Liz."

KATE SHOULD BE HERE in fifteen minutes. Her supervisor had admitted that Alex was her only client. Who could make enough money to live working eight hours a week? The least he could do was give Kate plenty of hours.

The doorbell rang and he pushed away from his keyboard. She was early.

He hurried through the house, yanked open the door and frowned.

"Gabe? What are you doing here?"

His friend, in khakis and a blue golf shirt, his hair all

windswept, looked like he'd come from a golf course. "Hey, Alex."

"Shouldn't you be at your office creating ads, encouraging people to want things they don't need?" Alex held open the door but peered outside for Kate.

Gabe slapped Alex's shoulder as he brushed past him and headed down the hallway. "I thought I'd let you know how the Larson Lighting presentation went."

"Really?" Normally Gabe called him on the client's reaction—he didn't show up on his doorstep. An itch grew between his shoulders.

"Yeah, got any coffee?"

"Sure." He'd made a large pot for Kate.

"Wow," Gabe said, glancing around the kitchen. "The place looks a lot cleaner than it did a couple of weeks ago. Found someone to replace dear old Martha?"

Alex nodded. "Started this week."

"Good. I worried you'd need a fumigator soon."

"Yeah, yeah." He liked the way the house looked now. And he was picking up after himself.

Gabe grabbed a mug, poured a cup and sat at the counter.

"So, what happened? Did they hate the jingle?" Alex filled his mug, settling onto a barstool. Gabe wouldn't have come to the house if the client had liked the song.

"They loved it. And we storyboarded a series of ads with a young girl growing up." Gabe wouldn't look him in the eye. His knee jiggled against the counter. "Perfect idea. Client loved it."

Alex squinted. Why was Gabe twitching? "That's good."

"Yeah. Good. Great." Gabe pleated his slacks. "Damn, you still make the best coffee around."

Alex raised an eyebrow. "I knew you before your voice changed. What happened?"

Gabe took a deep breath and let it out. "They want Meredith to record the song."

The muscles in Alex's face froze as if Novocain filled each nerve ending. Meredith? The woman who'd fucked up his life? "How did she get involved?"

Gabe held up his hands. "The team designing the campaign had no idea she's now your ex. When I found out, she'd already cut a preliminary demo."

"She's good." Her voice was the one honest thing about her. And the music fit her range.

Had he done that? Written the song for her? The coffee curdled in his stomach. God, he hoped not.

"It's my fault. I authorized searching for voice talent." Gabe leaned closer. "I never would have used her. I hope you know that."

Alex did know. He forced his mouth into a smile. "Seems sacrilegious. Maybe she'll get struck by lightning while singing a song about kids."

"I'm sorry." Gabe shook his head. "Are you okay with this?"

Alex pressed his hands against the granite, trying to stop the spinning. "Sure. I'm … just a little shocked, that's all."

"Your marriage has been over for almost two years." Gabe fingers bounced on the countertop.

"I know."

"I'll make this up to you. How about we hit a bar tonight?"

"Not tonight," Alex said. "Of course if you could get Timberwolves playoff tickets I might forgive you."

"That's a pretty hot ticket. I'll try." He finished his coffee. "What are you working on now?"

"My sonata." Alex pursed his lips. He was struggling, but at least he was working. That was an improvement. "Plus, I'm working on something for Central Standard Time."

"I heard them last month. They're good. I didn't know they played any of your songs."

Alex twirled his mug. They hadn't yet. He hadn't finished any of the songs he'd started. "I'm … branching out."

"Excellent, my friend."

For a while he'd composed exclusively for Meredith and her band. How many songs had he written? Two dozen? They'd recorded a dozen. The memory of their hours in the recording studio, Meredith perfecting each phrase, slapped against him like the sub-zero wind of a Minnesota winter.

The doorbell rang. *Thank you, Kate.*

Gabe followed him to the door. "I'll head out. I wanted you to hear the news from me."

"I appreciate that." Alex opened the door.

"Hey." Kate didn't sound too friendly.

"Hey back at 'cha." Alex tipped his head.

Gabe patted his heart.

Kate leaned down and grabbed her equipment.

Gabe mouthed *she's hot* and rushed to lift the vacuum into the house.

Kate shot him a thin smile. "Thanks, but I can get it."

"Sure." Gabe backed down the sidewalk, waggling his eyebrows.

"See you later." Alex shook his head at Gabe.

"Thanks for coming," he said to Kate.

He swore she muttered, "The client's always right."

"Coffee's on."

He should head to his office and let Kate work. Instead he followed her into the kitchen. He couldn't keep the expectant smile off his face.

What did the money from four more hours each week mean to her? And why was she cleaning in the first place? Was the economy this bad? Was she a student?

She headed for the cupboard with the mugs. The door shut with a sharp crack and he winced. She grabbed the coffeepot, her actions jerky, her shoulders hunched up to her ears. She didn't glance at him as she tipped the mug to her lips. Then she set it on the counter with a bang.

Even he could tell she wasn't happy, and Meredith had always told him he was clueless to other people's emotions. "Everything okay?"

"Peachy." She rolled her eyes. Today they were more golden than green, and they shot death rays at him.

"What's wrong?" he asked.

"You requested more hours." She threw her hands in the air.

"The house needs work and … and I wanted to help you out." She should have figured that out.

"I don't need that kind of help." She jerked open the dishwasher and started to unload the dishes.

"Wait, those are dirty." He moved toward her.

She shot him a lethal look and reloaded the dishes she'd taken out.

"When I talked to Lois, she said I was your only client. I figured you needed the money, and the house needs the attention."

"Well, I'm here." She pulled Martha's list from the laundry room. "I'll start with the vacuuming."

Why wasn't she grateful? "Don't you want the extra hours?"

"There's no—" Her jaw snapped shut. "I'm sorry. I shouldn't be taking my frustrations out on you. It's not you."

She took a deep breath. Her eyes closed. Man, she was angry.

He waited, wanting to smooth out the furrows on her forehead. He hadn't meant to complicate her life.

"Thank you." She didn't look him in the eye.

"You're welcome. You figure out what kind of hours you can work." He pulled out the extra key he'd made. "Just come … whenever."

Her eyes went wide. When she didn't take the key, he picked up her hand and placed it in her palm. She stared at him, and he curled her fingers around it.

His thumb swept her knuckles. They were softer than he expected. Her rubber gloves must protect her skin.

Her eyes flared open. She took in a breath and held it.

Heat radiated up his arm.

This was a … he was … a client.

He forced himself to let go.

"Just don't get here before seven in the morning or you'll catch me in my boxers," he added.

Kate jerked away from him.

Stupid. His comment was almost more suggestive than holding her hand.

He turned, almost running to his office.

THREE

"Amen," Kate repeated after Dad asked for the blessing on their Sunday family dinner.

Stephen handed her the au gratin potatoes. "So, Katie, you can't avoid my question. They added hours because you just can't get everything done, right?"

"Obviously I'm good at everything I do." Her cheeks ached from the smiling she'd done since walking into the house. Her brothers kept teasing her. "Isn't it a pity you can't say the same?"

Stephen growled.

Her family gathered around the dining room table, everyone in their childhood seats. Dad occupied the head of the table while Mom anchored the end nearest the kitchen door. Michael and Timothy sat on one side. She and Stephen on the other. The arrangement was permanent because Stephen and Timothy used to fight at the table.

"Oh, I can multitask," Stephen said. "Ask my date last night."

"Stephen Murphy MacBain." Their mother's voice

stopped her brothers' laughter. "This is not an appropriate dinner conversation."

Stephen shook his head. "We were playing a video game, carrying on a conversation and I was on the phone." His eyes twinkled. "Mom, what a dirty mind you have."

Kate couldn't help laughing. "Hey, Timothy, I talked to the Lotus Blossom owner. They're interested in expanding."

"Great," Timothy said. Even from across the table she could feel the vibrations as his foot bounced on the floor.

Mom waved a finger at them. "No business at the table."

"I didn't get a chance to let anyone know before my Friday cleaning penance," Kate explained.

Her comment drew her mother's laser gaze. "The rule's been in place since your father and I married. Just because you're working for the company doesn't mean the rule has changed. Understood?"

Kate heaved a sigh. "Yes."

Stephen and Timothy nodded. Michael said, "It wasn't me."

Her father laughed.

"And I suggest you stop thinking of cleaning as a penance." Her mother passed the potatoes around the table. "I wish someone would bring a date to dinner. What about the woman you were with last night, Stephen?"

Stephen's face was so frozen, it could have been carved from ice. "I don't think so."

Michael smirked, took a long drink of his wine and then refilled his glass. "How's the hot seat feel?"

Mom turned to Michael. "What about you?"

"No way." He took another drink.

Mom bit her lip. "It's time to move on, Michael. Sarah wouldn't want you to go through life alone."

The table grew quiet at the mention of Michael's fiancée. She'd died not quite two years ago.

Michael took another slug of his wine. "No."

"We're not ogres." Mom was trying to lighten the mood. "We won't devour your dates."

"I wouldn't want any woman I dated to get the wrong idea. I'm never settling down." Michael cut his ham and stuffed it in his mouth. Probably so he wouldn't have to answer any more questions.

"Are you feeling old, Mom?" Stephen asked. "Looking for grandchildren to play with?"

"I would like to be a grandmother." A wistful tone infused her mother's voice.

Her brothers would have to fulfill her mother's wish. Kate was going to run MacBain. Although being a doting aunt might be fun.

"I'm not sure I want to sleep with a grandmother," Dad said from his end of the table.

"You won't have a choice." Her mother smiled at her dad. "Time is short. Your father and I aren't getting any younger."

Kate stared at her mother. Makeup failed to cover the purplish shadows under her eyes. Her face looked thinner than normal.

The peas she tried to swallow stuck in her throat and she drank some water before asking, "Mom, is everything okay?"

Her mother brushed back her hair. "Let's finish dinner first."

"What is it?" Kate's muscles tightened like a spring.

Michael leaned forward. "What's wrong?"

Timothy's fork clattered to his plate.

Mom waved a hand. "Later."

Stephen pushed away from the table. "Mom?"

"Patty," Dad said. "I don't think the children will enjoy their meal if you keep them in suspense much longer."

Everyone looked at her.

"I found a lump. A couple of weeks ago." Her mother gave

a sharp nod. "I had a mammography last week. They confirmed that it's suspicious. Because of the family history, they're being cautious."

"Mom." Kate squeezed her hand.

Her father moved around the table and stood behind her mother. His big hands covered her shoulders.

"My biopsy is Tuesday. We planned to tell you after the results."

"Everything will be fine," Stephen said.

Timothy nodded.

"Yeah." Michael's face had gone pale.

Sometimes Kate forgot how much she loved her family. They were her bedrock, allowing her to build her sky-high dreams.

"You weren't supposed to notice I looked like a hag," her mother said to Kate.

"Hag? You're the prettiest mom ever."

"Ever," Timothy added.

"We're assuming the best," Dad said, but worry lurked behind his smile.

Her mother couldn't have … Kate refused to name the disease that had stolen her maternal grandmother. She barely remembered Grandmamma. She'd died when Kate was eight. All she remembered was her grandmother's twinkling eyes as Kate handed her a homemade Christmas card. And a smile on her thin face. And her long skinny fingers.

"Where will the biopsy take place?" Stephen asked.

They got the specifics.

"Everything will be okay." Timothy tapped his fingers on the table so hard the silver chimed.

"Of course it will," Stephen said, his deep voice rumbling.

"Absolutely." Kate pasted on a smile. Once she got home, she would start checking the internet for information.

Michael drank and refilled his wineglass.

"Stop with the solemn faces," Dad ordered. "It's a biopsy. We don't have anything to worry about."

Kate could almost hear the word *yet* at the end of her father's sentence.

"Everyone—eat," her mother insisted.

Kate brought a forkful of potatoes to her mouth.

This might explain why her parents wanted her to learn more about Murphy's Maids.

"I DON'T KNOW why *we* had to do the dishes." Stephen pushed the dice toward her. "It would be good practice for Kate."

"You're so funny." Kate refused to let her brother push her buttons.

She rolled the dice and moved her shoe around the Monopoly board, crossing Go and landing on Baltic Avenue. Damn.

Her father had hotels on his properties. "You owe me $450," he said.

Her mother, always the banker, handed her two hundred dollars for passing Go.

Kate counted out money to pay her rent and pouted as she handed it over to her father. "Why do you always have to have those two measly properties?"

"Haven't you learned anything in our business?" her father asked. "It's not always the biggest and flashiest property that brings in the best profit margin. Start small and build big."

Michael rolled, skipping past her properties and landing on his railroads.

The dice rattled in Timothy's hand. "How many Monopoly games do you think we've played?"

"Anytime it rained," Mother recalled. "Hundreds?"

"All I remember was not being allowed to play Battleship with you guys." Kate glared at her brothers.

"You're a girl," Timothy said.

"And that means what?" Kate shoved his shoulder. "That you hated to be beat by me?"

"Yeah. You always won. I never figured out how you did it. It should be a game of chance," Stephen said. "But you always won."

"Well of course I won. I worked in quadrants to scope out your ships. Didn't you?"

"Not back then," Stephen said.

Dad chuckled. "Let's get back to this game so I can continue my supremacy. Then you can dig out the old Battleship game and challenge one another. He winked at her. "My money's on Katie."

She'd always wanted to hear those words from her father, but not about a game. She wanted to be his acknowledged successor.

Well, if her parents needed to put a succession plan in place sooner than any of them had anticipated, Kate would just have to make it easy for them. She had to be the obvious choice.

"That's my property, Timothy," she said when he landed on Park Place. "Pay up."

"THERE'S a map of our properties in the glove box if you want to look," Kate told Liz as they drove to meet with the owner of the Lotus Blossom on Monday morning.

"Great. Thanks for bringing me along." Liz bounced a little in the passenger seat.

"No problem. This is a family business, so we'll meet with

Mr. and Mrs. Sung, Prem and Dao, and possibly their son. They've been leasing their space for—"

"Seven years. I also checked their reviews. People love their food."

Kate flipped on her turn signal, exiting onto Johnson Street. Normally the facts and figures for the restaurant's lease would be at her fingertips. She should have compiled the information last night, but after Mom's news she'd scoured the internet for biopsy and cancer information until early in the morning.

Now she worried because they were performing the biopsy in the hospital. Why the hospital and not a clinic?

Her phone rang, playing over her BMW's speakers. "Kate MacBain."

"Hey, Kate, Eric Sorenson. I'm getting back to you about those Timberwolves tickets. My son and I would love to attend Friday's game."

"I'll messenger the tickets to your office. We'll pick a restaurant around Target Center and eat before the game." They settled on the time. "See you then."

Liz shot her a thumbs-up. "Do you think taking the managing partner to the game will help wrap up the lease renewal?"

"It can't hurt having Eric at my mercy for three or four hours." Especially since the tickets were almost impossible to get. The Wolves hadn't been in the playoffs for years. Maybe this year they'd go all the way to the NBA finals.

If Sorenson brought his son, who should she bring? She hadn't dated in … forever. Wow, when was her last date? She'd probably have to ask Meg. Her friend kept better track of Kate's dating than Kate did.

Alex came to mind, with his dark hair and hypnotic eyes. Of course he thought she was a starving house cleaner. She didn't want him knowing she was the owner's daughter. She didn't want *anyone* knowing she was cleaning.

Right before she'd left his house last week, he'd asked whether there was some sort of evaluation he could complete on her. He was determined to make sure she didn't lose her job, and wasn't that ironic? She didn't want the job.

But she *would* excel at her real job. To do that, she needed Sorenson's signature on his lease extension.

The law firm had already requested some remodeling. If the firm wanted additional construction work done, Stephen should be involved. He could join them at the game.

Kate turned in to the strip mall. "Are you ready?"

Liz smoothed down her black pencil skirt. "Absolutely."

They walked into the nearly empty restaurant. The tables were set for the lunch rush. Seascapes painted on screens hung from the ceiling, giving each table a sense of privacy.

The Sungs sat near the back, drinking from large mugs. More mugs and a teapot waited for them.

"It's great to see you again, Prem and Dao," Kate said.

"Thank you for coming." Prem's voice carried the lilt of Thailand.

Kate introduced Liz and they both took the offered tea. Then she opened her folder. "As you know, Hanson Toy's isn't renewing their lease."

Prem nodded. "He talk to me already. He'll be out in three months?"

"Yes," Liz said. "At this time there's another tenant that has right of first refusal on the space." She checked her notes, but Kate doubted she needed to. "Trencher's Comics."

"He is not interested." Dao stumbled over the words. "He come for lunch every day."

"That's good. We'll need to go through the steps of negotiating with you and then offering to let him match the lease, but

I don't anticipate any problems." Kate smiled at Dao. "We want to see you expand."

As if they'd worked together for years, Liz pulled out the offer sheet. "We've developed an offer for your review. It includes leasehold improvements to tear down the walls and the refit of the space."

"My brother Stephen did your initial remodel. He'll be stopping by to talk to you," Kate continued. "We've done some prelim work, but you need to let us know if this fits your vision."

Liz pulled out Stephen's rough drawing. It showed an archway between the spaces. She pushed it across the table with the offer letter.

"Look at that," Dao said. Then she and Prem quietly debated whether they should have a private room or more tables. Their hands touched. They smiled into each other's eyes. The couple reminded her of her parents.

Prem looked between Kate and Liz. "You work fast."

"Timothy adores your pot stickers," Kate said. "Stephen refuses to let your restaurant move. It gives you a negotiating advantage."

Everyone laughed. The bell on the door jangled and the first lunch guests walked in. Dao popped up and sat them near the windows.

"I will have my son look at these," Prem said. "He is in law school now."

"That's wonderful," Kate said. "You can give Liz or me a call if you have questions."

"I better get into kitchen," Prem said.

They shook hands. Dao went to welcome more guests.

"So, we're waiting for your family, right?"

"Right." Family. How was her mother doing today with the biopsy scheduled for the next day?

"Are you okay?" Liz asked, her forehead furrowed. "I thought that went well. Did I miss something?"

"No," Kate said. "You did great. I was thinking of something else."

"Well, you know I'll help you any way I can, right?"

"You already are."

Stephen walked into the restaurant and dropped into the empty seat beside Kate. "Let's eat."

By the time Dao handed them menus, Michael had arrived and sat next to Liz.

"Two days in a row. I don't think I can stand all this familial bonding," Michael said.

Stephen shifted in his seat.

"Where do you usually sit?" Kate rolled her eyes.

Stephen waved to the back of the room. "I'm good. I'm flexible."

"Okay. Here's the deal," Liz said, looking around the table. "No inside jokes. No family … whatevers. Don't make me feel stupid."

"I thought you were a twin." Michael picked up one of the menus.

How did Michael know that?

"I am. And no, my brother and I didn't have our own language. Although according to our parents, we were quadruple the trouble."

Michael flashed a lazy smile at Liz. Kate blinked. Michael was smiling?

"What kind of trouble did you get into?" he asked.

"I could open childproof locks when I was two." She wiggled her fingers. "Fine motor skills."

"Really." Michael leaned closer.

Liz looked down at her place setting.

Kate kicked Michael under the table and he winced.

"Stephen, I told the Sungs that you'd walk them through your ideas," Kate said, changing the subject.

"How'd it go?" he asked.

"Good," Liz replied. "We'll stop at Trencher's Comics on the way to the office and let them know they'll be getting a right of first refusal letter." She grimaced. "Sorry, Kate. I should have let you tell them."

Kate loved Liz's enthusiasm. "Go ahead. You're doing great."

They ordered, agreeing to eat family style so they could try one another's choices. "You can eat everything but the pot stickers," Stephen said, snapping his napkin open and spreading it on his lap. "I'm bringing them home for dinner."

"How long will it take to remodel the space next door?" Liz asked.

"We'll work around their hours. We can demo next door without opening the walls. Then start the rebuild." Stephen scratched his head. "We'll do all-nighters if we have to. Maybe a week of work. It's dependent on how much plumbing and electrical is needed."

Liz grinned. "I can't wait to follow the whole process, from the proposed lease agreement to the changes in the space."

Had Kate ever been that energetic?

Liz was a couple of years younger than her. But with Kate's parents forcing her to clean houses and her mother facing a biopsy, she felt as old as the men who played chess in the park across from her apartment building.

"Where are you from?" Stephen asked Liz.

"A small town in Iowa." She nibbled on her bottom lip.

Both brothers stared at her mouth.

Kate jabbed Stephen in the side and shoved at Michael's foot.

"I grew up on a farm." Liz didn't notice the exchange between the MacBains.

"That explains the enthusiasm," Michael said.

"I worked for Colfax Property Management, but once I learned who's who in property management, I knew I wanted to work for your company."

"Who'd you work with at Colfax?" Stephen asked.

"I worked in leasing there too." Liz rearranged her napkin.

Kate knew why Liz was uncomfortable but wondered if she would tell her brothers. She waited a beat, but Liz didn't add anything.

"Their growth has been phenomenal in this economy. Why did you leave?" Timothy asked.

Liz pleated the napkin in her lap. "I … I quit."

Michael's jaw clenched. "Any particular reason?" His words came out low and slow.

Liz stared at her lap. "I … I …" She looked up, her eyes the color of bruised eggplants. "I wasn't comfortable working in their organization. Working with Jerry."

Her brothers slid back in their chairs. Maybe this would stop them from hitting on staff.

Dao arrived with a tray of steaming dishes.

Stephen snatched the pot stickers. "These are mine. And I'll need a box."

Dao patted his back. "Sure thing, Stephen."

Everyone dug in.

"God, this is good," Liz exclaimed.

The talk around the table shifted to business.

A line formed near the cash register. Numerous customers carried out bags. "They need to expand," Liz added. "What's their dinner service like?"

"Just like this," Stephen said. "Maybe more takeout. They have a great reputation."

Kate gathered her files. "Lunch is on Michael. Right?"

Liz dug into her purse. "No. I can pay."

Kate held up her hand. "I'm kidding. Family joke. This is

on the company. The employee with the most seniority at the table always pays."

And unfortunately, right now that was Michael.

"MOM, WHY ARE YOU WORKING?" Kate leaned her hands against her mother's desk. "Shouldn't you be relaxing … prepping for tomorrow … something?"

"This is routine. Besides, I need to be here. Otherwise I'll drive myself nuts with *what ifs*." Her mom's red highlights in her brown hair caught the sunlight as she shook her head. "If I'm gone for a while, I want everything in order."

Gone? Kate refused to think that way. But … "Would they operate tomorrow if they found something?"

Her mother moved around her desk and tugged Kate to the sofa. "We won't know the results for up to five days."

"I want everything to be okay." Kate sat on the sofa and set her head on her mother's shoulder.

"Don't worry." Mom took Kate's hand. "I've been vigilant with my mammograms. You need to be too."

"I am." Both her great-grandmother and grandmother had died of breast cancer. Now her mother had a lump. It seemed inevitable she would end up with breast cancer too.

She should be comforting her mother, not the other way around. "I think we need massages this week. My treat."

Mom bounced a kiss on the top of her head. "Maybe. I'll get through tomorrow and see how I feel."

The silence seemed to wrap them in a warm cocoon. Kate couldn't imagine anything bad happening to her mother.

"I'm worried about Michael," her mother said finally. "I think he'll equate this lump with Sarah's cancer."

Kate nodded. "He got awfully quiet on Sunday."

"Will you keep your eye on him?"

"Sure." Kate chewed her lower lip.

"Good. That's a relief."

They both took a deep breath, making them laugh.

"Okay." Her mother hugged her. "I don't want to explain to the boss why we're relaxing on the sofa."

Kate chuckled. "Yeah, our boss is an ogre."

"Hey, I heard that." Her father leaned against the door-frame. His gaze zeroed in on his wife.

"So what time is the biopsy?" Kate asked.

"One," Mom said, "but I don't want anyone coming to the hospital with us."

"Mom," she protested. "I want to be there for you."

Her mother held up a hand. "I refuse to give this too much weight. You don't sit in the lobby worrying when I have a mammogram, do you?"

"No," Kate said.

"Then we won't make a big deal out of this."

Dad came over and stood next to Mom. Together they were a wall of strength. How could she live up to the examples they set?

"I'll let everyone know how things go, but your mother and I aren't worrying. Things will be fine," her dad said.

Plastering on a smile, she hugged her mother. "Of course."

She touched her dad's arm and headed to the door. "I'm going back to my grindstone, ogre."

ALEX CHECKED THE CLOCK. It was only 9:30. Would Kate be on time this Tuesday? On Friday she'd come and gone without saying hello.

Of course he'd given her a key.

Handing out keys had always been hard for him. It wasn't just his expensive instruments and electronics he risked. He was allowing someone to enter his home. Even when he'd seriously dated, it had taken him forever to give that kind of trust.

Yet he'd handed Kate a key after knowing her for a few days.

Alex pushed away from the console. He wasn't concentrating on this latest song. He grabbed his mug and went for a refill.

Central Standard Time was getting national recognition. Their female lead had a great voice. The group thought he had a reputation of getting things done. Boy, they didn't know he'd been struggling for almost two years.

Maybe if he wrote about a struggling woman making it on her own. The flash of Kate's coppery curls filled his mind. And the way her eyes sizzled after she'd discovered the mess in the washing machine.

He added milk to his coffee and stirred, carefully putting the spoon in the dishwasher.

Kate had been the first woman to point out he was a slob. Even Meredith had never complained. His ex had had the cleaning service come every day.

Kate. Why did such a sharp woman end up cleaning houses? Bad love affair? No education? Economy? And if he was her only client, how could she pay her rent? Unless cleaning was a side gig for her. Maybe she was trying to make it as an actor, or musician doing this on the side …

Of course she could be living with someone. Roommates. Boyfriend?

The idea that she had a boyfriend didn't sit well, but how else could she survive? He'd request more hours, but he didn't want to face her anger.

He didn't understand women.

How do you understand a woman? A melody line rang in his head fully formed. He froze. Letting it play out. *They burrow into your head, leaving you dead.*

Okay, maybe not. But the melody grabbed him by the balls.

He rushed into his office, careful not to spill his coffee. It might not be the rock tune the group had requested, but the music pulsed inside his head. He put the mug on a coaster, then slapped on his headphones.

His fingers flew across the keyboard. Waves of the tune ebbed and flowed like the ocean, sometimes gentle, sometimes battering against the walls of his mind. He scribbled notes as fast as he could, bracketing phrases, rearranging, caressing the tune to wrap around words that flowed like a raging river.

"Yes." Sweat ran down his neck, and he scratched at the irritating sensation.

He fought with the melody, forcing it to modulate for the chorus when it wanted to stay in the minor key. Emotions bashed into quarter notes and trills. Despair bled pain into a driving chorus.

In the dark you come to me,
Moonlight in your hair.
Love tangles in our silence,
Words unspoken on the air.
You never say a word, never say you care.

His foot tapped out the syncopation of brushes on the drums. A pulsing bass.

You never say a word, never say you care.

Shutting down, he rolled away from the keyboard. This song needed the haunting tone of a piano. He gathered his note-dotted papers and moved across the room.

His fingers took a moment to get used to the piano keys' harder action. With a deep breath, he crooned the words, hating that he didn't have a singing voice.

The melody sounded different on the piano. He made changes, emphasizing the bass, the dark tones, to convey the sadness. Love unrequited. Love denied. Love undiscovered.

His shoulders slumped. He leaned his elbows against the music desk.

"Wow. That's incredible."

He jerked his head up. No one was allowed in his office while he worked. Hadn't he explained that to Kate?

He swiveled to look at her.

She stood in the open doorway. She hadn't crossed the threshold.

He'd left the door open. He never made that mistake.

"I …" She waved her hand. "That sounded amazing."

"Thanks." He rose from the bench. His legs quivered. He needed to move, needed exercise. Needed something.

"I'm heading out." Kate's eyebrows knitted together.

How bad did he look?

Then her words sank in. "Heading out?" He glanced at the clock. "Nine-thirty?" He'd worked twelve hours?

"No." She gave him a perplexed look, still not stepping into the room. He must look like a mad man. "It's a little after two."

Ah. "Guess I need to put a battery in the clock," he said, a little sheepishly.

He shook his head, trying to clear away his creativity haze. He hadn't been this wrapped up in a song since … since before the divorce.

"Well, from what I saw, you were in a battle." Her gaze softened. "The song is … beautiful. Sad, but beautiful."

Her phone rang. She checked the screen and sank against the doorframe. Her face paled.

He moved to her side as she answered the call, worried she'd had bad news.

"Hey, Dad," she said.

Alex pulled up before he put his arms around her. Why would a phone call from her dad shake her up?

"But they stopped the bleeding, right?"

Something was wrong with Kate's mom?

"Is this bad? Is bleeding a sign that it's malignant?" Kate asked.

That sounded like cancer.

"You're sure?" Kate didn't look convinced at whatever her dad said.

"Can I talk to her?" Her teeth chewed on her lower lip.

"Of course. I'll … talk to her tomorrow." Kate stubbed her toe on the floor.

"Sure. Are you going home now?" She nodded. "Okay. Give Mom my love."

She tucked her phone in her pocket and closed her eyes.

"Bad news?" he asked, touching her arm.

She took a deep breath and it shook her whole body. "No."

She pushed away from the door, but her legs wobbled and she set a hand on the doorframe to steady herself.

"Sit." He wrapped an arm around her waist.

Her body melted into his side. He half-carried her, her softness molding to his hardness.

It would be easy to pull her into a hug. Only her solemn face kept him from doing something stupid. She hadn't looked this bad when she'd dealt with the laundry last week.

He guided her to the kitchen and eased her onto a barstool. She didn't look like coffee would help, so he pulled out a couple of sports drinks. Electrolytes.

"Try this." He took a stool on the opposite side of the island.

"Thanks." She took a sip, blinking as she stared at the counter. "I should go."

She didn't move off the stool.

"I don't mean to intrude … but is your mother all right?" he asked.

"No. Well, we don't know. She had a biopsy today," she said, her voice brittle. "There was some bleeding, so they held her longer than normal."

"Is that bad?"

"My dad said no, but it doesn't sound right." She swallowed. "My great-grandmother and grandmother died from breast cancer."

"If they do a biopsy, don't they know right away whether it's benign?" He didn't know much about cancer but thought they knew in the operating room.

"She had a needle biopsy. It's less traumatic, leaves a smaller scar." Kate picked at the label on her bottle. "The downside is you need to wait for the pathology report."

"You're kidding?"

"Wish I was."

"How long does it take to get the results?"

"Five or six days." She sighed. "I should go."

She stood as he came around the counter. He couldn't imagine the turmoil she was going through.

"Are you okay to drive?"

"Sure." Her voice was small.

He stepped toward her, his arms open. She looked so sad.

"What are you …?"

He pulled her into a hug.

She leaned into him, pressing her face against his chest. Her breath shuddered. "Thanks," she mumbled into his shirt.

He rested his cheek on the side of her head. Her hair smelled earthy, with the faint hint of bleach.

She took in a deep breath. He did the same. They both pulled apart. Placing a finger under her chin, he tipped her face up. "Better?"

Something changed. What had started as a comfort hug, morphed into awareness. Something sparked between them.

Her eyes widened, the gold flecks glittering.

He had to know what her lips felt like. It was just a brush but enough to know they were soft. Soft, smooth and tempting.

She stood on tiptoe. And her mouth was right there.

He licked the seam of her lips and they opened, inviting him in. Mint exploded against his tongue, heat exploded in his groin. He took her weight in his arms as she angled her head. Their tongues tangled and one of them groaned.

The dryer buzzed, a discordant blare.

Her eyes fluttered open. The dark pools of her pupils drowned out the hazel of her irises. He couldn't see the gold rings he'd discovered around her eyes.

She froze.

Crap.

"I'm sorry. I shouldn't have done that." He swallowed.

She broke away. "No. It's okay."

It's okay? Alex fought the urge to pull her back. For the first time in two years, he wanted to hold a woman.

"Thanks for the … hug." A flush tinted her skin a lovely pink. "It helped."

She snatched the bucket of cleaning supplies, her movements rushed and jerky. Okay … that put the kiss in the *too stupid to live* column of his life.

"Wait," he called.

When she turned around, her eyes were wide.

Was she afraid of him? God he hoped not. "I'm sorry. I was out of line. It won't happen again. It was …" he waved a hand between them, "it was just the moment."

"Yeah. Yeah. I get that." She didn't look convinced. "Thank you."

"If I'm your only client, why don't you leave the supplies here? At least on Tuesdays."

"Good idea." She set the vacuum and bucket in the laundry room. Turning, she said, "We know you don't use that room."

"Ha ha." But her joke broke the tension arcing between them. "I hope your mother is okay."

"Thanks. I'll … see you tomorrow."

He followed and watched her make her escape.

"KATE?"

She started at Michael's voice. They were reviewing the first quarter budget overruns, but she'd zoned out.

"What's got you so jumpy?"

Alex. His hug had been … perfect. The brush of his lips had knocked her socks off. What a kiss. His tongue on hers had made her want to rip off his shirt. Heat filled her face.

Then he'd apologized. *Apologized.*

She'd *wanted* to kiss him. Really kiss him and see what those plump lips of his could do. Now she wanted more. She wanted to know what his lips would feel like on her body.

But she couldn't tell Michael any of this. "I'm worried."

He leaned back in his chair. "Me too. Mom's too young and full of life to … you know?"

"Yeah."

He sank a little deeper into his chair. She frowned. The collar of his shirt no longer fit. Her brother was losing weight, and Mom wanted her to watch over him.

"Does Mom's biopsy bring back memories?" she asked.

He stared at the papers. "Of what?"

She put her hand on his arm. "Sarah."

"I don't want to talk about her." He slipped away from her and stalked to the windows. "It's Mom I'm worried about."

Great. He had been opening up to her—they'd been having an honest moment—and she'd blown it by being too direct. Maybe she wasn't as good a people manager as she thought. *Hm.* She'd try to sign up for an online Human Resources workshop to build that strength.

Kate pushed away from the conference room table and

joined him at the windows. "I can't concentrate on budget overruns right now. Let me run an idea by you."

Michael shut the folder. For a CFO, her brother was eager to ignore a numbers discussion. "Sure."

She wanted her mind off her mother's biopsy and Alex's kiss. A kiss that would never, *ever,* be repeated. Maybe if she voiced some of her ideas, it would be easier to get through the day.

"The economy's picking up," she said.

Michael shrugged.

She paced across the room and set her hands on the table. "I can almost sense hope from our clients. What do you think about running an advertising campaign around our retail construction business?"

"We were just talking about budget overruns." Michael raised an eyebrow. "You want us to spend money? Now?"

She had to think about the future. A future where her mother was healthy, and the company thrived. "Hear me out."

FOUR

"Gabe, over here!" Alex waved from the table.

Gabe threaded his way through the crowd at Harry's Pub. "Glad you got a table," he shouted. "This is a madhouse."

It might be crazy, but Alex liked the rhythm of the restaurant. He heard music in the clash of silverware and the clinking of glasses. There was a driving pulse to the background noise. If he created a piece based on the sounds he'd call it *The melody and counterpoint of urban living.*

"Look at this mob." Gabe slid onto the stool at the high-top table Alex had secured. "Are they all going to the game?"

Most of the crowd wore Timberwolves jerseys or gear.

"Looks like it. Are we sitting in the nosebleed section?" Alex asked.

"Hell no." Gabe slapped his back. "We're about ten rows up from courtside. We'll be splashed with sweat, my friend."

"Way to score."

"Gave up my firstborn child for the tickets, but they'll be worth the price."

Gabe's quip was like a punch to the diaphragm. Alex stiffened.

"I'm sorry." Gabe held up his hands. "I didn't think."

"No, it's okay," Alex said. "I'm good. Don't worry."

"I mean it, man. It was a turn of phrase. I would never …"

"I know." Alex amped up his smile. "But that will cost you the first round. Maybe even the second."

He wouldn't let his best friend's comment ruin the evening. He wouldn't think about his ex-wife either. Tonight was about getting out again, reconnecting with the world.

"Hi, I'm Missy. What can I start you off with?" The server stood close to Alex's shoulder. Almost too close, but it was probably because the place was noisy.

"Surly's Axe Man," Gabe said.

"Make it two."

"You got it." Her smile almost blinded him. No one had teeth that dazzling. She brushed against him before turning and heading to the bar.

"She's pretty cute," Gabe said.

"Her teeth must glow in the dark."

Gabe laughed. "Speaking of glowing in the dark, how's your love life?"

"You're kidding, right?" Alex's fingers played the tabletop. All he could think of was his inappropriate kiss with Kate.

All week Alex had kept his encounters with Kate professional. Neither of them discussed what had happened, or not happened, in the kitchen. He never told her he'd lain in bed each night wondering what she would look like minus the raggedy blue jeans she wore when she cleaned.

He couldn't tell Gabe about that kiss. "The last person I went out with was you. People are starting to talk."

Gabe smacked his own chest. "You're playing for the other team. I'm out of here."

"Ha ha."

Gabe gave Alex a punch in the shoulder. "We'll hit a

couple of clubs after the game. We could swing by The Shout House. You could play for drinks."

"I've graduated from those days." The tension between him and Gabe melted away. Alex let the background percussion soothe him.

Missy brought their beers and took their order, still standing too close for Alex's comfort. She barely looked twenty-one. He wasn't into robbing cradles.

"So, what are you working on now?" Gabe asked.

The sonata deadline was closing in on him. "I'm still working on tunes for Central Standard Time."

He'd spent the end of the week cleaning up the melody. Then he'd worked on the harmonies and instrumentation. "I … like it."

It was hard to judge his own work. Although Kate had liked the song.

"That's great." Gabe saluted him with his beer before taking a swallow.

"Hopefully I'm out of my drought. It might have been your jingle that pulled me from the funk." Or Kate.

He spent too much time thinking about his house cleaner. Alex rested his chin in his hand and checked out the crowd as they waited for their dinner.

"So, you owe me?" Gabe asked. "Pay for dinner."

"I planned on it. You scored the tickets."

Missy brought their burgers. "Let me know if you need anything else." She flipped her blonde hair off her shoulder. Her smile looked like an invitation.

Gabe watched Missy walk away. "God, how do you do it?"

"She was just friendly." Alex poured the last of the ketchup onto his burger. He wasn't a chick magnet. "Hell, she's probably looking for a better tip."

Gabe snorted. "Ten bucks says she adds her phone number to the check."

"No way." Alex hadn't even looked her in the eye.

"Put your money where your mouth is, big guy."

"Sure. Easy ten."

Missy swung back to the table before he'd even picked up his massive burger. "How's everything?"

"Could we get more ketchup?" Gabe held out the empty bottle.

Missy didn't even look at Gabe as she grabbed the container. "Yeah."

Gabe leaned over. "I should have made our bet a hundred dollars."

"Right."

Alex glanced at Missy and a flash of coppery curls caught his eye. *Just like Kate's.*

He had to stop thinking about his house cleaner.

"Are you checking out her ass?" Gabe asked.

"No. I thought I saw someone I knew."

Gabe bit into his burger. "Good luck in this crowd," he said around a full mouth.

A woman with auburn hair had been standing near the entrance. It couldn't be Kate. She was just on his mind.

But she could have a date.

He sank back in his chair. If she did, what did she think about the kiss they'd shared?

God, it would be terrible if he were the only person thinking about it.

KATE SPOTTED Eric Sorenson standing by the hostess station and waved. Thank goodness she'd arranged for an early dinner. Harry's Pub was packed.

They could have eaten farther from Target Center, but Harry's was within walking distance. Unfortunately the noise level wouldn't allow them to talk about the law firm's lease renewal.

"How are you?" she asked when Eric joined her at the table.

"Great." He shook her hand. "This is my son, Nathan."

She couldn't judge how old the boy was. He wore a Timberwolves cap and jersey but only came to her chest.

"Hey, Nathan, nice to meet you." She'd hoped Eric's son was college age. She didn't like dealing with kids. She'd had enough kid time babysitting her two younger brothers. "Looks like you're a fan. Just like me."

They wore matching jerseys except the kid's looked a little newer. Her jersey might be older than the kid. Yikes.

She tapped his cap, and he gave her a blank stare. Okay. Not the right approach.

Eric frowned. "He is a fan. Plus, he plays traveling basketball."

"I don't understand why we can't just go to the game." Nathan's sullen look made the kid seem older. "Besides, women don't know anything about basketball."

"Nathan," his dad hissed.

Kate smiled. She might not know how to talk to kids, but she did know basketball. "Oh Nathan, you have a lot to learn. I do know my basketball."

He sneered. "No way."

"Oh way. I played point guard on my high school basketball team. Four years starting varsity." Did she have to prove something to this pip-squeak? "I still take my brothers in one-on-one."

Nathan didn't need to know that she played as dirty as possible. Her brothers had qualms against elbowing her, and she took advantage whenever possible.

And where was Stephen? "My brother's joining us. You've met Stephen before, haven't you, Eric?"

Eric looked up from the stare-down he was having with his son. "I don't think so."

"Stephen heads up the construction arm of MacBain," she told him. "I thought we could discuss your ideas for changing your space."

In theory a casual dinner to review the lease extension had sounded great. Now with a sour-looking kid, the deafening background noise and Stephen a no-show, her stomach bounced like a trampoline.

Eric looked around. "We can try."

Their server took their drink order. Kate was tempted to order a martini. After this week, she wanted straight alcohol.

Following Eric's lead, she settled for a beer.

Nathan pulled out his cell phone. His thumbs flew across the keyboard. Wasn't there a minimum age on cell phone usage?

"How old is your son?" she asked, hoping she didn't sound judgmental.

"Twelve." Eric rolled his eyes. "His mother and I thought getting him a phone would help with the logistics of picking him up after practices." He leaned across the table away from Nathan. "I don't know what he and his friends talk about. I swear it's in code."

"Kate."

Thank God. Stephen to the rescue.

She made the introductions. Nathan looked up from his phone to mumble a hello. More than she'd received.

As everyone sat, someone kicked her. Pain radiated up her leg. She stared at Nathan, but the kid was texting.

Kate made a show of checking her watch. "I think we should order."

"Sure, sure." Eric checked the menu. "What do you want, Nathan?"

"Tacos."

Kate checked through the menu. No tacos. "Since they don't have tacos, maybe there's something else you're interested in."

"No. I want tacos. They sell tacos at the game."

"Hey, bud. Do you like nachos?" Stephen asked. "They're pretty close to a taco."

Nathan shrugged.

"Why don't we get an order of nachos while we check out what else you might like to eat?" Stephen suggested.

"I guess." Another shrug.

Stephen cajoled Nathan into picking a menu item. Then the kid went back to his phone.

Finally. The adults could talk.

"Eric, what do you have in mind for changing your space?" The toe of a pair of sneakers caught her shin again. She forced a neutral expression onto her face through the pain.

"We'd like to add stairs in our leased space between our floors. Something nice behind the lobby on the sixteenth floor. And the same on the upper two floors but not necessarily as showy."

"Is this for clients or employees?" Stephen asked.

"Both. With stairs, we'd consolidate reception on sixteen. And our employees wouldn't have to use the elevators." Eric laughed. "Someone's always forgetting their security cards."

"I get that," Stephen said. "Have you seen the stairs we built for Forest and Forest on the eighth floor?"

"That's what got us thinking." Eric sipped his beer.

Her brother pulled out his phone. "I've scanned your blueprints … the reason I was late. Let's take a look."

Stephen opened a file. Kate was pretty good at reading blueprints, but Stephen had gone to the HVAC and wiring schematics. She left that to the experts.

Kate pictured the lobby of the law firm. There was a

conference room behind the receptionist's desk. "Are you giving up conference room space?"

"If this works, we would probably lose two conference rooms." Eric winced. "The partners want the convenience of having a fully enclosed space."

Kate took a sip of her beer. She might be able to swing tenant switches and get Sorenson his conference rooms. She'd make some calls, give them a solution without them asking.

Nathan frowned at her. *What was his problem?*

The nachos arrived and the kid dug in. At least he'd stopped kicking her. Maybe he was taking out his sullenness on her brother's shins.

Stephen looked up from his phone. "I won't get your hopes up but adding a staircase might work. I'll review the blueprints this weekend and have an engineer take a look too."

"Great." Eric grinned.

"Are there other changes you're looking at for this renewal?" Kate asked.

Eric pulled out his phone. "We've compiled a wish list. I'll send it to you."

"Good."

Their food arrived. As Kate passed the ketchup to her brother, a man with curly black hair headed to the door. It almost looked like Alex.

Whoever it was, they were leaving the restaurant.

She flushed and then went cold, the sweat chilling her skin.

Stephen bumped her shoulder. "You okay?"

"Yeah. Just ... yeah."

It couldn't have been Alex, right? The man whose mouth she'd never forget? Too coincidental.

ALEX SETTLED INTO HIS SEAT, beer in hand. "Great seats."

They were ten rows up from the floor. Must have cost a fortune. Especially since the T-Wolves hadn't made the playoffs since the 2003/2004 season. Hard to be a fan.

"Corporate tickets." Gabe shed his jacket. "I needed to thank you for helping land the Hanson Lighting account. They loved the idea of having the little girl grow up. We should be able to run with it for a while."

"Well, if I didn't say thanks—I am now," Alex said.

He watched the cheerleaders. They were so … peppy. And none of them had curly auburn hair. He scratched his head. He'd never been fixated on redheads before.

People were filing in to their seat in front of them. "What the hell?"

Gabe looked at him. "What's wrong?"

It *was* Kate. And she had two men and a boy following her. They were decked out in T-Wolves jerseys and sitting in the best seats in the house.

"Nothing. Just recognized someone."

Gabe craned his neck. "Who?"

"Kate."

"Your house cleaner?"

"Yeah."

Gabe smacked his shoulder. "That's Eric Sorenson, the managing partner of Sorenson Law."

Hell, even Alex had heard of the law firm.

"She's Kate MacBain." Gabe elbowed him. "I didn't recognize her before."

MacBain? She'd never said her last name. "MacBain. Why do I know that name?"

"MacBain is a property management company. They lease buildings, have a construction arm and own strip malls. They're huge."

Alex's head hurt. "How does Kate fit in?"

"Daughter. Second oldest child. Since they're real estate royalty—that would make her a princess. She's their leasing director and a hell of a negotiator." Gabe elbowed him. "Why's a millionaire cleaning your house, Double A?"

Alex's eyebrows rose. "That's what I want to know."

WHAT INCREDIBLE SEATS THEY HAD, courtside. Unfortunately Kate ended up next to the kid.

She whispered to Stephen, "Switch places with me."

He frowned. "Why?"

She tipped her head at Nathan and raised her eyebrows.

Stephen gave her a guppy stare. "You need to get over your kid phobia."

"There isn't any getting over this." She rolled her eyes. "You and Timothy scarred me for life."

"I can't help that the parental units forced you to babysit."

"Come on." She leaned closer. "My shins are black and blue from dinner."

Stephen rolled his eyes. "That's what you get with barstools and high top tables. People swing their legs and you got kicked."

She handed her brother the box of popcorn and shook off her jacket. "You owe me for all my years of babysitting. Forever."

Stephen waved a hand and she squeezed past his legs as they traded spots. At least she wasn't next to Nathan. Now she could enjoy the game.

The back of her neck itched. Almost as if someone were staring at her. She glanced around but only saw a sea of faces.

Eric leaned around Nathan and Stephen. "Great seats. Thanks for bringing us."

"You're welcome. MacBain appreciates your business."

If she could lock up their renewal *and* add additional square footage to their lease, they would be even more appreciated. If she accomplished it, maybe Dad could appeal to Mom to let her out of her cleaning penance with Alex.

Alex. She touched her lips, still able to feel his kiss. A kiss that had turned her into a puddle.

Then he'd apologized. It had been *inappropriate*. It wouldn't happen again, yada yada yada.

The players were introduced with enough hoopla to rouse the crowd. Kate stood and clapped along with the rest of the fans.

"No wonder you like this job," Stephen said. "Want to trade for a while?"

"Like you could stand sitting in an office." She took a handful of popcorn.

"I could stand catching live games every week." Stephen indicated the playing floor.

"Anytime you want, except during playoffs. Those tickets are taken. We've got plenty of Twins tickets available. Next time read the memos I send out."

"Yeah, yeah. Can I bring a date?"

"You know the rules, you bring clients or vendors. Otherwise the ticket price gets included in your taxable income."

"Get out."

The tip-off saved her from explaining tax law. The Wolves captured the ball and made the first two points. A Spurs player took the ball upcourt.

Kate let the game take her away from the humiliation of cleaning houses and the memory of Alex's lips on hers.

A San Antonio player elbowed the forward as he shot. The refs didn't call the blatant violation.

"Foul," she cried. "Get your eyes checked!"

She jumped up and shook her fist at the ref for another bad call.

"It's just a game," her brother whispered as she sat.

The blare of the buzzer signaled the end of the first half. The teams left the court, replaced by a dance group. Their music pounded the air.

"Just immersing myself in the game, 'cuz if I think about what's going on with Mom, I'll wallow."

Stephen rubbed her back, and she tipped her head to rest it on his shoulder. For all the trouble he'd given her as a child, they were the closest of the siblings. Stephen didn't have Michael's melancholy or Timothy's frenetic energy. He was a big teddy bear.

"Mom will be fine," he said.

"I know, but waiting is hard."

"You know Dad took her to the lake, right?"

"Yeah." The MacBains' lake house, Solitude, was the family's sanctuary near Brainerd. Just thinking about Solitude made Kate's muscles relax.

"Dad will take care of her."

"Is the ice out on the lake?"

"Yeah."

She patted his thigh. "I need to hit the bathroom before the second half."

What she wanted to do was go home, crawl in bed and sleep until Monday.

As she scooted past Eric and Nathan, she asked, "Can I get you anything to eat or drink?"

Nathan nodded. "Tacos."

She smiled. "Sure." Now she would have to find a taco stand. "Eric, what can I get you?"

"Just a beer."

Stephen got up behind her. "I'll get the beer if you find the tacos."

She stepped close to her brother, letting someone pass. Too bad they made the steps so narrow. "Yeah, give me the tough job. I don't even know where they sell tacos."

"You're resourceful. You'll find them." He grinned.

"Thanks." She stared at each step, avoiding the people returning to their seats. At this rate, she'd miss the beginning of the second half.

"Kate!"

Her head jerked up. *Alex?* She stopped on the stairs and looked around. He stood in the middle of the row to her right.

"Alex?"

He began to move toward her.

Someone bumped her shoulder and she wobbled. Stephen steadied her. "I'll get the beers."

"Kate." Alex stepped over the last pair of legs separating them.

"What are you doing here?" she asked.

"Watching the game," he said.

Okay, that was sarcasm. First with the client's kid and now with this guy who'd kissed her.

"I always kind of wondered why you didn't give me your full name. Tell me," he said, "why is Kate *MacBain* of MacBain Enterprises, cleaning my house?"

FIVE

ALEX WATCHED KATE'S MOUTH OPEN AND SHUT, TWICE. Someone hurrying down the steps bumped her shoulder, and she took a little stutter step. The heels of her boots clicked on the steps. Even he recognized her designer purse as one that cost hundreds of dollars. Meredith had owned something similar.

She didn't look like a woman who cleaned houses.

"Heading up?" he asked.

She nodded. Her bewitching eyes looked green tonight. She had on formfitting dark blue jeans and the requisite T-Wolves jersey, worn over a deep green turtleneck. On her, the sports gear was high fashion.

He took her elbow, pursed his lips and took a deep breath. What kind of game was she playing?

When they reached the concourse, she tried to shake off his grip.

He didn't let go, just tugged her to the opposite side of the hall, and they stopped next to a napkin dispenser.

"Hey." She yanked her arm back.

"Why the hell is Kate *MacBain* cleaning my house?" he

asked again, his lips next to her ear. "Is this some sort of reality show gimmick like *Undercover Boss*? Is that why you didn't tell me your last name?"

"I … I …" Her shoulders straightened. With heels on, she came up to his nose. "What difference does it make why I'm there? Your house is getting cleaned, right?"

"I. Won't. Be. Played." Until he'd mouthed the words, he hadn't realized that was his fear. That he was some kind of sick means to an end.

"Played? What are you talking about?" She drew closer and the gold in her eyes looked like fireworks sparks. "I'm doing a job. My reasons are none of your business."

"None of my business? Fine." He dragged in a breath. "Then how about this? Why the hell did you kiss me and then hang on the guy next to you at the game?"

Shaking her head, she backed away. Damn it, now he'd scared her. A man trying to get to the condiments knocked into her and she stumbled into Alex's arms.

His hands automatically steadied her.

"You idiot. That's my brother." Her soft voice cut through the corridor noise.

"Your—"His anger deflated like a popped balloon. "Brother? Really?"

"Stephen, my younger brother." Her eyes sparkled, but she was chewing on her upper lip.

"Brother," he repeated, feeling like she'd pulled the rug out from under him. "I thought … assumed …"

Someone walked between them to get napkins. They both stepped around the guy and met on the other side. No one could get between them now.

"You know what assuming does." She smirked.

"It makes me an ass." Alex winced. Maybe if he hadn't been looking through a jealous haze, he'd have seen the similarities between Kate and her sibling.

As if he had a right to be jealous. His anger took him by surprise. His wife had left two years ago, but it had been even longer since he'd felt this kind of emotion over a woman. To be honest, the only emotions he'd felt had been over his music.

"What about the other guy and the kid?" Lord, don't let her be married.

Really? Did he really just think that about this woman he barely knew? Hell, he'd just found out her last name.

"Client and his son. Their lease in the Daschle building is up for renewal. Scoring tickets for the playoffs may not help the negotiations, but I'm hoping it can't hurt."

The television screens in the concourse showed the second half underway.

Her eyebrows knit together like sixteenth notes written across her forehead. "I need to go find tacos for the brat."

"Brat?"

"The client's son."

He hooked her elbow and looked down at her. "I'm sorry I rough-handled you a minute ago. I … Is it okay if I take your arm? I know where they sell tacos."

She pushed her hair behind her ear and slowly nodded, studying his face.

He led her down the concourse, weaving through the people moving in every direction. "What kind of taco does he want? Hard shell or soft? Beef or chicken?"

She stopped abruptly. "Shoot. I didn't ask."

"Come on," he said, moving her forward again. "We'll get a couple of each. I know where you can get it all, but I'll only let you in on the secret if you tell me why you're cleaning houses."

She tipped her head and looked up at him. Her curls brushed against his shoulder. "That story will take more time than we have. The second half's already started."

"Let's grab a drink after the game," he suggested.

"Okay."

Thank goodness she wasn't relying on cleaning his house for a living.

He wasn't taking advantage of someone who depended on him for their livelihood.

~

KATE LOST track of the game. Alex's gaze tickled the back of her neck. Would it be too much like high school if she turned around or asked Stephen to turn around and check on him?

Oh yeah. Stephen would razz her until she was doddering and senile.

Her brother sat next to Eric discussing renovations. She ended up next to Nathan for the second half. Joy. For the first time watching a game, she wanted the damn thing to end.

When the Wolves sank a three-pointer, the crowd clambered to its feet. Kate stumbled as she belatedly stood and cheered. A quick check of the scoreboard showed Minnesota was behind. When had that happened? They'd been ahead by seven after the first half.

That was it; she would concentrate on the game. A ball got away from a Spur's player and bounced directly at Nathan. She slapped the ball back onto the court.

"I could have stopped the ball," the kid whined.

"With your face," she muttered. The kid hadn't even thanked her for the tacos.

With two minutes left and the Wolves down by two points, the time-outs started. *Get on with the game already.* Even Nathan paid more attention to the game than his phone.

She should be loving this. The excitement. The noise. The thrill of courtside seats at the first playoff game in ten years. She should be in fan heaven. Instead she kept checking the clock and worrying she wouldn't find Alex after Target Center emptied.

The seconds ticked off. The Wolves dropped a three-point shot to take a two-point lead. The sooner the Wolves won, the sooner she could find Alex.

The crowd stood for the remaining seconds of the game, clapping and chanting. The teams exchanged the lead with each basket made. At the ten-second mark, San Antonio nailed a three-pointer and pulled ahead by one point. She moaned. They had to make the next basket.

As the clock ticked down the last five seconds, she bit her lip. If they shot too soon, the opponents would have another chance to score. If they shot too late and missed, they wouldn't have a chance to rebound and recover.

"Come on." Kate's hands were in tight fists at her sides.

The point guard faked a pass and suckered his defender. He drove for the basket and executed a perfect turnaround layup. The noise blasted her ears. Every fan was on their feet. The opponents grabbed the ball with 1.6 seconds left to play and lobbed the ball to their downcourt teammates, but a Wolf intercepted.

Game over!

She bounced up and down, giving high fives to the fans behind her and over Nathan's head to Stephen and finally to Nathan who was actually grinning. Who would have guessed that would happen.

"Great game," she shouted as the players worked their way off the floor.

"That's about as exciting a finish as I've seen," Eric yelled. "Thanks for inviting us. What a night."

"You're welcome." Turning, she looked up in the stands, an excuse to see if Alex was still there.

"I'll wait for you," he mouthed with exaggerated lip motions.

Heat shot through her. She nodded and gave him a thumbs-up.

At least she'd worn her most flattering jeans. And she loved the fact that her boots made her taller.

Eric shook her hand. "We're heading out the east exit. It's closer to our parking ramp. Thanks again." He held out his hand to Stephen. "I look forward to hearing your ideas on the changes we've requested."

"Give me a week. I'll check with Kate on who should get the analysis."

"Nathan?" Eric said.

"Thanks for … bringing us to the game." The kid forced the words out of his mouth.

To prove she was above the jerkiness of a twelve-year-old, she smiled. "You're very welcome."

Stephen waited with her as they watched the Sorensons leave. "You want me to walk you home?" he asked.

With the arena almost clear, Alex and another man came down the steps.

"I ran into someone I know," she said. "We're stopping for a drink."

"The guy who called your name?" Stephen checked out the men walking toward them.

Alex must have heard the question because he had his hand out. "Alex Adamski."

"Stephen MacBain." Her brother raised his eyebrows.

She ignored his look.

"And this is Gabe Mauer." Alex waved at the man next to him.

"Unfortunately not related to Joe." Gabe held out his hand to Kate. His smile was easy, and his face looked familiar.

She shook his hand, a nice firm grip. "Kate MacBain. I'm sorry, have we met? You look familiar." His name sounded familiar too, but maybe that was because of his last name. Oh, crap. He'd been at Alex's house. Maybe she didn't look like Alex's cleaning lady. *Please, please don't say anything in front of Stephen.*

"We met about five years ago at Knight Ad Agency."

She sighed in relief. "Clare introduced us."

"Right. I hear we're stopping for a drink."

Her eyes widened. Stephen grinned. Alex scowled.

"No, Kate and I are stopping for a drink." Alex crossed his arms. "Go home, Gabe."

"I'm up for a drink," Stephen said. "Where?"

"How about O'Dair's?" Gabe said.

The arena's security team closed in on them.

"Come on, let's go before they throw us out." Kate led the way and Alex fell into step with her.

He whispered as they walked up the steps. "This wasn't what I had in mind."

She looked at her brother and Gabe. "Not what I had in mind either." But she didn't whisper.

She wanted her brother to hear.

"WHEN I ASKED you for a drink, I didn't anticipate chaperones," Alex complained as they walked into O'Dair's Pub.

Kate bumped into his side, her voice low as she said, "Can we ditch them? At least my brother?"

"Doesn't look like it." Alex looked over his shoulder and raised his voice. "Don't you have to go home, Gabe?"

"Nope. I'm good."

"Stephen, wouldn't you like to get right on those changes for Sorenson?" Kate asked.

"Not at all."

Stephen's grin reminded Alex of a shark. And Alex was the chum. Not good.

"There's a table." Kate led him into the crowd.

"Where?" He didn't see anything, but she drew him away, losing Gabe and Stephen.

Standing on tiptoe, she tugged his head close. "Don't talk about cleaning with my brother, okay?"

The smell of her hair made him think of summer nights.

"Alex, okay? Don't mention how we met. Don't talk about me cleaning your house. Please?"

"Why?"

"He's my brother." As if that explained everything. She grabbed his hand and waved to a woman standing next to an empty table.

"No problem."

If he couldn't talk about why the daughter of the MacBain family cleaned his kitchen, he decided to try something better. A small Irish trio played a soul-wrenching song, nice, slow and perfect. "Let's dance."

He didn't wait for her response; he pulled her into his arms. He wanted to feel her body move against his.

"I still have my coat on." But she wrapped her arms around his neck.

The concertina carried the melody in a minor key. He rubbed up and down her spine. She was as stiff as a backboard. Shoot.

She twisted her head away from his.

He loosened his grip.

"Is this okay?" It had been a while. Maybe flirting had changed. Hell, maybe sex had changed.

She rested her cheek against his chest, and he couldn't help smiling. "Yes. I'm just trying to figure out what my little brother is up to. Stephen and your friend found a table with Meg."

Alex pulled her closer, his thigh between her jean-clad legs. "Who's Meg?"

"The woman I waved to. My best friend." His chest muffled her reply. "She'll want to meet the hot guy I'm dancing with."

"Hot?" He pulled her into a tight circle.

"I've had too many beers. I shouldn't be telling you that. I'm sure you already know that you have this tall, dark, brooding thing going. And the five o'clock shadow."

"I shaved this afternoon." He pulled her hand up and rubbed it across his face.

Her fingers danced across his cheek. "I think you missed a spot." She trailed a finger to his lip.

His body reacted to her touch. He tried to shift his groin away, but they were molded together.

He nipped the finger resting on his lower lip.

She took in a sharp breath but didn't pull her fingers away.

The song ended and the band took a break. Her hands slid along his shoulders and down his arms to his hands. Those cat-like eyes never blinked.

He could barely think. He knew everyone was clearing the dance floor and didn't care.

Whatever had been wrong with his libido was fixed. Fixed and wanting action. Kate, a green-eyed, copper-haired woman had fixed whatever ailed him.

He cupped her face. The sounds of the crowd faded. There was only him and Kate.

"Can we leave?"

She swallowed. "That's probably not a good idea."

He stroked a thumb along her delicate cheekbone. "I think it's a stupendous idea."

She laughed, a joyful sweet sound. "Stupendous. Who uses a word like that?" She didn't wait for an answer. "Come meet my best friend. Plus, you promised to buy me a beer."

"Kate!" A woman with bright blue eyes and light brown hair waved from a table.

Kate dragged him through the crowd.

Stephen and Gabe were pulling chairs over to the small high-top table. Then Kate's brother sat in the middle of the three empty stools.

Kate elbowed the guy. "Move."

Stephen grinned like a Cheshire cat, and then slid into the seat next to Kate's friend.

"Meg, meet Alex Adamski," Kate said. "Alex, this is Meghan Davis."

"Nice to meet you." Meg's infectious grin had Alex smiling.

"Nice to meet you," Alex replied. "This is Gabe Mauer."

Both he and Gabe said, "Not related to the baseball player."

"Too bad," Meg said. "I'd sure like to meet Joe."

After the server took their orders, Meg leaned around Stephen and asked, "Tell me about how you two met."

Alex let Kate handle the question, curious what she would say.

"We met … at the liquor store."

Was he the only one who heard her hesitation?

"Wait, I thought …" Gabe started.

Alex kicked Gabe's foot under the table and shook his head.

He may not understand why she didn't want people to know how they'd met, but he would honor her request. His need to know why she was cleaning his house irritated him like an unresolved chord.

"What do you do?" Meg asked him.

"Composer." He didn't talk about his work. "That's how I know Gabe. I sometimes help him out with songs."

"Are you a musician?" Meg asked Gabe.

Good, keep the conversation away from Kate's lie. He rolled his tense shoulders.

"Advertising."

Meg asked about Gabe's firm. Their beers arrived and the pressure he felt eased. Ever since his wife's lies, he'd vowed to live his life fully in the truth.

Apparently Kate didn't suffer the same need. He watched her eyes brighten as she talked about a client's lease with Meg.

She sipped her beer, licking a drip off the mug, and his groin tightened. She caught his eye and he glanced away, afraid she would see his lust.

Why this woman? Why this time?

Kate leaned over. "Want to dance again?"

"Yeah." He gulped his own beer and then helped her off her stool.

"I can climb off a stool," she mumbled.

"And I can offer a hand."

The tune being played wasn't slow, but he still pulled her into his arms. He leaned down and her silky curls smoothed along his cheek. He whispered into her ear, "Why don't you want to tell anyone how we met?"

"Because of my brother." She tipped her face to his. Her pink lips begged him to relive their kiss.

"I don't understand." His voice scratched like a bow against a bass fiddle.

"I … I don't want to get teased. Luckily no one asked any more questions." She touched his cheek. "Thanks."

"Your family knows you're cleaning, right?"

"Of course." She closed her eyes. "I'm just not sure why my parents want me to clean."

"Oh." He truly didn't get it. But his body didn't object to her explanation. Gabe would tell him to go with the flow, although he wasn't always comfortable with that approach.

"How are you getting home?" He pulled her close, her feet keeping up with the little turn he executed.

"I'll walk." She rested her head against his shoulder. "I only live a block and a half away."

"If we dump the chaperones, can I walk you home?"

"YOU DON'T HAVE to walk me to my door," Kate said as they stood outside her apartment building. She keyed in the security code and the door buzzed.

"Of course I do." Alex put an arm around her shoulder and guided her into the building. His touch made her knees weak.

"What floor?" he asked.

"Tenth."

She let him lead her to the elevator.

He toyed with the rings on her hand and each stroke of his fingers sent little earthquakes into the center of her body.

She wanted to yank her hand out of his, she wasn't used to reacting so—quick and strong to a guy, but she also wanted him to keep up this foreplay.

"Is this one of your family's buildings?"

"Yes."

He waited as she stepped into the elevator and then followed her in.

"Why do guys do that?" she asked. "Then women are in the back of the elevator and have to walk around the guys to exit."

"It's respectful?"

"Medieval, more like."

"We'll have to agree to disagree on that point," he said. "Does your brother live here?"

"I'm the only one in this building."

The doors closed and he linked their hands together and pulled her closer. "That's good. The chaperones got a little old tonight."

His deep brown eyes watched her.

"So, do you have more siblings?" he asked.

"I have an older brother. Then me. Then there's Stephen and the baby is Timothy."

She kept watching him and he looked at her expectantly. Finally he said, "Do you think we should push a floor number?"

The way he looked at her had her brain fritzing out. "Probably."

She tugged but he didn't let go of her hands.

"I think I need at least one finger."

He tugged her close, tucking her hands behind her back. His thighs lined up with hers.

Her chest tightened as he brought his mouth to hers.

His tongue circled her lips. Heat poured through her, sending any of her objections up in smoke. Sipping at his lips, she savored the taste of beer on his tongue. He clasped her butt, pulling her tight. With his erection jutting against her stomach, there wasn't a question this attraction was mutual.

The elevator door rumbled. Alex pulled away and Kate collapsed against the wall. He shifted so she stood in front of him as the doors opened.

One of the fifth-floor residents gaped at them. "Going up?"

Alex's voice rumbled in her ear. "I told you we should have pushed a button."

The woman looked like she planned to wait for the next elevator. Kate wondered what her own face looked like.

"You're on the fifth floor, aren't you?" Kate asked.

Her comment got the woman's feet moving. "Yes. Thank you."

Kate pushed the buttons for the tenth and fifth floors.

The older woman huddled in the corner as far from them as possible.

Alex's hands were still on her hips. She wanted to sink against his body but feared she'd rip the man's clothes off in front of a woman old enough to be her grandmother.

Alex tapped his fingers on her hips in time with the elevator music. She'd lived here for almost two years. Had she ever noticed the music piped into the elevator?

As soon as the door opened the woman hustled out.

"Have a nice night," Kate called to her retreating back.

Even before the doors closed, Alex caught her shoulders and backed her against the side of the elevator. Her arms snaked around his neck, and he crushed his wonderful lips against hers.

There was a little more desperation in this kiss. A little more heavenly pressure wherever their bodies met. His low growl rumbled through her body like a vibrator and settled deep in her pelvis. She tightened her grip on him, wanting that agile mouth on her body.

At the ding of the elevator, Alex broke away and leaned his head on the top of hers. "Wow."

His arm settled around her waist as she guided them out and toward her door. Damn, he'd just kissed her socks off. She couldn't let him in her apartment. They'd sleep together and they hadn't even dated. She couldn't do it. Too … slutty? Too … soon. Or maybe too much.

"This is me." She dug for her keys, struggling a little because he didn't let go of her waist, but truthfully she didn't want to move out of the warmth of his arms.

"Am I invited in?" he asked.

There was something different about Alex. When he touched her, her brain took a vacation.

He moved so their bodies were once again chest to chest. Raw need filled his face, probably reflecting her own.

"Tell me why you're cleaning my house," he whispered.

"I wish I knew." She wrapped her arms around him. "It might be because of my mom's biopsy."

"Any word on that?" He stroked her hair off her forehead.

"No."

"Am I coming in tonight?"

"Not tonight. Not … yet."

Disappointment flashed in his brown eyes. "Okay."

He tipped her head and kissed her. "Do you like jazz?"

SIX

KATE TUGGED A RUST-COLORED DRESS OUT OF HER CLOSET. Holding it up, she checked her reflection. It looked good with her coloring, not too formal, not too casual. If she added a gold belt and her chunky gold necklace, the outfit should work for wherever they were eating.

Or she could wear her black sheath. She fingered the fabric. Too light for spring. He hadn't said where they were going, just asked if she liked jazz. She pulled out a pair of pants and then her blue suit.

Spinning around, she was appalled at the clothes scattered on the bed. Enough. If she planned to run MacBain Enterprises, she had to be decisive. Of course work decisions were based on logic, facts, financial projections and intelligence.

This decision involved something else … attraction.

Maybe after their date, she could relegate Alex to *been there, done that* status. And hopefully she wouldn't be thinking about him every spare minute. It was embarrassing to daydream about him all day. She had to stay focused on the prize and becoming involved with anyone would ruin her chances of succeeding her father.

"Fine." She whipped the rust dress off the bed and slid it over her head. She added a little gold to her blush and eye shadow. "It's just dinner."

She moved into the living room and flipped on the television. CNBC came on with the show *Greed*. This episode was on another Ponzi scheme.

She was so engrossed in the story, the knock on the door jerked her to her feet. She checked the time. Six-twenty. Alex was ten minutes early, and someone had let him through the security door.

She turned off the TV and hot-footed it to the door. Then she took a deep breath so he wouldn't know she'd run to answer his knock.

"Hey," she said as she opened the door.

"Hey, sis." Timothy pushed past her into her apartment. "Have you heard anything from the parental units?"

"Not yet." Her smile turned into a frown. "What are you doing here?"

"I met friends for a drink and was in the neighborhood. Thought I'd see if you wanted to grab dinner."

Timothy prowled her apartment, touching the family pictures adorning the bookshelves and checking out the magazines scattered across the coffee table. He tapped her copy of *Forbes*. "Good article on the recovery signs in the construction industry."

Timothy's habit of talking about ten things in one breath drove her nuts. "I've read it. That's why I want to initiate an advertising campaign. Get our name out early in the recovery. And no, I don't want to get dinner." She waved her hands down her body. "My ... date ... is coming in a few minutes. Out."

"Date? You have a date?" Timothy stared at her and whistled. "Looking good. Who's the guy?"

"No one you know." She moved toward the door and yanked it open. "Out."

"Hi." Alex's hand was raised to rap on the door.

"Hi." She forced her scowl into a smile. "Come on in."

Timothy sauntered over, so different from his usual pace. She glared at her brother.

"Alex, this is my brother Timothy, who is leaving. Timothy, Alex Adamski."

The men shook hands.

"Where are you having dinner?" Timothy asked.

"Dakota Grill." Alex smiled and stared at her so long the room temperature jumped ten degrees.

"I hear the food is as good as the music," Timothy said.

She grabbed her purse and shawl. "I'm ready."

"I came to see if Katie wanted to grab dinner and catch the game." Timothy grinned.

Her brother was not coming with her and Alex. "Go bother Stephen. He's probably at home."

Timothy turned to Alex, but Alex deferred to Kate. Her brother rolled his eyes. "I can take a hint."

They walked to the elevator. "If you could take a hint, you would have left when I first asked," she whispered.

Her brother was still grinning when Alex caught her elbow as they left the building.

"See you later, Katie," Timothy said as he headed in the opposite direction.

Thank goodness.

"Finally." Alex wrapped a hand around her waist and pulled her into an embrace.

Her arms snuck inside his blazer. Alex made khakis and a blue jacket look good. She didn't care that they were standing on the sidewalk. She sank into his kiss. His tongue slid along hers, leaving a trail of mint and sparks in its wake. He pulled away and she moaned. The kiss had been too short, too hot and too public.

"Hi," he whispered, cupping her face.

"Hi back at 'cha." Everything in her body lit up like a pinball machine. What was it about Alex? This wasn't normal.

"You look incredible," he said.

"Thanks." She blushed. She never blushed.

"The restaurant is on Nicollet Mall. Can you walk that far in heels?" he asked.

She'd picked an open-toed wedge in case. "I'm good. Lead on."

He took her hand.

When was the last time she'd held a man's hand?

"Tell me about where we're eating," she said. "Since they don't open until dinner, I don't take clients there."

"The owner is a big jazz supporter. Has been for years."

"I don't know much about jazz. Were you in a band or ensemble or whatever you call a group that plays in a jazz club?"

"I don't play in bands, but there are groups that play my songs." His fingers tightened on hers. "What kind of music do you listen to?"

He'd changed the subject. She didn't know him well enough to press him on the sudden tension that stiffened his body.

"I guess easy-listening stuff. I like to understand the words and I hate heavy metal." She listened to classical music when she took a bath, but that was a little too intimate to mention on a first date, even if she'd folded his underwear.

They talked, an easy conversation bouncing between topics. They were standing at the hostess station before she knew it.

She'd pictured a dark smoke-filled low-ceilinged room, even though Minnesota had banned indoor smoking years ago.

It was nothing like that. The large restaurant had tiered tables directed at a stage containing a piano and drum set.

A good-looking blonde led them to a table close to the stage. "Nice to see you, Alex. Enjoy your dinner and the show. Craig is your server."

"Thanks, Dar. Great table." Alex shot Dar a smile that had his dimple making an appearance.

Dar run her hand along his back as she walked away.

"Friend of yours?" Kate asked.

Alex raised an eyebrow, looking more like a pirate than a composer. "I used to come here a lot. I know most of the staff."

Craig introduced himself, filled their water glasses and recited the specials.

"I'm trying the chef's tasting menu," Alex said. "Do you want wine or something else? The tasting menu comes with wine."

"The tasting menu sounds good," she said.

Craig looked pleased at their choices.

"We're staying for the show, so don't rush anything," Alex said.

"Good. Oh, the performer scheduled tonight called in sick."

"Who's replacing Jeff?"

"They're working on it," Craig said.

Alex really was a part of this scene. Kate shifted in her seat. She was usually the one most familiar with the environment. It felt strange to have her date be so … connected.

Alex leaned back in his seat. "Okay, I've waited almost twenty-four hours. Why are you cleaning houses?"

"It's only *your* house." She shook her head. "My parents want me to understand the business, from the ground up. Apparently that means cleaning. My brothers worked in the construction side of the business to learn the business. I worked in the office during high school, but now I get to work at

Murphy's Maids. My mom's the founder." She mimicked her father's voice. "Your mother cleaned, are you too good to work like her?"

Alex covered her hand in his big one. "Do you hate cleaning my house?"

"It seems like such a waste. I've got an MBA."

"I'm glad they chose my house." He smiled. "Especially since you found out what the smell was."

"Yeah, one of my finer moments." She shivered even as she smiled.

"Well, like I said, I'm glad." Alex gazed into her eyes.

She took a deep breath. She'd never been this attracted to a man. Ever. "I'm worried my cleaning is connected to my mother's biopsy."

He squeezed her fingers. "Have you asked?"

"No." Her lips trembled, and she pinched them together. "I hate that my parents might be thinking worst-case scenario. Honestly? I don't want to know that."

"What's your normal job?"

"Director of Contracting and Leasing." She twisted the candle on the table. "The guy from last night is one of our biggest leasees. We're negotiating an extension with their law firm. I'd like to nail down their account for another ten years 'cuz putting up with his son was not fun."

"Early teens," Alex managed to say, clearing his throat. "Hard to impress."

"I didn't want to impress him. I'd hoped Eric would bring his wife, not his son."

Alex frowned. "Don't you like kids?"

"Nope." She opened her napkin and laid it on her lap. "I plan on running MacBain Enterprises when my parents retire. That's enough for me."

He paused, and then said, "I'd like a house full of kids."

~

ALEX SIPPED the wine that had arrived with their appetizers. Kate didn't like children.

In that rust-colored dress, she sparkled. An auburn curl slipped off her shoulder and onto her breast. He wanted to wrap his hand right there. Even sitting across the table, he caught a hint of her perfume. Her scent drilled right into his chest.

The most interesting woman he'd met in years, and she didn't want kids. Why was he *always* attracted to women who cared more about their careers than family?

Well, at least he knew his libido was working again. He'd just have to work very hard to make sure he didn't let infatuation stray into love. Hard though, since every time he touched Kate, their connection overwhelmed him. And his body didn't care that she couldn't be long-term.

"I like this appetizer." Kate tapped the printout of their menu. "Fig and Brie."

"It's good," he said. "What's next?"

"Salad and then short ribs." She grinned. "Can't wait."

"Great." One word answers. He'd lost the easy give and take of their conversations.

"So … what are you working on?" She pulled a face. "Is that okay to ask a composer? Are you sensitive about your current work in process?"

She made him laugh. "I'm writing some songs for Central Standard Time. You caught part of one."

"Impressive." She tipped back the remains of the champagne that had accompanied their figs.

He stared at the pulse beating along her throat. "I'm also toying with a sonata." Or trying.

"A sonata? You write classical music too?"

He shrugged. "I'm an eclectic composer. Rock and roll,

classical, ballads and jingles. I even wrote a piece for Zenith Ballet a couple of years ago."

"Get out!" Her eyes glowed a soft green in the candlelit room. "I loved the song you were working on the other day."

She touched his hand, and he laced their fingers together.

"I'd love to hear more of your music," she said.

"Maybe when you're at the house." Although he didn't like people watching him create.

Meredith used to make suggestions and lyric changes and generally drove him crazy until he'd banned her from his music room. But maybe Kate was interested in his music, not because it could improve her career, but because she enjoyed it.

Maybe Kate could help him get back in the saddle. He didn't need to think long-term.

Craig brought their salads and another wine, a crisp pinot grigio.

"Do you travel much for your work?" she asked.

"Sometimes, but not often." When he'd been married, he'd followed Meredith to all her performances. "How about you?"

"Occasionally for a property auction, but that's usually my father's role."

"Auctions?"

"Sometimes properties are auctioned off in blocks, especially if it's held by a bank."

"You mean foreclosed property?"

"Not necessarily, but sometimes. Last year, we bought a building and a strip mall. Just last week I finally leased the last floor of the building."

As they ate their entrees, she talked about the lease and construction economy and how her family had protected their company during the downturn.

"These short ribs are so tender." Kate tucked another forkful in her mouth. "God, I need to stop eating. I'm so full."

He eyed her plate.

She pushed it toward him. "Here, finish mine."

"Thanks." He finished off her meal and then leaned back in his chair, more relaxed than he'd felt in ages.

"They're starting to set up," Kate said, nodding at the stage.

Alex was surprised to see Andrew taking his place at the piano. Hell, he hadn't seen him in a couple of years. "That's a friend. I'd like to say hello."

"You go ahead." She gathered her purse. "I'll visit the ladies' room."

Heads turned as she made her way through the restaurant. She was gorgeous. And easy to talk to.

But they didn't want the same things in life.

It wasn't something to solve right now, so he went to greet his friend.

KATE REAPPLIED HER LIPSTICK. Alex had gotten quiet for a while, but everything seemed fine now. Maybe she would invite him into her apartment tonight.

The thought of stripping off his shirt and running her hands along his massive chest … She'd never dated anyone built like Alex.

Back in the dining area, she let her eyes adjust to the dim lighting. On the stage, Alex was talking to his friend. Who would guess that a man built like a football player could look so natural on stage. He had a great voice. She could listen to him all day.

Of course, listening to his music was more fun than cleaning his floors.

Two more people walked out onto the stage, an older man and a stunning brunette. The woman had a tiny waist overshadowed by unnaturally large breasts shown off by a low-cut sparkly red dress.

The brunette jerked to a stop. Then she threw her arms around Alex, fusing her lips to his.

Kate's mouth dropped open.

Obviously she knew nothing about Alex. She slipped back to their table.

"Are you ready for dessert?" Craig asked as he stopped beside her.

She looked up. "Ask him."

She pointed to the stage where the woman was still attached to Alex.

Craig swallowed. "I guess you want to wait."

Maybe. Or maybe she should leave.

"YOU CAME TO HEAR ME SING!" Meredith hugged him again. "I'm so, so happy!"

Everything his ex-wife did or said happened in exclamation points. She stood on tiptoe, her lips homing in on his.

He carefully pulled away from her embrace. "I came to hear Jeff …"

He glanced to their table. Even from the stage he could see Kate's crossed arms as she stared at them. *Uh-oh.*

"With Kate."

"Kate?" Meredith turned to see who he was looking at. "You're on a date at one of my gigs?"

He frowned. "You weren't performing tonight. It was supposed to be Jeff."

Meredith bit her plump lower lip. That used to make him wild. "Okay, I get it. Well, anyway, thank you for that beautiful jingle you wrote for me. It's perfect."

"Meredith, I didn't write it for you." He started to move away but she clutched his arm.

"Y-you didn't write it for … I thought … Well, clearly I need to speak to Gabe." She studied his face before letting go of him. "But you'll be there next week for the recording, right?"

"No."

She pinched her lips together. "But … it's your song. You're always there when we record your work …" She trailed off, still staring at him.

They were standing on stage. She was not going to pull him into an argument.

His eyes went back to Kate. He could sense Meredith following his gaze.

"Great to see you, Andrew," he said as he stepped off the stage.

"Alex, I need to …"

He looked at Meredith over his shoulder.

Her eyes filled with tears, but he wasn't buying it. She'd used tears on him one too many times during the four years of their tempest-filled relationship.

"Our attorneys said it all," he whispered, just loud enough for her ears.

"I've left the band. I'm going out on my own."

"Congratulations."

He turned away, but she pulled on his jacket.

"I want to sing your songs." She stared into his eyes. "Please. We're good together. Look at the songs you wrote for me. We can do it again."

Yup, everything came down to Meredith's career. "Not even if hell froze over."

"Alex, you know the divorce was for the best—for both of us. Can't you forgive me?"

He ignored her question, hurrying back to the table. Back to Kate who was holding her shawl and purse. Fuck.

"Please don't leave," he said.

"There's one too many women kissing you tonight," she said, refusing to look him in the eye.

Alex stepped closer. "Wait."

She turned away, but he caught her hand. People around them were staring.

"Stop," he whispered.

"Who is she?" she whispered.

Alex held out her chair. "Please?"

Kate closed her eyes and took a deep breath. Then she sat on the edge of the chair, her shawl and purse clutched in her lap.

Out of the corner of his eye, he saw Meredith taking the spotlight. Talk about being between a rock and a hard place.

Craig walked up. "Are you ready for dessert?" He looked between their faces and grimaced. "Or not."

Alex took Kate's fingers. "Let me explain."

She tugged her hand out of his, pushed her stuff onto the extra chair and crossed her arms. "Go ahead and bring the damn dessert."

"Thank you."

"So?" Kate tipped her chin.

"Meredith's my ex-wife."

Her eyebrows shot up. "Ex-wife?"

"If I'd known she was singing tonight, we wouldn't have come here. I thought Jeff was singing." He leaned forward. "I haven't spoken to her since the last settlement meeting."

Meredith had called numerous times, but Alex wasn't about to mention that to Kate.

Now he knew why Meredith had been calling. She wanted his songs. Nothing had changed. She wanted him to make her a star.

He grinned sheepishly. "Someday this will be funny."

How did Kate's eyebrows climb even higher? Pretty soon they'd be buried in the curls on her forehead.

"Interesting greeting if you haven't talked to her for—"

"Six months."

"It … surprised me."

He nodded. "Since watching you lean your head on your brother's shoulder bothered me, I can see why Meredith kissing me might … make you doubt that I want to date you."

"Do you still want to?" she asked. "Date, I mean?"

"Absolutely. And exclusively," he added.

Craig slipped a raspberry and chocolate confection in front of each of them. "We have a lovely raspberry liqueur that would complement your dessert," he offered.

"No thanks. Decaf coffee with cream." Kate's voice was still chilly but not as icy as earlier.

Alex hoped she meant to drink the coffee and not pour it in his lap. "Nothing for me, thanks."

The lights dimmed and the stage lights came up.

"Hello. I'm Meredith Anderson. I'm sorry if you came to see Jeff Saber. He's caught the crud. I'm filling in. Give it up for Andrew Giley on the piano and Sam Dolman on the drums."

Meredith must have put together her own combo.

A smattering of applause ran through the audience. People were still finishing their dinner, but the conversational buzz dropped.

Kate picked up her fork and poked at her dessert.

Boy, didn't he know how to show her a good time? "Look, we can go."

"Oh no, we came for the music. We should stay." Her smile didn't reach her eyes.

Yeah, he was in big trouble. But damn, this wasn't his fault.

"Let's take a stroll down memory lane." Meredith started

out with "God Bless the Child." Her voice carried more depth than the last time he'd heard her.

He watched Kate's face. She stared at the stage, not giving a hint of her feelings.

Not liking the distance between them, he scooted his chair so they both sat on the same side of the table and faced the stage.

He stretched his arm across the top of her chair. Leaning close to her ear, he whispered, "Let's get out of here."

"Not yet." She settled into her chair.

Meredith winked in their direction.

"Nice," Kate whispered. "Was she always this desperate?"

"Umm." He wasn't sure what she was driving at. "Her ... career was always more important than our marriage."

The song ended, and they applauded with the rest of the audience. Once the applause died, Meredith said, "We're lucky to have the composer of the next song in the audience tonight. Put your hands together for Twin Cities' own Grammy winner, Alex Adamski. He wrote this song for me."

Kate turned and looked at him, a smirk on her face.

He closed his eyes. Then he half stood and waved at the crowd before retaking his seat. Damn Meredith. What would she sing?

He played with the curls on Kate's shoulders. The melody of "All My Heart" filled the quiet.

You turn to me, in the dark of night,
A shadow drenched in starlight.
Our love lights up the room,
No more sorrow, no more gloom.
My heart is in your hand.
Through all of time, all I need is all your love,
And all your love is mine.
All your love is mine—forever.

If people weren't staring at them, he'd leave.

He leaned close to her ear. "I'm sorry."

"I'll bet." She turned, but this time she was holding in a laugh.

Their mouths were inches apart and he wanted to lean over and kiss her. "You think this is funny?"

"Yes." Kate pressed her lips together, but a snort escaped.

Meredith finished the song, and the crowd roared their approval. Kate's chest bounced a little as she stifled her chuckles.

"Can we leave now?" he asked, refusing to look at the stage.

She grinned. "You don't have the bill."

He caught Craig's eye and mimed writing.

Why couldn't he have picked another restaurant for their first date? Now it looked like this would be their last.

Meredith started another song. Christ, did she only sing his love songs?

"Did you write this song too?" Kate whispered.

Craig arrived with the bill. Finally. "Leaving so soon?"

Alex didn't even look at the amount. Tucking his credit card into the pocket, he handed the folder to Craig. "Yes, thank you."

Kate leaned in. "You didn't answer my question."

He didn't understand what Kate wanted from him. "I wrote both those songs. Years ago."

"Years?"

"Years."

How long had he obsessed over Meredith? Her band had tried out a few of his early songs in his salad years and then they'd commissioned more. He'd kept asking Meredith out but she hadn't given him a chance until after he'd written their first hit.

Everything had always been about Meredith or her career or what he could do for her career. They'd dated for two years and been married for the same amount of time. He'd thought they were on the same page. Love, family, music.

Alex scrawled his name on the credit card receipt and added a generous tip.

Kate looked up at Meredith and then took his hand. Meredith missed a word in the song.

They moved through the tightly set tables and left the restaurant.

When they stepped out onto Nicollet Mall, Alex stopped and took both her hands.

"I'm sorry," he said. "I wanted to take you out for a great dinner and enjoy some music." His first real date in years. "I … wanted to take you somewhere where they would know me. I wanted to impress you."

She nodded, still with that half smirk on her face. "I was impressed."

"If I'd known Meredith was singing, I wouldn't have gone near the restaurant."

"I gather the divorce wasn't her idea."

"Did you take my hand in there to spite Meredith?"

Now her smirk turned into a grin. "Maybe."

"Thanks, I think." Maybe Meredith would stop calling him now that she'd seen him with Kate, not that he ever answered her calls.

"She's a good singer." Kate swung their hands as they moved down the sidewalk.

"She is." He truly didn't understand women, at all. "So are we good?"

"I think so."

Now he was second guessing everything Kate said. "And you'll go out with me again?"

"If you promise no more ex's will show up."

"That I can promise you." He didn't have that many.

She stopped in front of her building and input her security code.

The door clicked and he pulled it open. They rode the elevator in silence and walked to her door.

"Thank you for a lovely … dinner." She stood on her toes and brushed her lips on his.

Before he could deepen the kiss, she unlocked her door.

"See you Tuesday." She smiled as the door shut in his face.

SEVEN

Kate took a deep breath and then trudged up Alex's sidewalk.

It was hard to admit, but last Saturday she'd been jealous of Alex's ex-wife. The love songs he'd written for Meredith had made her feel like she was watching the couple having sex.

But it had been fun to watch him squirm. Alex had sent her beautiful flowers—on Sunday. Sighing, she unlocked Alex's front door. The card had said, *Sorry about Meredith.*

They'd talked every night and it had been—nice. This was unusual. She didn't necessarily want to get to know the guys she dated because she wasn't looking for anything permanent. She had to keep her focus on impressing her parents.

But having a little fun with a guy who she was attracted to was just fine.

She checked the time. Alex was probably in his office. Opening his front door, she paused and listened. Nothing.

The smell of his coffee lured her into the kitchen. She had to find out where he got his beans.

She stopped and frowned. Something was wrong.

The kitchen was clean.

No dishes in the sink. The counters sparkled.

Kate poured a cup of coffee. She hadn't slept well since their dinner … followed by jazz sung beautifully by his wife. Ex-wife. Beautiful ex-wife.

Not that she had any right to be jealous. But she was human.

Time to clean. She hurried to the second floor, stripped his bed and grabbed his laundry. How nice not to open the washing machine to find everything green and slimy.

With the laundry started, she pushed in her earbuds and flipped on some music. Humming along with Dave Matthews, she emptied the dishwasher. Alex must have rinsed off his dishes. They were clean. Amazing.

She sprayed the counters with granite cleaner. Pulling out a big garbage bag, she tackled the fridge. She'd avoided this task until now. Tossing unidentifiable items covered with growth, she sanitized the shelves and wiped down every jar and bottle. Then she reorganized the contents.

Stepping back, she assessed her work. It wasn't a multi-million-dollar lease, but it felt good to make something shine. She could see why Mom took pride in the work her company performed.

A tap on her shoulder made her jump. She turned, pulling out her earbuds.

A photographer taking Alex's picture would have captioned this image: *Remorse*.

"Morning." He searched her face as if he didn't know what she was going to do.

She liked keeping him on his toes. "Hi."

She stripped off her gloves and tossed them into the sink. "Thank you again for the flowers. They're beautiful."

"You're welcome." He poured coffee and pulled milk out of the fridge. "Wow. Martha never organized my food."

"I thought about organizing everything alphabetically."

"What?"

"Instead I color-coordinated the jars and bottles." She topped off her coffee and doctored it to her liking. "It's interesting that your blue energy drinks and the brown beer bottles were the most prolific."

In her fridge it would be white yogurt containers.

"So, did the ex call you after Saturday night?" she asked.

"I wish we'd eaten someplace else." He blew out a breath. "How did you know?"

"Just a guess." She should let him off the hook. "It's not your fault. What's her agenda?"

"She wants me to write more songs for her." He sipped his coffee and stared at her over the rim. "I screen her calls, but she called from an unknown number. I know better than to answer those."

She couldn't help but laugh. "Afraid?"

"Deathly." He stroked her cheek.

She stepped closer. "Alex …"

"Are we really okay?"

"We are." She understood why his ex wanted to kiss him. The man had an amazing mouth.

He cradled the back of her head. "Kate."

She reached up and slowly stroked his lower lip. "Alex."

And they kissed.

A knock on the kitchen door interrupted them.

"Damn it." His forehead rested on hers. He kissed her nose. "Hold that thought."

"I need to work anyway." She sank against the counter. Thought? When they kissed she didn't think. All she did was feel.

He opened the door.

A short towhead boy waited on the deck. He bounced a basketball way too big for his small hands.

"There's my man." Alex gave the kid a high five. "Why aren't you in school?"

"We don't hafta. We got to thtay home 'cuz the teachers are talking to our parents."

The boy tucked the ball under his arm and stepped onto the rug. "Want to thoot hoopth?"

Alex shot a look at her. "Sure. Let me grab my shoes."

He headed out of the kitchen and called, "AJ, that's Kate MacBain. Kate, my friend Arthur James Cane."

"Hi, AJ." She tapped her fingers on the counter. "How old are you?"

"Thix," he lisped through missing front teeth.

"Looks like the tooth fairy's been spending time at your house."

"I get a buck for every tooth."

They stared at each other. Time crawled as they waited for Alex's return. AJ stuck his tongue in and out of the gap between his teeth.

Alex came back, grabbed a couple of sports drinks and handed one to the kid. "Showing off your smile, buddy?"

AJ nodded. "Mom says the big oneth will grow in thoon."

Alex held the door open. "Yup. Your mom knows you're here, right?"

AJ nodded.

They headed across the grass to a hoop and cement half court in Alex's backyard. While she watched, Alex lowered the basket. Sweet. Now the little boy had a chance.

The man owned a house and played with neighbor kids. He'd already been married.

She shouldn't be attracted to him. Damn chemistry.

ALEX BOUNCED the ball to AJ. "Last shot."

AJ faked a move right and then drove left. His dribbling was improving. The kid took a shot. The ball circled the rim, dropping in.

AJ bounced up and down. "I won! I won!"

Alex gave him a high five. "Great job."

On their way across the alley, he ruffled AJ's hair. God, he wanted a child. He'd had an unusual but great childhood. Sure, his two sisters wouldn't play basketball or anything that might interfere with their music, but his dad had spent time on the court with him, when he wasn't in court. And Mom taught him any instrument he'd wanted to play.

He should call his mom and dad and maybe his sisters. Maybe head out to Minnetonka to see them.

By the time he'd chatted with AJ's mother and let himself back into the house, Kate was gone. He could tell. There was an empty ring to his footsteps as he walked through the kitchen. Since when did his house feel empty if he was alone? This house had always been his sanctuary.

He caught the hint of Kate's perfume. He closed his eyes and inhaled.

Back in his office he battled with the sonata's counterpoint. Pushing his headphones off he ran his hands through his hair. Why couldn't anything in his life be easy?

"HAVE you heard from Mom or Dad?" Kate sank into Michael's guest chair. She couldn't concentrate this afternoon. Between kissing Alex this morning and waiting on Mom's pathology report, she was … anxious.

"Nothing."

She traced the pattern on Michael's mahogany desk. "Do you think they're waiting for the results at the lake because they think it's bad?"

Michael shoved his fingers through his hair. "I don't know. What do you think?"

"I think they're worried." She stood and paced to the window. Even the sky looked ominous.

She laid her head against the cool glass. "I can't bear thinking Mom might …" she couldn't say cancer, she didn't want to jinx the outcome, "… might be sick."

Michael came up behind her. "I know. She doesn't seem ill."

Kate rested her head against his shoulder. "She looks tired."

"Yeah," Michael agreed. "But that could be from worry."

She nodded thoughtful. "Did they ever say anything to you about why they wanted me to clean?"

His eyes narrowed. He leaned against the window so they were face to face. "What are you thinking?"

"That she suspects the worst." Kate took a deep breath. "That she wants me to run Murphy's."

Michael frowned. "Has she said something like that?"

"No." She rubbed at the ache in her temple. "I just wondered if they'd said anything to you, that's all."

His eyebrows pinched together. "Want to get the sibs together tonight and compare notes?"

She swallowed. "Yeah."

A knock on the doorframe of Michael's office made them both turn. Michael straightened and shot his cuffs.

It was Liz. She had a small apologetic smile on her face. She glanced at Michael, but then looked straight at Kate. "Sorry to interrupt. Eric Sorenson's on the phone wondering if you're available."

Kate frowned, visualizing her schedule. "I didn't miss a meeting, did I?"

"No." Liz shook her head. "I can tell him you're busy."

"I'll take it." She looked at Michael, who couldn't seem to

take his eyes off her assistant. She bumped his shoulder as she left. "Round up the sibs and let me know where we're meeting."

"I'LL HAVE THE LAMB STEW," Kate told the server in O'Dair's. The calendar might say April, but there was snow in the air. It wouldn't stay on the ground, but come on, Mother Nature. Last year it had been in the seventies most of April.

"Make it two stews, Amy," Stephen said.

Michael nodded and Timothy said, "Might as well make it stew all-around."

"You got it." Amy checked the level of their beers. "Another round?"

Kate declined, but her brothers said yes. Easy for them to burn off the calories when they outweighed her by fifty pounds.

Stephen whispered to Michael, "Change chairs with me, man."

"Jesus, Stephen," Timothy complained. "When will you outgrow this?"

"Never." Stephen stood and waited behind Michael's chair.

Everyone groaned, but Michael slid his beer mug over and sat next to Timothy.

"Kate, tell them your theory." Michael resettled in his new chair.

She raised an eyebrow. Theory? "It's odd that Mom has me learning the inner workings of Murphy's right before her biopsy."

"Are you getting the dirt on running that division?" Timothy grinned, his fingers rattling against the tabletop.

She slapped her hand on Timothy's to stop the noise. "Ha ha. The cleaning jokes are getting old. I'm serious. I'm afraid they'll want me to step in and manage Murphy's if Mom goes into treatment."

That wasn't the career path she'd imagined, but she would go where the family needed her most.

Stephen balanced on the back legs of his chair. "Hunh."

"Didn't any of you think it was strange?" she asked. Were her brothers this clueless? "Mom and Dad have never said anything about me getting," she used her fingers as quote marks, "ground-up experience."

"We started as construction helpers," Stephen said.

"You were in high school," she reminded them.

Michael took a pull of his beer. "Didn't you work in the office when you were in high school?"

"Yes." She'd thought she'd paid her dues. Maybe that was why this insistence she clean houses was like a splinter under her skin. "Dad didn't want me on any of the construction sites."

"I'd forgotten about that." Timothy's bouncing leg jiggled everything on the table. "Maybe you're on to something."

She rolled her eyes. "And …?"

Stephen gave her a long look. "And what?"

She took a big breath. Then let it out. "Do you think it has something to do with Mom?"

"Maybe." Timothy said.

Stephen leaned back and crossed his arms.

Michael drained his beer and rested his head in his hand.

These three men had been the nemesis of her youth, but they were family.

But what would the family be without Mom? Her boundless energy, her unrelenting love. If their mother was sick, what kind of hole would that leave in their lives? Her mother had to be okay.

Stephen set his mug down. "We might be getting ahead of ourselves."

"What should we do?" She pushed away her beer.

Michael's changeable eyes turned a bleak gray-green. "Whatever Mom and Dad ask of us. Kate, that means you learn about Murphy's from the ground up."

"I guess." She sighed.

Amy brought over a tray with their stews and a bowl of bread. "Here you go."

They all thanked her.

Timothy drummed his fingers against the side of his mug. "Dad's given me more autonomy with the new strip malls coming online this summer."

"He's not making the site visits he did two years ago." Stephen rubbed his chin.

They looked at Michael.

"Nothing new on my end." Michael finished his beer and pointed at her abandoned mug.

She nodded, pushing her mug to him.

"Are these changes because we're evolving or because of Mom?" Stephen asked.

Kate spooned up some carrots and potatoes and blew on them. "I don't know."

Michael and Timothy shook their heads.

"Bring any issues to me," Kate looked around the table, "and Michael. Let's keep Mom and Dad's work lives stress-free."

"As much as I don't want to add another meeting to our lives, it sounds like we should get together on a regular basis." Timothy shuddered.

"Not at the office," Stephen said. "How about dinner every week."

"That's a good plan." Michael held up Kate's empty mug and caught their server's eye.

"Are you driving?" Kate blurted.

"Stephen drove," Michael growled.

She frowned. How many beers had Michael already had? "I'll have Liz schedule weekly dinners on our calendars. Send me issues and I'll create an agenda."

Timothy rolled his eyes. "Of course."

Kate pulled out her phone and sent Liz an email. "Did anyone hear whether Mom and Dad are home yet?"

"Still at the cabin," Timothy said.

Michael took a swig of his freshly delivered beer. "We'll probably hear tomorrow."

Tomorrow.

Tomorrow Kate had to put in another four hours at Alex's.

EIGHT

WHEN KATE LET HERSELF INTO ALEX'S HOUSE ON WEDNESDAY, he was leaning against the counter, sipping his aphrodisiac coffee.

In jeans and a black T-shirt, he looked relaxed and in control. The shirt was soft as silk—she'd folded it yesterday.

"Morning." She dumped her purse on a stool and headed to the laundry room to claim her equipment.

"Do you have a minute?" He intercepted her as she walked by him.

"I really don't." She smiled with regret. "I have to finish here and get back to the office for a meeting."

"I was hoping we could talk." He stroked a finger down her cheek. "You didn't return my call last night."

"I was with my brothers." She hoisted the vacuum and tried to move around Alex.

"Hey," he said. "Are we okay?"

"I'm sorry. I'm just preoccupied with ..." She finally looked into his eyes.

He took the vacuum from her hands. "Is your mother all right?"

"We haven't heard." She tried to take the vacuum back, but Alex just held it.

"That must be hell." Concern filled his dark brown eyes.

"It is." She bit her lip. "But we're doing what we can to take the pressure off our parents. If that means I clean houses, so be it."

"That's nice of your family." He lifted the vacuum. "Where do you want this?"

"Your bedroom." This was way too intimate.

He set the machine inside his bedroom door and then leaned against the hallway wall.

He watched as she fumbled with the cord.

"Can we get together tonight?" he asked.

"I should catch up at work." She wasn't sure how to juggle this thing with Alex and trying to take pressure off her parents. She didn't know how much time she would have.

She flipped on the vacuum, hoping he'd leave her to her work.

He walked over and turned it off. "How about tomorrow. Lunch? Dinner?"

She closed her eyes. "Alex, with everything going on, maybe we shouldn't start anything."

"We already did." He hugged her. "Let me help you through this."

"Why are you so irresistible?" She curled into him, wrapping her arms around his waist.

"I am?" He chuckled. "I'm also good for hugging, kissing and meals."

"I didn't even know I needed this." She hugged him tighter and her breath slowed. Her shoulders relaxed.

He tipped up her chin. "I'm here for you. Think about dinner."

"Thank you." Her throat got tight. He was basically a

stranger, and yet he was reaching out and trying to help her. "I should get your house clean."

He stroked her cheek. "Work whatever hours you need to."

He kissed her, a firm press of his mouth against hers. Then headed down the stairs.

"You're too nice to me," she whispered.

She worked her way through the bedrooms, then ran downstairs and grabbed the glass cleaner. As she climbed the stairs, she checked her phone, worried one of her parents might have called while she'd been vacuuming. Nothing.

When would they hear from the pathologist? She spritzed the cleaner on a hallway mirror and rubbed. Her stomach churned. Cleaning left too much time to think. Maybe she should be brainstorming possible solutions to the Sorenson Law firm's leasing demands. They were asking for numerous concessions, rent reduction *and* remodeling dollars. She wanted a win-win solution that would make the firm feel like MacBain had listened to them while still ensuring a profitable lease.

Of course if Sorenson pulled out of the Daschle building, they wouldn't make *any* money.

Normally she would ask her father for advice.

Dad and Mom. Were they back in town yet? She checked her phone one more time.

No messages. Maybe that was good news.

After cleaning windows and mirrors she rolled the vacuum to the top of the stairs. Using the wand, she worked her way down each riser, vacuuming the runner held in place with brass posts. If Alex wanted children, the brass holders were a hazard. Children could trip on the posts set at each end of the steps.

Not her problem.

Her phone buzzed. She switched off the vacuum and yanked the phone out. *Timothy.*

"Hi," she said, smiling so her voice didn't project her worry.

"Dad called," he said. "Dinner at the homestead tonight. Six-thirty."

She swallowed. "Did they hear from the doctor?"

"They didn't say, but they're on their way home."

"What did Dad sound like?"

"I couldn't tell." Her brother let out a big sigh. "Wouldn't he have said if the report came back clean?"

Her chest ached. "Maybe. Probably."

"They wanted me to call everyone. Oh, fuck, Katie." His voice cracked.

"Don't. Don't think worst-case scenario." Her fingers strangled her phone. "I'll see you tonight."

She sank onto the step and her phone slipped from her fingers.

If it had been good news, Dad would have texted the all clear.

Oh God. Mom had cancer. It was the only reason she could think of that Dad wouldn't tell Timothy over the phone. Her breath shuddered as she inhaled and exhaled. Tears dripped onto her jeans.

She never cried. Burying her head in her lap, she let the tears fall. Her mother was too young and vital to have breast cancer. Damn it, the family needed her. Kate needed her.

A text buzzed on the phone at her feet. Stephen. She couldn't dredge up the energy to respond.

"What happened?" Alex's voice reverberated from the foot of the stairs.

She raised her head, unable to speak. Instead she buried her face in her hands.

He took the steps, two at a time. Crouching at her feet, he asked, "Are you okay?"

"I ... I'm ... I'm fine." Her voice creaked like an old rocking chair.

He sat next to her, his body crowding hers. "Your mother?"

She nodded, her body shaking. "I think so."

His arm wrapped around her shoulder. "You *think* so?"

"Dad and Mom requested a family dinner. Tonight. If it was good news, they'd tell us on the phone."

"I'm sorry." He swallowed. "Cancer?"

"We think so."

He tugged her closer and his warmth seeped into her back. She set her heavy head on his shoulder, just for a moment. She could lean on him for a moment.

"My grandmother died of breast cancer when she was forty-three," she said. "My great-grandmother too."

He squeezed her shoulders. "The treatments must be better than when your grandmothers were diagnosed."

"I suppose." She got to her feet, and his hand slid down her back. "I just ..."

He stood below her.

"You need to think positive thoughts. If you guessed correctly, you need to send your mother positive energy." He set his hands on her hips. "She'll get through this."

"I know." She clenched her teeth. "Theoretically I understand that the odds of surviving breast cancer are higher the earlier you catch it. If the lymph nodes aren't involved, very high. There's a seventy-five percent survival rate at ten years. But ..."

"But ...?" he encouraged.

"This is my mother." She clutched his shoulders. "What if she's the one woman in four who doesn't survive? What if it's worse? What if the lymph nodes are involved? The odds then ..."

He pulled her into his chest. The man was like a furnace.

"Okay, you've spent too much time on the internet," he

said. "Stop. You'll make yourself crazy. You don't even know why your parents want you over for dinner."

She nodded, her arms wrapped loosely around his waist. She took a deep breath. "You're right. It's just …"

He rested his chin on her head. "Turn it off, at least for now. Wait until you hear what they have to say."

"Easy for you." She inhaled his woodsy aftershave. This was not the time to be noticing Alex's scent. She tried to push herself out of his embrace, but he tightened those outrageously muscled arms.

"Wait." Somehow his face was beside hers. His chin no longer rested on her head. His breath feathered the hair around her face.

"I have to finish cleaning." The words coming out of her mouth wouldn't make the flame on a birthday candle flicker. *She was in trouble.*

Alex tipped up her chin. "Kate?"

He kissed her.

His tongue eased into her mouth, skimming against her tongue, then delved deeper. Her head tipped, allowing him better access. She wound her arms around his neck.

He lifted her and she wrapped her legs around his waist. One of his hands stroked her bottom, tugging her against his erection. The other curved around her breast. His thumb found her pebbled nipple, and he brushed against it.

Her phone buzzed. Another text message. "Alex."

He groaned.

She slid down his body. "Crap," she said, pulling out her phone to read the text.

His hands settled on her shoulders. "Is it your mother?"

"My assistant. I need to finish and then handle some things at the office before …" She swallowed. "Before I go to my parents' house."

"I'll do whatever I can to help." He kissed her forehead.

"Thank you." She closed her eyes. "Let me finish the vacuuming, and then I need to leave."

"Sure." He started down the steps but turned. "Promise you'll answer my call tonight, whatever happens. I need to know you're all right."

Warmth pushed away some of her fear. "I will."

PATTY MURPHY MacBain gazed at her children as they filed into the family room. Her babies—all grown up. They gravitated to their own chairs. The spots they used to claim even after they'd gone off to college. Michael and Katie were on the sofa, Timothy sprawled on the floor and Stephen hunkered in the corner wingback chair.

Her three gorgeous sons and beautiful daughter were wonderful. And it wasn't their good looks, it was their inner goodness.

She and Mac had made a fine family.

She moved closer to the blazing fire. Ever since the doctor had called, she'd been cold. As if he could hear her thoughts, Mac draped his arms around her, sharing his warmth.

God, she didn't want to do this to them. She didn't want their lives to change. But the evil growing in her body altered everything.

"Mom, please tell us what's going on. What did the pathologist say?" Katie asked.

Of course it would be Katie to get straight to the point.

"The lump was malignant."

Katie flew off the sofa and wrapped her arms around her. "Mom."

Everyone hugged her and she gathered strength from their love.

"Sit. Sit down," she said.

"Okay." Katie slapped her hands on her legs after moving back to her chair. "What do we need to do to beat this?"

"We're meeting with an oncologist tomorrow to review options." She took a deep breath. "I will beat this monster."

Timothy nodded. "Absolutely."

"How can we help?" Katie asked. "What do you want us to do?"

Mac's hands stroked her arms, pouring strength into her. He kissed her forehead. "We'll talk about it later. Tonight, we want to be with all of you."

"Don't you fall apart on me now, Mac," she warned her husband.

"Never." His voice was sad, and she didn't know how to take away his sorrow.

"Whatever you need from us," Michael said, and each of the children echoed the thought.

"What I need everyone to do right now is eat. Maria's made a Mexican feast. We're together, let's celebrate that."

Patty stared at her children's faces. She wanted to see them happily settled, maybe with children on the way. She wanted all that. God, she wanted the chance to be a Grandma.

She pushed off from the sofa. "Come on."

They trailed after her into the dining room. Missing was the normal kidding and family jokes. No one even threw a verbal punch. She actually missed their bickering.

The food smelled delicious. Patty planned to fuel her body for her upcoming fight. "It looks fantastic."

She grabbed a plate off the sideboard. The array Maria set on warming plates could have fed a family of twenty. She looked at the fajita makings but changed her mind. Digging into the enchiladas and adding black beans and rice, she said, "Anything that's not eaten will be sent home with you."

After everyone had their plates, Mac said grace, finishing

with, "God, help Patty with her fight. And help us, her family, help her."

Amens echoed around the table.

The kids stared at their plates, pushing around the magnificent food. She took a big forkful of enchilada, chewing on chipotle peppers and cheese. "This is wonderful."

Mac rolled his fajita and took a big bite. "Fabulous." His eyes were like a stormy day on the lake.

Why did she and Mac always sit at opposite ends of the table? When the kids were growing up it was so they could each take a child in hand. Stupid habits. Now that they had an empty nest, she wanted to be near him. She wanted to touch him, feed off his vigor.

"How can we take the pressure off you at work?" Timothy's fingers drummed on the table. Someday he would find a place to focus his energy.

"We're at the dinner table." Patty raised her eyebrows. "I may be heading into battle, but the rules haven't changed. We will talk about this another time."

Michael jabbed Timothy in the side. "Idiot."

"Sorry, Mom."

"How was the lake?" Katie asked. Her diplomat. No wonder she was good with clients. When Stephen and Timothy had fought as kids, she'd always distracted them. Why didn't Katie know how good she was with people, with children?

"It was quiet. Very relaxing." Mac winked at her.

She grinned. At least Mac hadn't told the kids they'd made love on any available surface. They hadn't been that—uninhibited—since before they'd had children. The threat of mortality had broken something free in them.

"So, what did you two do?" Stephen stuffed most of a tortilla in his mouth.

"Took walks, read. Did a little cleanup around the cabin." If she could call dusting the dining room table with her back, cleanup. "I'd like to celebrate Mother's Day at the lake this year."

"Sounds great." Katie pushed pieces of enchilada around her plate, mixing it with her black beans and rice.

"No *sopaipillas* if you don't finish your meals," Patty said.

Timothy smiled. "Come on, Mom. That's not fair."

"I get your share," Stephen joked, his plate half-empty.

"Pass me the wine," Michael growled. Her oldest wouldn't look her in the eye.

Patty's hand fisted around her fork. Ooh, she worried about him. After Sarah had died, he'd suffered. How would he react to her cancer?

"So, K-K-K-Katie," Timothy said, "how's the cleaning going?"

"Wonderful," Katie snapped.

"No work discussions," Patty reminded them.

"Then how was your dinner date Saturday?" Timothy sported a huge grin until he cried, "Ouch!"

Someone kicked him under the table. Patty had her money on Katie.

Mock surprise covered Stephen's face. "You went out with someone on Saturday? But you had drinks with a guy on Friday."

When they were young, Stephen had instigated most of the trouble between him and Timothy. And Timothy had always exploded first. Now Stephen leaned back in his chair, after throwing oil onto the fire brewing in Katie.

"Shut up you two." Katie shoved food in her mouth and chewed with a rebellious frown. "It was the same guy."

This was what Patty had missed earlier.

"Alex Adamski," Timothy said in a singsong voice.

Katie was dating Alexander Adamski? Patty had met him when Murphy's bid on cleaning his house. The man made a Kodiak bear look small. Her daughter and Adamski?

Maybe that was a good thing. Katie needed something in her life besides the family and the company.

"Did he play you a love song?" Stephen asked, adopting the same lilt as his brother.

"Why would he?" Katie snapped.

"That's what he does, right? He's a songwriter?" Stephen asked.

"Yes." Katie took a sip of her wine.

Mac shot Patty a look, eyebrows raised, an appealing smile filling his face.

"When will we meet this guy?" Michael asked.

"Like I would introduce him to morons," Katie said.

"If Timothy and Stephen have met him, you should bring him to a family dinner." Michael tipped his wine glass at her. "I'd like to grill … I mean … meet him."

"Not in this lifetime." Katie tipped her wineglass at him. Besides, I don't have time to date."

"Of course you should make time to date. There's more to life than work." Patty shook her head. "I liked him."

Stephen headed back to the buffet with his plate and piled on more enchiladas. "When did you meet him?"

"When I bid on his work. He's Katie's client."

Katie closed her eyes. "Mom."

Everyone laughed. Everyone but Katie. The tension in the room evaporated. Mac grinned at her.

Timothy inhaled and started coughing. "You're dating a client?"

"No." Katie spit the word out.

Michael tipped more wine in his glass, spilling a little on the white tablecloth. "Come on. He needs to meet the rest of the family. Only Dad and I haven't had the honor. Be fair."

"Sucks to be you."

"Kathleen Patricia MacBain, you're at the dinner table." Patty used her best mom voice.

"Sorry, Mamma."

If nothing else the teasing had leached the sadness out of their dinner. Patty only reminded the kids once more not to talk about work. God, she loved her family.

Katie was the last one to leave. "Mom, let me know what you need me to do. I love you."

"I love you too, Katie bear."

After they closed the door behind Katie, Mac wrapped an arm around her. "Are you okay, love?"

"Yeah." She sighed. "I wish we hadn't needed to tell them."

Mac pulled her into a hug. "We had no choice. You can't keep something this big from the ones who love you. They want to help." He held her face in his big, scarred hands. "I want to help."

Their kiss had everything melting inside her like chocolate dropped on a summer sidewalk. She gasped for breath. "You know how you can help me?"

Mac scattered kisses along her collarbones. "How?"

"Take me to bed. Make love to me."

Mac swept her into his arms and headed for the stairs. "I was waiting for you to ask."

NINE

THIS WAS STUPID. ALEX BEAT HIS FINGER ON HIS STEERING wheel and glanced up at Kate's condo. Sitting in his car outside her place was like stalking.

He pulled out his phone and found her number. His finger hovered over the *call* symbol. Kate could still be with her family. He didn't want to interrupt. She was dealing with a lot.

But he didn't want her to be alone tonight. He could help her … defuse.

Not sex. Just letting her talk, vent. Keep her from bottling everything up.

His head dropped to the steering wheel. What a liar he'd become. He wanted to hold her in his arms and comfort her.

He checked the time. Okay, he'd see if she was home. Find out if she wanted to talk or needed a shoulder to cry on. Then he'd leave.

In the building's vestibule, he found her apartment number and pushed the button. He hummed the bass line of the phrase he'd been working on as he'd waited.

No answer. He pushed again.

Nothing. He turned to leave.

"Alex?" Kate's hand was on the outer door. "What are you doing here?"

"I was worried about you."

He closed the distance and stroked her cheek. She'd been crying.

Kate's eyelids fluttered shut. Her head leaned into his hand. She sagged against him. Damn.

Wrapping an arm around her shoulder, he said, "You're exhausted. Let's get you upstairs."

She handed him her keycard and keys. He swiped the card and guided her to the elevator. Maybe she was allowing him to take care of her, but he couldn't help feeling this *rightness* whenever he held her.

She was silent through the elevator ride and the walk to her door. He made short work of the locks and then led her into her living room. Stripping off her coat, he encouraged her to sit with a nudge. "I'll get you something to drink."

He didn't need to ask what her mother's diagnosis was. One look at her face and he knew.

Shrugging out of his jacket, he hung their coats on the ornate coatrack. The coatrack looked out of place in her modern setting. Like the owner herself, the decorating was a puzzle. And he wanted to put the pieces together.

In the kitchen he found her alcohol stash. He warmed a mug full of milk in the microwave. God how could anyone stand drinking *skim* milk? While waiting, he poured a snifter of brandy. One sip and he grimaced. She needed to upgrade her brandy. The microwave dinged, he added a good slosh of brandy to her milk and a spoonful of honey.

She'd curled into the corner of her sofa.

"Here." He sat on the coffee table and set his snifter down. The table creaked and he moved to the sofa, pulling her feet onto his lap.

She took a deep breath before opening her eyes. She

frowned at the mug in her hands. "Thanks, but I can't handle any more caffeine."

"It's warm milk with a bump." He nudged the mug to her lips. "My mum's recipe for what ails you."

Her expression crumbled a little, but she sipped and made a face. "You drank this when you were little?" She took another sip.

"Well, not the brandy part. What did they tell you? Can you talk about it?"

Her chest rose and fell. She shifted her feet off his lap and curled them under her.

"The lump was malignant." Her lips trembled. "They'll find out tomorrow what the treatment plan is."

He eased open her fist and laced their fingers together. "I'm sorry. She's a lovely woman."

She stared at their linked hands. "It was hard not to bawl. My mom's amazing. She kept talking about battling the evil in her body." Her fingers tightened on his. "She comforted us."

Tears coursed down her cheeks. Alex took the mug out of her hand and pulled her into his lap. He rubbed her back as she cried. Better to let her cry it out here than in front of her mother.

"C-c-crap. I never cry." Her curls shook.

"I know." Although he'd seen her cry earlier today.

She snuffled into his shirt, and her fingernail traced a pattern there. "I'm glad you were waiting for me."

"I'm glad I came."

She sank into him. He rested his head on the top of hers, just holding her.

Why did being with her comfort him? Yeah, he wanted to sleep with her. No, make love to her. But there was something *right* about the way she curled into his arms. Something *right* about the way she looked him straight in the eye and told him to pick up after himself. Something *right* about her not needing him to advance her career.

She stirred. Damn, he didn't want her to move. Not yet.

"Thank you." She looked so sad. She turned so they were as close to chest-to-chest without her straddling his legs. "I didn't think I needed someone to lean on."

His body went on alert. Shit, he hoped Kate didn't realize what was happening under her butt. Not the time for all the blood to rush to that particular organ.

"Everyone needs help at some point in their lives." He kissed her upturned mouth, careful to keep it friendly with Kate so vulnerable.

She pulled him down, sucked his tongue into her mouth. She stroked his chest, leaving his skin too tight for his body.

He broke the kiss and just held her. Her breasts were soft pillows against his chest.

Although the sofa wasn't wide enough, there was a rug in front of her fireplace. He could imagine starting a fire and watching the light from the flames flicker over her pale skin.

He drew in a breath, shutting his eyes tight on the image he'd painted. Kate needed comfort, not lust.

"I should go." Before he did something she would regret.

"Can you …" Her head buried in the hollow of his shoulder. "Can you hold me for a while?"

He sighed. "My pleasure." Or pain.

She reached for her mug and drained the milk. Then she sank into his arms. The perfect fit. He hummed the jingle he'd just written, hoping the sound of his voice didn't grate against her nerves.

Her body grew lax, heavy in his arms.

He didn't know how long he sat there, humming ballad after ballad. Even when he shifted away, she didn't wake.

Carefully he stood, cradling his precious bundle. He headed down the hallway and found her bedroom. Moonlight reflected off the gauzy drapes hanging over railings along the top of her bed. Kate, the take-charge go-getter, had a fairy bower bedroom.

Holding her in one hand, he pulled back the bedding. Then he set her on crisp white sheets. He almost threw the covers back over her but decided he should remove some of her clothes.

He unbuckled her short boots and set them next to the bed. His fingers drummed against his thighs. He should take off her jeans. It would be as if he were seeing her in a bikini, right?

Pushing away his doubt, he unbuttoned and unzipped the jeans that molded to her body. By the time he grasped the pant hems and tugged, sweat dotted his brow.

He quickly covered her long legs with the sheet. Swallowing, he wondered if he should remove anything else.

She curled onto her side. Her eyes blinked open. She reached out to him. "Alex?"

He linked their fingers together and sat on the edge of the bed, keeping space between their bodies. "Yeah?"

"Don't go." Even in the dim moonlight, he could see her lips trembling.

He closed his eyes. "I really should."

"Please." Her voice cracked. "I don't want to be alone tonight. If you could hold me, it doesn't have to mean anything."

Doesn't have to mean anything? How could she do that—have someone sleep with her and not have it mean something? He just couldn't. And he didn't want to. She meant something to him.

But her eyes were huge, vulnerable. She was hurting.

Alex found himself toeing off his shoes and pulling off his socks. Then he tugged up his shirt. He'd leave his jeans on, no need to tempt fate.

He moved to the other side of her bed and slipped under the covers. He rolled onto his side and she wriggled closer.

Didn't she know what she was doing to him? He tucked her into his body and draped an arm around her waist.

She sighed.

His cheek rested against her hair. Inhaling, his nose filled with her scent. His body reacted, oblivious that Kate was emotionally fragile. *Christ.*

This would be one hell of a long night.

KATE JERKED AWAKE, her heart beating like a jackhammer. She was pinned to the bed. Trying to catch her breath, she gathered her strength and shoved.

A man grunted. A man connected to a big hairy arm. She wasn't pinned. A man was asleep—in her bed.

Taking a deep breath, she caught a whiff of cologne. Alex?

She glanced at the alarm. Three a.m.

Alex rolled over.

Had they slept together? Her hands went to her chest. Nope. Her sweater, shirt and bra were still on.

She rubbed crust from her eyes. She must have been crying.

The night before crashed into her like waves battering a cliff. She let out a ragged breath.

Her mother.

She'd begged Alex to stay. He'd comforted and held her like she was precious. She'd felt his arousal, but he hadn't made a move.

Sitting, she wrapped her arms around her legs. Her jeans were missing. Vaguely she remembered Alex taking them off. But he hadn't taken off her bra. The straps cut into her shoulders.

Her mother. Oh, God.

She didn't want to lie in bed, thinking about what the next weeks would bring. How would she get back to sleep?

She glanced at Alex. He could help her forget. At least for a night.

She stripped off her sweater. Her breath came a little faster. Not thinking too deeply about her actions, she whipped off her shirt and unsnapped her bra.

Alex faced her. With one hand, she touched his chest. Oh, man, he was so broad.

She buried her fingers in his chest hair. She'd never slept with someone so … hairy. What would the brush of that hair feel like on her breasts?

Her nipples pebbled. She found Alex's nipple and brushed it with her thumb. It stood erect under her attention.

Alex moaned, still asleep.

Her hand wandered down a path of soft hair. He'd left his jeans on.

The top of his jeans was unbuttoned. Taking a deep breath, she explored farther, finding his erection pressed against the zipper. *Poor man.*

She eased down the zipper, giving him room to grow. And he did. She set her palm along the hardening ridge. He wore a pair of his silk boxers. *My, oh my.* He could take her mind off her troubles.

Obviously her parents wanted her to run Murphy's while Mom went through treatment. She was done cleaning Alex's home. They might never see each other again.

Her chest twisted a little. Cleaning hadn't been so bad. She stroked a hand up his chest. Not so bad at all.

Alex was her reward. Short-term only.

Leaning toward him, she kissed him. With her hand, she explored the hard planes of his chest.

He rolled closer and kissed her. His lips opened, tongue delving into her mouth.

Her hand sank lower. She rubbed along the hard ridge framed by his open zipper.

Alex tore his mouth away. "Kate? Kate! I'm sorry. I didn't mean to … I swore I wouldn't."

He started to roll away.

She grabbed his shoulders and let him take her with him. Now he was on his back, and she was his blanket.

She pushed off his chest. Sitting, she tossed back her hair.

His eyes fixed on her chest. Her breasts ached under his scrutiny.

"How? Did I?" His words carried an edge of panic.

Poor man.

She placed his hands on her breasts. His fingers flexed, easing the ache. He kneaded them. Good man. Her head dropped back. "Oh, God, yes."

"You …" He was so damn cute. "You want this to happen?"

She wiggled. "Absolutely."

His hands slid down to her thighs. He wrapped those large, competent hands around her butt and held her. Then he sat.

Wow. Nice core strength.

He pulled her flush to his chest. Not many men made her feel petite. Alex did. His hands spanned her back as he tugged on the ends of her hair, and she tipped her head.

There wasn't anything tentative in his kiss. He sucked her tongue into his mouth. Then he nibbled on her bottom lip.

Her breath rasped as his tongue trailed down her neck to her collarbone. Lightheaded, she wondered if they'd sucked all the air out of the room. Arching back, she prayed he would take the hint.

He did. He nuzzled his way between her breasts. His beard

rubbed against the tender skin on the sides of both breasts. He latched on.

A moan erupted. From her.

One hand massaged her breast, his thumb and forefinger pinching and rolling her nipple.

Her fingernails dug into his shoulders. His talented mouth moved to the other breast, and she groaned. She didn't want him to stop, but she wanted more. She wanted him inside of her.

She let one hand drift down, rising so she could touch his erection.

Alex gasped.

She pushed onto her knees, forcing him to bury his face against her stomach. He licked and wonderful chills coursed through her body.

Her fingers dug into his silky thick hair. "I think we need to get rid of your jeans."

His arms tightened around her waist. "I'd say we're moving too fast, missing the best parts of seduction, but … it's been a long time for me. I don't know if I can wait."

He almost squeezed the air out of her lungs. And she didn't care. She didn't ask if he'd slept with anyone since his wife. She didn't want to be that important. She just wanted him to take her mind off her mother.

"It's been a while for me too," she whispered. *Keep it light.* "Let's see if we can figure out if our parts fit together."

She rolled, tugging off her thong.

He'd already stumbled off the bed and pushed his jeans and his boxers off. Then he stopped.

They stared at each other.

Moonlight caressed each hard plane of his face and chest. Her eyes dropped to the erection jutting out. He was a big man, a wonderfully big man.

Lying back, she held out her arms.

His voice was as solemn as a priest's during a particularly dire homily. "You're lovely."

He knelt between her thighs. His hands, those hands that could create such beautiful music, played her face, her breasts, and made her body sing. Each touch took her higher. She closed her eyes, unable to look into his serious dark eyes. Afraid of what she might see there.

"You're pretty lovely yourself," she said.

Sitting, she pushed him down to the mattress. Her fingers mimicked the journey his hands had taken over her body. She traced the lines and angles of his face. Smoothed along his neck and toyed with his nipples until they were hard beads between her fingers. Sliding down, she trailed a finger along the sharp line of his hip. Then she taunted him, drawing patterns along his inner thigh, between his hips, brushing next to his balls but never touching his erection.

Alex growled like the bear he'd reminded her of at their first meeting. He rose and flipped her under him.

"Enough." His voice was a low rumble. The drapes above their heads shimmied.

She accepted his hard kiss. Nipping his lower lip, she guided him into her body.

"Slow down." Alex captured her hands, shackling them above her head. Then he took control.

Inch by torturous inch, he opened her, invaded her, joined with her. His face strained above hers. His muscles were etched in deep relief as if he were Atlas holding up the world.

She arched her hips, trying to take him deeper. When that didn't work, she squeezed her inner muscles around him.

Alex groaned.

"Hurry," she urged, trying to tug her hands free.

"No," he whispered, nudging a little deeper. "I don't want this over too quickly."

Alex kissed her, slow and deep. She sucked on his tongue,

raked her teeth against his lip, but nothing sped up his glacial pace.

He ran his lips down her cheek, along her neck and back to her breasts.

Her head rocked back and forth. Pressure built, in her chest, in her belly and where they were joined.

"Let me touch you," she begged.

He let go of her wrists. She clutched his hips, trying to tilt her pelvis and fully seat him. Her body was nitroglycerine; volatile, shaken and ready to detonate.

Nothing made him hurry.

She dug her fingers into his ass. If he would shimmy a little higher, she'd relieve this wonderful agony.

Alex's chest heaved. He started to withdraw, still moving at the pace of a turtle.

"Alex, move!" She rolled her hips.

His jaw clenched. "You. Are. Driving. Me. Crazy."

Thank goodness. "Higher."

He slid in a little faster with a little more thrust. She met him with a pulse of her own. And again. And again. Agony and ecstasy combined.

She erupted. "Oh, God."

Waves of delight rocked her. Fireworks exploded behind her eyes.

He sank into her, freezing as her body squeezed around him.

Then he started again.

His mouth found her nipple, biting down, and the agony flared like gasoline on an open flame. His other hand wandered south, his thumb hitting a spot so sensitized she would have jumped if she hadn't been pinned to the bed.

The waves began again.

Alex thrust deeper, harder. "Look at me. Stay with me."

Her eyes were glued shut, but she pried them open. His

eyes looked black. She didn't want to look into them, but she couldn't tear her gaze away.

He thrust one last time, setting off new explosions.

"Kate," he called.

He sealed their mouths together. His kiss barreled into her, invading her heart. A place she'd sworn no man would touch.

Never. Never before.

Her body shook, both from the orgasms that had rocked her and her reaction to Alex.

Their hearts pounded. Breaths whooshed in and out. She wrapped her arms around his back, holding on, relieved she wasn't staring into his emotion-filled eyes. She didn't care that she couldn't breathe.

His gasps slowed and he wrapped his arms around her and reversed their positions. She drew in a deep breath and rested her head on his broad chest.

"Amazing." Alex kissed her ear and let out a huge sigh.

"Yeah." Her voice trembled.

A tear sneaked down her cheek. She brushed it aside. Her face heated in embarrassment. She was a hard-charging executive, she didn't cry after sex.

"Are you okay?" Alex swept another kiss on her hair.

Damn the man. Why couldn't he roll over and sleep?

"I'm fine. Fine."

She rolled off his chest. Alex tucked her head into the hollow of his shoulder. Between her legs, she was wet and sticky.

"Oh, God," she gasped. "We forgot … condom!"

"Shit. Shit." Alex rolled toward her. "I … I didn't even think. I woke up and …"

And she'd taken advantage of him. Had him rocking and rolling before he'd come to his senses.

Shit was right.

"I'm clean," she said, her stomach twisting at the thought that she'd had unprotected sex.

She was Miss Plan Everything in Advance.

"I use an IUD." She was part of that small percentage of women who got sick from birth control pills. They should be okay. She chewed her lip but couldn't remember the start of her last period.

"I'm clean too." Alex brushed her hair off her face. He dropped a quick kiss on her lips. "I was so … turned on. I didn't even think. It's just … you surprised me. And pleased me."

He rolled so they lay on their sides. "Get some sleep."

She returned his kiss and shifted so her back was to his chest.

What had she done?

THE GAUZY DRAPES SHROUDING Kate's bed shook as Alex plumped his pillow.

He was in Kate's bed. Heat zipped through his body, zooming to his erection. *She'd* turned to him. *She'd* wanted to make love. God, he hadn't felt this content in … ever.

When he'd been married to Meredith, he'd always felt like he was on an emotional rollercoaster. She'd … guilted … him into everything. Sex came with emotional strings attached. And he'd let her manipulate him, just to stay within her orbit.

A melody flitted through his consciousness. He tried to grab at the notes, but they floated away.

Unfortunately he was alone. His sigh made those drapes shake again. He hoped Kate had gotten some sleep. Her mother's diagnosis had rocked her.

He threw off the covers and headed for the bathroom.

A piece of paper was stuck to the mirror.

What can I do today to improve MacBain Enterprises?
What can I do today to prove I'm capable of running MacBain?
Interesting.

A new toothbrush sat on the counter. He frowned. How often did Kate supply a toothbrush to a man who stayed the night?

No. She was an organized woman who'd graciously had an extra toothbrush available. No problem.

How the hell had they forgotten a condom? He'd awakened in the middle of the night with her lips on his, and her hands wrapped around his dick. He hadn't been able to think —only feel.

His body still coursed with want. He wouldn't mind pulling her back into bed for another bout.

Alex made his way to the kitchen. Kate sat at the table with her arms wrapped around her legs and her head resting on her knees. She didn't need sex right now, she needed sympathy.

He stopped next to her chair. "Good morning."

"Morning." She didn't quite manage a smile. This was the face of someone whose loved one had received a cancer diagnosis.

He kissed her knee. "How're you doing?"

Kate closed her eyes. Her chest rose and fell in a big sigh. "Not so good."

The coffeepot emitted a gurgling burp. "Let me get you a cup of coffee."

Her fingers stroked her lips, lips swollen from last night's kisses. A tremor went through her body. He'd never seen someone who looked so alone.

Mugs hung from a rack, and he grabbed two. He added a dab of milk to his and a little more to hers. He'd noticed she liked more milk than he did. Probably because she didn't have the coffee source he did.

He'd gift Kate a couple of pounds of his custom-roasted coffee. He got it directly from a Seattle distributor.

He hoped to spend some nights here. Or have her stay at his place. Then he could bring her coffee in bed. He liked the vision of her in his big bed. And he'd be a little more comfortable. Her bed was too small. His feet had hung off the end of the mattress.

Plus, he wasn't an urban kind of guy. He rolled his shoulders. The spot between them itched. Living in an apartment in the sky wasn't him. He liked looking out his windows and seeing his yard. Liked playing ball with AJ whenever his buddy knocked.

And maybe … Okay getting ahead of himself. One night didn't make forever.

He poured their coffee and brought it to the table. She still had her arms wrapped around her legs.

"Here you go."

"Thanks." She didn't look at him.

Was she embarrassed about what happened last night? Or was she worried about the condom, well the lack of a condom.

"I'm sorry about forgetting protection."

"I'm not … in the right time of my cycle."

"Good. That's good." That itch between his shoulders grew … itchier. "Are you worried about your mother?"

"Yeah. I feel like the world blew up, and I don't know what I'm supposed to do or where I'm supposed to go."

He set his hand on her knee. "You'll figure it out. And I'll help."

"Thanks." Those green eyes of hers finally looked into his.

"I mean it. Anything I can do to make your life easier."

"There's nothing right now." She sighed. "I should get ready for work."

"Of course." He would get out of her hair. "Can I take you to dinner tonight?"

149

Her eyes shuttered. "I don't know what's happening. My mom sees the oncologist today."

"Um, sure."

She stood, forcing him to take a step backwards. "I need to hop in the shower."

"I'll go." He kissed her. "Last night was incredible."

"Yeah." She sighed against his chest. "Thank you."

"I'll call this afternoon. See how your night's stacking up."

"You don't have to." She headed down the hallway.

He pulled on his shoes as her shower went on. Letting himself out of her apartment, he made sure her door locked behind him.

Damn. She'd just brushed him off.

TEN

"Mom, what are you doing here?" Kate asked.

Her mother had folders spread out on her desk as if this were a normal workday. It wasn't normal. Her oncology appointment was this afternoon.

Mom smiled as if she didn't have a care in the world. "I work here."

"I thought you had a doctor's appointment."

"Not until this afternoon."

Her mother signed a document, set it in her outbox and then got up and moved away from her desk. She looked slim and healthy. She'd paired a gray sweater and pants with a silky cranberry top. How could she have cancer?

She touched Kate's cheek. Taking her hand, Mom tugged her to the sofa. "How are you doing, Katie?"

How was *she* doing?

She blinked. Could Mom tell that she'd slept with Alex? Now Alex thought they were seeing each other tonight … Her stomach threatened to spew the muffin she'd bought at Caribou on her walk to the office. "Not at the top of my game. Didn't sleep well last night."

"I don't want you or your brothers worrying," her mother insisted. "I'll get through this. I need you to keep the faith."

"It's just …" Kate couldn't sit anymore. She stood and paced to the windows. How many of the people twenty floors below were going through something like this? "It's a lot to take in right now."

"I know," her mother said, "but each day is a blessing."

One breath at a time. Kate had read that somewhere. She inhaled and her neck muscles relaxed a little. "So what time is your appointment?"

"Two o'clock at the university."

"And have you checked out your physician?" Kate could do a quick search if her mother would give her the doctor's name.

"Yes." Her mother walked over to the windows and wrapped an arm around her waist. "Katie, let go a little. Business as usual."

Kate's laugh sounded raw and rough to her ears. "I don't think business has been *usual* since you insisted I start cleaning houses."

Another smile broke across Mom's face. God, her mother was beautiful. Not a gray hair on her head. Her eyes looked more green than golden right now.

"Is it getting any easier?" Mom asked. "I know Mr. Adamski is hard on our cleaners."

"Alex is fine." Kate's face grew warm. If her mother found out she'd slept with her client, she'd be disappointed. "Should I tell Lois to find him a new cleaner?"

"Why would we do that?"

Kate raised an eyebrow. "So I can take on more of your administrative duties."

"No. We'll keep things as they are. You'll still be cleaning."

"But why?" The knot in her throat became the size of a fist. "Didn't you get me involved with Murphy's because you'd found the lump?"

She'd assumed she was done cleaning. She *wanted* to be done with cleaning.

"It wasn't *just* because of the lump. We want you to expand your company knowledge."

"But … you told us about the lump right after I started cleaning." Hadn't they?

"Coincidence." Her mother squeezed her fingers. "Honey, I want life to be as normal as possible."

How can it be? "I thought you wanted me to take over the management of Murphy's. I figured that's why you had me cleaning."

"Oh, sweetie, we do want you to have more experience in the company, the whole company. We want your brothers to have more experience too. The last thing we want is a family business that can't survive into the next generation." Her mother's laughter filled the room. "I'll say it again, your cleaning isn't just because Dad and I thought I had cancer."

"It's not that funny." Kate couldn't help frowning.

"Laughter is the best medicine." Her mother's eyes twinkled. "Laughter and work."

At least she'd done something right. She'd made Mom laugh.

Kate perked up. "So Michael, Stephen and Timothy will have to clean too?"

"We haven't decided how to help them." Mom rested her back against the glass.

Kate would still work for Alex. That wasn't what she'd expected. She'd assumed she was through.

She couldn't think about seeing Alex again. Work, she'd focus on work. If work helped her mother get through the day, she'd run some ideas by her.

"Mom, I've been toying with a plan. There's a lot of turnover in our cleaners. Even in last year's slow economy we had an eighteen percent turnover."

153

"I know." Her mother shook her head. "Unfortunately you get that with entry level positions."

"What if we developed work/study programs with some of the smaller colleges. I talked to the Augsburg dean of student affairs last week."

Her mom crossed her legs. "Tell me more."

FOR THE SECOND time in a week, Kate headed up the walkway of her family home. Mom and Dad had requested another dinner. Stephen and Timothy's cars were already in the driveway. Michael had probably grabbed a ride with one of them.

Her stomach churned. She hadn't eaten much lunch, too worried about her mother. What had they learned at the oncologist appointment?

The entry smelled of her mother's homemade vanilla and lavender potpourri. A recipe great-grandmother had taught Mom.

Kate swallowed a rush of emotions. Her mother had wanted to teach her how to make the potpourri, and Kate had poo-pooed the attempt. She hadn't wanted to be *domestic*. She was an executive. Baking cookies, making a home smell sweet. Those things weren't in her master plan.

Maybe she should learn to make her mother's potpourri. Then when her brothers had children, she could pass the art down to them. The recipe wouldn't die.

She gritted her teeth. No thoughts of dying. Only positive energy around Mom.

She shed her coat and hung it in the front closet. Voices carried from the family room.

She didn't want to know what the doctor had said. Her

world would change. She wanted everything to return to before her mother's biopsy.

Her siblings sat in the same seats as the previous night. Dad stood behind Mom, his hand on her shoulder. Michael had one side of the sofa. Timothy sprawled on the floor, and Stephen had claimed his wingback chair.

There was a tray with a bottle of cabernet and glasses. She poured a glass, moved to the sofa and sat with Michael. "Hey."

Her mother smiled. "Glad you could make it."

"Sorry, traffic was bad." Really, she'd procrastinated leaving the office.

"Let's get to it, shall we," her mother said.

Dad squeezed her shoulder. "Go for it, love."

"We caught the tumor in the early stages." Her mother's head bobbed up and down, making her curls dance. "The plan is to perform a lumpectomy and then do radiation therapy but with a different technique. It's called brachytherapy and involves implanting radioactive seeds into the breast right after surgery. With luck, I only need radiation therapy and no chemo."

Kate rested a shaky hand against the top of her own breast.

"That's good, right?" Stephen asked. "If they're talking about a lumpectomy, that's good?"

"What is it?" Timothy asked, his foot tapping on the rug.

Dad explained, "Instead of a mastectomy, they remove only the lump and the tissue around it."

"What if they don't get the entire tumor?" Kate asked.

"If they need to, they'll do the mastectomy. It would be based on the pathologist's report once they remove the tumor."

Michael sipped an amber drink from a tumbler. "Are they worried about your family history?"

"They're taking my mother and grandmother's deaths into

consideration." Mom sipped her wine. "But we've caught this early."

"This is good news," Dad said. "They're planning the least invasive procedure for your mother."

"But will they get all the cancer?" Kate repeated. She'd explored too many breast cancer websites over the last few days. "What about lymph nodes?"

"They'll check them." Dad took Mom's empty wineglass and refilled it. "If they have to do a mastectomy as a next step, they will."

"Thanks." Mom smiled up at Dad.

"When is the surgery?" Timothy asked.

Mom and Dad said together, "Next Monday."

EVER SINCE ALEX had made love to Kate, he could barely scribble notes fast enough. For the last four days, the music had demanded release. The counterpoint and percussion filled his head, and his fingers danced across the keyboard.

Apparently sex had helped him break through the road-blocks and false starts. The next movement in his sonata swamped his senses. He let the piece jump from E minor into major. Triumphant broad chords, big, brassy chords, marched like soldiers across the page.

No. He slashed out an entire phrase. Sweat dripped on the keyboard. He swiped it away with his elbow.

He returned to the original theme that had haunted him from the moment he and Meredith had broken up. Slower now. It started in the oboe, echoed in the violas. The violins would pick up the melody, but in harmonics, like a ghost of the original strong notes that had opened the piece. The harp would have the last say. The rest of the instruments droned a low E minor with only the harp plucking out the melody.

Finally. After two years, he'd finished the second movement of *Sonata to a Child Unborn.*

He pushed away from the keyboard and rolled his neck. Vertebrae cracked in protest.

Then he set up the recording module on the keyboard. Now to add in the sections he'd just slaved over.

He recorded the melody and harmonies. Then he changed the instrumentation on the keyboard and added the wind instruments. Once more he flipped switches, adding the bass and the percussion. Finally he laid down the harp.

Done.

Rolling his chair away, he grabbed his mug and sipped. "Fuck."

The coffee was cold and stale. How long had he been working?

He glanced at the clock behind him. Still 9:30. He needed to buy batteries.

Was Kate here?

She hadn't been able to chat the last couple of days. Each time he'd called, she'd rushed off the phone after saying hello. Now that it was Friday, hopefully her life would have settled down. She'd barely had a chance to tell him how her mother was doing. Just that her surgery was Monday.

Easing from the chair, he stretched out his lower back. Everything hurt.

He headed to the kitchen, mug in hand. His stomach grumbled. He'd better eat. Passing the living room, he could see the lines in the carpet were straight and even. No footsteps.

The kitchen was spotless and smelled lemony. He rinsed out the mug and set it in the now empty dishwasher.

"Kate?" he called.

Silence.

Maybe she was upstairs. He took the stairs two at a time.

He wanted her to hear the latest movement, see what she thought.

After all, she'd helped him break through the roadblocks.

He checked his bedroom. Empty. Clean towels hung in the bathroom. He frowned. Where else could she be?

He checked every room on the second floor and then headed downstairs. Nothing—no one.

She'd cleaned and left.

He sank into his family room lounge chair. No note. She hadn't said hello or goodbye. His fingers drummed the opening notes of Beethoven's Fifth.

Was she still under the assumption that he shouldn't be interrupted while working? That would explain why she hadn't even said hello.

What if she'd tried to interrupt and he hadn't heard anything? His headphones were really good.

In the kitchen, he grabbed a beer. Damn, everything sparkled in the fridge too. How had he missed her?

He popped the top off a Surly.

Out of habit, he'd closed his office door. Of course she wouldn't have disturbed him. He'd seen that on Martha's notes. It was the number one bullet point—don't disturb him while he worked.

But he wanted Kate to disturb him.

He pulled his phone out. Blank screen. Shit. He'd meant to charge the thing.

Retrieving the charger from his bedroom, he plugged it in, waiting until it acquired enough charge to open. He took a long pull of his beer, but it didn't give him the pleasure it should have.

He waited for the initial screen.

After unlocking it, he checked his missed calls. Mom had called. And Aubrey, his business manager.

No Kate.

Six-fifteen. With quick keystrokes, he called Kate's cell. It rang twice and then went to voice mail.

Fuck. She'd just ignored his call.

KATE SILENCED HER PHONE, knowing it would send Alex to voice mail, and dropped her head into her hand.

She flung herself onto her sofa. Why had she slept with him?

Yes, she'd been upset. Yes, he'd offered comfort. Yes, his body was incredibly sexy. All that *bigness*. His chest was so wide if she laid her hands and stretched out her fingers like she was reaching for keys on a piano, she wouldn't reach his side. And no fat. He must use the weightlifting equipment in his fitness room.

She sighed. Normally she would have avoided Alex. She avoided guys who wanted relationships.

The only relationship she intended to have was working toward her ultimate goal—CEO of MacBain Enterprises. She couldn't split her focus from her long range plan.

If he didn't get possessive, she wouldn't mind taking him for a spin again. He was so … thorough.

Rolling her eyes, she pounded the cushion. Friday night. At home. Alone.

Grabbing her cell phone, she called Meg. "Let's have a girl's night."

"Sure," Meg said. "I'll be there in thirty."

"I'll call for pizza," Kate said. "And find a chick flick on Netflix."

"Wine or margaritas?" Meg asked.

Alcohol. Lots of it. "Margaritas."

"I'll bring the makings."

Kate ordered a large chicken Alfredo pizza. Her brothers

hated any pizza with white sauce. Although they would steal all the bacon they threw on it. Everything was better with bacon, right?

She'd exercise tomorrow.

She scanned the available movie options, settling on *You've Got Mail*, an old standard. It wasn't too sappy. She didn't want a tearjerker.

A pounding on her door stopped her wallowing.

From the hallway Meg called, "The booze is here."

Kate smiled as she opened the door. "'Bout time."

Meg kicked off her heels and gave her a one-armed hug. The scent of Crystal Noir, Meg's favorite perfume, filled Kate's nose. "Let me get the drinks going and you can tell me about your week."

Kate followed her friend into the kitchen.

Completely at home, Meg dug out the blender and threw things together.

"I brought the good stuff," Meg said. "Nothing but the best for you, my friend."

"Thanks." Kate pulled out the pitcher and glasses. They worked side-by-side like old times. "Salt or sugar on the rims?"

Meg patted her flat stomach. "Neither. You do what you want."

With pizza coming and figuring they would have more than one drink, Kate chose to go bare too.

Kate organized everything on a tray. "Just waiting on you."

Meg sampled her concoction and added another slug of tequila and a little more amaretto. The blender gave one last burp and Meg sampled again. She smacked her lips. "Perfect." She transferred the mixture to the pitcher.

"Okay, liquid sustenance is ready." Meg grabbed the tray and headed to the living room. Setting the tray on the coffee table, she plopped onto the sectional.

The sectional where Alex had held her, comforted her.

Kate almost moved to an arm chair, but it wasn't as comfortable. Trying to forget the memories, she sat next to Meg.

Meg made a production of pouring their drinks. Maybe being with her friend would stop the voices in her head.

Kate took her glass and sipped.

"Wait!" Meg held up her glass. "To your mother. To getting through her surgery on Monday without any surprises. To a quick and uncomplicated recovery."

Tears sprang to Kate's eyes. "To my mother."

They drank. The mellowness of the amaretto softened the bite of the tequila. Fantastic combination. From prior experience, Kate knew she should drink slowly. These were lethal.

"So anything new since you gave me the last update?" Meg asked.

"Nothing. She had a pre-op physical today. Everything's a go for Monday."

Meg had on her favorite clubbing clothes. A sparkly black top and blue jeans that made her legs look long and her ass perky.

Kate set down her margarita glass. "You were going out."

"Nothing special, a party with some associates," Meg said. "You did me a favor."

Kate twisted her hands in her lap. "You should have told me."

"You're my best friend." Meg set down her drink and turned to Kate, catching her hand. "I'm here for you. But you'll have to put me up for the night. I plan on getting you drunk, girl."

"No wonder we're besties." Kate squeezed her hand and then picked up the remote.

Waiting for the movie to start, Meg asked, "What's happening with you and that big hunk of sexiness?"

"Alex?" Kate hit fast forward, avoiding the previews.

"Yes, Alex. Give me the dirt."

"That's it. Dirt … you know." She and Meg had always talked about Kate's dates. For some reason she couldn't tell her best friend she'd slept with Alex. "You know, cleaning his house."

"Ha ha. You sure didn't look like you were cleaning his house at O'Dair's. Looked like you were planning on cleaning out your pipes." Meg leaned close. "The guy couldn't take his eyes off you."

Kate swallowed her mouthful of margarita and coughed. "He's a client."

"You're still cleaning his house?" Meg asked. "I thought you were stopping because of your mom."

"It doesn't look like my parents are letting me off the hook very soon."

"Well, why should that stop you?"

"Meg." She rolled her eyes. "Would you date one of your clients?"

"Two problems here." Meg held up a finger. "One, I don't date." She held up a second finger. "Two, all my clients are over fifty." She tipped her head. "Although there is this fascinating CFO. He climbed Mount McKinley. Loves to snorkel off the Florida Keys."

"Marital status?"

Meg pleated the front of her jeans, gorgeous jeans too. "Married. First grandchild on the way. He looked great in a tux at his daughter's wedding."

"Do you bill these people when you're," Kate made quote marks with her fingers, "building client relationships."

Meg's head reared back. "Of course not. Why do you think I put in the late hours? Got to meet my billable quotas."

Kate raised her hands in surrender. "Sorry. And I know for a fact that you never have trouble meeting your hours." Her friend had a job with Thornton Law Firm, one of the region's most prestigious firms. "Nothing's changed on the partner track, has it?"

Meg stood and paced to the fireplace. She flicked on the gas and stared at the flames as they caught hold. "No, I had a great review for my third-year anniversary."

Something was going on. Kate had been so focused on her own troubles, she hadn't paid attention to her friend. "But—?"

Meg nailed her with her laser blue gaze. "I thought I would feel like I was contributing more."

"To the firm?"

"No. To society."

Uh-oh. Meg had changed her major three times before she'd figured out her undergrad program. And then she'd applied to both law schools and MBA programs. It wasn't that she was flighty—she was so bright, she got bored.

"What do you want to do?" Kate asked.

Meg rubbed her fingernail along the mantel. "Something more thrilling than SEC filings."

"But you worked hard to get into the corporate side of the firm," Kate reminded her.

"I thought there'd be," her shoulders rose and fell on a sigh, "more excitement. Instead I'm verifying that corporations can back up each claim in their management discussions." She sat on the brick hearth. "If my clients were merging or launching new products, it would be more fun."

"I thought they were." Kate remembered how excited Meg had been when one of her clients had done a stock offering. "You were jazzed working on that prospectus a couple of months ago."

"But it's not all the time."

Kate crossed to her friend and rubbed her back. "They can't all live with constant adrenaline. Not like you."

"I know. I'm just ..." Meg bounced her head on the mantel. "I'm restless."

The door buzzed. Meg pranced to the intercom. "Pizza!"

Kate slid the tray with the drinks to one side of the table and went to the kitchen for napkins and paper plates.

"Look who I found," Meg called, her voice tinged with glee.

"I'm hoping its Pizza Lucé's and not one of my mooching brothers." She wasn't sharing her pizza with her brothers. Besides, they hated Alfredo. And she wanted weekend leftovers.

"Hi, Kate."

Her head snapped up.

Alex stood in the archway of the kitchen. He wore one of the silky black T-shirts she'd folded this afternoon underneath a buttery soft leather jacket. His jeans formed to his thighs.

"Alex," she said.

He stared at her with those dark eyes. "Thought I'd see how you were doing." He glanced at the pitcher of margaritas. "Guess you're doing okay."

Heat flashed across her face. "We're having …"

"When you didn't answer your phone, I worried something had happened to your mother."

"Nothing new with my mother," she mumbled.

"Sure. That's good." He took a deep breath. "I'll leave you to your fun."

Alex turned and almost bumped into Meg.

Her friend juggled the pizza box balanced on one hand. She frowned at Kate. "Hey, we've got plenty. This is an extra-large from Pizza Lucé, the best pizza in the Twin Cities. Stay. Right, Kate?"

"No. I just wanted to make sure everything was okay." Alex headed to the door.

"Kate," Meg hissed.

Kate felt like a worm. "Sure. Stay. There's plenty."

Meg pushed Alex into the living room. "Let me get another glass. We don't do girls' night very often," she blabbed. "It's

164

just, you know, with the kind of week Katie's had, we thought we would blow off steam."

Meg set the box on the coffee table and left the room to get him a glass.

Alex stared at Kate. "Do you want me to leave?"

Okay, now she felt like a flea on a worm. She was such a lowlife. He was nice, and she—she wasn't. She should have left him a note after she'd cleaned or taken his call.

Mom would be giving her that disappointed look. And what was taking Meg so long?

Alex shook his head. He turned, leaving.

She wanted him to leave. Right?

"Wait." The word popped out of her mouth.

He turned back.

"Stay." She took a step closer, and his heat filled the space between them. "It's the best pizza in town."

"Are you sure?"

"Stay."

"Thanks." He seared her with an intense stare. Then he shrugged off his coat and hung it on the coat tree.

She shoved her hands in the pockets of her hoodie. A hoodie. Alex never saw her dressed like herself, a successful businesswoman. Well, except for their dinner. The one where she'd watched his ex-wife sing two love songs to Alex that he'd written for her.

"Finally found another glass." Meg's too bright voice preceded her into the living room.

Kate raised her eyebrows at her friend, who'd obviously been eavesdropping from the kitchen.

Meg ignored her. "Alex, you're a composer, right?"

He nodded as he took a seat next to Kate on the sectional.

"Are there any songs I would recognize?" Meg asked, opening the pizza box. She removed a piece, snagging the strings of cheese with her finger.

"Possibly. Do you listen to the band Foresight?"

Kate's eyes widened. "Foresight? You've written for them?"

"What have you written for Foresight?" Meg mumbled around her pizza.

"'Secrets of the Night.'" Alex slipped a couple of pizza slices on his plate. "'Girl Next Door.'"

Meg squealed. "Didn't they win awards with those songs?"

"Yeah." Alex shifted, embarrassed.

"Have you been to the Grammys?" Meg bounced on the sofa.

Alex swallowed a mouthful. "Couple of years ago. I've been working on other things since then."

"Your sonata?" Kate asked.

He shot her a little smile. "Took me two years, but I finished an important movement today." He gazed at her. "I broke through a block a couple of nights ago. Everything came together."

"Good, that's good," Kate muttered, unable to take her eyes off him. A couple of nights ago? Like after they'd slept together? What was he trying to tell her? That sex with her had helped him break through his composer's block?

She wasn't responsible for something like that. She wasn't responsible for someone's creativity.

Kate dropped her gaze from Alex's and took a bite of her pizza. She could barely swallow over the lump in her throat.

She wasn't proud she'd slept with Alex to keep from obsessing over her mother's diagnosis. But it should have been a one-time event. She wouldn't have time for a relationship with her mother in treatment.

When she'd been writing her final paper for her MBA, she'd interviewed several female CEOs in the area. Every woman had talked about their sacrifices; family and relationships. How could she expect her quest for the top position would be any different than others?

She swallowed the bite and took another, not paying attention to the questions Meg kept asking Alex.

He'd been so kind, holding her while she'd cried. She never cried.

When Meg stopped firing music industry questions at him, he asked, "How's your mother?"

"She's … amazing. I don't know how she stays so positive."

"Is her surgery still scheduled for Monday?"

Kate nodded.

He took her hand and laced their fingers together. "Do you want me to wait with you?"

It would be comforting having someone there holding her hand, someone to take care of her. Alex would do that. Bring her coffee, make her smile.

His brown eyes searched hers. What did he want from her? Whatever it was, she couldn't give it.

"I'll be fine," she said. "My brothers and dad will be there."

He pushed her hair away from her face. "I know you'll be fine. I want to help."

She leaned into the large hand cupping her cheek. Alex made her long for things that weren't in her life plan.

ALEX SHOVED the paper plates into Kate's garbage. Obviously she didn't want him here. Conversation had been stilted at best. At worst he'd just stared at her while she'd avoided his eyes.

Meg carried in the margarita pitcher. "Hey, big guy, don't give up."

"She doesn't want me here."

Meg peeked around the corner, checking that Kate was still

in the bathroom. "Sure, but that's because you've gotten under her skin."

"You mean like a sliver?" Something she'd pluck out and throw away.

"Listen," Meg whispered, "you slept with her, right?"

How did he answer that question?

"I'm only guessing, based on her prickliness."

He nodded.

"Normally she'd tell me but she didn't. Plus, she won't look you in the eye." Meg patted him on the back. "This is good."

"Doesn't feel good." Her rejection hurt like hell.

"Hey, did she give the *I'm not looking for long-term* speech before you did the deed?"

Alex frowned. "Not that I can remember. She …"

He didn't want to share their intimacies.

"She wanted to be held after she found out about her mother." The water ran in the bathroom and he lowered his voice. "That's all I did. But in the middle of the night …" He shrugged.

"Wow." Meg nodded. "This is good. I know it doesn't feel like it, but it is."

Alex leaned against the counter. "Really?"

"I'm leaving. Tell her I—whatever."

Alex didn't know whether the pressure in his gut was excitement or gas. Who ate pizza without red sauce?

The front and bathroom doors closed in unison.

"Meg, did Alex leave?" Kate's voice carried down the hall. The relief lacing her words cut into him like a dissonant chord.

"No." He'd let another woman make a fool of him. The breath he drew in felt like there were tiny razor blades slicing through him. "I didn't leave, Meg did."

Kate turned the corner and stopped in the entrance of the kitchen. Her face went pink.

He tossed the towel he'd used to dry his hands. "I'll leave."

He brushed past Kate, heading for the door. He should have guessed from the short phone calls and the lack of enthusiasm in her voice. But, like an idiot, he'd hung around waiting for her to feed him scraps.

Hadn't Meredith taught him anything?

"Alex." Kate reached out but he sidestepped her. "I'm sorry."

Putting on his jacket, he didn't turn around. "What are you sorry for?"

"I'm not sorry we slept together." Her lips pinched together. "I'm sorry I can't be what you want."

"What I want?" He turned toward her. "You don't have a clue what I want."

"Yes, I do. You told me." Fire glittered in her changeable eyes. "You want a wife and children. I'm not interested."

"We went on *one* date. Had a couple of dances. I came over to see if I could comfort you since you were going through something horrible." He stepped closer. "You asked me to stay the night." Stroking a curl off her cheek, he curved his hand around her face. "You seduced me."

"I ... I ..." She covered his hand. "I did ..."

He pulled his hand away and slumped against the wall. "What do you want?"

"I don't know." She wrapped her arms around her stomach as if she were freezing. Staring at the floor, she said, "I thought I wanted you to leave."

He pushed away from the wall. "I'll do that."

She stepped in front of him. "But now I don't want you to."

His breath caught.

"Alex?" Her voice barely carried over the pounding of his heart in his ears. "Could you hug me?"

The gust of breath exploding from his lungs feathered the hair around her face. He wrapped his arms around her.

She trembled.

He kissed the top of her head, inhaling her scent, now tinged with the citrus of margarita and pizza.

Her head burrowed into his shoulder.

They fit together like a melody and harmony. The beat of their hearts was the tympani. Their synchronized breaths were the brush of a snare drum.

Did she feel their connection? Probably not. He should be building walls around his feelings.

"Now what?"

He didn't realize he'd said the words aloud until she tipped her face and looked at him. "Could we maybe watch a movie or something?"

The *or something* was his vote.

Shrugging out of his jacket he hung it on the coatrack. "The basketball game should be tipping off in a half hour. Want to watch the Wolves beat San Antonio?"

KATE DRAINED her glass of ginger ale. No more alcohol for her.

Why had she asked Alex to stay? He'd given her the opening. His speech at the door could have been their finale. Instead she'd clung to him like a wimpy girl.

At least they were watching the least romantic thing around —basketball. Her head nestled a little deeper in his shoulder. Her muscles softened. He was easy to cuddle.

"Foul! Come on, ref!" Alex leaned closer to the television, bumping her head. "Oh, sorry."

He tucked her head into the curve of his shoulder and stroked her hair.

"No problem." Shoot, she didn't even know what the score

was. She checked the screen. Timberwolves were ahead by five. "I don't think the refs can hear you."

"Yeah? I bet a million other people saw them miss that foul." He brushed a kiss on her forehead.

Kate tossed some popcorn into her mouth.

He caught her fingers and licked the buttery, salty tips. Her body woke up.

His gaze was locked on the game.

"You're good at multitasking, aren't you?" she asked.

He smiled. "I can be."

A beer commercial came on. She eased out of his arms and stood. "Do you want another beer?"

"Not if I'm driving tonight." The smile that had creased his face disappeared. "Am I driving tonight?"

She hadn't thought beyond watching the game. Hadn't thought about the ramifications of asking Alex to stay. She'd spent her whole life planning for the future, and now she didn't know what she wanted for the next few hours.

Her teeth worried her thumbnail.

"It's okay." Alex stared at the television, engrossed in a BMW commercial.

Embarrassed, she headed for the kitchen and leaned against the counter. Alex thought silence was her answer. Didn't he understand how tough this was for her?

Her body wanted Alex to stay. Her head insisted she usher him out the door and her heart—that stupid body part had no vote.

Staring into her fridge, she picked out a can of ginger ale for herself. Hesitating, she finally drew out a beer for Alex.

A roar from the television muffled the pop and sizzle of the bottle.

As she walked into the room he glanced up. He frowned at the beer in her hand.

She handed it to him, her lip tucked between her teeth.

He set the bottle on the coffee table. Then took her ginger ale out of her hand and set it down too.

Pulling her onto his lap, he cradled her face in those big hands. "Are you sure?"

"No." She kissed him. "Just don't read too much into tonight. Please."

"Okay." He kissed her. His tongue stroked hers.

He tasted of pizza and the hoppy bite of beer. She sucked his tongue into her mouth and heat pooled between her thighs.

It was better when they let their bodies do the communicating.

His hands slid down her arms, then came up underneath to cup her breasts. His palms rubbed lightly against her nipples, too lightly. She wanted him to press harder, wanted to feel him hard between her legs.

She tried to straddle his body, but he wouldn't let her.

"Alex."

His lips trailed from her earlobe to her collarbones. She tipped her head back, encouraging him lower.

He buried his face in her neck. With a big sigh, he turned her so she sat on his lap, facing the television. "Game's back on."

"The game?" She sank deeper onto his erection.

"Fourth quarter. Five minutes to go." He chuckled, but his hand slipped under her top and unsnapped her bra. Then he pulled her against him and rolled both her nipples between nimble fingers.

"Clever boy." She whipped off her top and bra and tossed them over her shoulder.

Even though she was at a disadvantage sitting on his lap, she stroked his thighs. So much muscle there. So much man.

"Lean forward," he murmured in her ear.

She complied, taking a moment to set her hand against his erection. It pulsed under her fingers.

He shifted her back and she rested against bare skin. She wriggled, enjoying the silky hair rubbing against her back.

His hands slid down her stomach and under the loose elastic of her sweatpants.

"What's the score," she gasped as his hands circled around her hips and headed for home.

"Who gives a damn?"

Alex laid her on the sofa. While resting on his haunches, he tugged off her pants. Then he sat back and looked. There was a man kneeling between her legs staring at her. His deep brown eyes sparkled.

A blush heated her neck and face. If she looked down, it probably covered her chest. Not the sexiest image.

Alex traced a finger on her cheek and then down her neck.

She leaned her head back, wanting him to kiss instead of touch.

He didn't take the hint. His finger traveled along her collarbone. Slowly he scraped it along her breast and over the tip of her aching nipple. Arching her back, she offered her body to him.

He still didn't take the hint. That slow finger, now trailing fire in its wake, circled the underside of her breast and headed south.

Thank goodness.

She forced her eyes open, and all she could see was his thick black hair. She pushed her fingers into his curls, shifting through and finding a wealth of deep colors. But it didn't take her thoughts away from his fingertip tracing a path around her bellybutton and lower—*oh, yes*.

Her hips jerked and his finger slid a little closer to the heat pouring out between her legs.

But he didn't slip inside her. Instead his palm covered her mound. And stopped moving. *Come on.*

Alex looked into her eyes. "You're beautiful."

His words were a long deep whisper. Had anyone else ever said something so touching, stopping just to admire her?

She raised her hips, trying to entice Alex.

His eyes took the same journey his finger had made.

"Alex," she whispered.

He leaned forward, grinning. His face hovered above hers. "I didn't get a chance to look last time. As much fun as that morning was, I'm not making that mistake again."

The warmth in her belly soared to flashpoint. "Okay."

His lips followed the path his finger had taken, pausing to lick or nibble. What had taken mere seconds, now took a lifetime.

His mouth on her breast dragged a long hiss out of her. She moaned as his tongue drew patterns around her hip bone. Her fingers flexed in his hair as he dropped lower. He pulled down her thong, sliding the offending material away. It dangled around one ankle.

Finally.

Alex swept his tongue and lips up her inner thighs, coming close and then withdrawing. Time and again until she dripped with passion and frustration.

"Alex, please." She pushed herself onto her elbows.

He slid away and stood. Shucking off his jeans and boxers, he dug in his wallet and pulled out a condom. Ripping it open, he said, "Not forgetting tonight."

He settled between her legs.

If there had been enough space on the sofa, she would have helped him put on the condom. Maybe with her teeth. But he rolled on protection and lowered himself over her.

Her breath came in small fast pants. "Would you please—"

She didn't finish the sentence before he entered her. Slowly each small movement eased her open. She tilted her pelvis, wanting him to go faster, deeper.

Her body wasn't used to him, his size, his breadth.

Please, no hip cramps.

She Kegeled around the tip of him. Alex pushed in a little deeper on a groan. She wrapped her legs around his hips, the stretch and position forcing him deeper.

He slid back and then advanced. His jawbone stood out in sharp relief. His gritted teeth and sweat were the only indications he was suffering as much as she was.

The muscles under her hands contracted. She pulsed her hips and he slid further into her. Just a little more.

"I don't want to hurt you," he grunted.

"Do I look like I'm hurting?" Her hands clutched his butt.

He thrust once more.

She arched against him. "Yes."

His shoulders shook as he hovered above her. His eyes were squeezed shut. "Don't move."

Had she brought him to this? This big strong man shuddering? She squeezed around him.

"Stop, please," he whispered. "Or I won't last."

She didn't care. She rocked against him. Sparks set off small explosions in her body.

He growled. Leaning back, he pulled one of her legs onto his shoulders. Clasping her hips, he manipulated her like a ragdoll.

The sensations were hot, wonderful. She couldn't do anything but tighten her muscles around him. Waves started in the core of her body. She tried to hold him inside, tried to wiggle him into the perfect friction.

Alex stopped thrusting.

Her hands clutched his thighs, holding on as her body surged out of control.

His fingers rolled one nipple, and everything exploded. "Alex!"

Fireworks ignited behind her closed eyelids.

Alex thrust as she came apart. Her legs shook. Her head thrashed back and forth.

And it didn't stop. Whatever he was doing had her orgasm rising from one peak to the next. She couldn't breathe. She could barely hang on.

Alex moved her legs to either side of his hips. He wrapped his arms around her back and pulled her onto his lap so now she rode him. Every slide against her sensitive body set off a mini explosion.

"Kate," he yelled as he thrust one more time. "Jesus."

His head was buried between her breasts. The only thing keeping her upright was his iron grip. She wrapped her arms around his neck and hung on.

Their breaths heaved together. Sweat dripped from Alex's forehead. He feathered a kiss on the side of her breast.

"We could have held off a lot longer if you'd stopped moving." He cupped her face between his hands and kissed her, a solid firm kiss.

"I didn't want to drag it out." She started to move away from him.

"Wait." He hugged her. "Give me a minute to enjoy."

She sighed. "Probably not a good idea with a condom." But she relaxed into his embrace.

He slipped out of her body, kissing her as he did. She sank into the sofa. He was gorgeous in a big, hunky sort of way. And what he could do with his upper body. Yum.

"I'll be back." He bounced a kiss off her nose. "Don't think so much."

How could she not? He was a complication she didn't need.

But she admired his butt as he walked away.

Sure, her body hadn't felt this good in—ever. What did that say about the previous guys she'd slept with? Had they been inadequate, or was Alex that much more skilled?

She rolled onto her side. Her fingers searched for her clothes. They were too far away to bother. The corner of the afghan her grandmother had made hung off the back of the sofa.

"Sorry, Grandma," she whispered as she covered up. She was sure her grandmother hadn't intended the afghan to be used after sex. Although when Grandma MacBain got a glass of wine in her, she'd told some pretty bawdy jokes.

She smiled at the memory.

"I hope that smile means you're not kicking me to the curb." Alex pulled her legs up and sat on the sofa.

"Just thinking about Grandma MacBain."

"Nice." He stroked her arm.

The silence settled over them, a comfortable intimate silence.

"Don't get the wrong impression. Remember, don't read anything—long-term—into this …"

"Yeah?" he asked, frowning.

She wanted Alex to hold her. "Can you spend the night?"

ELEVEN

Alex woke to the smell of coffee. Excellent. Well, the coffee wouldn't be excellent, but waking in Kate's bed was —satisfying.

Of course she might kick him to the curb. Again. She'd said not to read anything into her invitation to spend the night.

He rolled out of bed and threw on his jeans. He needed to stay in the present, not be building future fantasies around children with auburn curls and changeable eyes.

His toothbrush was still here from the last time he'd spent the night. Maybe that was a good sign. She hadn't thrown it away.

As he walked into the kitchen, there was a déjà vu feeling to the scene. Kate sat in the same chair with her arms clutched around her legs. Her chin rested on her knees. She looked a little lost, a little sad. And far, far away.

"Morning." He dropped a kiss on top of her curls.

She started.

"Sorry, I didn't mean to startle you."

"No." Her smile didn't reach her eyes. "I was thinking."

"Your mom?"

She took a deep breath, nodding. "I can't imagine …"

"Don't. Don't imagine." He took her hands. "Take each day as something precious. Stay in the moment."

Words to live by. Especially since he didn't think he and Kate were heading in the same direction. Maybe they were on the same path, but their end goals were different.

She was right. He wanted marriage and children.

Based on her bathroom inspirational notes, she wanted the top spot in the family business.

He'd better take his own advice, enjoy the path and forget about the future.

"I know I should stay in the moment," she said. "It's … hard."

The coffeemaker gurgled. He poured two mugs, doctoring both with milk. "Here."

"Thanks." Kate stuck her nose in the top of the mug and took a deep sniff. "My coffee smells better than it tastes."

"I'll give you some of my beans." He sat next to her at the table.

"Really?" This time the smile crinkled the corners around her eyes. "Your coffee is fantastic."

"But you need a grinder."

She scrunched up her face. "Okay, I guess."

"I'll walk you through it," he said. "How have you lived to be …?"

"Twenty-nine," she filled in.

He frowned. "Almost thirty without grinding your own beans?"

"I avoid anything domestic."

"That's just stubborn."

"As the only girl in a family of four, I chose not to learn how to cook. I didn't want to become my brothers' short-order cook."

"You have three brothers, right?"

"Yeah." She wrinkled her nose. "You met Stephen at the basketball game and Timothy here. There's one more, my older brother, Michael."

"You've got an older brother and you want to run the business?" he blurted out.

She rubbed a spot off the side of her mug. "I'm the only one with an MBA."

He sipped his coffee, wishing he could take back his words. "It's … I would think … he's the oldest?"

"You should stop right now and pull your foot out of your mouth."

"Good idea." His stomach growled. "Can I take you out to breakfast?"

"I'd planned to stop in the office to catch up on my mail." She sighed. "Normally I'd be there by now."

It was only eight o'clock. At least she hadn't rushed him out the door this time. "You need to eat something."

"I know, but lately I'm not hungry." She pressed on her stomach.

"Have you ever been to Al's in Dinkytown?" he asked.

She smiled. "Sure, when I was in college."

"Want to brave the crowds?"

"I love their blueberry pancakes."

"Let's go."

KATE SHUFFLED along the back wall of Al's as they waited for seats. Alex's hand rode on the small of her back, spreading warmth through her body.

"At least we're in the door," he whispered.

With thirteen or fourteen stools, diners had to be patient and ignore the claustrophobia.

She leaned into Alex's body, and he wrapped his arms

around her waist. "How wide do you think this place is?"

He looked from one wall to the other. "Nine, ten feet?"

"Unbelievable. And they're a Frank Beard recipient."

He pointed at the award on the wall.

She inhaled the smell of coffee, syrup and fried foods. Somehow after college, she'd stopped enjoying places like this. Dining had become a tool for bringing in new clients or keeping old ones.

Alex was right. She needed to *stay in the moment.*

Three people jostled them as they exited the diner. She and Alex took the open seats.

A waitress swept away the plates and tip left on the counter. "What're you drinkin'?"

"Coffee," they both said.

"Two cups of Joe coming up."

Mugs clattered in front of them and were filled with dark rich coffee. Alex handed her the cream jug.

"Do you know what you want?" Alex asked.

"Blueberry pancakes."

When their server crossed in front of them, Alex ordered a veggie omelet with hash browns and her pancakes. He called the waitress by her name. Usually she would bristle at a date ordering her food, but Alex was … different.

She swiveled on her stool and faced him. Their knees rested against each other in the cramped space. "Come here often?"

"I used to." Something crossed through his expression. Sadness? Regret?

"With your ex?" she guessed, keeping the question neutral.

"She wouldn't eat this many calories in a day, maybe even a week." He shook his head. "Gabe and I. But we haven't been here in a while."

He took her hand and kissed her knuckles.

She swallowed. What made Alex tick? He was different

from any man she'd ever met. A composer who created classical music, pop and jiggles. And he played basketball with the kid next door. "Why?"

He sipped his coffee and stared over her head. "I kind of stopped leaving the house."

"Like … never?"

"No." He grimaced. "But for a while I avoided people." He tipped his head at the crowd behind them. "It's kind of hard to do that here."

"And this was because of your divorce?"

"Partly." He turned and smiled. "Gabe kept hounding me. I had no choice but to start leaving the house."

"Can I ask," her finger doodled on the Formica countertop, "did you leave your wife, or did she leave you?"

"I left her." His harsh response slammed the door on any follow-up questions. Did he still have feelings for her?

Alex's ex was gorgeous and she was part of his musical world. Her voice was incredible.

But could Alex's ex-wife prepare a ten-year present value analysis on a lease agreement? Suddenly that didn't sound like such an accomplishment.

A plate of pancakes appeared in front of her. Steam curled from the golden stack along with the heavenly smell of fried cakes and hot berries. She spread on butter, and it melted into the thick cakes. She dribbled on a little syrup, then added a pool. "What the heck."

Alex didn't have his omelet yet. She waited, her mouth watering. Holding her knife and fork at the ready, she scanned the two griddles for evidence his omelet would arrive soon.

"Don't wait for me," Alex said. "Eat while they're hot."

She didn't need a second invitation. She cut through the stack with her fork. Sopping up more syrup, she brought the huge bite to her mouth.

A fat blueberry exploded as she chewed. The sweetness

mixed with the maple syrup. The crispy fried edge of the pancake crunched in her mouth.

"This is better than I remember." She took another bite, closing her eyes to shut out the chaos of the diner.

Alex chuckled.

"Try some." She circled her plate with her fork.

"Thanks." Taking a small nibble, he closed his eyes too. "They do taste better with your eyes closed."

She jabbed him with her elbow. "Don't make fun of me. These are great."

"So, you came here when you went to school."

She swallowed the food in her mouth. "I lived on the west bank, but we'd come over for breakfast."

"You went to the U?"

She nodded, her mouth full again. It was as if she hadn't tasted food for—forever.

His omelet arrived. As he cut into it, he asked, "What did you study?"

She swallowed her mouthful. "My undergrad was entrepreneurial management. My MBA specialization is management."

He held a forkful of omelet to her lips.

She took the bite. "That's good too."

"We might have to make this a weekly event," he said, not looking at her.

She snorted. Had great sex made him forget this wasn't long-term? But the thought of having a weekly date didn't bother her as much as it should. "Where did you matriculate from?"

"Juilliard."

Juilliard? "Wow. Isn't that the elite of arts colleges?"

"They sure believe it."

"What did you study?"

"Composition and Jazz Studies." He rocked his head back

and forth. "The double major added another year to my studies, but it was worth it."

"I remember a teacher saying that in the early years of computers, music majors were hired as programmers."

Alex tipped his head. "That makes sense. Composition is mathematical, especially harmonies. You're working in exact intervals." He nodded. "I could see it."

She pushed her plate away. She'd nearly devoured all three pancakes, cakes the size of the plate. "I'm stuffed."

"I'm getting there." Alex had polished off his hash browns and most of his omelet.

"Do you want to catch a movie tonight? Or go to a club?" he asked. "Or … do you need time to yourself or with your family?"

"Timberwolves lost last night." She took a sip of her coffee. "They play tonight at eight."

He brushed back her hair, and she wanted to lean her cheek into his palm. This thing with her mom must have her unbalanced.

"How 'bout we watch at my house. I'll pick up dinner." He leaned in and whispered, "And I'll make breakfast tomorrow."

Sleeping together two nights in a row? Every body part Alex had explored last night went on high alert.

One more night shouldn't give him the wrong idea. Besides, she'd had a tough week. She deserved to enjoy herself, didn't she?

And she wanted to sleep with him again.

ALEX FLIPPED THE BACON, smiling. He'd smiled a lot over the weekend.

Kate was sleeping in his bed. They'd watched the basketball game there the night before.

He'd had to check the score this morning. They'd missed the second half of the game. Timberwolves had lost. Their season was done.

"Wow, you weren't kidding about breakfast." Kate walked into his kitchen. Barefoot and in one of his T-shirts, he wanted to forget breakfast and take her back to his king-sized bed.

But she was skittish. Who or what had made her that way? He'd like to ask, but she'd probably bolt.

He grabbed the mug he'd pulled out for her and filled it, leaving room for her milk. "I bagged some beans for you. Thought we could buy a coffee grinder today."

"I spent most of yesterday with you. I need to get into the office."

"Isn't most of what you do on the computer?" he asked, trying for nonchalance. "You could use my laptop. I have some ideas bouncing around in my head. I'd like to get them down."

He already had a title for the piece. "Second Chances." Perfect range for Central Standard Time's lead singer.

Kate circled her finger around the top of her mug.

He didn't look at her as he poured the eggs into the hot fry pan. Then he pushed the toaster lever down.

She moved to the stove and took the spatula. "You plan to put me in a food coma, don't you? Then I won't be able to leave."

"No ulterior motive." That he would admit. He kissed her pouting lips.

He loaded the bacon onto a plate lined with paper towels. The toast popped and he added it to the plate. "Would you rather eat in the dining room?"

"God, no. Sunday mornings are for the kitchen. Do you get a paper?" she asked, spooning the eggs into the bowl he'd set out.

He pointed to the stack on one of the stools.

"Dibs on the business section."

"All yours." He topped off their coffee.

She hopped onto a stool and sorted out the sections. "You want the sports pages?"

"Arts."

She pulled out his section, then served herself eggs and handed him the bowl. "I don't know what to make of you."

Good. "What do you mean?"

He handed her the bacon, then started eating.

"You're obviously exceptional at your career. You love basketball. You love the arts and you're not gay."

He choked on the eggs he'd swallowed. "Gay?"

She frowned. "You aren't gay, right? I mean, you're fantastic in bed. It's not just a big ruse, is it?"

He set down his fork. Turning, he pulled her knife out of her hand. Then he stood, tugged her to her feet and kissed her. His tongue swept into her sweet mouth. She clutched his back, widened her stance and he nestled his erection between her legs.

He pulled away. "I. Am. Not. Gay."

Her eyes blinked open. "What?"

"I'm not gay." He caught her hand and wrapped her fingers around his erection. "Got it?"

She squeezed and her lips formed that perfect seductive O.

He moaned.

"Got it."

"Good." No one had ever asked him outright. Only Kate. "Eat before your food gets cold."

"Sorry, I'm stereotyping." She added jam to her toast. "You've got to admit there is a higher percentage of gay men in the arts."

"True. And a lot of them are my friends." He shifted on the chair, but that didn't relieve his discomfort. Maybe he should demonstrate how heterosexual he was and make love to her in the kitchen.

She smiled. "You're … intriguing."

That was good, wasn't it?

"I've got a question," he said. "Even though neither of us is thinking long-term," what a crock of bull, "as long as we're … seeing each other, we're exclusive. Right?"

He didn't look at her. He wouldn't hint at how important her answer was to him.

Her gaze burned a hole in the side of his head.

"Alex?"

He didn't have a choice. He looked at her. "Yes?"

"We're exclusive." She aimed her fork at him. "Just don't be getting all emotional on me, or we're through."

ALEX REREAD THE EMAIL. Frederick loved the sonata's second movement.

He'd spent the last two years battling his demons. It was great to have a clear vision of this piece. The third movement was taking shape. He just might meet his deadline.

Things were looking up.

Hadn't he convinced Kate to keep seeing him? Sure, she was fighting anything that looked like a commitment, but she no longer ignored his calls.

Kate's mother was heading into surgery right about now.

It would be overstepping the boundaries she put around their … friendship, but maybe he should stop at the hospital and wait with her.

Or not. Her father and brothers would be there. Too much pressure on poor Kate.

She'd promised to call. He'd have to trust her.

He tilted his head. Yeah, maybe not such a great plan. Who knew what was going through Miss MacBain's head. She probably regretted spending most of the weekend together.

Well, he didn't regret their weekend. And he'd keep hounding her until she realized she could have her future *and* a relationship.

～

KATE HANDED over her money and picked up Short Line Railroad. Not one of her favorite properties, but she would work with it. She didn't want to play a board game while her mother was in surgery, but Mom insisted.

Mom needed to be thinking about herself, instead of focusing on the family. Kate could never live up to her mother's accomplishments.

"I can't believe Mom packed the Monopoly game for us." Stephen moved the hat around the board. Mom wasn't there to pay out the passing Go money, so Michael had been promoted to banker. "Ah hah. I'll buy Baltic." Stephen shot his dad a look of triumph.

Dad didn't react. He took the dice and rolled. Moving his race car, he landed on Park Place and purchased the property. "Your mother knew you'd be climbing the walls and driving the other people in the waiting room nuts without something to occupy you."

Monopoly was something for Dad to do too. He was a pacer. He would wear a path in the carpet without this game.

The family had taken over one of the waiting room tables. The smell of overcooked coffee had Kate's stomach churning. She took a sip of her ginger ale. Stress was wreaking havoc on her stomach.

Timothy snatched the dice. "Come on, six."

Kate grinned. As usual Timothy wanted the orange property. He already had one, but she owned New York. She would make Timothy trade. She had her eye on his red property.

Playing the game still didn't keep her from worrying about

her mother. They were trying a lumpectomy first. If the tumor came away clean, maybe they wouldn't perform a mastectomy. She rubbed the side of her breast. What a terrible decision. Sure, you could do reconstructive surgery, but the size and status of the lump would determine the course of Mom's future treatments.

Her dad rubbed her knee. "Positive thoughts only, Katie."

How could he be so upbeat? "It's … not fair. She's been careful. She doesn't deserve this."

Stephen bumped her shoulder. "That's the good thing. She's caught it early."

Dad nodded. He waved Park Place at Stephen. "Ready to trade Park Place for Baltic?"

Everyone laughed. It wasn't freewheeling joy, but it was good.

A doctor in scrubs entered the waiting room and everyone turned. The doctor made her way to the reception desk, and the volunteer directed her to the appropriate family.

Not them.

Kate checked her watch. Twelve-thirty. How much longer? They'd said goodbye almost an hour ago. A bitter acid burned the back of her throat. She needed to eat something, get her stomach settled down. "Anyone hungry?"

"I could eat," Michael said.

"How about Michael and I grab soup or sandwiches and bring everything back here," she suggested.

They headed to the cafeteria. She and Michael loaded soups and sandwiches on a couple of trays. "I'm claiming the potato soup."

Her brother paid as she added utensils and napkins. Then they each took a tray and headed to the elevator banks.

"She has to be okay." Michael hit the button with his elbow. "She's strong. She'll lick this."

"It's hard to imagine her sick or going through treatment."

God, what would radiation therapy be like? "I can't imagine her not at the office."

"Neither can I." Michael's gaze was unfocused.

"Does this … remind you of Sarah?" she asked. His fiancée had died from brain cancer.

The look he shot her was so haunted her heart ached. "Let's not go there."

"Okay, positive thinking." If only that would be enough to eliminate Mom's cancer.

Michael held the door to the surgical waiting room open with his back.

A doctor sat on the coffee table in front of a woman dabbing her eyes. Kate hoped the tears were of happiness.

"What did you buy?" Timothy asked, sorting through the food.

"The potato soup is mine," she warned.

"Fine by me." Stephen took the tuna fish sandwich she'd picked up because he liked those gross slimy things.

Dad held up the chili. "Any takers?"

Everyone shook their heads, so he opened the lid and crumbled a packet of crackers on top.

She took a couple more packages, hoping for relief from the queasiness that had haunted her since her mother's announcement. She wouldn't complain to her family. She didn't want them to think she was weak. Now was the time to be strong and in control.

The crackers helped, so she took a spoonful of soup. A little bland, but not bad.

"Hey." Michael pointed at the Monopoly board. "Why isn't my piece where I left it?"

Stephen grinned. "We took your turns for you. We even bought you new property."

Michael frowned. "I don't want Water Works."

"Too bad." Timothy elbowed him. "Kate bought

Boardwalk."

Now she wouldn't have any cash.

Her brothers broke out in good-natured arguing.

Another doctor, this time male, walked in and went to the volunteer's desk. The woman pointed him to their table.

Every muscle in her body locked in place.

He pulled over a chair. "You're Patty MacBain's family?"

The doctor sounded exhausted. What was he doing operating on her mother? Was he competent?

Dad nodded. "That's us."

The doctor smiled. "Mrs. MacBain's surgery went well. We did the lumpectomy. The tissue edges were clean."

Her dad clutched her hand and she squeezed back.

"Clean?" Dad's voice quivered.

"The initial tissue exam shows we got the tumor. Everything's looking like we caught the cancer early." The doctor nodded. "Over the next few days, we'll get additional pathology reports on the tissue and lymph nodes to verify these results."

"Thank goodness." A weight lifted off Kate's chest. The breath she released shook.

Timothy slapped Stephen on the back. Michael closed his eyes and a tear snuck down his cheek.

"Can I see her?" Her father started to stand.

"Not yet. The recovery nurse will get you once the anesthesia wears off." The doctor ran his hand over his head, pulling off his surgical cap. He crunched it into a ball. "She caught this early. It's great, really."

"What follow-up treatment will she need?" Stephen asked.

"Five to seven weeks of radiation therapy. But assuming the pathology comes back negative on the lymph nodes, that should be it." The doctor nodded. "Normally I wouldn't have taken lymph nodes, but with Mrs. MacBain's family history, we're being proactive."

"How long will she stay in the hospital?" Kate asked.

"We'll observe her after she wakes, but barring complications, she'll go home today. She should rest for a couple of days. And we'll give her aftercare instructions." The doctor stood. "Everything looks good."

"Wow." Timothy smiled after the doctor walked away. "She can go home today."

"Home is the best place to heal." Stephen grinned. "Should I call Maria?"

Dad looked stunned. A tear slid down his cheek, another one followed. "Please. She wanted to know as soon as we heard anything."

Kate dropped a hand on his knee and squeezed. She'd never seen her father cry. She swallowed back her own tears. "This is wonderful."

She wrapped her arms around his neck and hugged him. The comforting scent of soap and his aftershave eased her tension.

"Oh, Katie." Her dad held on. His body shook and she hugged him tight.

With a jolt, she recognized that her father had been scared.

"Everything's good," she murmured. "You were right."

What would the fear be like if the one you loved was facing cancer? The woman you'd lived with for thirty-five years? They completed each other. Her father's gruffness, her mother's energy. What happened to a marriage if all that changed?

He patted her back. "We should finish our lunch."

They settled back to eat, and the smiles on everyone's faces came more easily. Everything would be fine.

"Damn, we should have brought champagne," Michael said.

Okay, maybe not *everything* was fine. Mom still wanted Kate to watch over Michael.

TWELVE

"How's your mother?" Alex asked once Kate opened her apartment door.

"Good." She held the door as he came in. "They removed the tumor and there weren't any abnormal cells in the edges of the tissue they excised."

"That's great news." He kissed her and handed her the bag of takeout. "Per your request, Thai food."

"Thanks."

She carried it into the kitchen. "So, what's next?" he asked, following.

"She'll have radiation therapy. Five to seven weeks, but it looks like she doesn't need chemo." She set the bag on the table and pulled out white boxes of food. "They still have pathology reports to come."

"It's terrific that she's not going through chemo. I had a friend's wife who really struggled with the treatments. It was brutal."

"Yeah." Kate sighed.

They worked together, pulling out plates and silverware.

"What would you like to drink?" she asked.

"Beer is fine."

Kate grabbed a beer and a glass for him. Then poured a glass of water and set it by her plate.

"Why don't you look happier?" He took a spring roll and handed her the box. Locating the peanut sauce, he dipped the roll into it.

"My stomach's still upset. I thought that hearing something definitive today would settle it down, but no luck."

"Glad I didn't select any of the spicier items on their menu." Stress could destroy a person's stomach. "You've been internalizing a lot."

Maybe he was adding to her stress. He hoped not. He hoped he'd reduced some of her worries. "Does my hanging around make your stress worse or better?"

She blinked those blue-green eyes. Surprise flickered like a flash of lightning across her face.

"No, it's not you." She gave a tiny shake of her head. "I don't usually notice when you're around." Her mouth dropped open. She slapped a hand across it. "I mean … you're easy to be around."

"Good." He grinned. "Really good. Why don't you try the lo mein? Maybe the noodles will calm your stomach."

He opened boxes, finding rice, lo mien and the pho he'd ordered. And chicken wings. Crispy, deep-fried wings.

"I'll try the soup." She spooned soup into a bowl and added bean sprouts. "It should go away now that we know Mom's diagnosis. Guess I was more upset than I realized." She twirled her spoon in the soup mixture. "My dad cried."

Alex wasn't sure how to respond. He tried the old therapist trick. "He cried?"

"We got the good news and he cried." She swallowed. "His being strong was all an act for my mom."

He took her hand. Her fingers were cold, and he pulled them to his lips. "Or maybe it was for his kids."

"Maybe." She squeezed his hand then withdrew and spooned up some of the soup. "You haven't told me about your family."

Subject closed. Sometimes he felt like he would take a step forward with Kate, then she'd realize and push him three steps backward.

"I'm the oldest of three children," he said. "I have two sisters."

"Do they live here?" She frowned. "Did you grow up here?"

"Lake Minnetonka. My parents still live there. I have one sister in the area. The other is in Chicago."

"Are they all musical?"

"Yes. When I was younger, Mom played cello for the Minnesota Orchestra. She taught us to play." He shuddered. "That wasn't my instrument. I begged her to let me take violin and we took piano lessons. I took guitar and the oboe." He shrugged. "Whatever instrument we wanted to play, Mom taught us or they gave us lessons."

"Wow."

As he talked, she ate. She added lo mein to her plate.

"How did you do all that and school?" she asked.

This was the part of his history he didn't like talking about, but if it kept her eating … "My sisters and I were tutored."

"Tutored? We're not talking homeschooling, but Victorian-era style tutors?"

He took the last spring roll and dipped this one in soy sauce. The soft wrap gave way under his teeth.

"We were …" Could he tell her they were considered musical protégés? Other people's reactions had ranged from thinking he was a snob or thinking he was rich. "We were … gifted. Mom thought it best. She and Dad brought in teachers for us." Their music lessons were a priority.

He scooped up a serving of Pad Thai, keeping his eyes on his plate.

"I've never met someone who was tutored. I wonder if that's easier or harder."

"I think it was both." He took a forkful of the Pad Thai. "In grade school it was okay. We probably learned faster. But I wanted to play basketball. I talked my dad into letting me play park board ball. He convinced Mom. She was freaked I would hurt my hands."

"Well, sure. Did you?"

"Jammed a couple of fingers." He swallowed another forkful of noodles. "Mom would watch my games, but she hated it." She'd sit on the top row of the bleachers, twisting her hands in her lap.

"In high school my parents cut a deal with the school district. Since I was ahead in my course work, I was allowed to attend school part-time, still do my musical training and play on the varsity basketball team." He grinned. "I played two years and got to take classes. It was great."

"I thought I had it bad." Kate added Pad Thai to her plate. "You were homeschooled?"

"No, worse. I got stuck babysitting my younger brothers—all the time."

"I thought Michael was older than you."

"He is." She squinted. "He figured it out faster than I did."

"Figured out what?"

"Getting involved in school and sports. If you had practice or a game, Mom and Dad couldn't force you to babysit." She pushed her plate away. "Stephen and Timothy were better birth control incentives than any lecture my mother ever gave me."

"That much trouble?"

"They're only fifteen months apart. Timothy always wanted whatever Stephen had. Plus, Timothy can't sit still. He and Stephen fought constantly." She took a sip of her water. "They shared a bedroom too. It was like refereeing a wrestling match."

"I always wanted a brother." Alex pushed his plate away too. "My sisters wouldn't play one-on-one with me. They believed Mom about hurting their hands."

"Oh, we all played basketball." She winked. "My brothers had to work to keep up with me."

"Oh, yeah?" No wonder she liked watching basketball.

"Once I figured out what Michael was doing, I went out for sports." She pointed to her chest. "Starter all four years. All-state champs my junior year. All-state guard my senior year."

"Impressive. We'll have to play some one-on-one." His mind went automatically to the intimate games they'd played all weekend. Not something she'd be interested in after the stressful day she'd had.

"I might have to see what you've got." She cleared the table. "At least I learned something from babysitting my brothers. I'm never having kids."

THIRTEEN

Kate made one more correction on the Sorenson Law renewal offer and then saved her file. It had taken Stephen three weeks to give her the remodeling estimates, but his numbers had been the last pieces of the puzzle.

It had been two weeks since her mother's lumpectomy. This afternoon Mom would have her first radiation treatment.

It had also been two weeks since Alex patted her on the head and told her to *get some rest*. The night they'd eaten Thai food.

She saw him at his house, they'd met for drinks, but they hadn't slept together again.

Kate should be happy to move on. But she wasn't. Alex Adamski had gotten to her. She couldn't stop thinking about him.

Picking up her phone she scrolled to his number, then stopped. Instead she opened a text message. *Sally is cleaning today —please be nice. Mom has 1ˢᵗ treatment.*

She tapped her fingernail on the screen and added, *Dinner?*

Before she could second-guess herself, she hit send.

She stared at the screen, hoping for an answer. Nothing.

He was probably working, like she should be.

Liz stuck her head in the door. "Got a minute?"

Kate put her phone down. "Absolutely."

"The Sungs called. They've signed the agreements. I sent a courier to pick up the documents." Liz sat in the guest chair. "I let Stephen know. Construction starts on the expansion space in two weeks. They're hoping to break through the adjoining walls in three weeks."

"Nice work." And she hadn't worried about any of the details. Liz had brought her the big picture issues, and Kate had given her the parameters. "What's our final ROI?"

"With the change in capital we made last week, it brought the return on investment up to 15.5 percent."

"Nice." Liz had suggested their cost of capital in the models was too high. Their borrowing rate had dropped substantially. That ROI change had made a difference in their offer to Sorenson.

She sure liked having an assistant.

"Anything else you need before your mother's appointment?" Liz asked.

"No, but thanks. Hopefully she'll sail through her treatments."

She'd done more research on radiation therapy. The side effects weren't as bad as chemo. She'd worried her mother would have hair loss. The websites suggested there could be arm pit hair loss. It didn't sound like there would be nausea.

Liz looked her straight in the eye. "Are you taking on her duties?"

"See." Kate pointed a finger at her assistant. "You and I are on the same wavelength. That's what I assumed when we found out Mom was going in for a biopsy."

"I'll do whatever I can to lighten your workload." Liz grinned. "It will show you how amazing I am."

"I already know you're amazing, but thanks."

If Kate didn't have her sights set on a higher goal, she'd worry about her ambitious assistant. But having someone ready to take on her position gave her the ability to leap up the corporate ladder.

She smiled. Michael didn't have a successor in place.

"Great work with the Sungs, Liz."

"They're easy to work with and they have delicious take-out." Liz headed for the door. "Anything else you need?"

"I finished constructing the offer to Sorenson. Are you available to meet with them tomorrow?"

"Our biggest client? Sure."

"Why don't you grab the offer off the printer and we can review it."

Liz almost ran out of the office.

Oh yeah, Michael, I have a successor in place. What about you?

THE MUSIC FLOWED. It was like his creativity had been dammed for two long years waiting for Alex to find the spigot. Okay, that was a mixed metaphor, but he sure couldn't worry about words now that he was composing again.

Last week he'd finished "Second Chances" for Central Standard Time. The band loved the ballad. Now he was working on an up-tempo number, more in line with their other songs.

Since CST had both male and female singers, it was a duet. A melody had stuck in his head for most of the week. He could almost pull the notes out like the line on a rod and reel. And the words weren't far behind. "Steamy Dreams". The song had a driving beat like the pulse of a racing heart during sex. Title needed work, but the melody wouldn't leave him alone. But it needed to percolate.

Percolate? Maybe coffee would help. Unfortunately

pouring a cup of coffee always made him think of Kate. The way she would inhale the scent and then get a dopey smile on her face.

In the kitchen he found a clean mug and filled it. He pulled his phone off the charger. Kate had sent him a text. His heart picked up a couple of beats.

"Sally?" Someone named Sally was cleaning his house. He shrugged off the twitch in his shoulder. And why would she remind him to be nice?

Her mother's first radiation treatment was today. He sent positive thoughts out to Mrs. MacBain.

Kate wanted to have dinner.

He set the phone on the counter. He didn't have plans, but it was hard seeing Kate and not *being* with Kate. He paced to the door and stared at the deck. She didn't want anything long-term.

But he did.

If they had takeout, they'd end up sleeping together. He blew out a breath.

He wanted to hold her, comfort her, share her pain and happiness, but when she pushed him away, could he handle the heartbreak?

IT DIDN'T MATTER how welcoming a medical setting was, it still smelled of cleaning solutions and that sickly sweet scent of disease. Kate flipped the page of the contract she was reviewing, but the words blurred together.

Her dad glanced up from his phone. "You don't have to be here."

"I want to be."

She and her brothers had established a rotating schedule of accompanying her parents to Mom's treatments. Michael should be here, but he hadn't been able to rearrange a meeting. So she was up.

"Did the oncologist say anything else?" she asked.

"She confirmed your mother's treatment schedule ... five weeks, five times a week. Then she explained the survival odds with and without radiation treatment."

Kate swallowed. Her mother had a five to ten percent chance of recurrence. Low, but this was her mother.

She stuffed the contract back in its folder, concentration impossible. "I saw vending machines in the hallway, do you want anything?"

"Water."

She'd been thinking of coffee, but water was probably better. Coffee reminded her of Alex. Pulling out her phone, she checked for messages. Still no response.

Her stomach churned, so at the vending machine she bought crackers with peanut butter too.

Handing Dad his water, she asked, "Did you see Stephen's estimate for Sorenson's remodel?"

He cracked the seal on the bottle and took a drink. "Yeah. A lot more costly then when I suggested the stairs ten years ago."

She sat on the sofa and set her head on his shoulder. "Didn't you tell me the customer's always right?"

He put his arm around her shoulders. "Yes, but they're not always smart."

She walked her dad through the terms of the Sorenson offer.

"You're doing good work, Katie girl."

"Liz is a real asset."

Dad's phone buzzed. He pulled it out and read the text. "I need to call Michael. He's got a question."

Kate pulled out her own phone and saw a text message. From Alex.

Taking a deep breath, she opened the message. *Hope your mother is okay. Dinner is a go.*

She heaved out a relieved sigh. Now she could admit she'd been afraid he would say no.

I can grab takeout she sent back.

His answer pinged before she'd tucked her phone into her purse. *Got a place I want to try. I'll pick U up. Let me know time.*

ALEX PULLED to the curb in front of Kate's apartment. She was waiting on the sidewalk.

"Hi." Kate slid into his car.

He gave her a quick kiss. "How's your mom?"

"So far so good."

She chewed her lip and he wanted to kiss her again.

"My brothers and I decided that one of us would always wait with Dad."

He laced their fingers together and pressed a kiss on her hand. "That's good, your mother comes first."

She nodded. "Where are we going?"

"A little place in Uptown Gabe suggested." He pulled into traffic.

She stared out the window as they headed south on Hennepin Avenue. He left her to her silence. What was going on inside that complicated circuitry that was her brain?

"I don't get to Uptown often," she finally said.

"I used to live in the area." He and Meredith had owned a condo nearby. They'd walked to most of the Uptown restaurants and shops. Since neither of them was much of a cook, they'd eaten out a lot. "I like the energy in the neighborhood. Plus, the lake is great."

She turned toward him. "Where did you live?"

He turned into the ramp, easiest solution since street

parking was hard to find. "I had a condo across from Lake Bde Maka Ska."

"With Meredith?"

He took the ticket the machine printed for him. "She moved in after I'd been there for a year or two."

"And you sold it because you couldn't stand to live there with your memories?" Her voice sounded teasing, but her expression was serious.

He concentrated on pulling into the first available parking spot. Once he shut the car off, he shifted, looking her in the eye. "I didn't want to live there anymore."

"Oh."

"Meredith had an abortion." He took a deep breath. "Without telling me she was pregnant."

The twist in his gut was as fresh as it had been the day he'd opened the payment information from the insurance company.

Meredith hadn't thought that one through. She'd paid cash for the co-insurance, but she hadn't realized the insurance company would send an explanation of what they'd paid for.

She reached across the console and held his hand. "I'm sorry."

"We were *supposedly* trying to have kids." He closed his eyes.

"Wow." Kate opened her mouth and then shut it.

He shook his head, shaking away the memories. "I let her have the condo in the divorce settlement, just to be done."

"I'm so sorry."

"Let's eat." He didn't want to discuss it. "You've had a long week."

KATE LET Alex link their hands together as they walked along the crowded sidewalk. She didn't know what to think.

She believed in a woman's right to her body. Guys didn't go

through nine months of a baby growing inside them. They could take the high road on the question of right to life because their bodies weren't involved.

She'd helped Meg with the decision. That one had been easy. A guy had spiked her drink at a frat party. Meg hadn't even known who'd raped her. Kate had been at the clinic holding Meg's hand during her procedure.

After that Kate had been even more diligent at parties. No one touched her drink. There had been too many rumors of guys using the date rape drug.

The Uptown area was so wonderfully diverse. A man with dreads halfway down his back wearing colorful tribal clothing moved toward them. He was with a woman with more piercings than Kate could count in one quick glance. As they approached the corner, a man with a guitar played and sang. His case lay open, money spread along the dark blue velvet lining.

Alex dug in his pocket and threw in a twenty-dollar bill. "Great job."

The man kept singing, a smile creasing his face.

"That's a hard way to make your rent payment," she said as they waited for the signal to change.

Alex's generosity didn't surprise her. He played with the neighbor boy, took care of her and supported street corner musicians.

What would he do next, save the children in Haiti?

Alex wrapped his arm around her shoulders and pulled her a little closer. "I played on a few street corners in New York. It's kind of fun, until it rains or snows."

"Was your hair long and stringy?"

"No. It might have been a little longer." He squeezed her shoulders and she curled into the half hug. "I didn't always remember to cut it."

She looked at his hair. It brushed his shirt collar. "I hate to break it to you, but that hasn't changed since you were in college."

"Hey. I'm an artist." He brushed a kiss on her nose.

She wished they were alone, and he'd aimed a little lower. It had been two weeks. She wanted one of his mind-blowing, drop your drawers kisses.

The signal changed and they crossed the street. "I thought we could try this Indian place, Serenity."

She almost groaned at the thought of spicy foods. She hoped they put pictures of chilies on the menu to indicate the heat level. But now that her mother was getting treatment, her stomach should settle down.

Alex held the door, and they worked their way through the crowd.

"Let me put our name in and then I'll grab some drinks. What do you want?" Alex asked.

"A ginger ale."

She backed against the wall. Most of the Indian restaurants she'd eaten at had used a lot of red. Serenity's walls were blues and gold. Sheer gold fabric draped from the ceiling, separating sections of the restaurant. The dividers had a fringe of little bells. There was a faint jingle each time someone brushed against the material.

Right behind the hostess, a small fountain splashed. Lights focused on a Buddha. Soft sitar music played in the background.

Alex waved her to the bar on the right. It was made of light wood carved into intricate airy designs. Kate followed him into the lounge. A couple left and she sat on a small pillow-strewn sofa with a postage stamp-sized table.

"Oh, good." Alex handed her a glass and joined her on the couch. "You found a spot. The hostess thought it would be a ten- to fifteen-minute wait."

"Thanks." She took a sip. Setting the drink down, she asked abruptly, "Are you a pro-life advocate?"

His eyes took on a hooded look. "I guess I'm pro-choice. Is this about Meredith?"

"It's easy for men to frown upon abortion. They're in and out, so to speak, but a woman's committed forever."

"You agree with Meredith's decision?" His voice came out low.

She leaned forward. "I'm saying I understand some women making the choice to terminate a pregnancy."

"The child was mine too." His lips formed two straight lines, a little white around the edges. "What about my rights?"

"You were married." She pulled one of the jewel-colored pillows from behind her and hugged it. "She should have talked to you."

"Thanks for that." He took a swallow of his beer, staring at a point over her shoulder.

The silence built around them. She took a drink. Twirled her glass. Kate had never had an abortion discussion with a man.

Finally she said, "There are situations when I think abortion is right."

"Like when?" he asked, his voice void of emotion.

"Like when my friend was drugged and the guy must not have used a condom." Her hands closed into fists on her lap. She couldn't tell Alex this was Meg. Meg still hadn't recovered from the trauma. She surrounded herself with friends but never let a man get close. "She was pregnant and couldn't remember anything."

Alex set down his glass. "Did they prosecute the bastard?"

"It took her days to realize she'd been raped, and she didn't remember anything. The cops couldn't do much. It wasn't an option to take DNA swabs of the guys who'd walked into the frat party."

The hostess hovered right behind Alex's shoulder. "Your table is ready."

"Thank you." Alex stood and held his hand out to help her up. He smiled, but it didn't reach his eyes.

Their evening had soured. She asked, "Are you sure you want to eat?"

"I'm hungry." He dropped her hand.

She slid to the back of a small table, not much bigger than the one they'd been sitting at in the bar.

The hostess handed them menus. "Your server will be right with you."

Kate stared at the menu, avoiding looking at Alex. This was a mistake. Dating was a mistake. She would get through dinner tonight and then end this ... thing they had going. They'd been ... out of balance ... for the last two weeks.

"I can understand what your friend did. I can." Setting down his menu, he reached across the table and linked their fingers together. "I hope you can understand how ... betrayed I was. This was my child."

She looked up. His eyes seemed darker, sadder. "I'm sorry."

"Thanks." He kissed her palm.

She sighed. "I don't know what to do with you."

"I don't know what to do with you either." He smiled and this time it reached his eyes. Pulling in a deep breath, he added, "But I have some ideas."

FOURTEEN

"How was Mom's treatment this morning?" Kate asked Michael as they walked into the company's break room.

Her brother grabbed the carafe and emptied it into his cup. Damn him. "Her skin is getting tender, like she has a sunburn, but Mom says that's expected after two weeks of treatment." He buried his face in his coffee and took a big gulp. "She looks tired."

"Yes," Kate agreed. Mom's face looked drawn. Was that from the surgery, anesthesia, radiation treatments or worry? "She's been coming into work every day. Maybe she needs to cut back."

"Yeah." Michael slouched against the counter.

She frowned. He looked awful. "Are you sick?"

He shrugged. "A little under the weather."

She dumped the coffee grounds and got one of the packages of ground coffee out of the cupboard.

"You didn't stay at the bar last night after we had dinner, did you?"

"Ran into a couple of friends. Played darts."

Cryptic wasn't her brother's style. When she'd walked into

O'Dair's, he'd already been drinking and he'd had two more drinks with dinner. "Everything all right?" she asked, trying for a casual tone.

"Fine. Just had a late night." He stalked out, almost knocking Liz down as she walked in the room.

Liz watched Michael walk away. "What stick's up his butt?"

Kate shook her head. "I don't know."

"As my mother would say, he looks like something the cat dragged in."

Kate turned back to the coffeepot. Not good when the staff commented on how awful the CFO looked.

Only a month ago, she would have sworn her family was perfect. Now her mother had cancer and her oldest brother was drinking too much. Was the family falling apart without Mom riding herd?

She'd corral Stephen and see what he thought. Timothy might not notice.

The coffeemaker gurgled and steamed. When it finished, she pulled out the pot and poured a cup and then added coffee to Liz's mug.

"Sorenson sent the next volley of requests," Liz said.

"Great." She wanted to finish this negotiation. Instead the law office kept asking for more and more concessions. "I wonder if the firm has another space in mind or if they're trying to see how far they can push us."

"If they were looking at other spaces, they'd work with a broker, right?" Liz asked.

"Probably."

"I know a commercial leasing broker." Liz added milk to her coffee. "Do you want me to see if she's heard anything?"

There were probably hundreds of brokers out there trying to lease space. Okay, not that many worked the downtown spaces. "Sure. I'd be interested in knowing if we're bidding against ourselves."

"Moving would cost the law firm a fortune." Liz stared at the ceiling. "I could run the numbers."

"I like that idea." Kate nodded. "We want our clients to make fully informed decisions."

Michael stuck his head in the door. "Still lollygagging in the break room, Katie? We need to set a better example for the staff."

Anyone who looked as hungover as he did, shouldn't talk about appearances. "We're working here. Did you need something?"

"Mom and Dad want a meeting at twelve-thirty. They're bringing in lunch."

Kate looked at Liz. Other than working another two hours at Alex's late that afternoon, she couldn't remember what was on her calendar.

She was tired of cleaning, but somehow working for Alex didn't bother her. It should. Cleaning his house had the potential to make her feel like his servant, but he never made her feel that way. She sighed, unsure of what she felt for Alex. It could be lust, God he made her body sing, but then there was his kindness. Sometimes he would hug her for absolutely no reason. Those hugs were the best.

Liz had her phone open. "You have a lunch meeting with the marketing intern."

"Can you handle it?" Kate asked her.

"Of course." Liz grinned. "Now I'm glad I booked your reservation at Cosette's. I love their food."

"Enjoy." Kate looked at Michael still leaning against the doorframe. "I'll be there. What's the agenda?"

Michael shrugged. "They didn't say. You call Stephen, I'll catch Timothy."

Before she could agree, Michael walked away.

In her office, she dialed Stephen. "Can you get here for lunch?" She raised her voice over the screech of a saw and the thump of nail guns. Good sounds. "Mom and Dad called a lunch meeting."

"I'll be there," Stephen shouted.

"Stop in my office before the meeting," Kate said. "I need to talk to you about something."

"I'll try."

Kate filled the rest of the morning with troubleshooting and updating the lease alert calendar with notification deadlines on a small lease that had been signed in the Maple Grove strip mall. Then she tackled her emails.

By twenty-five after twelve, Stephen hadn't arrived. She saved the file she'd been working on and headed out.

"I got hung up." Stephen ran down the hallway, stopping her. The scent of new-sawn wood and sweat filled her nose as they stepped back into her office. "What's up?"

"Michael's drinking too much." She didn't have time for subtlety.

Stephen's head jerked back. "What?"

"He's drinking too much." She bit her lip. Was Michael an alcoholic?

Her brother crossed his arms. "Explain."

"Last night he had a drink before we arrived and two drinks with dinner. Then he stayed and played darts with friends. He looks like hell today."

Stephen took a deep breath. "All of us have had a little too much to drink during our lives."

"Yeah, when we were twenty-one. I'm worried. Mom is too." She touched Stephen's arm. "Watch and see what you think."

"Sure." He looked at the clock on her office wall. "We'd better get down there. Do you have any idea why we're meeting? Nothing happened at Mom's treatment today, did it?"

"Not a clue. Michael said she looked tired." But she didn't trust her oldest brother's observational skills right now.

By the time she and Stephen walked in, everyone was eating. A bowl of salad and a tower of sandwiches were set out on the side table. Bernice's doing. Bernice had been her father and mother's assistant for as long as Kate could remember. If something happened to her parents, Bernice could probably run the company. Maybe better than she or Michael.

She grabbed a plate and placed half of what looked like a turkey or chicken sandwich on one side. Then she filled the rest of her plate with salad. She stuck a packet of raspberry vinaigrette on her plate.

"That can't be all you're eating." Stephen looked appalled.

"Some of us don't do manual labor." She hooked a bottle of water and headed to the conference room table.

Stephen laughed. "But you clean houses."

"Come on you two," Dad called.

Kate took a seat across from her mother. "How was your treatment today?"

Her mother's smile was forced. Makeup camouflaged the circles under her eyes, and her blush was too bright on her pale skin. "My skin feels like it's sunburned, but they gave me some cream."

Kate squeezed her mother's hand, wishing she could infuse her with energy. "Let me know what I can do."

"Eat," her mother said.

"Aye, aye." Kate forced herself to take a big bite of her sandwich. She knew it was delicious, but all she tasted was sawdust.

Dad finished his sandwich, stood and picked up his trash. "Patty, can I get you anything else?"

The tender look in her father's eyes had Kate swallowing. She may not want the hoopla that went with love, but she wouldn't mind some guy looking at her the way her father looked at her mother. Dad looked at Mom like she'd invented the next iPhone or had found a cure for cancer.

Talk about wishful thinking.

"I'm done." Mom pushed away her half-eaten sandwich.

"Try one of these. Bernice got them from Figlio's." Dad set a plate of brownies on the table. Brownies were Mom's weakness.

Her mother looked at Dad. The shoulder of her sweater slipped a little, revealing her too defined collarbones.

"Bernice is a devil." Mom put a brownie on a napkin, picking a small corner off and popping it in her mouth. "I swear Bernice and Maria are fattening me up for slaughter."

A shiver ran through Kate's body. Her mother *was* losing weight.

Timothy ran a hand through his hair and turned his worried gaze to her.

"What are we meeting about?" Stephen pulled the brownies closer and took two.

Dad squeezed her mother's shoulders one more time and then took his seat. "Your mother is following the pattern of most radiation patients. The fatigue may have hit a little sooner because she's hardly changed her work schedule."

"I didn't want to change my schedule," Mom said.

"I refuse to see her wear herself out." Dad's jaw jutted out, a sure sign he didn't want anyone disagreeing with him. "Starting next week, I'm banning her from the office."

"I still think I can come in halftime."

"Patty. I don't give a damn about the company." Conviction ignited Dad's blue-gray eyes. "For the next couple of months, your job is to heal."

He turned Mom's chair so it faced him. "You're more important than the company."

Mom stroked his face.

Tears filled Kate's eyes. It was such a private moment, but she couldn't pull her gaze away.

Dad pulled Mom's hand to his mouth and kissed it, never tearing his gaze away.

Her dad stood. "Katie, you'll have authority over Murphy's."

"Whatever you need," she choked out. "Mom, conserve your strength for getting well."

Mom gave her a small smile. "Let's spend time together this afternoon."

Kate pulled out her phone and sent Liz a message to clear her calendar. If she didn't get to Alex's until late, he wouldn't mind. She planned to clean for a few hours and then they were having dinner. "Absolutely."

Dad stared at Michael and frowned a little. "Still think you have the flu?"

"It might have been something I ate." Michael shrugged but didn't look Dad in the eyes.

Stephen's eyes widened. He looked at Kate and gave a small head shake.

"Rest this weekend because starting Monday I'm cutting my hours in half," Dad said. "I'm delegating all responsibility for transactions under a million dollars to you."

Kate's mouth dropped open. Her brother? Michael would be second-in-command? But she was the one trained to replace her father.

She wasn't even sure Michael wanted to run MacBain. Everyone knew that was her ambition.

Michael straightened in his chair. "I'll rest."

Timothy's finger tapped the notebook set in front of him. He leaned forward, as if he were about to say something, but then slid back in his chair and crossed his arms.

"Since Michael is already the primary check signer, Kate, you'll take over the second signature duties for checks over five thousand dollars," Dad continued. "Stephen, your backup."

"Sure. Whatever you need," they said together.

"We need your signatures on a couple of documents." Dad pushed a folder to Kate.

She opened the file and found bank forms. Michael had already signed the documents—yesterday. He'd known this was happening and he'd gotten drunk last night? He could have given her and the brothers a heads-up.

She signed and handed it to Stephen who also signed.

"That's it." Dad rapped his knuckles on the tabletop.

"I know you children have a rotating schedule to accompany us to the clinic." Mom's gaze circled the table. "I love you for the thought, but starting Monday, only Dad and I will go to my appointments. This disease will not suck any more of the family's energy than it already has."

"We want to be there for you," Timothy said.

"I know." Mom set her hands on the table and pushed out of her chair. "But we're putting more work on you. You have two strip malls coming on line in the next ninety days. You'll be up to your eyeballs. Stephen is in his busiest season."

Mom dusted off her suit pants. They were loose on her. Too loose.

"Michael and Kate, I want you to rely on your brothers." Dad stood behind Mom, setting a hand on her shoulder. "Maybe you should have your weekly dinners at the office. Bernice can cater in the food."

Her brothers had a stunned look on their faces. She probably did too.

"What?" Dad laughed. "You think your mother and I don't know what's going on in your lives?"

"Speaking of which, Sunday dinner at the house. Every week from now on." Her mother looked at Kate. "We would like it if you would bring Alex this Sunday."

"Ummm, I'll see if he's available." How did they know this stuff? "Who's your spy?"

Her mother laughed. The first time Kate had heard her

laugh in a while. "I'm not giving up my sources." She stared at each brother in turn. "And it would be nice if you would each bring a date."

Her brothers stuttered and stammered out explanations. Well, at least she had a date, except she hadn't planned to have him attend a family event. That was such a ... relationship step. A step she'd never planned on taking.

But she would invite Alex to their family dinner. For her mother.

"SO, you've met everyone but Michael." Kate buckled her seatbelt.

"I haven't met your dad. Guess that happens today."

"Yeah, sure, sure."

She flipped down the passenger visor and checked her hair. Might as well add a little more lip gloss. She dabbed on her favorite pink color. With a flick of her finger, she folded the visor back into place. "Thanks for driving."

Alex glanced at her. "No problem."

His glance looked skeptical, like he was deciding whether to drive Kate to her parents or to the hospital for psychiatric evaluation.

"Maria will be there too. She's been with my parents," Kate had to think, "since I was in tenth grade."

"Maria ...?"

"Maria Vanseula. She's their housekeeper and cook. I hope we're having Mexican. She's second generation, but her mother taught her to cook and she's fantastic."

"Kate." He dropped his hand on hers, forcing her hands back into her lap.

Had she been swinging them around? Alex probably should take her to the hospital. "Why are you nervous?"

Her fingers fisted around the straps of her purse. "I've never … you'll be … don't get the wrong idea."

"You're an MBA, don't they teach you to use full sentences in business school?" He squeezed her fingers. "Take a deep breath and start over. Please."

She inhaled, held it. Then exhaled slowly. "I've … I've never brought anyone I've dated to meet my parents."

"Never?" A big grin broke across his face as he focused on driving.

She frowned. "Of course not. I never wanted Mom and Dad, *or my date*, getting the wrong idea."

He merged with the traffic entering I-394. "I get it. But it's kind of nice being the first."

"Somehow Mom knows we're dating. Probably from Stephen or Timothy. It would be just like them to rat on me." She pursed her lips. "I'll find out which one and get back at them somehow. Payback will be sweet."

He gave a mock shiver. "Let's get back to the fact that I'm the first man you've introduced to your parents."

She groaned. "See, that's why I don't do things like this."

"I'm flattered." He laced their fingers together.

She moved his hand back to the steering wheel. "I'm doing this for my mother. Don't think this means anything."

He flashed her a quick smile.

She rolled her eyes. "Just don't get any ideas, okay?"

"I've got lots of ideas." His voice took on a husky tone that made her body hum. Damn him.

He headed south on Highway 100, then she guided him home.

As they headed up the curved driveway, Alex ducked his head to look at the house. "Nice."

It was impressive. Gray-beige rock covered the front of the first story. The next three stories were covered with tan brick. Stone pillars flanked massive red double doors. She'd always loved the brightness of the doors. It broke up the neutral colors. If you looked closely, the stone had flecks of gold, black and maroon.

But Alex was probably used to mini mansions. If his parents lived on Minnetonka and had hired tutors for the kids, there was serious family money.

Alex pulled under the portico next to Stephen and Timothy's cars. Maybe Michael had caught a ride with one of them. Had he already started drinking for the day?

"Looks like we're not the first," Alex said.

She hoped they were the last. She wanted to spend as little time as possible looking like a couple.

The unkindness of her thoughts hit her like an elbow in the face as she went up for a basket.

Taking a deep breath, she said, "I'm sorry I'm being weird. I appreciate you coming. Thank you."

He put the car in park and unsnapped his seatbelt. "You don't have to thank me."

"Yes, I do."

"I like being with you." The kiss he brushed against her lips was soft and sweet.

He kissed her again and this kiss wasn't sweet. He licked her bottom lip and she opened, inviting him in. Heat arrowed to all the right parts of her body, leaving an ache that wouldn't be relieved in the near future.

"Okay, that was a mistake." He pulled in a gulp of air. "We'll sit here for a few minutes."

She laughed, bounced a kiss off his nose. "Thank you. How do you always talk me off the ledge?"

"I'm brilliant. Child protégé and all that."

When the front door opened, they both turned to look. She sighed. "Sucks to have brothers."

"Mom says to stop making out in the car and get in the house," Timothy called, leaning against the doorframe.

"Ha ha. Mom wouldn't say that." She stepped out but turned to grab her purse off the floor and the changes of clothes she and Alex had brought along. There was a b-ball game planned for later.

"You okay?" she asked Alex in a whisper.

"I'm fine. Let's go face the family." He had a grin as big as the state of Texas on his face.

And damn him, he was laughing as they walked to the door. She checked to see if he was still aroused, but apparently laughter was the best medicine for everything.

"Good to see you again," Alex said, holding out his hand. "You're Timothy, right?"

"You got it."

"I'll take your coat," she said to Alex.

"Come on and meet the rest of the family," Timothy said.

Kate hung his jacket in the closet. She brought it to her nose and sniffed. It had the rich smell of leather and wood and some cedar-piney scent. It reminded her of all the wonderful things they'd done last night. Sitting together watching an old movie and feeding each other pizza. And the night. Her cheeks warmed with the memory of the way he'd made her wait for release.

Had she ever had such a generous lover? Someone who cared more for her pleasure than his own?

Shoving his coat in the closet, she tossed her own on a hanger.

She hurried down the hallway, not wanting her brothers to grill Alex. As she neared the family room, her mother laughed. What a wonderful sound.

She came around the corner. Alex held her mom's hand. Michael slouched in an armchair, his eyes closed, still looking like something the cat had dragged in, just like Liz had said on Friday. Timothy paced between the window and the fireplace.

Dad stood, probably to shake Alex's hand. Stephen wasn't in the room.

She should have introduced Alex. Instead she'd been sniffing his coat.

"… you're going through this," Alex was saying. "If there's anything I can do to help, I'm more than willing. Take you to appointments, sit with you. Whatever you need."

"That's so kind." Mom had more color in face. Maybe it was her deep green shirt, but she looked—better. Hopefully she'd rested over the weekend. "I would love to hear your music."

Alex stood. "That's an easy request. I can send you CDs through Kate."

Mom pointed to the baby grand angled in the corner of the room.

Kate had always thought of the piano as an instrument of torture. All the MacBains had learned to play. It wasn't her thing sitting the required thirty minutes each day to practice a piece that never sounded like music to her ears.

"Would it be too much to ask if you'd play something before dinner?" her mother asked.

"For you, I'll play for my supper." He headed over and lifted the keyboard cover. "What kind of music do you like?"

"Anything." Her mother leaned back. Dad sat and wrapped his arm around her.

"Okay." Alex folded up the keyboard cover. "You'll start hearing this one in commercials soon."

He ran the scales.

"If I'm spending all this time at home, I'll get the piano tuned," Mom murmured.

Who would play? Mom had better not assume Alex would be having dinner here every Sunday.

The tune he played was the first one she'd heard. He sang, his voice had a Bob Dylan kind of growl.

Mom closed her eyes and leaned on Dad. Was there a therapeutic element to music? She would check. If so, she'd load Mom's phone with music to help her heal.

Kate went and stood in the curve of the piano. Alex smiled at her, his fingers flying over the keys. She leaned on her elbows, cradling her chin in her hand. The song made her think of families gathered together at the end of a day.

He finished and everyone clapped.

"Could you play something else?" her mother asked.

Alex nodded. "I'm working on songs for Central Standard Time. They're a pop group."

She'd heard parts of this song too. The score she'd guess it would be called, but she hadn't heard the lyrics.

In the dark you come to me,
Moonlight in your hair.
Love tangles with the silence,
You never say a word, never say you care.
I touch you, just tonight,
You swear we just can't last,
But morning comes and I'm still here,
Remembering the moonlight in your hair.

He stared into her eyes. She couldn't tear her gaze away. He'd written a song about her, about them.

She didn't want to open her heart to him, didn't want to be thrilled that he'd written music that shattered her resolve. But he was unlocking everything inside her.

"That's lovely," Mom said. "Sad but lovely."

"Thank you."

Stephen came in with a tray of drinks, chips and guacamole. "Maria says dinner will be at two." He looked at his watch. "We have an hour."

Alex folded down the keyboard cover. "You okay?"

"I'm fine." But she wasn't. She was becoming too dependent on Alex. "Hurry, before my brothers eat all the dip."

~

ALEX RAISED HIS EYEBROWS. "That's why you wanted me to bring my sneakers, and athletic gear? To play basketball?"

"Didn't I tell you?" She pointed him down the hall. "You can change in the bathroom."

Now he wished he hadn't eaten that second plate of enchiladas, but they'd been damn good. He hoped he didn't lose his dinner while they played. He pulled on his T-shirt and the sweatpants he'd thrown into a bag.

Kate leaned against the hallway wall, a couple of water bottles in her hands. She handed him a bottle. "Our court's out back."

"Lead the way."

They walked through a bright kitchen. A small, dark-haired woman loaded a dishwasher.

"Maria, fantastic meal." Kate gave her a one-armed hug. "This is Alex Adamski."

"Nice to meet you," Maria said.

"Dinner was delicious." He shook her hand. "I don't suppose I could hire you to cook for me?"

Maria's laughter filled the room. "If I had a dollar for everyone who tried, I'd be a rich woman."

Alex winked. "Well, if you ever change your mind."

Maria waved them away. "Out of my kitchen. I'm going to clean and then put my feet up."

"This way." Kate pointed to another short hall. He set his arm on her shoulder, but she elbowed his side. "My mother likes you and you try to steal Maria. I could tell Mom on you, you know."

"I'd just play her another song." He pulled her to a stop before they headed outside. "Come here."

She resisted, but only for a second. Then she sank into his arms.

223

Everything settled into place. His tongue brushed hers. She tasted like the spice of dinner and the wine she'd drunk. Her breasts nestled into his chest.

Home. Comfort. Perfect harmony.

How had he ever thought he could stay away from her?

For two weeks he'd tried to be only a friend. But he couldn't. She was becoming as important to him as his music.

He sighed and pulled her closer. He felt more than heard her matching sigh.

"I don't know what to do with you." She rubbed his butt.

"Right back at 'cha."

"Come on or one of my brothers will search for us." Kate took his hand and pulled him out of the door onto a patio. Not a wooden deck, but a stone patio with a concrete bannister.

Mrs. MacBain lounged in the sunlight, a book unopened on her lap. "Katie, remember that Alex is a guest."

"Of course." But Kate had an almost evil smile on her face.

"What's going on?" he whispered.

"Nothing."

Steps led to another patio. An expanse of grass rolled away from the house. To the side was a fenced-in full basketball court. "Wow."

Kate grinned. "Dad put the court in when we moved here." They started down the steps and she called back. "Mom, you have to referee those cheating brothers of mine."

Without opening her eyes, Mrs. MacBain called back, "Kate, you're the worst offender. I'm soaking up the sun. Behave."

Alex stared at Kate. "What kind of game do you play?"

Kate slapped his shoulder. "A friendly family game."

He held open the fence door and a ball shot toward them. Kate snatched it before it hit him in the gut. *Good hands.*

"Katie, you're on my team," Mac called. "Come on, Timothy, huddle up."

Kate jogged to her dad and gave him a high five.

"Alex, you're with Michael and me," Stephen called.

He joined Stephen, giving Michael a curious glance. Michael had been quiet through most of the afternoon and the meal. His eyes were bloodshot and his skin had a greenish cast that looked suspiciously like a major hangover.

Stephen sighed. "Ideas on containing Kate?"

"Kate?" Alex said.

Michael blew out a boozy breath. "Trip her every time she gets the ball?"

"You're kidding?" Alex asked.

"No." Michael released a deep breath, and Alex caught the whiff of whiskey.

"Have you played much?" Stephen asked him.

"High school. Point guard."

"She's good, real good," Michael said. "Four year starter in high school."

"I guess she did tell me," Alex said. "I never ..." better not complete that sentence where Kate could hear him.

Stephen stared at his brother. "Can you play?"

Michael nodded.

"Michael, you'll take the ball in," Stephen said. He raised his voice. "Half-court, right?"

"Sure, sissies," Timothy called back.

Stephen rolled his eyes. "We're going to get killed."

They put their hands together. Michael and Stephen chanted, "Stop, Katie." And they broke.

What the hell?

Kate took the ball out first.

"Alex, guard Kate," Stephen called, heading toward his father. Michael showed a spurt of energy and moved toward Timothy.

Kate bounce-passed the ball to Alex. "You ready, big guy?"

"Show me what you got." He bounced the ball back to her and gave her space.

With his arms up, she went low, sending the ball to her dad. She banged into him as she moved onto the court, knocking him off balance.

"Don't let her in, Alex!" Stephen hollered.

He scrambled to get between Kate and the basket.

Her dad sent the ball back and Kate dribbled, faked left and then spun right. Since she was a step ahead of him, she had a clear path to the basket and did a perfect layup. The ball dropped sweetly into the net.

She retrieved the ball and sent it to him. "That's two."

Stephen shook his head.

Alex jogged to the line. When he turned, Kate crowded him. At least he had height on her. Stephen got open and Alex passed the ball.

Kate jumped as he let go and got a piece of the ball sending it off course, but Stephen scrambled, getting there before Mac did.

Alex moved toward the basket but couldn't get around Kate. She had one hand up. He stepped back and Stephen sent him the ball. Kate had her hand in his face.

He dribbled away from her and moved the ball to Michael. Timothy almost intercepted the pass, knocking Michael in the shoulder.

Alex grinned. "You all play dirty."

Michael got around Timothy, but Mac blocked the money shot. Michael sent the ball across court, and Stephen winged it to Alex without looking.

He snatched it just before Kate could slap the ball out of his hands.

His teammates were covered so he took the ball in. Spinning, he drove to the basket. Kate's shoulder smacked into his chest, but he kept moving.

He took two steps and went up. Kate was in his face. He shot. The ball arced over her outstretched hands, hit the backboard, circled the rim and dropped.

"Nice shot." Kate slapped his butt. Then she pulled off her sweatshirt and tossed it beyond the court boundary.

Her tight-fitting shirt and sports bra left nothing to the imagination. Her black pants hugged her hips as tightly as he had last night.

He didn't want to play the game of basketball.

"Devil woman," he muttered.

Kate laughed and took the ball to half-court.

This time he crowded her, but she still got the ball to Timothy. She moved next to him, her breast pressed against his arm. He jerked away, aware this was another weapon in her distraction arsenal.

Luckily Stephen stole the ball from his brother. Alex got clear and made the shot, a sweet swish from the top of the key.

He stripped off his sweatshirt, pulling his T-shirt off at the same time. Two could play Kate's game.

She ran her gaze up and down his chest. As they walked to half-court, she said, "Nice."

He would never have believed that playing basketball with his lover and her family could be foreplay.

When Kate and her team had taken a six-point lead, Stephen took a timeout. Leaning over his legs and dragging in deep gulps of air, he said, "Okay, we can't let Kate get to the basket. Alex, use those elbows God gave you. You're giving her too much space to shoot." He turned to his brother. "Michael, get your feet moving. You look like you're eighty years old. Dad's outplaying you."

"Yeah, yeah. Still fighting the bug." Michael drained his

water bottle and threw it near a garbage can by the gate. He couldn't even make that basket.

"No one believes that lie except maybe Mom. Clean up your act."

Alex wiped the sweat off his forehead with his arm. Should have brought a towel. "We could switch up. You guard Kate and I'll play in." For a big man, Stephen was fast and had good hands. "We might get more shots."

Stephen drained his bottle and threw it into the trash. Perfect two-point shot. "Let's try it."

Stephen took the ball out and Kate called, "Hey, Adamski, did I wear you out?"

"In your dreams." And his.

Stephen faked a pass and then sent the ball to Alex. Kate's brother had no qualms against blatantly fouling his sister. Since there weren't any refs, Kate jabbed an elbow into her brother's abs as he shot past her on the court. Alex couldn't pass the ball to Stephen. Michael was guarded too tightly, so he took the ball in, shouldering past Mac for a textbook layup.

Their deficit was down to four.

"Change up, Dad," Kate called. Sunlight made the gold strands of her hair blaze like precious metal. Her eyes twinkled like Christmas lights.

She passed the ball to her father, and he took it out. She guarded Alex.

"Couldn't stand to be away from me?" he whispered. The scent of lemons and her musky sweat had him wishing the game was over and they were already home.

She pouted. "Keep dreaming."

God, he wanted to nibble on that lip.

"I'm defending the most dangerous player." He flipped her ponytail over her shoulder.

He stayed right with her, deflecting her elbow when she tried to plant the pointy weapon in his belly. He slapped Timothy's pass out of her hands, but unfortunately Michael wasn't fast enough to steal the ball.

The battle raged, but Alex's team never took the lead. And he didn't care. Kate's competitive spirit filled him with joy.

He'd judged so many women in his life based on Meredith. His ex-wife wouldn't touch any sort of ball, much less played a hard-hitting game of physical b-ball.

Kate was a woman he could love.

He stumbled, tripping on his own feet. Went down hard on his knees. Damn. It wasn't that he *could* love her. He *did* love her.

Hell. He'd fallen in love with Kate.

A fist to his solar plexus would be more comfortable. How many times had Kate told him she didn't do long-term?

He scrubbed his face. Maybe he could change her mind.

Kate laughed. "We've got him on his knees team, let's finish him off."

Her dad scored, but Alex couldn't move.

"Are you all right?" Kate asked. She patted his back.

He looked into her eyes. "Tripped. I tripped."

"We saw."

He couldn't be in love with her. She would push him away faster than a bee circling a soda can.

She pulled him up and checked out his knees. "You're not bleeding. You want to stop?"

"I give up," Michael gasped out. He collapsed where he stood.

"Great, just great," Stephen called out. "For once I thought we could take you, K-k-k-Katie."

Kate brushed his knees. *A little higher. Without an audience.*

"You look okay." She stared at him. Her eyes flared open at whatever she saw in his face. She glanced at his groin.

Yeah, he was reacting to her. Standing in front of him, she gave him cover.

He constructed a succession of minor seventh chords, pictured them dotting his score. Better than thinking about stripping those skintight clothes off Kate's sweaty body. *Whoops.*

"Well, Dad, you and I are still supreme champions." She raised her hand and flashed a victory sign. "Be glad you picked the right team, Timothy."

Her team exchanged high fives.

Alex grabbed his shirt and sweatshirt, slipping them on. By the time he returned to the court, his body had settled, mostly.

"Good game, Adamski. Next time listen when I say to take my sister down." Stephen slapped his back. "Next game, Mom referees. Then you," he pointed a finger at Kate, "can't cheat all the time."

"Wah-wah. Tell it to someone who cares." Kate pulled on her sweatshirt. "Ready to go?" she asked Alex.

She'd used the same words last night. Right before she'd stripped off his belt. Was that a coincidence?

"Absolutely." His voice cracked.

Kate hugged her father. "See you tomorrow."

"I'll be working from home. And then there's your mother's appointment." Both of their smiles faded.

Alex stretched out his hand. "Thanks for inviting me to dinner."

"Anytime," Mac said. Did he see some sort of warning in Kate's father's eyes or was it his guilt for the things he planned to do as soon as they were alone.

Kate climbed the stairs in front of him, making her way to her mother. She gave her a hug. "Let me know if you need anything."

"I'm good. See you next Sunday." Her mother winked at Alex. "I hope you'll come again."

≈

"CAN'T YOU DRIVE FASTER?" Kate asked Alex for the third time. She wanted her hands on his body.

"Do you want me to get a speeding ticket?"

"No." She slouched in her seat. "But head to my apartment. It's closer."

"Agreed."

She pulled his right hand to her mouth and licked one of his fingers. "I can't wait much longer."

"Are you sure that was basketball?" he asked.

She snorted and licked his pinky, her tongue swirling around the base. He groaned. She didn't plan on waiting for a bed.

"I've never had so much fun." She worked over another finger. "Damn it, when you took off your shirt and I saw your chest all sweaty and nummy, all I wanted to do was bite you."

His hand formed a fist. Then he yanked her hand to his mouth. "You've got to stop. I'll drive off the road."

Good to know Alex was as crazed as she was.

There weren't any parking spots in front of her apartment building.

"Damn it," she muttered as they circled the block. Craning her neck, she spotted a possible opening. "Try this street."

"This is why I live in a house with a garage."

Alex pulled in front of the spot. It looked too small for his car. With pursed lips, he wedged his Lexus into the space, easing back and forth until it was snug to the curb.

Kate unlocked her door as he parked the car. "Hurry."

She gathered their clothes and the leftovers Maria had sent home. "Sustenance for after."

They moved in tandem along the sidewalk. She pushed the bags into Alex's arms and retrieved her keycard. She punched the elevator button. Then hit it again.

Alex grinned. "Me too."

231

They were in perfect accord. She'd think about the ramifications of that later.

The bell dinged. They waited. Solar systems were born and died. Could the doors take any longer to open?

Finally they screeched open. Always the gentleman, he waited for her to enter first. She pressed the button for the tenth floor. "Go."

Turning toward him, she stroked his face. "If this cranky machine stops, we're getting it on right here."

He kissed the top of her head.

Too little. Too sentimental. She wanted raw, no-holds-barred sex.

She clenched his butt.

"Keep that up and this will be over too soon, love."

Her breathing stopped at his endearment. Had to be his pheromones talking. Or the testosterone, or any of those *'rones* that had been activated as they'd played basketball.

Even as the elevator door opened, she had her key in her hand and ran down the hall. The door was open by the time he joined her. She took the bags out of his hands and forced him against the closing door.

Alex welded their mouths together. Their tongues clashed, and they both gasped for air.

He whipped off her sweatshirt and pulled the band from her hair. He growled as he worked the stretchy T-shirt over her head.

Meanwhile she tugged off his shirt. The sweatshirt was easy, but their hands tangled as they fought his uncooperative T-shirt.

"Wait." He stepped away and jerked off his shirt, flinging it to the floor.

"Good idea." She snaked out of her clingy sports bra.

Before she pushed off her pants, his hands wrapped around

her waist. He spun her around and pressed her against the door.

"There you are." His hands stroked and molded her breasts. His lips opened hers for a deep kiss.

Heat washed through her. Alex slid kisses down her neck. She leaned against the cold door, arching her back, begging him to put his mouth to her breasts.

He chuckled. "Not so fast."

He toyed with her nipples and his mouth did seductive things to the shell of her ear.

She wrapped a leg around his thigh, bringing the hardness of his body against her heated core.

"Alex," she groaned.

He kissed her again. His answer that he would do things on his own damned timeline.

She'd show him. Kate worked her fingers down his pants and under his boxers. Silken steel filled her hand. She rubbed the tip of his penis, spreading his lubricant around the head.

"Jesus," he swore.

His hands dove down the insides of her pants, taking her underwear with them. She dropped her leg and her pants slid to her feet.

Laughing, she repeated the action on his pants. Drawing in a deep breath, she pulled away and looked.

He was a feast. Golden skin dewed with sweat. She licked his nipple and tasted salt.

His erection nudged between her legs. Alex picked her up. "Guide me into you," he grunted.

Against the door. *Oh my God. A fantasy come true.*

She grasped his thick head and placed him at the heart of her body. Only his heat could cool this fire building inside.

He rocked his hips, entering her with a smooth slide. Tingles spread to every muscle in her body. Her head banged

NAN DIXON

against the door and she didn't care. She tried to arch into him and draw him deeper.

He pulled her legs higher. She couldn't move. Couldn't breathe. His fingers pulled her wide. He pulsed his hips, small gyrations causing minor earthquakes in her core.

But it wasn't high enough, deep enough or quick enough.

"Harder. Alex, please."

Sweat dripped from his brow. His eyes flashed with golden flecks. His gaze captured hers. "Just wait, love."

No. She closed her eyes against the passion in his. She grasped his head between her hands and kissed him. Her tongue moved in and out of his mouth the way she wanted his body to work over hers.

His hips mimicked their mouths. She hung on, her hands slipping on his sweaty shoulders.

She tilted her hips, trying to get him to hit the one spot that would blast her off like a rocket.

Alex buried his lips on her neck. A curse vibrated through his chest. His muscles shook under her hands.

Then it started, a magnificent curl of pleasure. She tightened her legs around his waist, not wanting him to move at all but also wanting him to move harder. She arched and rolled. Fireworks exploded behind her eyes. "Alex!"

He pumped into her, causing the explosions to go on and on. His body shook. Their breathing crashed, big deep gasps. She drew in the scent of the lovemaking, the scent of his sweat and the wonderful musk that was all Alex.

She kissed him. "Oh God."

He opened his eyes. The muscles of his arms shook.

"Jesus," he gasped out.

"Nope, just me."

He helped her down. Her legs wobbled and then collapsed under her and they sank to the floor. The tile was cold on her bare skin, but at least Alex had doused the fire inside her.

"Shit," he muttered, resting against the wall.

"Really?" she groaned. She thought her bones had lique-fied from Alex's assault. Hopefully they would re-form some-time in the next hour.

"We forgot the condom. Again."

Her body wouldn't do anything more than roll toward Alex and settle into his shoulder. Her brain was fogged with sex, but she should be getting her period any day now. "We should be okay."

His hand rubbed her bottom. "I didn't hurt you, did I, love?"

"Enough with the endearments. I'm good. Just don't have full control of my body right now."

And that was a first for her. Sex *never* destroyed her. Yet each time Alex touched her, she wanted more.

Something to think about. Later. Right now she needed food. "Let's check out our leftovers."

"I need water." He kissed her. "Between you and basket-ball, I'm as dry as the Mojave Desert."

"You'll have to get the water." She snuggled into his shoul-der. Just for a moment until she could get her feet under her.

"Yeah. Soon." He bent and kissed her, a sweet chest-tight-ening kiss. Nothing like the mad kisses they'd shared moments ago.

"I had fun today. I liked playing basketball with your fami-ly." He twisted her hair around his fingers. "Our children will have to play basketball from the time they can walk, just to keep up with their mom and uncles."

The bones in her body re-formed with a snap. She put a hand on his chest and pushed away from him. "You must be thinking of another woman you're sleeping with."

Every female CEO she'd met talked about their sacrifices. To get to the top, they'd given up so much. It was what she had to do.

235

She snatched her clothes and dashed for the bedroom.

He followed, not bothering with his clothes. "Kate. You have such a great family. Why wouldn't you want to pass on that tradition of love?"

She pulled in a tortured breath, her nostrils flaring. "Because I'm a woman. I can't do both. I come from a family of successful executives. I'm choosing success. I don't need babies to complete myself."

Look what had happened to her mother. She'd gotten breast cancer. Was it from trying to do it all? Run her own company and a family?

And the grandmother she could barely remember had done the same thing. Worked all her life and breast cancer had killed her when she was in her forties.

On the day Grandmother had died, Kate had one sharp memory. Her mother on the floor sobbing, Dad holding her in his arms.

Both her mother and grandmother had been spread too thin, working full-time or more than full-time, and having a family. Even her great-grandmother had died when she was in her forties. Murphy women's life expectancy weren't long.

She would never force a husband to go through what her dad was enduring. She would go her road alone. Obviously she would end up with breast cancer, but no one else had to suffer her death. Her brothers would have their wives. They would carry on the MacBain name. And while she could, she would be the aunt everyone loved to visit.

She pulled on her robe and belted it, hard. She'd made the decision years ago that she wouldn't ever be placed between the proverbial rock and hard place. Alex wasn't changing her plans.

He closed the distance between them. She stumbled back and his face fell.

"Kate, life isn't about denying yourself pleasure. Sure, your mother is successful in business, but more important than her work, she's successful in family and love."

She threw up her hands and paced to the window. Clouds covered the sun, leaving the city streets gray and dingy. "My mother has cancer!"

He settled his hand on her shoulders. "That has nothing to do with her success or happiness."

"Of course it does." She shrugged off his touch. Her skin itched with irritation. "How many years did she spend denying her body sleep, stressing over my brothers and me. That weakens a person's immune system."

He laughed, pulling her into his arms.

She evaded and stalked out of her bedroom. Why didn't the man put his clothes on?

He followed her. The smile faded from his lips. "You can't be serious."

"Dead serious."

"Why?"

"Every female CEO I've met has had to sacrifice to get there."

"What about your mother?"

"Sure, but ... I want ... bigger." She wanted to be bigger than Murphy's.

She'd never thought of it that way. She'd always thought in terms of her dad's position and growing the company.

She sank to the sofa. She needed time to think and couldn't do that around Alex. "I don't want to do this anymore."

"Do what? Fight? I don't want to fight either," Alex said. "But you're strong. You can ... forge a new path for female CEOs."

"Women have been trying, but even though I'm the best candidate, my dad is giving Michael more authority." She sighed. "Would you please put some clothes on?"

"We ripped each other's clothes off. We couldn't wait to get inside the door. Hell, we almost made love on the basketball court. Now you want me gone?"

"That was just sex."

"That was making love."

There was that damn word again. Love. "We didn't *make love*. We had 'back against the door' sex."

Alex yanked on his sweatpants. "I made love to you."

Why was he bringing up love? "Stop. I can't do this anymore."

His voice grew louder. "Are you saying we're through?"

"Yes!" He was making everything too hard. "I told you I never wanted a long-term relationship."

He closed his eyes, drew in a deep breath. "I'm in love with you, Kate."

Weight settled on her chest. She couldn't breathe. Spots filled her vision. When she drew in a breath, it was in quick shallow pants.

Alex shoved her head between her knees. He knelt, rubbing her back. "Obviously you're thrilled with my confession."

She gasped for air. Her body shook.

Alex needed to leave. She would get her life back the way she wanted it if Alex left.

"Please," she croaked. "Please go."

He dipped his forehead to hers. She wanted to push him away. She wanted to let him hold her and make everything better.

"Don't do this," he pleaded. His brown eyes were so close she could count the golden flecks that formed a circle around his irises. "Not to us."

She closed her eyes, refusing to look into his. "Alex, there is no *us*."

FIFTEEN

ALEX TOSSED HIS BAG IN THE HOUSE AND HEADED OUT TO HIS basketball hoop. He threw free throw after free throw. The ball banged against the backboard with a finality of a bass drum.

He sure knew how to pick 'em. *Bam. Swish.*

Falling for another woman whose only concern was their career. *Bam.*

No children in her future. *Swish.*

He needed to fall out of love. *Bam. Bam.*

His chest hurt like someone was drilling into each rib. He didn't remember this kind of pain when he'd walked out on Meredith.

For an hour he shot the ball. His dribble was a syncopated dirge. He shot until the light faded. He didn't turn on the flood lights. He didn't want to see.

He tucked the ball in the garage and went into his empty house. The pulsing beat from the ball echoed in his head.

Grabbing a beer, he headed for his office. Sitting at the keyboard, he slipped on his headphones. And stopped.

He wouldn't close himself off from the world. Wasn't that

what he'd been doing for the last two years? Creating a world without pain, but also one without love?

He cranked up the volume. No more.

He played. The melody came as a trickle, then a flood. Waves of pain translated into phrases, harmonies, dissonant chords that resolved, always returning to the home key of A minor.

His hand couldn't write fast enough. He shoved back his hair. Dry mouthed, he tipped the beer bottle, but it was empty. He set it aside, his eyes never leaving the sheaves of paper covered in musical notations.

At least his creativity was back. Because of Kate.

He paced. Moved to the piano, then back to the keyboard. The notation sheet was a mass of notes slashed out and rewritten.

And everything coalesced. He closed his eyes. Pictured the melody moving through the orchestra. Heard how it changed, grew, evolved. Until the strings set it free.

The solemn sad music filled his home. It filled the empty corners that should have held laughter and children's footsteps. Page after page fell to the floor. The music flooded out of him like tears. His fingers made the piano weep until there was no more sorrow, no more pain.

His breath came in shaky gasps. Done.

He threw his head back and shouted, "Take that."

He hit record. Again and again, he layered in harmonies. The undercurrent of two quarter notes started in the strings and then moved to the horns. The basses took it next and finally the pulse ended with the violins. The cry of the clarinet floated above the beat and echoed in the French horn. The tympani was last. He laid it down like a heartbeat, driving through the music, rising to a crescendo when the full orchestra took on the theme from the first movement. Then each instrument died away until only the tympani remained. Boom boom. Boom boom. Boom boom.

Silence, then one final beat. A heart-breaking final beat.

Alex's shoulders sagged. He shut off the power and rolled away from the console.

He'd finished the sonata.

Lightheaded, he found his phone. He should eat or maybe sleep, but he had to tell Kate. Had to let her know he'd finished the damn piece. The monkey that had clung to his back for two long years had finally returned to his jungle.

He hit her speed dial.

"Come on, answer," he muttered. He closed his eyes, but the room spun a little.

"Alex?" Kate's voice crackled with sleep.

"I finished it."

"It's four in the morning."

Four in the morning?

"Are you drunk?" she asked.

"I'm not drunk. It's my sonata. I finished it." He cradled his head in his hand. "It's done."

He sank into the chair.

"I'm happy for you, really. Congratulations."

"It's because of you."

"Don't say that. I've … I've got to get more sleep." Kate hung up.

I'm an idiot. His head smacked the back of the chair.

He staggered to the sofa. He didn't trust his legs to carry him upstairs to bed.

∽

KATE EASED BACK in her office chair, rubbed her eyes and hoped her headache would disappear.

No luck.

241

Between fighting with Alex, her mother's cancer and her parents giving Michael more authority, she'd barely slept. And when she'd finally drifted off, Alex had called.

What didn't he understand about breaking up?

When her phone had rung, she'd shot up in bed, adrenaline coursing through her. Her first thought? Something terrible had happened to Mom.

She rubbed the ache under her breastbone. Maybe now that she wasn't stressed by how dependent she'd become on Alex, she would feel better.

Alex had finished his sonata. She was happy for him, really. She would miss him.

Work would get her though this—confusion. She opened the present value projections Liz had completed.

A rapping at the doorframe pulled her away.

"Kate, do you have the projections on how the Sorenson deal affects Daschle's yearly revenue?" Michael asked.

At least he looked better than he had the day before but still not a hundred percent.

"I'm reviewing it right now." Or trying to. "I need to respond to their last offer by tomorrow."

She hadn't decided if she should give them any additional remodeling money.

"I need the five-year projections this afternoon." He walked into her office and collapsed into one of her guest chairs. He handed her a sheaf of papers. Under the harsh fluorescent light, his eyes were red. Probably matched hers.

She flipped through the papers. It was the forecast materials she'd developed a couple of years ago. Hadn't Michael made any changes to her worksheets?

"Which projections do you want?" she asked. "The offer we've made or the offer Sorenson made?"

Michael ran his fingers through his hair. "Um, maybe

Sorenson's offer? Or do you have a version where you think we'll end up? Maybe that would be better."

If Michael wanted to run the company, he needed to be more decisive. "What are you doing with the info?"

"Dad wants an update on the multi-year forecast. I need to project any draws on our line of credit in the next five years."

"When did he ask for this?"

"Last week." Michael winced.

And he couldn't have told her last week? She rubbed her chin. "I'll give you three versions. Basically a low, medium and high. Will that work?"

He nodded.

"I think you should project additional marketing for the residential building arm," she suggested.

"Oh, we did talk about that." He rubbed his chin. "Can you give me something on that?"

"By this afternoon? You want me to develop a marketing forecast in a couple of hours?"

"Yeah." He smiled, but it didn't soften the blow.

"Sure. Any more of *your* work you want me to do?"

"Ha ha." Michael stood. "I'd owe you."

She looked at the sheets in her hand. She'd created these before they'd brought two of the strip malls online. "Where are Shamrock Square and Otis Court?"

"Aren't they on there?" Michael flipped the pages around. His fingers ran through the list of properties.

"Not that I see."

"Crap. Do you have anything on them?"

"Just the budget we pulled together last November." Six months ago. What was Michael's department doing? Shouldn't they be on top of this stuff?

"Could you check for other changes?" he asked.

She glared at him. "Anything else?"

"I think that's it." Michael stood. "I'll leave the model with you. You'll double-check everything, right?"

She closed her eyes. "You owe me."

"Yes, I do—I will."

She readjusted her day. Thank goodness she wasn't cleaning Alex's house today.

Alex. God, she was going to have to clean his house later in the week. What a nightmare.

She stuck her head out her office door. "Liz, do you have a minute?"

Liz spun around. "Absolutely."

"We need to work on the Sorenson present value model and integrate it into the Daschle budget model."

Liz grabbed a folder off her desk. "Got it."

Kate joined Liz at the conference table in the corner of her office. Thank goodness she'd developed a present value template with all the assumptions on one page. Before, it had been for her own sanity, now she could easily discuss changes with Liz.

But the company's financial head, Michael, never even asked about the assumptions. He just wanted the end result. She loved her brother, but she didn't respect his work ethic or the way he ran his life. If it came to worst-case scenario, how would she report to him?

She couldn't. She wouldn't.

Liz pulled out her assumption sheet. "What's up?"

"Michael's asking for forecasts by this afternoon. The sticking point is the Sorenson lease negotiations."

Liz nodded her head. "We're still almost a million dollars apart."

"We can put together a low and high forecast. That will be Sorenson's request and our currently offered lease terms. The challenge will be to approximate where we think we'll end the negotiations."

"They seem determined to get the remodeling cost paid by us, maybe we backload the annual increases?"

Kate headed to the windows and stared down at the street. "That was my initial thought. Run through a couple of scenarios and see what happens. I don't want the ROI to drop below twelve percent."

"Will do." Liz made notes on her printout.

They walked through possible options. It was nice having someone who understood what she was doing.

"I'll drop everything and get this done. It shouldn't take long." Liz gathered her papers and placed them in the folder. "Anything else I can do for you?"

"Could you see if Jake in marketing can give me a half hour, ASAP?"

"Absolutely." Liz walked to the door and turned. "You don't happen to have any quarters I can borrow." She grimaced. "I need to keep a box of tampons in my drawer. That darn machine in the bathroom is hungry."

"Sure. I always keep change in my center drawer." Kate moved back to her desk and pulled some out for Liz. "Any time you need them, they're there."

"Thanks. I'll pay you back."

"Don't worry about it." She'd probably have the same need soon.

She sat and pulled out her notes on the marketing campaign she'd discussed with Michael almost five weeks ago. Or was that six? Ever since her mother had announced she had a lump her sense of time had been distorted.

She frowned. Two months ago? She'd gone from the bathroom to Michael's office because she'd had her period and hadn't wanted to have any accidents during their meeting.

She flipped through her calendar, looking for the smiley face she used to help her remember having her period wasn't a bad thing.

She had to flip back to March. Cold sweat pooled at her temples. It was May. Her mouth dropped open as she looked at the date.

She couldn't remember having her period since March.

She set her fingers against her abdomen.

She and Alex had had unprotected sex the first time they'd slept together.

And again last Sunday.

Pain throbbed behind her eyes. She couldn't be pregnant. Children weren't in her future.

She stood and paced. This couldn't happen. It was … stress.

But she was always regular. Every twenty-eight days.

She leaned her head against the cool windowpane. For once she couldn't think beyond the next minute. She didn't have a plan.

Well, she had one. She needed a pregnancy testing kit.

ALEX STOOD next to the coffee pot, inhaling the steam. He should get one of those pots that allowed a person to pour a cup while the coffee still brewed. Instead he waited in his shorts for the morning's first elixir. Well, not morning, two in the afternoon.

Where did he go from here? The sonata had been his Prometheus's rock for so long, he didn't know what to do with himself now.

First coffee, then food. After, he would send *Farewell* to Frederick. The title of the sonata had come to him after his phone call to Kate.

Then he'd move on with his life.

He picked up his phone and called his mother.

"Alex, how are you?"

Hard to answer that question. "I finished the sonata."

"Oh, that's fantastic. Wonderful." There was a catch in her voice.

"Are you crying?" he asked.

No." She sniffed. "Well, maybe. But they are happy tears. I know how hard this was."

He rested his head on the cabinet. "It was."

"Come to dinner. We'll celebrate. I'll try to get your father out of the office at a reasonable time. Tomorrow, does tomorrow work?"

"Perfect." It would be good to see his parents. Good to be around people who'd never met Kate. "I'll see you tomorrow."

Somehow, he had to forget Kate. Somehow, he had to stop wanting her.

He closed his eyes. The machine gave one last gasp. He poured and doctored his drink, then took a sip.

It burned his tongue.

KATE NODDED, praying she had the information she needed from the head of marketing. How could she think when she wanted to run to the nearest drugstore to buy a pregnancy test?

Back in her office she input the information for Michael, knowing she was enabling him by doing work *he* should be doing.

What else could she do? She couldn't tell her parents their son was an alcoholic. They had enough to worry about with Mom's treatments.

Kate looked at her hand clenched into a fist on her keyboard. No, she, Stephen and Timothy would handle Michael. They would make sure he acknowledged his problem.

And what about her problem? She shook her head. One issue at a time. Pull the forecasting information together.

Liz knocked and walked in. "Can we walk through these projections?"

"Absolutely." Anything to take her mind off her family.

Liz set up her laptop on the conference table. "I've printed out copies for you but wanted to make any changes as we talked." She checked her watch. "Michael stopped by when you were meeting with marketing. He's hoping we'll have the numbers by four."

"Okay, let's see what you've got."

Liz had labeled each of the scenarios. It was easy to follow her logic. They tweaked one small assumption.

"I've already linked the Sorenson projections into the Daschle budget files." Liz gave a small smile. "I hope that's all right. As soon as you give me the go, I'll send Michael the file."

"Fantastic." Kate had worried it would take most of the afternoon to reload the Sorenson lease into the forecasts. "Send the last model to Michael."

Liz typed on her keyboard.

Kate leaned back and let the clack of the keys lull her into a state of relaxation. Or as relaxed as she'd been since making love with Alex.

Sex. Not making love. Love didn't happen that fast. And love hurt once you did fall. Her dad was falling apart, couldn't do his job because the love of his life was ill.

And Alex wondered why she didn't want a relationship?

"Done." Liz closed her laptop. "I'm getting lunch or maybe it's an early dinner. Want anything?"

She'd forgotten to eat. "Sure. Soup. Chicken noodle if they have it." Something bland. Oh shoot. Maybe her upset stomach hadn't been from stress.

No. It had to be.

She dialed Michael's extension. "You have everything from my department now."

"Great. Stephen just sent me his data. Timothy is almost done too. Do you want to review it before it goes to Dad?"

Kate raised her eyebrows. She wanted to do her own work. But she didn't want to fail her parents. She would protect the company for them until they were back in charge. "Sure."

The receptionist waved at Kate from the doorway.

"Okay," Michael said. "I'll call as soon as we've compiled everything. Might be late. Then we can walk through it one more time, finalizing."

"Give me a heads up on an ETA."

"Will do."

The receptionist still hovered by the door. "Jenny, can I help you?"

Jenny turned around, holding a flower arrangement that stood almost two feet tall. "Someone's got an admirer."

The arrangement was huge. Jenny had her fingers wrapped around the vase and her hands didn't meet. Pinks, purples, yellows and bright greens. The colors were almost too vibrant.

Jenny set the flowers on Kate's conference table and pulled out the card. "Who are they from?"

Kate moved to the table and brushed her finger against a deep red rose. Her stomach churned. "I'm not sure."

Jenny handed Kate the envelope with a big grin. The card wasn't the tiny florist version, this was letter-sized.

Kate bounced it on her palm. "Thanks, Jenny."

The grin slid off Jenny's face. She backed out the door, looking like she wanted to snatch the card out of Kate's hand and rip it open. "You're welcome."

The envelope was sealed.

Toss the damn thing. The flowers had to be from Alex. No one else sent her flowers. Her parents might on her birthday, but she couldn't remember a man sending her flowers. She'd never allowed anyone to get that close.

Standing next to the trash, she held the envelope above the rectangular surface.

Her fingers wouldn't let the thing drop.

"Oh, hell." She sat in her chair and turned her back to her door. Loosening the flap, she slid the card out. Damn it, the card smelled like him, that woodsy pine scent with a hint of something extra.

Dearest Kate,

I think what we've discovered is worth fighting for. You're worth fighting for. I will always be here for you, whatever you need.

Know that you are loved. That I only want what is best for your life. If that means you are better off without me, then this is as it should be.

But if you aren't, if you miss me like I miss you, then call.

You are more than I ever hoped for, more than I ever knew I wanted. You're strong, committed and loyal to your family. You're intelligent, hardworking and dedicated. Christ—you even love the game of basketball.

But you don't believe you can have love and a career. There are other women who have both.

I think you can. I think we can. I want to try.

Please don't be afraid.

Love, Alex

The paper dropped onto her lap.

Why did he have to do something sweet? She couldn't handle sweet. She'd been cruel. Last night they'd made love and he'd spoken *those words*.

Now he'd done this. Woven love around her like a noose. Why couldn't he have left everything the way things were? They could have enjoyed each other. *Why?*

"Oh, what beautiful flowers. They're stunning," Liz said, adding, "I've got your soup."

Kate stared at the letter in her lap without turning. "Thanks. Leave it on the table, please. I'll grab it when I'm through."

"Sure thing."

Kate listened as Liz's footsteps receded out of her office. She should take the flowers to the break room for everyone to enjoy. Then Alex wouldn't always be on her mind.

She refolded the note and tucked it into the pocket of her briefcase.

SIXTEEN

KATE PUSHED OPEN THE RESTAURANT DOOR AND SEARCHED FOR Stephen and Timothy.

"Can I help you?" asked the hostess.

"I'm looking for my brothers."

"Tall, good-looking and brown-haired?" The hostess had that starry-eyed look her brothers brought out in women.

"Yes." She wasn't in the mood. All she could think about was the pregnancy test she was going to buy as soon as this dinner was over.

Stephen hadn't shared why they were meeting. Just that she shouldn't mention this to Michael. Guess she knew the meeting topic.

The hostess led the way through the maze of tables and booths.

"I see them," Kate said.

"I don't mind bringing you back. Are either of them dating anyone?" the young woman asked. She was pretty, in a too-young-for-her-brothers kind of way.

Kate rolled her eyes. "They're both taking their vows—for the priesthood."

"No!" The woman's smile slipped off her face. "What a waste."

If the hostess was too dumb to realize Kate was pulling her leg, she wouldn't disabuse her. Her brothers were too hedonistic to take vows. "There aren't enough priests."

Maybe Michael should take vows, although priests could still drink. That wouldn't help him.

"I'll just …" The hostess sent a longing look back to her brothers. "What a shame."

"What did you say to Kari?" Timothy asked as she sat.

"Who's Kari?"

"The hot hostess. She looked over here and shook her head."

Kate set her briefcase under the table. Alex's note was in the side pocket. "I told her you two were joining the priesthood."

Stephen choked on his beer. Timothy put a hand to his heart and then slapped Stephen on the back.

"What! Stephen said.

What the hell!" Timothy said at the same time.

She shrugged. Maybe if her life wasn't in such turmoil, she wouldn't have done it, but … "You can tell her I was kidding, but Lord, if she believed me, do you want to date someone so clueless?"

They looked at each other.

"She's hot. What more do I need?" Timothy asked.

"And you'll be carrying on the family name?" Kate said, disgusted. "The MacBains are in trouble."

"We didn't say we wanted children with her." Stephen winked. "But practice does make perfect."

Children. Her hand shook and she tucked it under the tablecloth. Why had she mentioned children?

Time to change the subject. "What about Michael?"

Her brothers exchanged a look. Sometimes she swore her

younger brothers shared a secret language. One that didn't require words.

The server took her drink order.

"Just ginger ale for me, thanks." This couldn't be morning sickness because it lasted every waking hour.

Once the server left, Stephen said, "You're right. Michael's drinking is out of hand."

Timothy nodded. "I was with him last night after we left Mom and Dad's. He knocked back enough whiskey to put us both under the table."

"I don't know why I didn't see it. He and I have had a few beers after our Thursday dinners. I always left the bar first." Stephen ran his fingers through the condensation on his beer mug. "I didn't see what was happening. I'm glad you did."

"It was Liz," she said. "She made a comment."

The server dropped off Kate's drink and took their order. She settled on a grilled chicken sandwich. Her brothers ordered like it was their last meal: steak, potatoes and salad.

When they were alone again, Timothy said, "We have to deal with him. Mom and Dad don't need this crap."

Kate nodded.

Stephen picked up his beer and then set it down without taking a drink. He pushed it to an empty spot at the table. "Hell, maybe I drink too much."

"When did it get this bad?" she asked. "How did we *not* notice?"

Stephen took a deep breath and let it out with a loud hiss. "He always liked having a good time. If I wanted a drink, Michael was available."

"He was bad the first summer after Sarah died," she said. "But not this bad."

"I wasn't even twenty-one, and he always bought the booze for my friends and me." Timothy grimaced.

"He still talks about her, about Sarah. Mostly when he's

been drinking." Stephen rested his elbows on the table and lowered his voice. "I think he still talks to her."

"What?" she asked.

Stephen ran his fingers through his hair. "The other night he was in the pub bathroom, but I could hear him … carrying on what I hope to God was a one-sided conversation."

They sank into their chairs.

Their food came and they settled into the business of eating. Her stomach churned. She cut the chicken into little pieces and rearranged them on her plate. Stephen frowned and she put a piece in her mouth.

It tasted like she was eating rubber. She drank her ginger ale.

"He's not getting his work done in the office," she said. "I just put together the forecasts. Apparently Dad asked for them last week."

Stephen set down his knife and fork. "Why in hell did Dad put Michael in charge?"

Timothy pointed with his knife. "It should have been you."

Kate wanted to cheer. "Mom asked me to watch out for him. Maybe they're hoping he'll straighten up."

"That's not happening," Stephen said. "Christ, did you see him Sunday? Smell him?"

"I thought I would get drunk as the sweat rolled off him," Timothy joked.

No one cracked a smile.

"What do we do?" Kate asked. She held her head. How much more work could she handle?

"We have to confront him." Stephen cut into his steak, scraping the knife on his plate with a squeal.

"What do we know about having an intervention?" Timothy asked.

"I guess we'd better find out," Kate said.

"You look tired," Stephen said. "I'll do the research. You don't have to do everything, Katie."

"Thanks." She didn't say anything about the tired comment. She'd looked in the mirror.

Timothy nodded as he said, "We'll talk to him Thursday night."

"Good. That gives us a couple of days." She let her shoulders relax. "Maybe we shouldn't meet at the pub. We should take Dad's suggestion and have Bernice order in food."

"Good idea. Hey," Timothy said, his mouth full of steak, "I liked Alex."

She wasn't discussing Alex with her brothers. "Chew your food before you talk."

"Yeah, yeah." Timothy took another huge bite. "Once he figured out how we played basketball, he did pretty well. Too bad he didn't take you down. When Mom doesn't ref, you get away with too much crap."

Alex had taken her down. Or at least taken her against the door. She wiggled in her chair. Then she'd annihilated him.

"I've got some errands to run, can one of you pick up the check?" She had to get out of here.

"Yeah," Stephen said. "Wish we could get charged based on what you ate. Do you want a to go box?"

"No. See you Thursday." Kate heaved a deep sigh as she walked away from the table. Maybe Michael would recognize his problem, and everything would return to normal.

Her stomach twisted. Apparently her body didn't think normal was possible.

KATE WANTED Alex to be here with her. Ridiculous.

She stared at her phone's timer, trying to ignore the pregnancy test stick on a tissue on the bathroom counter. It was like ignoring an elephant in the room.

Who knew three minutes could take this long?

She brushed her teeth. Washed her face. Started on her makeup. Whatever the stick said, she still had to work this morning.

Her timer trilled. Swallowing, she looked at the small window. *Pregnant.*

Her fingers squeezed the offending plastic wand. *No.*

She sank to the bathroom floor. Black spots filled her vision, and she tucked her head between her knees.

This couldn't happen. The test must be wrong. What was it called? A false positive. She'd screwed up the test somehow. Hadn't followed the instructions.

Her stomach jerked and heaved. She wrapped her arm around her belly.

The cold seeped in through her thin pajama pants. She rocked back and forth. This wasn't what she wanted.

She would take the test again. Her life couldn't be this screwed up.

She drank water, hoping to be able to pee, but couldn't. Apparently she didn't have anything left in her.

She would get ready for work and take the test again in the next half hour. It wouldn't be the hallowed waters from her first pee of the day, but maybe it would show she wasn't pregnant.

Kate pushed herself off the floor and finished her makeup, carefully blending concealer under her eyes.

She dragged herself out of the bathroom. A toasted bagel settled her churning stomach, the first food she'd eaten in almost forty-eight hours. That could be why she was light-headed. It couldn't be because she was pregnant. Her body must be one of the few that gave inaccurate results.

She wasn't supposed to have children.

What about her IUD? When she'd first tried birth control, she'd had trouble breathing. Her ob-gyn said it was a reaction to the hormones. Between that and her family history of breast cancer, her doctor advised alternatives to birth control pills.

She rubbed her eyes with a trembling hand. The odds of getting pregnant with an IUD were higher, but not that much.

She and Alex had had unprotected sex. Twice.

She took another bite of her dry bagel. This was stress.

Choosing an outfit, she zipped the skirt. It hung off her hips. See, she was losing weight. If she was pregnant, wouldn't everything be getting tighter?

The last thing she did before leaving the condo was take another test. This time she checked her emails as she waited.

Pregnant.

She'd buy another test tonight. The results had to change.

ALEX HANDED the envelope to the florist. He'd decided to send tulips and daffodils. "Send this with the arrangement, please."

"She'll love the flowers," said the woman who'd helped him.

Alex doubted it. Kate was stubborn. What she didn't know was Alex could be stubborn too. Hell, when he'd wanted to play basketball, he'd taken on both his parents. That had been a battle of wills like no other in his life.

"You know what? I think I'll send flowers to my mother too." Alex picked out an arrangement.

"Do you want a Mother's Day card with these?" the clerk asked.

"Mother's Day?"

"It's a week from Sunday."

"No, I'll send something next week." He hoped he

wouldn't have forgotten the date. Of course his mother would likely forget if left on her own. His sisters would remember, and then he would have become a scapegoat for their jokes.

He should be sad. The woman he loved had pushed him away. Instead he hoped her knee-jerk reaction hid strong feelings for him.

For some reason she had antiquated concepts of women, working and love. They would have to get past them. It was only after he'd said he loved her that she'd freaked out.

So, he would send her gifts each day until she agreed to talk to him.

He whistled as he walked out of the shop, a tune that had haunted him since Sunday. Kate-inspired.

You can push me away, but I'll always be there,
I'll catch you if you fall.

The pulse of a basketball slamming against the court drove through him.

Push all you want, but I'm here to stay,
You know I'll have it all,
And the all includes you.

Yeah. It would work for Central Standard Time. The lead male singer could carry the range Alex envisioned.

He turned the radio off before he drove to his next stop. Lyrics and melodies were enough to fill the space as he headed to the coffee shop to meet Frederick. The artistic director had called but hadn't given his reaction to the completed *Farewell*.

It was his best work, ever. If Frederick didn't like it, too bad. He'd completed his obligation. Something he hadn't thought possible two months ago.

Inside the coffee shop, the enticing scent of beans wrapped around him. Frederick waved from a corner table. Ordering a plain coffee, he doctored it with milk and then joined his friend.

"Congratulations." Frederick shook his hand.

"Thanks." Alex took his seat.

Their chairs scraped the floor as they settled at the table.

"I'll admit, I never thought you'd finish the sonata," Frederick said.

"Sometimes miracles happen." But did Frederick like the piece?

"I like the new title too. The last one would have been a problem with our audience." Frederick took a sip of his coffee. His eyes closed as he savored the brew.

"But did you like it?" Alex blurted out.

Frederick's eyes blinked open. "Of course I did. I told you on the phone."

"No, I would have remembered that." Alex relaxed back in his chair.

His friend slapped his palm on the table. "I loved it. And I played it to some of the principals. They loved it too."

Alex wanted to call Kate and let her know. Let her know she'd been the catalyst.

Frederick stuffed a piece of coffeecake in his mouth. Again he closed his eyes, savoring the experience. Just like Kate had done with her pancakes.

"Will you guest conduct when we perform the piece?" Frederick asked.

Something clicked inside him. Something right. "I'd love to."

"I'd like to see if your mother would come out of retirement and bring both your sisters in too." Frederick had a sharp canny look on his face. "Playing up the musically gifted Adamski family could get the orchestra additional press."

"You want me to conduct the three women in my family?" He'd never worked with any of them, other than playing around at home.

Frederick laughed. "I think it would be great, for your family and for the Chamber Orchestra."

"I'll talk to them." It could be fun.

"I'll have my assistant coordinate contracts and schedules. We'd like to use the piece at the beginning of next season. We'll play up the local composer and musician angle in the season renewals."

"You sure that won't drive your ticket holders away?"

"It will drive up our box office. We'll want your bio and media packet."

"I'll get Aubrey to forward it to you." Hell, Alex had forgotten to let his business manager know he'd completed the sonata. He'd avoided talking to her for almost two years.

How had he let his business life slide out of control?

Well, he was back. And Kate MacBain didn't stand a chance.

"ANOTHER BOUQUET." Liz set a vase of flowers on Kate's desk. "Who is this guy, and does he have a brother?"

"Sorry, just sisters." But she didn't give Liz Alex's name.

Kate ran a finger on the petal of a tulip. She loved tulips. Lord, there must be three dozen. They were a riot of colors: red, yellow, orange. And all different shapes. Beautiful.

Why was he so ... persistent?

Liz handed her the envelope stuck in the center of the flowers. Another letter. Couldn't he use the small cards like everyone else?

Her hand shook as she reached for the damn envelope.

Liz must have seen something in her face because she backed out the door. "Let me know if you need anything. Like taking this guy off your hands ..."

As if Kate had a chance at wishing him out of her life. *Pregnant.*

And the father of her child had sent her flowers, two days in a row.

She slipped a finger under the flap and tugged, getting a paper cut in the process of opening the envelope. *That was Alex's fault too.*

She sucked on the cut as she pulled out the sheet of paper. He'd written the message on composition paper. Funny guy.

Dearest Kate,

I miss you. Funny how quickly I've come to need to hear your voice every day. I miss the quick flash of intelligence in your eyes as we talk. I miss the way you curl into my body as we watch a movie. I miss your scowl over the state of my house. I even miss the way you played basketball, intense and competitive—in the moment. Just like you make love.

She swallowed the lump in her throat. She missed him too. But he wanted too much.

I miss the smell of your hair. I would sometimes wake in the middle of the night and take a deep breath. Somehow it calms me.

I'd like to talk to you. I surprised you with my feelings. They're my feelings, you don't have to reciprocate. But we should talk. We should not waste something so special. It doesn't come around often. We need to grab all the happiness we can. Who knows what life has in store for us? I think we should latch on to the things or people that make us happy.

When had she last been happy? When she'd been with Alex. He made the chaos of her life better.

I should have sent you flowers before. But you came into my life like a combine through a wheat field. (Yeah – I've never seen one of those in real life. But it's how I feel—chopped up, harvested and flattened.) You forced me to look at my life and realize I wasn't living. You forced me to feel.

You gave me the gift of life—of living.

Thank you—all my love,

Alex

The gift of life. She touched her still flat abdomen. What he didn't know was he'd given her the same thing.

What should she do?

She'd made an appointment with her gynecologist. They were fitting her in this afternoon. She'd choked out the fact that she wanted to confirm she was pregnant.

She could have an abortion. No one would know. No one would ever be the wiser. Her lips pinched together, and the words of his letter blurred.

She'd seen Alex's face as he'd told her about Meredith's deception.

But this was her body. She and Alex weren't married. They hadn't talked about having children. This was *her* body, *her* life.

Her lips trembled. It was his child too.

She could let Alex have the child. He would do it. He would raise a child by himself, or with the next woman he loved.

Her hand fisted around the letter. She didn't want Alex to love anyone else. How sick was that? She couldn't see a place for him in her life, but she didn't want him finding happiness with another woman.

What a selfish bitch she was.

She tucked the letter in her briefcase.

What could she do?

The only thing she knew. Work.

Kate buried herself in all the things she'd set aside from the day before. She tweaked the next volley on the Sorenson lease negotiations. Then printed a number of copies.

Now what? She could send them an email, or she could exchange the terms face-to-face.

Pulling out a tablet of paper, she listed the pros and cons of a personal meeting. Looking at her list, she sided with face-to-face. Maybe they could finalize this renewal.

She needed a bathroom break. She needed caffeine. Her throat squeezed shut. Until she made a decision, she wouldn't harm the baby.

She stopped by Liz's desk on the way out of her office.

"Can you call Sorenson and see if they can meet for lunch. I've got the next offer ready. Hopefully this will be the last set of terms exchanged."

"Sure. Where do you want to meet?" Liz asked. "And do you want me there?"

Kate named a restaurant on the Daschle building's first floor. "Let's keep it easy for them. Show them how much they want to stay in their space." She brushed her stomach and then added, "I'd like you there too."

"Absolutely."

Kate pulled the copies off the printer and handed Liz the terms. "Here's what I'm proposing. It's still not our bottom line, but it gives them a little more leeway on the buildout. I've added ten more parking spots. Maybe that will be the leverage to sign this deal."

"Parking. Great idea."

Kate headed to the bathroom and then stopped by Michael's office. She hadn't seen him all morning. Her brother's back was to her as she walked into his office.

"Did you get the projections pulled together?"

Michael turned. Had he slept in his suit? His eyes were glassy.

"Almost," he said. "Can you look at it when I'm done?"

Normally she would have double-checked the forecasts and made revisions. After her dinner with her brothers, she knew she was enabling his sloppy work habits. That had to stop. "I'm sorry, I can't. I've got a lot going on today."

Shock filled his face. "But you always review the forecasts."

"I don't have time. I'm finalizing the Sorenson lease."

Her information was as accurate as she could make it. Michael would have to pick up his own slack.

"Oh, okay sure. It's just …"

Her fingers clenched into fists. This was the family business, and she wanted it to succeed. Succeed and thrive.

But she couldn't keep covering for him. Couldn't keep finding his mistakes. If Michael couldn't handle his job, they needed someone who could. She wasn't her brother's safety net.

Her stomach ached. This time it wasn't hormones. This was pure worry. "I've got to go."

She moved slowly down the hallway, nodding to her co-workers. Had Michael been in free fall since Sarah's death or had this started when Mom got her diagnosis? Had the family ignored all the signs, or was he hitting rock bottom? *Please, let that be the case.* She didn't want the family to go through any more stress. Between cancer, her pregnancy and Michael's drinking, that should be enough to satisfy the fates, right?

~

"WHAT CAN I do for you today?" the florist asked.

Alex rolled his shoulders. Kate may not know it, but this was full-out assault and damn the torpedoes.

"I want to send two more bouquets." He looked around the small showroom. "No, maybe flowering plants."

"Do you want help?" the woman offered.

"I know when I'm out of my element. Help." And being in love with Kate sure had him that way. He'd never, *never*, felt this off-kilter, like he was a composition and had been sitting in dissonance for way too long.

He wanted Kate to feel that way.

The clerk walked him around, discussing the pros and cons of different plants.

"Let's go with the two orchids," he said.

One of the spray of pinky-purple blossoms was for Kate's mom. He hoped it would make her smile. The other was for Kate at home. She didn't have any plants at her condo.

Pulling a slip of paper from his pocket, he added, "This envelope goes to the Edina address."

He handed over a large envelope with a note and a CD inside.

"Got it." The florist set the plants on the counter.

"And this one to the Minneapolis address." He handed her a smaller envelope.

He'd been dumped and was still smiling. There was something perverse about him.

But it was the expression on Kate's face when he'd said he loved her that had given him the glimmer of hope. Before her face had crumpled.

Kate gave so much of herself to her work and family, but she needed love too. Convenient, since he loved her.

"Do you want to pick out another arrangement for tomorrow?" the clerk asked.

He checked his watch. "You can pick the bouquet for tomorrow. And send it to her office address." He pointed to the paper on the countertop. "This is her condo."

"She's one lucky woman." She added up the total. He squirmed a little at the damage. Then she took his credit card. "What about a card for tomorrow's delivery?"

She would know they were from him. She'd better not be getting flowers from another man.

"No note for tomorrow." He struggled with each note, trying to find the right words to get her to pick up the phone. To get her to realize they were perfect together.

He would work on another note tonight after dinner with Gabe.

"I'M glad you could meet for lunch," Kate said.

Both Eric and Carol, the law firm's business manager, were

attending her impromptu meeting. She hoped that was a good sign.

"Liz indicated you'd come up with some creative solutions to our requests," said Eric.

"We have." A server hovered near the table. "Why don't we order?"

With drinks in front of them, Kate nodded at Liz. Her assistant pulled out copies of the latest and hopefully last offer.

"We've agreed to add another $50,000 to your buildout allowance," Kate said. She walked them through the changes and the items she agreed to change. She tried to decipher their expressions. Were they happy? Were they ready to pull the plug?

"I also reviewed all the calls we've received from your office. Although you've not mentioned this in negotiations, we'd like to offer your firm ten more ramp parking spots." Ten. The exact number of new partners in the firm.

A smile broke across Eric's face. "Parking has been an issue. But we wanted the remodel more than comfort. There are times that I've parked across the street. Usually when it's snowing."

Carol asked, "This won't affect the visitor spots we're allocated, will it?"

"No, although we should look at the traffic. You're being charged for those spots. I can have the ramp do an analysis on the percentage of use."

"Good. Good," Carol said.

Liz made a note. "I'll contact them."

Kate set her hands flat on the table. She knew how much Eric loved to negotiate, but MacBain couldn't take any bigger a discount on this deal. "MacBain loves the Sorenson Law Firm as a tenant. You're easy to work with." She smiled. "Tough negotiators, but fair. These terms are better than market, but it's because we appreciate your loyalty."

"And we like working with MacBain," said Eric. He frowned. "Although I was surprised Mitch Thornton asked to be shown around our offices. I hope you're not planning to rent our space."

Liz shook her head. "With their upcoming merger with the Burlington firm, they're looking to consolidate. I didn't realize Mr. Thornton would request a tour. I apologize. That's not the way I would have made the introduction."

My, my. Kate didn't blink. Her assistant was canny. Even though she hadn't known anything about this development, she pretended they were both in the know. Liz deserved a raise.

The managing partner looked a little mollified. "No problem because the Thorntons are not getting their hands on the best legal space in Minneapolis." He nodded at Carol.

Hope bubbled inside her. Maybe they'd found the right combination of perks and terms.

"We have a deal," said Eric.

"That's wonderful." She and Liz grinned.

"Maybe we should have a little champagne to celebrate," Eric suggested.

Kate agreed. The server brought their food and a very nice bottle of Cristal.

"To another successful ten years." Carol raised her glass.

The glasses clinked. Kate took a token sip.

They passed the rest of the meal with quiet conversation. She forced down half of her soup and salad.

She wanted her appetite back. She wanted her life back.

As she and Liz walked back to the office, she asked, "I wonder if it was the parking spaces or the fact that another law firm was interested in their space?"

"Who cares. We nailed a deal that's a win/win for both parties, and there's still a respectable return on investment. Nice work."

"Nice work, yourself. We're a good team. How did you get another law firm to ask to see the space?" Kate asked.

"I don't know if I did. When I talked to my real estate friend, she said she was working with the Thornton firm on space. I asked her to mention the Daschle building if she got a chance." Liz tapped her lip. "Maybe we could consolidate some of the tenants and have both the Sorenson and Thornton firms in the building."

"Go ahead and look at it."

They reached their office, and Kate stopped in front of the building. "I've got an appointment. Can you update the terms and finalize the lease extension?"

"Sure." Liz gave her a high five. "Great work."

"You too."

Her doctor's office was within walking distance, so she headed to Eighth Street.

Where was the normal euphoria that came with closing a big deal? This was what she lived for, this was her life.

In the elevator, she closed her eyes, light-headed again. She needed to get through the day. Tomorrow she would get excited. It was what drove her, that high of getting the best deal possible for the company. Of being the best, of knowing that only she could get the job done.

But Liz had been a big part of their success.

She registered at reception. The woman's cheerfulness grated against her like the incessant screeching of metal-on-metal. Didn't the receptionist understand not everyone was happy to be here?

Three other women filled the waiting room, all at different stages of pregnancy. She'd never noticed pregnant women until yesterday, now they were everywhere. Two wore suit jackets over their maternity clothes. One had a nice sweater and pants on.

God, she would have to buy new clothes.

She stared at their faces. They didn't look exhausted or depressed. They looked … happy. Even the woman who rubbed her hand on her belly, engrossed in a legal document. She looked like she'd swallowed a watermelon, an award-winning watermelon.

"When are you due?" Kate asked.

The woman looked up with a smile. "Two months."

"Two months?"

She laughed. "I'm having twins."

"Oh." Should she say congratulations to that kind of announcement? "Good luck?"

"Thanks." The woman pushed on her stomach. "Oof. Sometimes one of them gets their foot stuck under my ribs."

Kate's mouth dropped. How did women do this? How could a body stretch and grow like that?

"Kate MacBain?" a nurse called from the doorway.

She hurried toward the nurse. "That's me."

As they walked down the hall, the nurse smiled. "It looks like you're here for a pregnancy test."

She swallowed. "Yes."

"Okay, we'll get the basics done."

They stopped at a scale. Then her blood was drawn and her blood pressure taken. She peed in a cup. Finally she waited in an exam room.

The paper covering the exam table crinkled as she sat. She was too tired to grab a magazine from the rack on the wall. She didn't want to look at skinny models. If she was pregnant, if she kept the baby, it would be a long time before she was skinny again.

She pleated the paper and stared out the window, but because of the angle of the blinds all she saw was the colorless sky. She examined the posters on the walls, pictures of pregnant women's bellies. Gross. And there was a model of something that looked like a uterus on the small desk.

She swung her feet, took a deep breath, and then another. The smell of bleach and disinfectant burned the back of her throat.

Mom had done this four times.

But her mom was a super mom. Able to clean small buildings with the swipe of her hand.

There was a knock on the door and Dr. Waverley strode in. "Hi, Kate."

Kate nodded. "Dr. Waverley."

She'd been Dr. Waverley's patient for about five years, ever since she'd had problems with birth control. She'd liked her from their first meeting. Her hair might have a little more salt and pepper than five years ago, but the smile on her face was always friendly.

The doctor washed her hands and stood in front of her, pulling on a pair of gloves. "I understand we're verifying a pregnancy."

Kate nodded, not sure her voice would actually work if she spoke.

"I'd like you to lie down." The doctor pulled the stirrups around and directed her to move closer to the bottom of the table. Kate kept the paper blanket anchored at her waist, but a cool breeze swept underneath and chilled her.

She looked at the ceiling, still following Dr. Waverley's directions and adjustments.

A rolling tray set with instruments clattered across the floor. So did a stool. The stool cushion whooshed as the doctor sat.

"Spread your legs a little wider please."

The doctor stood and her fingers entered her body. She pushed from below and with the other hand, gently manipulated her belly. Kate held her breath, pinching her lips together. It took forever.

The doctor pulled away, and Kate heard the snap of the rubber gloves.

"You can sit up."

Kate struggled, pulling her legs under the paper and sitting cross-legged on the exam table.

Dr. Waverley set a hand on her thigh. "Your blood work and the physical exam confirm you're pregnant."

Kate wrapped her hands around her stomach. Goose bumps covered her arms and legs. "Okay."

"I take it this wasn't planned." Her voice was soft and warm.

"No." The word croaked out.

"First things first. We'll do an ultrasound and then I'll remove your IUD."

"Okay." She was pregnant. Her body shook.

Up until now she'd hoped the pregnancy tests, all three of them, had been wrong. That there was something in the chemistry on her body that elicited a false positive.

Pregnant.

KATE COULDN'T MAKE herself go back to the office. She walked back to her condo and gotten her car. A prenatal prescription sat on the passenger seat. Her blood was iron deficient. Dr. Waverley said it explained her light-headedness.

The doctor had asked whether she was keeping the baby. Kate hadn't answered.

Fate was derailing her plans.

She merged onto the freeway and headed west. The radio blared with news of the day's markets. She shut it off. She didn't care where the Dow Jones Industrial average had closed.

Merging into traffic, she blinked. Shoot, she was heading west at four-thirty in the afternoon. Rush hour.

This was why she commuted on foot. And it helped her stay in shape, especially as she didn't like going to the gym.

What would she do now? Where would she live? She swallowed. A baby didn't care if there was a backyard, but what about a toddler?

She might have a daughter. A girl with Alex's black hair and chocolate eyes. Or maybe she would get true green eyes like Timothy. Black hair, green eyes …

Or a boy? Someone who loved sports as much as she had. Or could create music like his daddy. Or maybe her daughter would be an athlete.

Oh, God.

She knew where her subconscious was taking her. Home. She needed to go home. To her mother.

SEVENTEEN

BEFORE GETTING OUT OF THE CAR, KATE REAPPLIED SOME makeup to cover up her paleness.

Closing the cover back on the visor mirror, she headed into the house. In the entry, she dropped her briefcase and made her way to the kitchen.

Their housekeeper was in the pantry. "Hey, Maria."

"What a wonderful surprise." Maria came out of the pantry, set an onion on the counter and opened her arms. "I didn't get a hug Sunday. You can make up for it now."

Kate pulled the small woman into her arms. Maria enclosed her in a warm hug.

"I sure wish Mom and Dad had found you when I was younger."

Maria patted her back and stepped away. "You told me that every day the summer before your first year in college. Sure made me feel needed."

She was needed, especially now. "Where are Mom and Dad?"

"After your mother's treatment, your father went to the

office. Patty's resting in the sunroom." She frowned. "Why aren't you working?"

"I had an appointment and decided to swing by. It's weird not seeing her at the office." At least one of her parents were always around. She missed seeing them.

"Well, you'll be staying for dinner."

"Okay." It hadn't been her plan, but Maria's tone suggested she shouldn't argue.

"Take your mother a cup of tea," Maria said. "What would you like to drink?"

She hadn't looked at the pamphlets Dr. Waverly had given her. She wasn't sure if tea was on the *No* list or not. "Water would be great."

With a beverage in both hands, Kate headed to the opposite side of the house. She pushed through the partially open glass door and stepped into the lush sunroom. Light flickered through the palm and ficus trees near the tall greenhouse windows. The earthy smell of dirt filled her nose. She caught the fragrance of oranges. Mom's trees must be in bloom. Water splashed from the small fountain near the lounge chairs.

Her mother lay on one of the chaise lounges, wrapped in a couple of throws. Her eyes were closed. Her skin was sallow.

A lump rose in Kate's throat. This had to be temporary, her mother's body battling the cancer inside her. Her mother would conquer this. She was just resting, that was all.

She tiptoed over and set her mother's tea on the table next to a beautiful orchid. Dad must have bought flowers for Mom. Maybe it was an early Mother's Day present.

Kate shouldn't wait for Mother's Day to send her mother flowers. Alex's bouquets should have triggered her to send flowers to her mother. She hadn't thought about anything but herself through all of this. Instead of worrying about her mother, she'd worried how her mother's cancer would affect her.

God, she was a terrible person. Why would anyone want to be around her? Why did Alex insist he love her? She didn't know how to love. She'd witnessed her parents' love fill the house, and she hadn't learned a thing.

Well, she was here now. Now wasn't about her, or Alex or the baby growing inside her. Now was about being what her mother needed her to be. Being here for her.

Placing her water on the floor she settled into a lounge chair. Even though the room was warm, she took the throw off the back and wrapped herself in its soft comfort. She toed off her shoes and stretched out her legs, letting her eyes close.

She matched her breathing with her mother's. Her muscles softened. Her thoughts slowed.

Alex would love this room. He would love the light, the music of the fountain, and for some reason she thought he would like the earthy smell.

She drifted, not asleep, but aware when her mother shifted and turned. Kate's breath sighed in and out and she relaxed for the first time in days. The sweet orange scent filled the air.

Her mother shifted again. Her breathing not as slow and rhythmic as it had been.

Kate kept her breathing deep and slow, unwilling to break her peace.

"What a wonderful surprise." Her mother's voice came out a little rusty.

Kate took a cleansing breath.

She wiggled her toes and moved her fingers. Then she opened her eyes.

Her mother grinned at her.

"Did you have a good nap?" Kate asked.

"The best. It's lovely in here. I've never had the time to enjoy this space." Mom waved her hand. "Oh, I take care of the plants, but enjoying the place I've created is something different. Now I have the time. Of course I fall asleep more often than not."

Her mother shifted and sat up a little more.

"That's because it's peaceful." Kate rolled her shoulders and slid a little higher in the chair. "I might have fallen asleep too."

"And look, Maria sent you in with a cup of tea."

"It's probably cold, do you want a fresh cup?"

Mom took a sip. "Lukewarm. No, I don't need anything more. If Maria had her way, I'd be floating in tea. I think she's adding healing herbs."

"I hope so." Kate swung her legs over the side of the chair and dropped her feet to the floor, facing her mother. "It's hard seeing you so tired."

"I know." Mom laid her hand on Kate's knee. "That's one of the reasons I don't come into the office. I don't want you kids worrying."

"I miss talking to you," Kate blurted out.

A smile broke across her mother's face, brightening everything in the room. "It's wonderful discovering that your grown children still want you around."

"I've taken you for granted." Kate pushed the throw off her shoulders. "It's only been a week and you're missed."

"That's sweet."

"Speaking of sweet, is Dad sending you plants?" She pointed at the orchid on the table.

"Isn't that beautiful? No, your father didn't send it, Alex did."

A jolt ran through her. "Alex?"

"Yes, with a lovely note and a CD of his songs. You've got a keeper there."

"I …" She couldn't form any words. Alex had sent flowers to her mother? She hadn't thought about sending flowers, but Alex had.

She rubbed her hands on her face. Ever since her parents had announced she would be cleaning houses, her life had fallen apart. Nothing fit in their organized boxes anymore. When would her life settle down? She pressed a hand to her belly. Oh God, probably never.

"What's wrong?" her mother asked. "You look upset. Are you sick?"

"I'm … I'm pregnant." She closed her eyes, afraid to see disappointment on her mother's face.

"Oh, my." Her mother's weight settled next to her.

Warm arms wrapped around her waist.

"A baby. Wow." She heard amazement in her mother's voice. "I'll be a grandmother."

"I'm sorry." Kate opened her eyes and stared into her mother's hazel ones. "This wasn't the way I wanted to tell you."

"You're having a baby." There was that wonder again infusing her mother's voice.

"I guess." Kate blew out a breath strong enough to ruffle the hair that crossed her cheek.

"You guess?"

"I never planned on having children. Ever."

"Children have a way of changing a person's priorities." Her mother stiffened. "Were you thinking of *not* having this child?"

Kate had been raised Catholic. She knew the stance of her religion teachers and priests. She wasn't sure what she believed. It was hard to accept cannon law formulated by only men. She believed in a woman's right to choose.

"I don't know," she admitted. "I haven't lived with the knowledge very long."

Her mother took her hand. "It's Alex's baby, right?"

Kate nodded her head.

"What does he want?"

"I know he wants children." It was why he was divorced. "But I broke up with him Sunday. He doesn't know."

"I'm sorry." Her mother's arm stole around Kate's waist for another hug. "What can I do to help?"

"You need to get healthy. I'll figure out what I'm going to do." She nestled her head onto her mother's shoulder. "As I was lying here, I realized how selfish I was. I haven't sent you flowers. It was all about *me*, not you."

"That's not true," her mother said. "When I told you about the cancer, the first words out of your mouth were *what can I do?*"

"Really?" She remembered the devastation but didn't remember offering to help.

"Of all you children, you're the one who hasn't figured out her boundaries. To you, being part of our family is living and breathing MacBain." Her mother squeezed her waist. "How much you are loved isn't based on how well you bring in the next lease deal."

"I … I don't think that." Did she?

"Oh, honey, you do. It's one of the reasons your dad and I thought you should get a better perspective on the company."

She grimaced. "That's shorthand for cleaning houses, right?"

"Yes. If you left the company today, I would still love you, Kathleen Patricia MacBain. I love you because you're *you*. Not because of your formidable negotiating skills." Her mother took her hand. "I love you because you love your family. You love the company, but you don't know how to balance your passion."

"But …"

"Let me finish." Her mother sighed. "I'm sorry you and Alex broke up. You seemed good together, in tune with each other. Happy. Don't you think it's strange that he sent me the orchid?"

Kate touched one of the petals. "Not strange. He's on a flower campaign. I've gotten bouquets at the office two days in a row."

"So, he doesn't think it's over."

Kate stood, no longer able to keep still. "He thinks he's in love with me."

She paced and stared at the basketball court. They'd almost stripped each other's clothes off in front of her family.

Her mother stood behind her. The stroke of her mother's hand on her back was familiar and comforting. "And do you love him? Is that why you've pushed him away?"

"I don't know." She turned into her mother's hug. "I don't understand why I'm such a mess. Why my life is such a mess."

Her mother's arms tightened around her. "Maybe this is one of those life lessons that aren't planned, but just happen."

"But I like everything planned."

Her mother patted her back. "Then you'd better plan how you're to tell Alex."

KATE GAZED at the orchid on the coffee table. She'd come home from dinner with her parents two nights ago and the plant had been at her doorstep. Along with another note.

Dearest Kate,

You'd think I'd be grieving. But I'm not. I'm glad I had you in my life. Glad we had so much joy together. And I'm not talking about making love. I'm talking about sharing a cup of coffee with you, a meal. Sharing my observations of my day and listening to yours.

As intense as you are, as directed, there is a calmness, a caring, that you exude. The way you cleaned my house and would leave it looking—inviting. The turned down sheets on my bed, the plumped-up cushions in the family room. You may think you're not domestic, but you knew how to make my house a home.

I want you to share my home.

I miss you. Love, Alex

Kate reached for her phone to call but stopped. She didn't know what to think of his vision of her. She didn't know anything about making a house a home.

Kate glanced around her condo. It was comfortable, but was it a home?

As a real estate professional, it was location, location, location. She'd picked this building because of its access to the office. She could be at her desk within five minutes. How many people could say their commute in a Minnesota winter didn't change?

She set the letter on the pile and picked up the one she'd received today.

My Kate,

You can push me away, but I'll always be there

I'll catch you if you fall.

Push all you want, but I'm here to stay,

You know I'll have it all

And the all includes you.

These are the lyrics of the song I'm working on. Kate's Song. *I won't call it that. I would never embarrass you like that. But that is the inspiration. It's unbelievable how meeting you has freed me to compose.*

Please call. I miss you. I love you. Alex

How could he be so upbeat when she couldn't even sleep? She pushed on her stomach. That was why.

Two days of living with this … news … still hadn't made it real. Two days of rehearsing what she would tell Alex and she hadn't come up with the words.

Her mother had been happy at the thought of becoming a grandmother. At least Mom had agreed to keep the news a secret, even though Kate knew she wanted to tell Dad.

She didn't want to disappoint her father. She didn't want her own dreams shattered by a baby.

A tear snuck down her cheek and she swiped at it with her shoulder. Fucking hormones.

She couldn't put off contacting Alex any longer. She sent him a text.

Can we talk—tomorrow? My condo at seven?

She hit send.

No taking it back now.

Her phone beeped signaling an incoming text.

I'll bring dinner. Love—A

She was too exhausted to tell him no, too worn out to beg him to stop using the "L" word. Too everything.

ALEX SHIFTED the pizzas and punched the elevator button for her floor. Hurdle one accomplished, Kate had buzzed him in the security door. Now to get her to let him in the condo.

Shouldn't be a problem. She'd contacted him. A text, but it was something.

What if she wanted him to stop contacting her? What if she had a *cease and desist* speech ready for him? Or worse, if she threatened him with, what were they called, an injunction. No, a restraining order.

He shook his head as he got off the elevator. She wouldn't have asked him to her home if she'd gone the legal route. They'd be meeting in court. Still, his hand wavered a little as he knocked on her door.

The lock clicked. The door swung open.

Kate wore sweatpants and a sweatshirt. Her expression was solemn enough for a funeral. His heart pounded.

She wouldn't look him in the eye as she held the door open.

Without a word, she took the pizza boxes from him.

He followed her to the kitchen. His arms itched to hug her. Instead he said, "Thank you."

She turned, a frown on her face. "For …?"

"For finally getting in touch."

Her mouth dropped open a little. "Yeah … well …" She opened the pizza box. "Thank you for all the flowers," she mumbled. "And thanks for coming. I don't feel like going out."

"You're welcome." Their politeness grated against his skin like the scratching of a novice violinist. "How's your mother?"

"She's …" Kate's eyes closed and she sank into her chair. "She's tired, but … amazing. She and Dad keep saying the treatments are going as expected."

He touched her cold fingers, then closed his hand around hers, warming it. "She'll get through this."

Her eyebrows raised a little. She tugged her hand out of his, shaking her head.

"Let's eat before the pizza gets cold." He set a couple of slices of pepperoni and sausage on the plate already on the table.

She took a slice of chicken Alfredo pizza. He'd picked it up, knowing it was her favorite. He wanted every possible advantage in his fight for their happiness.

He pushed away from the table and headed to the fridge. "Do you want a beer?" he asked.

"Umm, no. A glass of milk?"

He pulled a beer and the milk out of the fridge. Then he retrieved a glass from the cupboard.

She hadn't taken a bite of her pizza.

"Stomach still bothering you?" he asked.

She nodded, finally bringing the slice up to her lips.

"Maybe you should see a doctor," he suggested before taking a big bite himself.

She coughed, her face turning red.

He patted her back. "Are you okay?"

She coughed once more into her napkin. "Fine. Just went down the …" She pointed at her throat.

Could their dinner get any more awkward? Why had she contacted him? He'd hoped she would acknowledge they might have a future together.

"How is Sally doing?" she asked.

Sally? Oh, the dark-haired woman who had taken Kate's place housekeeping. He shrugged. "She isn't you."

She raised her eyebrows. "She doesn't yell at you to pick up after yourself?"

His smile was brief. "The place is clean. She doesn't do the little things, like flip down the corner of the bedding, or make a fresh pot of coffee." Or leave the scent of her perfume in the air.

"Oh." Kate blinked.

They sat in silence.

"I can't pretend to eat." He pushed his plate away and took her hand. "Kate, talk to me."

"Let's put this away first."

It took less than a minute to close the boxes and make room in her fridge. She pulled out a bottle of water. He took his beer and they headed into the living room.

He sat next to her on the sofa. She slid her legs around and faced him.

"How are you?" He took her hand, needing to touch her.

Her fingers squeezed his, probably an involuntary action. "Oh, I've had better years."

"You look unhappy." But that wasn't it. She looked like she was grieving.

Maybe she was. Maybe he'd added too much pressure at a time when she was suffering through her mother's cancer treatments.

"Alex." She pulled her hands away and scrubbed her face. "I don't know what to say, or how to say it."

"I want to be with you, Kate."

She tilted her head to the side. "I know."

"I'm sorry I upset you when I told you I loved you."

She drew in a sharp breath.

"I love you." He shrugged. "It's not the end of the world to have someone love you."

She pressed her hand against her chest. "Look at what my dad and mom are going through. Dad's in pain."

Was her father's pain keeping her from loving him? "Do you think your father would give up the good years, the good times, the joy, just so he wouldn't go through the pain he's going through today?"

"His heart is breaking."

God, she was stubborn. "I doubt he would give up one minute of the time he's had with your mother, or with his kids. I know I don't regret one second of the time I've spent with you."

She crossed her arms. "I don't understand why you want to be with me. I'm selfish."

Hope bubbled in his chest like a small melody trying to break free. "I don't see you as selfish. I see you as selfless. You don't know how to stop giving."

"You're wrong. Even when my mother was preparing us for her biopsy, all I could think of was how this disaster would affect my goal of attaining CEO. And while I waited for her to go through radiation treatment, I wanted Dad to notice how dedicated I was to the company because I was there reviewing agreements and keeping up with my work. I'm not a nice person."

He wanted to wrap his arms around her, instead he took her hand. She didn't shake his hand away. "That's not how I see you. That's not how your family sees you. It's okay to be ambitious. But you're not throwing your brothers under the bus to get there. They love you. Don't you trust your family's judgment?"

"They have to love me."

He couldn't stand their distance. He tugged Kate onto his lap.

She didn't push him away.

He inhaled the scent of her hair and his body relaxed. "Your family doesn't have to respect you, but they do."

"We shouldn't be cuddling." Her head rested on his shoulder. She wriggled a little, settling in.

He brushed his lips against her hair. "I've missed you."

"So you said, numerous times." She hugged him tight, giving him hope. "God, do you have to write such gut-wrenching notes?"

"Yes. I won't hold back." He smiled. "I don't suppose you'll admit you missed me, will you?"

She sighed. "Maybe."

"I don't want to lose you." He tightened his arms around her. "Since you wouldn't talk to me, those notes were the only way to let you know how I felt."

He kissed her temple. "Have I lost you?"

She stroked his cheek. "Alex?"

Her lower lip caught between her teeth, and he placed a kiss on the abused lip.

"Yes, love?" He touched her cheek.

"I'm pregnant."

EIGHTEEN

Alex's arms tightened around Kate, squeezing her so hard she let out a little, "Ouch."

"You're what?" His voice was almost a grunt.

"I'm pregnant. The IUD failed."

His forehead touched hers and his eye closed. "Are you sure?"

He wasn't asking if she was sure the baby was his. He wanted confirmation that she was pregnant. "Three tests and a doctor visit, sure."

"God." His chest shook as he took in a deep breath. "This is why your stomach's been upset."

"Probably." She breathed in his aftershave. How she'd missed his scent, missed his arms around her. Missed him.

He kissed her cheek, grinning. His brown eyes glittered. "How do you feel?"

"Awful." She couldn't look at his joy-filled face, so she closed her eyes. "I eat a lot of crackers."

He shifted so they were chest to chest. Then he hugged her. She wanted to burrow into his broad warm chest and never come out.

When she wasn't near him, she could analyze the impact of her pregnancy on the path she wanted her life to take. Her choices about the baby might either torpedo her career or she could lose her family's respect. But inhaling his scent, wrapped in his arms, all she wanted was for him to take away the confusion.

"Do you think it was our first time?" he whispered.

"Probably."

His heart pounded under her cheek. The steady beat, just a little fast.

He cupped her face and pressed his lips against hers.

His tender kiss brought tears to her eyes.

She should pull away. Instead she dug her fingers into his thick silky hair. The kiss spiraled into open mouths, tongues sweeping and sighs, lots of sighs.

"I was afraid I'd never kiss you again." Alex kissed her temple and settled her back on his lap.

She'd only wanted to tell Alex she was pregnant. Now they were locked in an embrace.

"When should we get married?" His voice sounded like he'd gotten everything he'd wanted for Christmas.

Get married? She scrambled to her feet. "What are you talking about?"

Her head swam and black dots danced in her vision. She staggered and bumped into the coffee table.

"Kate!" He steadied her.

She pushed him away. "Don't."

"You're carrying my child. I love you. I've been trying to tell you how much I love you for a week. Of course I want to get married."

"I can barely acknowledge I'm pregnant." She rubbed at the sharp pain between her eyebrows. "I broke up with you and because I'm pregnant, you assume we're getting married?"

"What did you think I would do? Say, *thanks for letting me know. Have a nice life?*" His voice took on a hard edge. "The reason you broke up with me was because you were falling in love with me."

Her head was shaking before he completed his sentence. "You kept pushing. Just like you're doing right now."

"And I'll ask again." His dark eyes were unreadable. "How did you expect me to react?"

"I ... I ..." She backed to the armchair and sat. Her body was so heavy. "Stop trying to overwhelm me."

In two quick steps he was in front of her and sitting on the coffee table. "I can't. Because that's what my love for you feels like. Like I'm overwhelmed. Like there's music assaulting me, never ending, and all I can do is hang on."

Is that what she was feeling? Love? She wrapped her arms around her waist. "This feels more like panic."

"Because you're fighting your feelings." He took her hands. "Let me love you. Let me love our child. I know you have dreams and plans, but the best plans come from the heart."

"I never planned on having kids." No, that wasn't right. "I don't *want* kids."

"Plans change."

Tugging her legs up, she wrapped her arms around her knees. "I know what I want. And this isn't it."

"Let me help you." Alex set his hands on the arms of the chair, caging her in. "Let me be part of your life."

"I don't want to be pregnant."

He sank onto his heels. Bleakness wiped his face free of expressions. "You wouldn't ..." He ran out of words.

When she'd helped Meg through her abortion, everything had been clear. Someone had drugged Meg. Raped her.

But this was Alex. Who she might love.

He pulled her hands free of her legs. "Don't do it, Kate. Please."

"Alex—"

"I'll take care of everything," he interrupted. "I'll take full responsibility. If you don't want to be part of our lives, that's the way we'll leave it."

Kate pressed her lips together. If she did this, what would her family think? Giving up her child could destroy her relationship with her parents. Could ruin her chances of becoming CEO.

"Please don't hurt the baby." Pain filled his dark eyes. "Give me our child."

She slid her feet to the floor. She had to escape his agony.

His head dropped to her legs. "Please."

She stroked his head. Leaning over him, she set her chest on his wide back, trying to comfort him.

She was destroying Alex. That was the last thing she wanted to do. But a baby could destroy her.

Could she do what he was asking? This was her body, her choice. With the turmoil in her family, how could she survive carrying a baby? This was a no-win negotiation. And her mother wanted to be a grandmother.

His shoulders stilled. She let him shift away.

Using his upper arm, he wiped his face. "Kate, please."

Maybe it was his breakdown, but she finally formed a coherent sentence. "I don't know what I'll do. I only know I needed to tell you."

"I'll do whatever you want, be whatever you want." Standing, he towered over her. "I'm here for you. Please don't …"

This was excruciating. "Can you give me some space?"

The shutters came down over his brown eyes. "Of course."

"Thank you." Her voice was weak.

He headed to the entry. "I love you, Kate."

The door clicked softly closed behind him.

Her head flopped back, and she stared at the ceiling.

He loved her now. But if she had an abortion, his love

would turn to hate. Her parents would despise her, and she could lose everything.

She buried her face in her hands. No win.

ALEX STUMBLED INTO THE ELEVATOR, pressing the ground floor button when he wanted to punch it. Punch anything. He had to escape.

This couldn't be happening again. He'd barely gotten through the grief of losing a child he hadn't realized existed, and now this?

He'd never been so powerless—ever. He didn't have any rights. Kate believed it was her body to do with as she would.

But it was his child. *His.*

And all he could do was wait. What words could he use to change her mind? Having a child wasn't in her long-range plan. And she loved her damn scheming plans.

But she wasn't scheming. The elevator door opened, and he nearly knocked down the man waiting to get on. "Sorry," he mumbled.

He stepped outside and the city noise assaulted him.

He wanted quiet. He needed solitude.

He hurried to his car and got out of the mass of humanity as fast as possible. Turning the car west, he headed out of the city.

Somehow he had to convince Kate to take a chance. Make her see their child wouldn't ruin her life.

He'd been sure she was softening toward him. She'd let him hold her, even kissed him. And then, as always, she pushed him away.

When he arrived, he didn't knock. He went in through the kitchen. The housekeeper was making a cup of tea.

"Dora, how are you?" he asked.

"I'm as good as I can expect." She rubbed her hip. "It takes a little longer to get out of bed each morning, but at least I wake up. Doctor keeps suggesting I get some of my parts replaced. I'm thinking about it."

"You could always retire." He knew she was pretty much retired already, but maybe she should move some place where there would be—less work. He gave her a hug.

"Not on your life. Who'd keep the staff under control?"

"No one does it better than you."

"What are you doing coming around so late?" she asked. "You were just here last week."

He glanced at the clock, surprised to see it was after nine. "Is Mother still up?"

"She is. I just took Natalie some tea. Thought I'd have a cup myself." The kettle boiled and she poured water into her mug. "Can I get you something?"

"No, I'm fine."

"Well, go see your mother. She's practicing."

He made his way through his childhood home. Each room took advantage of the stunning lake view.

As he headed to the music wing, the lament of his mother's cello drifted to him. His mother could make the instrument weep.

He stood in the open doorway and let the music of Natalie Simpson Adamski, his incredible mother, wash over him.

She leaned into the cello's neck, her eyes closed. Her hair, with its dramatic silver streak on one side draped over her shoulder. The bow flew across the strings. Her foot tapped out the measures.

How many hours had he and his sisters sat cross-legged on the floor watching their mother make her cello sing? She never closed the music room door. He had a vague memory of a bassinette in the room for his younger sister, but he wasn't sure.

Why had he insisted on solitude to compose? If Kate kept

their child, he would institute an open-door policy. Music should be shared.

Mom finished the piece with a dramatic flourish of her bow.

He applauded enthusiastically. She was so talented. He should write a piece for her. That would be his next work.

Her head jerked up. "Alexander!"

She set the instrument on its stand.

"Mother." He crossed the room and pulled her into a big hug.

She squeezed him back. "To what do I owe this pleasure? You're still coming on Sunday for Mother's Day, right?"

"Wouldn't miss it." He hugged her one more time.

She held his face between her hands and stared into his eyes. Her eyebrows snapped together. "What's wrong?"

How did she do it? Know when something was wrong. "Can't I come and see my mother?"

"Absolutely, but you're upset." She pulled him to the window seat. Lights twinkled from across the lake. Patting the seat, she said, "Talk to me."

Maybe this was why he'd come, to get a female perspective. His mom's perspective.

"Spit it out," his mother said.

"I've told you about Kate," he started.

She nodded. "I can't wait to meet her."

Okay, his mother was a little behind in the news department. He hadn't announced Kate had booted him out of her life, although he had hope. "That might be hard. She broke up with me ..."

His mother's jaw dropped.

"... but I'm working on changing that."

"I thought you said she was smart. What's wrong with her?" Annoyance passed through his mother's brown eyes. "Any woman who breaks up with my son isn't very bright."

"Her career comes first." He grimaced. "But she doesn't even understand her own priorities. Her family also comes first. In her mind that means ensuring the family's business thrives."

"Then you're better off without her." His mother's chin took on a stubborn tilt.

"I'm in love with her."

"Oh, Alex."

"I think I scare her. She doesn't believe love is worth it." He pushed away from the window seat and paced across the room. "How did you do it?"

"Do what?"

"Have a career and a family?" he asked. "She doesn't think she can do both."

"It's not easy. I had lots of help." His mother pushed back her long hair. For almost being sixty, she kept in great shape and looked good. "The toughest times were when the orchestra traveled. I missed you so much. But we had Dora. She was a godsend."

"I can do that for her." If Kate would let him. "I can get live-in help."

"Your dad and I were a team, but there was still a lot of negotiating and give and take." His mother smiled. "And arguments."

"We have those already." But they were about her pregnancy, and he couldn't tell his mother about that.

"If you have a strong foundation, you'll get through the tough times."

"I asked her to marry me." Hadn't he? Or had he asked *when* she wanted to get married?

"Then I hope she's as smart as you've said." His mother patted his cheek. "She'd be a fool to let a gem like you get away."

"WHERE'S MICHAEL?" Kate stared into his dark office.

Becca, the finance department's secretary, set down her phone. "He's not answering his cell. I know he had your meeting on his schedule. He had me make copies for it last night."

Great. Michael was a no-show. They were supposed to talk through capital commitments. Had he gotten wind that she, Stephen and Timothy were planning an intervention at dinner tonight?

"Let me know when he gets in." Kate started to walk away, but added, "If my parents call, don't tell them Michael's not here."

Becca gave her a small smile. "No problem."

How often had Becca covered for her brother?

Walking to her office, she called his cell. It rang and rang, finally rolling to voice mail. Odd.

In her office, she stared out the window. Her stomach growled. She needed to eat something. This morning she'd had actual morning sickness and hadn't been able to stomach toast after that stellar event.

What should she do?

Alex wanted this baby. When she'd told him she was pregnant, he'd beamed at her. He'd assumed they would get married.

Married.

Two months ago, she would have said an absolute no. But that was before Alex had barreled into her life. The thought of not seeing his slow smile, not being wrapped in his warm arms …

They'd made a baby. She rested her forehead against the window. Where was the crystal-clear vision of the future she'd always relied on?

She couldn't see beyond lunchtime.

And she worried her plans were changing because she was pregnant.

Alex loved her. He'd written it, said it and insisted it was true. This wasn't a tool to keep her from having an abortion. She cringed at the word. It was an ugly word.

She turned away from the window and the view of the bustling city and stared at the roses and tulips he'd sent.

He loved her. Not because she was pregnant. He loved her. He didn't even think she was selfish.

And she loved Alex.

But she didn't want a baby.

She couldn't think about that right now. What she could do was check on Michael. His condo was a block and half away.

The walk would do her good. On the way back, she would buy a sandwich. She grabbed her purse and stopped by Liz's desk. "Michael missed a meeting and isn't answering his phone. I'm going to check on him."

Liz frowned. "Do you want me to come with you?"

"No." She had a key to his place. "Hold the fort, would you?"

"Sure." Liz looked like she wanted to say more.

"Something else?"

"It's just … I'm sorry." Liz's words spilled out. "Your brother's drinking a lot. At the office, I think."

She hadn't noticed that. "My brothers and I will deal with him."

"Whatever you need me to do."

The family didn't need this crap from Michael. Her resentment multiplied as she walked down the street, boiling into a full-blown rant. What did he think he was doing going silent while the family concentrated on Mom's treatments? Where was his spine, burying his head in a bottle?

She looked at his condominium door. She was ready to

knock but changed her mind. She wanted to catch him sleeping off his night.

Digging through her purse, she tugged out her key. The lock clicked open.

"Michael Joseph MacBain, you're in trouble." She dropped her purse on the entry table.

She wrinkled her nose. His place smelled like a dumpster. As she came through the living room, she spotted pizza boxes and take out containers scattered on the coffee table. Bottles too. Whiskey by the look of it. One had tipped, leaving a sticky pool on the floor.

"Michael!"

She checked the kitchen and then his office. Peeked into the laundry area and bathroom. No sightings.

Damn it, she would have to dig him out of bed.

She pounded on the bedroom door. "Get your ass out of bed."

No answer. She pushed into the room flipping on the light.

The bed was a mess, the room was worse. The odor of alcohol and unwashed clothes had her breathing through her mouth. Clothes covered every surface. She swallowed. Even Alex's place hadn't been this bad.

But she didn't find Michael.

Only one room to go, his master bath. The door was partially closed. She pounded, yelling his name.

The door swung open until something blocked it.

"Michael!"

He didn't answer. Her pulse pounded in her ears.

She put her shoulder to the door, pushing whatever blocked the door enough to slip sideways into the room. The smell had her choking.

She slapped on the light.

"Oh God!"

Her brother lay sprawled on the floor. A pool of blood had dried on the floor next to his head.

"Michael!" She knelt, her knee slipping in vomit. "Oh, Michael."

His face was gray, scary gray. She searched his neck for a pulse. Her hand shook, but she found a thready beat. "Thank God."

She tapped his face lightly, worried about the massive gash and knot on his forehead. A trail of blood had dried in a line across his forehead and down his cheek.

He didn't come to.

She tried a little harder. "Michael. Wake up."

Nothing.

She pushed off the floor, trying to avoid blood and vomit. She grunted as she shifted and slid his lower body so she could open the door. Grabbing a clean shirt out of his closet, she wiped her hands as she ran to the entry. She dug out her phone and hit 9-1-1.

She was back in the bathroom when someone answered.

"My brother's unconscious. It looks like he hit his head. I can't wake him." The words rushed out. "There's blood and he's thrown up."

Things were a blur from then on.

She ran and propped open the front door. Then she found clean towels and wiped up some of the mess and gently dabbed her brother's head.

He didn't move, didn't make a sound.

His skin was cold to the touch. Kate pulled the comforter off his bed and covered him. She grabbed his pillow to get his head off the cold tile floor.

She wanted to call Alex, wanted to hear the comfort of his voice. Instead she walked into the bedroom and called Stephen.

"What's up," Stephen shouted over the screech of a saw.

"It's Michael." She kept her eye on his inert body from her spot in the bedroom.

"What's the bonehead done now?"

"He's …" Her voice cracked. "He's unconscious."

Her hands shook as she pulled up the bedding and straightened the room.

"What? I couldn't hear you," Stephen said.

Kate heard a shout from the EMTs.

"In the back bedroom," she called.

"What about a bedroom?" Stephen asked.

"I found Michael unconscious, bleeding in his bathroom."

"Fuck!"

A woman and man entered the bedroom and she pointed at the bathroom. There wasn't room for all three of them in the small space.

"The EMTs are here," she said to Stephen. "I'll call you back."

Kate moved to the doorway and gave the limited information she had. The woman ran out and came back with a gurney.

"Do you know how much he drank?" asked the EMT who introduced himself as Jeremy.

"I don't." She wrapped her arms around her stomach. "I came over because he missed a meeting."

Jeremy flicked a light in Michael's eyes. "That's a nasty bump on his head. We're transporting him to the hospital."

They bundled up her brother. She walked through the house that represented Michael's life—screwed up.

"Any chance I can ride with you?" she asked.

"Sure." They pointed her to a small bench in the front section of the ambulance. The radio buzzed. Jeremy monitored Michael and quietly updated whoever he was talking to on the radio.

At the hospital the staff directed her to registration. She

completed his paperwork, her hands shaking so hard her signature was illegible. Then she called Stephen.

"We're at HCMC," she said. "He's still unconscious."

"I'm on my way. Timothy's coming too."

"I'll let Timothy know where we are." She had to stay busy. She had to do something. "What about Mom and Dad?"

Stephen let out a rasping exhale. "I'm not too far away. Let's talk about it when we're together."

"Okay." Suddenly dizzy, she sank into the vinyl chair. "I'm in the waiting room."

She tucked her head between her knees and took deep breaths. She didn't know whether to blame her brother or her pregnancy for her sudden weakness.

Maybe she'd blame both, with the highest percentage going to Michael. He was the numbers man after all.

NINETEEN

"I'm looking for Kate MacBain,' Alex told the receptionist.

Kate had asked for space, but she needed to eat, so he hoped they could have lunch. When they were together, they were better.

"Oh dear." The woman's hands fluttered. "She's at the hospital."

"Hospital?" Oh, God, the baby! "Which hospital?"

"HCMC."

The woman standing next to her, hissed, "Jenny, you can't tell him that."

"What happened?" he asked.

"I'm sorry." The woman bit her lip. "We can't say anything."

"It's horrible." Jenny started to cry.

Alex ran out the door.

On the street level he glanced around. HCMC.

He pulled up directions on his phone and flipped the map to walk mode. Okay. Two blocks east and three blocks south.

As he ran, he pulled out his cell and called her. No answer. Damn it.

If she'd been in an accident ... He couldn't go there. She had to be okay.

He sprinted in between traffic. A driver blared his horn. He didn't care. He had to get to Kate.

KATE TRIED NOT to breathe through her nose. The woman next to her smelled like she'd slept in a dumpster. She looked like it too, her eyes red and weepy, her clothes stained and wrinkled. Kate wanted to change seats, but the waiting room was full.

Her sense of smell, especially foul smells, must be working overtime.

She should check on Michael, see if they would let her see him. She stood and the world wobbled. Grabbing the arm of the chair, she waited for everything to right. If she had to deal with dizziness for the next seven and a half months, she'd be pissed.

That was only if she kept the baby.

She took a deep breath and decided she was steady enough to walk. All the registration staff were helping people. She waited, standing back to let the patients and people have privacy.

She'd never been in the county hospital. Busy didn't begin to describe the place. Gun-toting sheriffs stood next to a shackled and bleeding man slumped in a wheelchair. A woman rested on a gurney holding a wad of bandages on her arm. Sirens grew near and a white-coated woman and a male nurse ran down the corridor.

"Kate!" Stephen hurried through the doors.

Tears welled in her eyes.

He wrapped an arm around her. "How is Michael?"

"I don't know." She wiped her cheeks. "They whisked him away and I haven't seen him."

The receptionist waved them to her desk.

Kate tugged Stephen's arm. "Maybe they'll tell us something now."

"Can you give us an update on Michael MacBain? We're his family," Stephen added, taking charge.

The woman asked for the spelling as she typed in Michael's name.

Stephen looked round. "Is it always so busy during the day?"

"There was a three-car pileup on 94." She glanced up, her smile forced. "Your brother's scheduled for an MRI. It will be a while."

"Did he wake up?" Kate wanted to lean over and read her screen.

"I don't know." The receptionist shook her head. "When he's back from imaging, a nurse will find you."

Kate took Stephen by the arm. "Let's walk outside for a bit. I can't take the waiting room smell."

"You look a little pale." He held the door for her.

She took a deep breath. It was bad when the smell of bus exhaust was a relief. "It's been a tough morning."

She leaned against the outside of the building, not sure if she could stand for long.

"Tell me what happened." Stephen leaned his shoulder against the building beside her.

And she did. As she was getting to her decision to walk to Michael's condo, Timothy hustled down the sidewalk, so she started again.

Both her brothers were shaking their heads once she finished telling them what she'd found.

"Fuck." Timothy paced to the wall and slapped the side of

the building. "We shouldn't have waited to talk to him. We should have forced him into treatment."

Stephen gripped his hair. "Maybe this is better."

"What do we do about Mom and Dad?" Kate pinched her lips together.

"Mom's at her treatment right now. Let's go back in," Stephen suggested. "Once we talk to the staff, we can decide if we need to call them."

At least the waiting room had cleared out a little and the smells weren't as strong.

"I'll get coffee," Timothy said, his foot bouncing. "Anyone want anything?"

"Coffee would be good." Stephen nodded.

Her stomach twisted. "Water."

But when Timothy returned with the bottled water even that tasted bad. They talked but finally lapsed into silence.

"MacBain family?" a nurse called from the center of the room.

Timothy stood. "Here."

The nurse walked over with a sheaf of papers in her hand. "Your brother is back from imaging."

"Is he conscious?" Stephen asked.

"No. I can let two of you back for a few minutes. The doctor wants to talk to a family member," the nurse said. "You'll have to take turns."

Stephen nodded. "Kate and Timothy, go ahead."

Timothy held out a hand and pulled her out of the chair. Black spots swam before her eyes and then settled. This was ridiculous. She couldn't work like this. She couldn't live like this.

They passed through security doors and moved through a maze of rooms until they were at Michael's bedside. He lay unconscious on a gurney.

Kate frowned. "No one has cleaned him up."

She'd wiped him down before the ambulance had arrived but hadn't scrubbed the dried blood. There was caked-on vomit by his mouth.

"It wasn't the first priority." The nurse patted her shoulder. "It looks like his head needs stitches. He'll be cleaned up for prep. I'll let Dr. Moore know you're here."

Kate moved to Michael's side; Timothy moved to the opposite side. She took his lifeless hand. "Wake up. I want to yell at you."

"That will keep him under," Timothy said. He sniffed. "God, he smells as bad as the drunk I passed on my way in here."

She squeezed Michael's fingers and then sank into the only chair in the room.

"How did it get this bad?" Timothy held out his hands. "I feel like a terrible brother."

"This is on Michael." They were all coping with their mother's illness. "He's self-destructing in front of us."

And was she much better? Pushing Alex away. Pregnant. A man she realized she loved?

A woman walked in. "MacBain family?"

"Yes." Timothy shook the doctor's hand first.

Kate pushed out of the chair to greet the doctor. Her head swam again. Shit.

The spots didn't clear. Her vision tunneled. "No."

Timothy turned. His mouth dropped open.

Her knees crumpled. In slow motion she wheeled her hands and then wrapped them around her belly.

Timothy reached for her. "Kate?"

Her head slammed the floor. Everything went black.

ALEX PUSHED through the emergency department doors and jerked to a stop. All the receptionists were helping patients or families.

Maybe her family was in the waiting room. His fists clenched as he walked, not ran, into the waiting area. Her brothers were huddled in a corner, their heads tucked together. He hurried toward them.

"Alex?" Timothy saw him first. "What are you doing here?"

"I was trying to have lunch with Kate, but the receptionist said she was here. How's Kate?" His words ran together. "How's the baby?"

Shock covered both brothers' faces. They rose, taking a quick step toward him.

Timothy's hands had formed into fists. "Baby?"

Whoops.

Stephen shoved him. "You got her pregnant?"

Alex stumbled back, his hands in the air. "Let's focus on what's important right now. How is she? Was there an accident?"

"She fainted," Timothy said. "Damn it, I almost caught her. She hit her head pretty hard."

"And they brought her to the hospital?" Alex was confused.

"We were already here. She passed out with a doctor standing right next to her." Stephen clenched and unclenched his hands. His eyes drilled holes into Alex's face.

Alex retreated another step. "Is she okay?"

"They're checking her out. At least she regained consciousness by the time they kicked me out of Michael's room."

"Michael's room?" Alex frowned. "What the hell is going on?"

"Kate found Michael unconscious this morning," Stephen explained.

"Shit. What happened?" Alex asked.

The brothers sat and Alex took a nearby chair. He listened to their story. Timothy kept looking at him like he was a slug.

Kate would kill him. He shouldn't have said anything about the baby. At a lull in the conversation, he asked, "Can I see her?"

Timothy's leg bounced up and down. "I'm guessing you probably should."

Alex nodded. Then he waited. And waited. What the hell were the medical staff doing? A nurse came in but went to another group of people.

A doctor walked their way. Finally.

All three men rose together. Alex took a deep breath and exhaled, saying a little prayer for Kate.

"I'm Dr. Moore. Your sister's all right." The doctor pushed her hair back. "She's resting, but we'll release her soon."

"Can I see her?" Alex asked.

"And you are?" the doctor asked.

A beat of silence sounded. "Family?" Alex said.

The doctor raised an eyebrow.

Stephen shrugged.

"How's Michael?" Timothy asked.

"Yes, my other MacBain patient. Your brother woke for a few moments too. He asked for someone named Sarah."

"Fuck," Timothy muttered.

Who was Sarah?

Dr. Moore looked at the three of them. "Your brother's blood alcohol was more than two times the legal limit."

"Jesus." Timothy punched a fist into his hand.

Stephen closed his eyes. "His drinking is out of hand. We planned on confronting him tonight."

"I can call in social services. If he agrees, we can facilitate getting him into treatment."

Alex itched to find Kate, but the doctor kept discussing

treatment options with the brothers. He wanted to scream, *What about Kate?*

Finally Dr. Moore said, "Why don't you follow me back? Two of you can see Mr. MacBain and one Miss MacBain." She held up her hand. "But no fainting."

Alex's fingers were beating on his leg as fast as thirty-second notes. The doctor led Stephen and Timothy to Michael's room. Then he followed her to Kate's.

Stopping in front of the door, he touched the doctor's arm. "Is the baby okay?"

She nodded. "As Kate fell, she wrapped her hands around her stomach. Mother Nature's designed a pretty good shock system, but we did an ultrasound. He or she is doing fine."

She'd protected the baby.

"You can let her know I'm writing up her discharge. And she needs to fill the prescription her OB gave her for anemia."

"I'll make sure she does." He knocked softly on the door, and then pushed it open. "Kate?"

She lay curled on her side, her eyes shut. Her skin looked as pale as the white sheets pulled up to her chin.

He moved the chair next to the bed. Brushing wayward strands of hair off her face, he kissed her cheek.

Her eyes fluttered open, unfocused and sleepy. "Alex." His name was a sigh.

"Hello, love." This time when he kissed her, he shook. He'd been afraid she was hurt—or worse. "I'm glad to see you."

She stretched. "What are you doing here?"

"I heard you were in the hospital. But at that point, you were only here with Michael."

She jerked upright, and her eyes almost rolled back in her head. "How is he?"

He raised the head of her bed and settled her into a sitting position.

"Dr. Moore said he was conscious for a bit." He rubbed her

shoulders. "They're bringing in social services. Why didn't you tell me he'd gotten so bad? I would have helped …"

"He needs treatment." She bit her lip. "I fell asleep while they were doing the ultrasound."

She squeezed his hand. "Is the baby okay?"

Joy bubbled in his chest, easing the ache that had started the minute he found out Kate was in the hospital. "The baby's fine. Doctor says you need to fill a prescription."

"That's good," she said, her voice soft.

He touched her stomach, rubbed gently and left his hand there. She laid her hand on his. The connection, the tenderness in her eyes had hope swelling in his chest. God, he wanted a lifetime with her.

"I was so worried I spilled the news. Your brothers know about the baby." He kissed her forehead. "I'm sorry."

Her fingers tensed around his and then relaxed. "Well, they would have figured it out eventually. Especially a few months from now when I looked like I swallowed a basketball."

"Oh, Kate." Happiness warmed every muscle in his body. He dropped his forehead to hers. "Thank you."

He wanted to ask her what this meant for them, their relationship. But this wasn't the setting.

"I'm sure you'll soon wonder what you've gotten yourself into." She stroked his cheek. "How do you always know when I need you?"

"We're connected." Hope burst out of his chest like an exploding champagne cork.

"Since everything is in working order, can you break me out of here?" she asked.

"The doctor's writing up your discharge."

"Fantastic." She let her legs hang over the edge of the bed. "I need to see Michael. We can wait in his room."

He looked at her pale face. "Hang on, I'll find a wheelchair. Don't move."

She frowned but didn't stand.

A nurse gave him a wheelchair.

"Your chariot," he announced as he backed into her room with the chair in tow.

He steadied her as she slid off the bed and settled into the chair. "I told the staff you would be in your brother's room. Since you have the same doctor, I'm hoping they'll overlook their two visitor rule."

"Hey, I'm still a patient. I don't count." She gave him a wan smile.

Stephen held the door as Alex pushed her into Michael's room. "Christ, Katie." Then he hugged her.

Timothy was right behind him with his hug. "Sorry I wasn't fast enough to catch you, sis."

Then the two men glared at Alex.

"Stop it you two," Kate warned. "How's Michael?"

Alex looked at the occupant in the bed. A line of black stitches took up a quarter of his forehead. Blood covered his shirt and God knew what else. Even from the doorway, the smell was foul.

"When they put the stitches in his hard head, he grunted." Timothy walked over and stood by his bed. "He's sleeping his drunk off. Did Alex tell you how drunk he was? Is?"

"I didn't have a chance," Alex said.

"Over double the legal limit." Disgust filled Timothy's voice. "How much do you have to drink to get that fucked up?"

Alex rubbed Kate's shoulder, wishing he could keep her from this.

There was a tap on the doorframe.

"Dr. Moore," Timothy said.

"Here are my MacBain patients." The doctor looked at Kate. "Wheelchair looks good on you for now." She tipped her head. "Let's step outside for a minute."

Alex wheeled the chair into the corridor.

The doctor said, "I'd like some privacy with my patient."

Kate reached for his hand, linking them together. "That's all right. He's the father."

His heart swelled with pride. *Father.* And Kate had acknowledged him.

"Okay. I know it's early in your pregnancy, but your hemoglobin is low. You already have a prescription, right?"

Kate nodded.

"Fill it. Or I can write you another one."

"No. I'll get it filled."

"I'll get it done," Alex said.

"You're dehydrated too."

"I had morning sickness today. That was a first. Otherwise I've just felt nauseous."

Alex massaged her neck, wishing he could ease her burdens.

"Try eating crackers before getting out of bed. Your OB will have more suggestions."

Kate nodded.

"Your brother told me there's a lot going on in your family right now. You need to get enough sleep and do something about the stress." The doctor glanced into Michael's room. "And don't use the crutches your brother is using."

Kate set her free hand on her stomach. "I'm not drinking."

"Good. You might try meditation or yoga. And you need to eat and get some liquids in you. Since I have the feeling you'll be here for a while with your brother, I've asked the staff to get you a bowl of soup."

"I'll make sure she eats it," Alex said as he crouched next to the chair.

"Well, my work with you is done." The doctor smiled. "Go forth and have a beautiful baby, you two. And don't let me catch you back in my ER."

"I'll try not to," Kate said, leaning into Alex's shoulder.

"Now to deal with your brother." The doctor headed into the exam room.

"How are you feeling," Alex asked, touching her face.

"Not dizzy anymore."

"Are we good?" he asked.

Kate's smile wiped away his fear. "I think we're getting there."

"KATE, GO HOME." Stephen's voice jerked her awake.

She blinked. "I was only resting."

Her neck ached from falling asleep in the chair.

Alex massaged her muscles, and she couldn't stop a small moan from escaping. He'd done what he could to help the family, from grabbing food in the cafeteria to helping her to the bathroom.

"We can handle it from here," Timothy said.

She checked the time. Four o'clock. They'd been here for hours. The nursing staff had overlooked the two-visitor rule, and they were camped in the small space.

About an hour ago Michael had awakened and grunted, "What the hell are you doing?" Then he'd fallen back into unconsciousness.

"I think it's better if Timothy and I confront him. Then we'll drag in social services." Stephen patted her hand. "We know you like to be in charge, but it's time to delegate. Let us do this."

"Keep me posted." She was tired. "Did Mom or Dad call while I was asleep?"

Timothy added, "We've decided they won't hear anything from us until Michael's in treatment."

If he goes into treatment.

Her brothers hugged her. The nurse walked them to the waiting area.

"I'll get my car. It's by your office." Alex brushed a kiss on her head before taking off at a jog.

"He's a nice man," the nurse said, watching him move away.

"Yes, he is."

Once Alex drove up, the nurse helped her into the car. "Good luck, now," she called, shutting the door.

"My house or yours?" Alex asked.

"Mine, please." She wanted to strip out of these clothes and soak in a long hot bath.

She relaxed into the quiet. The hospital had been noisy. "Thank you."

He took her hand.

His touch righted her world. She gave a strangled laugh.

"Are you sick?" he asked in panic.

"No, no." She squeezed his fingers. "I'm thinking what a mess my life is right now. With Mother's cancer, her and Dad stepping away from the business and now Michael's drinking."

And Alex made everything bearable.

"You'll get through this," he said. "You're a fighter."

"I am." Because she had a secret weapon, one that no one else in the world had. She had Alex by her side.

She was in love with Alex. She took a deep breath and tried the thought on like she would a pair of gorgeous shoes.

She loved Alex.

Everything clicked into place. A weight lifted off her chest.

"I noticed you didn't put your unwanted pregnancy in the mix." He shot her a quizzical look before he turned his gaze back to the road.

She nodded. "That's because I think … it's wanted."

"Oh, God, Kate. I want to kiss you right now."

"Drive." She smiled at him. "Let's get home."

They were quiet until they got to her condo. And it wasn't uncomfortable.

"I'll drop you off and walk you into the lobby."

"I can walk," she said with a smile.

"Indulge me."

He parked and was around the car before she unsnapped her seatbelt. And it didn't make her bristle. His caring made her feel loved.

She let him walk her into the building, even though she wasn't lightheaded. He pulled her into a hug. "Stay right here. I'll ..." He waved his hand.

She pushed him away. "Go park the car. I'll wait."

She didn't wait long.

Alex jogged into the lobby. "I found a spot right around the corner."

She laced their fingers together as they waited for the elevator. This was right. Why had she thought she couldn't have love and family and her career? Love and family made everything else ... easier. Mom and Dad had shown her the way, she'd just not believed them.

She did now.

Thank God Alex had never given up.

In the elevator, she leaned against his shoulder, and he wrapped an arm around her.

"Keys?" he asked.

She let him take control. Let him take over and escort her into her own home. It was a home with Alex by her side.

"Do you want to sleep or rest or what?" he asked.

"Let's talk."

He swallowed. "Sure."

Was it only last night they'd sat on this sofa and fought? "Thank you for being there today."

"It sounds like there's a but in there."

"But? No. What there is … is I don't want to go on like we have been."

He closed his eyes. "I can't lose you."

"You won't." She took a deep breath. "Will you marry me?"

His mouth dropped open.

"I love you," she continued. "It's taken me a while to figure it out, but I want you there to help celebrate the joy and help me through the sorrow. And I want to do the same for you because you make me a better person."

She took her finger and pushed his jaw shut.

"You love me?" His words were a whisper.

"Is that such a shock?"

He hauled her onto his lap. "It's a dream come true."

He kissed her.

She returned his kiss with all the love filling her heart. "I love you."

"I love you too." He held her close. "Do we need to negotiate anything else?"

She chuckled. "Probably."

"You asked me to marry you." He stared at her.

She hadn't closed the deal yet. "I haven't heard a yes or a no."

"Yes," he whispered. "Was there any doubt?"

"It helps that you *told* me we were getting married last night."

"I guess my negotiating skills need work." He hugged her close, brushing a kiss on her forehead. "I want you to meet my family, soon."

Families. She sighed. "Tomorrow. By then Stephen and Timothy will have confronted Michael. Mom and Dad will know what's going on." She tipped her face to his. "They'll want good news after that."

"I'd like to go with you. When you tell your family."

Absolutely. Because she was strong. But with Alex by her side she was stronger. "I wouldn't have it any other way."

"So, who will clean our house?" he asked.

"Now that I've got you trained, we'll keep Murphy's Maids, but I'm done cleaning. I hope my parents agree I've learned my lesson."

She'd bucked and fought learning the business from the ground up, but she'd gotten the biggest prize of all. Alex.

She still wanted to be CEO, but it was Alex that made life worthwhile.

"Thank you," she said.

Alex's brown eyes sparkled. "For what?"

"For loving me and not giving up."

She curled into his shoulder and sighed. She was right where she belonged.

Home.

LOOKING FOR MORE MACBAIN STORIES? Check out EDGE Of FRIENDSHIP. Come see if Michael can redeem himself.

ACKNOWLEDGMENTS

There are so many amazing people who help me in my writing. First and foremost my critique partners: Ann Hinnenkamp, Leanne Taveggia, Cat Schield and Lizbeth Selvig. And of course my editors Victoria Curran and Judy Roth. Your help is so appreciated.

I'm also blessed to have the Dreamweavers in my life. They are such an inspiration .

And of course my family — because they are everything to me.

And to my readers—thank you.

If you enjoyed Kate and Alex's story, please consider leaving a review at your favorite bookseller or book club website.

AMAZON
BOOKBUB
GOODREADS

ALSO BY NAN DIXON

POETIC JUSTICE - *Romantic Suspense*

DESIGNER CHILDREN - *Romantic Suspense*
DISCOVERY
CONNECTIONS
DECEPTION

THE MacBAINS - *Contemporary Romance*
MAID FOR SUCCESS
EDGE OF FRIENDSHIP
HOW WE STARTED (novella)

BIG SKY DREAMERS - *Contemporary Romance*
INVEST IN ME
STAINED GLASS HEARTS
DANCE WITH ME

FITZGERALD HOUSE - *Contemporary Romance with some Romantic Suspense*
SOUTHERN COMFORTS
A SAVANNAH CHRISTMAS WISH
THROUGH A MAGNOLIA FILTER
THE OTHER TWIN
UNDERCOVER WITH THE HEIRESS
TO CATCH A THIEF

A SAVANNAH CHRISTMAS WEDDING (novella)

Thank you for reading **MAID FOR SUCCESS**. (And again, I would love an honest review!)

Here's a preview of **THE EDGE OF FRIENDSHIP**, Book 2 in **THE MacBAINS** series.

CHAPTER ONE

Michael hung back from the crowd of people streaming into the Minnesota Twins stadium. It was noon on Friday. Maybe he should have stayed at the office or headed home. He didn't want to be part of this group. He didn't want to hear everyone laughing because he knew they would be laughing at him.

But both his therapist and AA sponsor had advised Michael against withdrawing.

Today was MacBain Enterprises' family day at Target Field. Every employee and their loved ones wore Twins caps and golf shirts with the company logo. As CFO, he should know what this party was costing, but he'd been *indisposed* when Mom and Dad planned the event.

Indisposed. In treatment. Drying out. Fucked up.

Kate, his sister, slowed and waited for him on the sidewalk. "How're you doing?"

He hated that question. At least one family member asked him that each day.

"I should be asking you that question." Kate was pregnant. She hadn't told him until he'd gotten through treatment.

She stroked her belly, even though she wasn't showing. "We're good."

Alex, her fiancé, set his hand on her shoulder. "Should I see if there's some kind of cart for you?"

Kate laughed. "I can walk."

Alex sighed.

Michael looked away. It was hard to be around Kate and Alex. He couldn't believe his career-minded sister had fallen in

321

love so hard and fast. Just watching them made him miss Sarah. If life had been fair, she would be by his side today.

Kate hooked her arm through Michael's and then Alex's. "Come on."

"I don't know why Mom and Dad insisted the whole company attend the game," Michael said.

"Because it's good for morale." Kate tugged him a little faster toward the queue of people at security having their bags checked. "It's a beautiful day, and we want our employees to know how much MacBain appreciates them."

"Yeah, yeah." Sometimes he didn't feel like part of the family company. Ever since he'd come back from Hazelton, he felt even more removed.

"Then how about this for a reason?" Kate stuck a bony elbow in his side. "Mom and Dad want to celebrate her oncologist's clean report."

"What? Why didn't I know this?" Michael held out his ticket for scanning.

"Sucks to be you," Kate whispered.

Alex raised one eyebrow. "I didn't know either."

At least he wasn't the only person out of the loop.

They followed the MacBain group to the concierge level.

Dad and Mom flanked the steps into their section, greeting all the people. Everyone was smiling.

His mother looked—healthy, not like she'd just finished her cancer battle. Thank God.

He bent and hugged her. "How come I have to hear from Kate that you got a clean bill of health from your doctor?"

He tried to keep it light, but hurt seeped into his voice. Hell, weren't there any privileges with being the firstborn?

"She was in my office when I got the call. I'd planned on giving an update either good or bad at dinner on Sunday." Her hazel eyes, so like his, glittered in the sunlight. "Cat's out of the bag."

His dad joined them and gave him a one-armed hug. "Great news, isn't it?"

"The best."

"Have fun today, Michael." Mom squeezed his arm, concern on her face. "Try and enjoy yourself."

Fun? He couldn't remember having much fun in the last four years. Not since Sarah found out she had inoperable brain cancer.

As he stood in the concourse, he swore everyone held a beer. His palms perspired, and a line of sweat slid down his back. He swallowed, almost able to taste the cold, hoppy brew.

"Michael, there you are." Becca, his assistant, came up to him. "I'd like you meet my fiancé."

Another woman who'd gotten engaged while he'd been away in treatment. "Congratulations."

The guy stuck out his hand. "Dave Benthal."

"Michael MacBain." Michael shook his hand, trying to come up with small talk. "What do you do, Dave?"

Becca shifted her feet.

"I'm a liquor distributor." He gave a crooked smile. "It's a family business, like yours. Genetic luck, I'd guess you'd say."

Becca's eyes were almost as large as saucers.

Michael set a hand on her arm. "I'm not going to roll him and steal any booze he's carrying."

Dave frowned.

"I don't … I wouldn't …" Becca stuttered. Apparently his assistant hadn't given away his secrets.

"I just got out of treatment, well, two months ago," Michael said.

"Alcohol?" Dave asked.

Michael nodded, hating this. "I've been sober for thirteen weeks."

"I'm sorry." Dave swallowed. "Is it tough to talk about?"

"No," he lied. "Today will be a test, being around other people drinking."

A whiskey to steady his nerves might help him get through the afternoon. But he was done with that.

"Congratulations on your sobriety," Dave said. "We're in the business, but we've had our share of alcoholics. I've seen what you're going through and I wish you luck. One day at a time."

"Thanks." More like one hour at a time. "You two have fun. Looks like the game's about to start."

"It's so great that your parents decided to do this," Becca said as she and Dave headed down the steps.

Becca was right. His parents were great. He moved down the stairs and found some empty seats, taking the one on the aisle and tugged his cap lower. He was like—oh what was that book called—*Stranger in a Strange Land*? He didn't feel part of any of this.

A server stopped next to him. "What would you like to order? Everything's on the MacBains today."

He *wanted* a Jameson on the rocks. "Ginger ale."

"You got it." She entered the order in a handheld computer. "Let me know if you need anything else." She flipped her blonde ponytail over her shoulder before moving to take another order.

"She's cute." His brother, Timothy, slid into the chair behind him.

"All yours." No one could replace Sarah. "How come you're late?"

"Stephen and I waited for the Moonlight Square inspector. The guy was two hours late."

"That's terrible."

The Twins were taking the field, the Milwaukee Brewers at bat. A fierce rivalry existed between Wisconsin and Minnesota. Even now, he could see the stands had more than the average number of opposing team fan gear.

"We got the certificate of occupancy—finally." Timothy clapped as the Twin's pitcher threw the first strike.

Michael tried to remember what had hung the CO up. "You and Stephen convinced the inspector the fire exits were up to code?"

"The guy was jerking us around. We didn't have any issues this time, and we didn't change anything."

The Brewer at the plate swung and missed. The crowd cheered.

"Is that seat taken?" Liz Carlson stood in the aisle pointing at the seat next to him.

Her company shirt was tucked into a pair of khaki shorts, and the ball cap stuck out of her purse. Michael gazed into familiar deep blue eyes, the most unusual eyes he'd ever seen. When she'd first joined MacBain, Kate had warned him and his brothers to stay away from her.

"Of course. Hi, Liz." He slid his legs sideways and she squeezed past.

Once Liz settled next to him, she turned to Timothy and said, "I hear Moonlight Square is a go."

"It is," Timothy said.

"I just found out." Michael frowned. "Why am I the last to get information?"

"Stephen called when he got the go ahead. I notified the signed tenants that they can finalize their move-in dates." She nodded to him. "Now that we have an occupancy date, I'll re-run the financial models."

"Yeah, good." Michael should be thinking of those things first. But it took so much energy.

While Liz and Timothy discussed the newly built strip mall he tuned them out, watching the crowd and the action on the field. That was another thing that had changed while he'd been gone. Liz wasn't Kate's assistant any more. She was now the leasing manager.

The company had gotten along fine without him. Probably better than when he'd stumbled around trying to figure out his place in the family dynasty.

His ginger ale arrived. Wonderful. Now everyone would wonder what he was drinking. As he set the cup in the holder, even his brother stared.

Liz glanced at him and ordered an iced tea.

"You don't have to abstain because of me," he whispered.

"It's a little early for alcohol."

Michael waved his hand at the group. "You're about the only one."

"I'm good." She clapped as the pitcher threw a strike. In a low voice, she said, "If you need to talk to anyone, you can ... talk to me. If you ... need a friend."

"Thanks," he said. With her reluctance, it hadn't sounded like she wanted to make the offer. "I appreciate that. Not many people know how to act around me right now."

"I get that. I've ... attended some co-dependency classes." She tipped her head. "I know how hard this can be."

"Thank you." Exhaustion stopped him from asking why she'd been at classes.

How could she understand what he was going through? To never have another drink? That was why they talked about one day at time. Forever was exhausting.

By giving up drinking, he'd lost contact with Sarah. He'd never told anyone why he drank. Never told them about Sarah.

He pretended to focus on the game but felt out of sync. He hadn't paid much attention to the Twins this season.

"Do you play sports?" Liz asked as the teams changed sides.

"Basketball. Football." Or he had. His therapist had told him to get physically active. He just didn't have much desire.

He did play pick-up b-ball games with the family. And he didn't do that very well. Everyone hated having him on their team. Or they had when he was drinking. Maybe that was a bright spot in being sober. He wouldn't be picked last anymore.

Liz had asked a question. He supposed he should reciprocate. "Do you play sports?"

"I wanted to dance, but farm life …" She paused. "I played basketball and ran cross country in high school and college."

Because she wanted to talk, he asked, "Do you still run?"

"Treadmill. Elliptical when I can." She smiled. "My neighborhood's not the best to run in, so I use the company gym a few times a week."

"Good. I'm glad people are using it."

He didn't ask the natural question—*Where do you live*? The noise of the game filled the silence between them. He'd depleted his daily conversation quota.

Timothy punched him in the shoulder. "You heard Mom's good news, right?"

"When did you hear?" Michael half-turned in his chair.

"Just now." When he leaned forward, Michael smelled the beer on his brother's breath. He inhaled the scent.

"Is your mother okay?" Liz asked.

She'd turned toward them, bringing their three faces way too close.

"All clear from the doc." Timothy pretended to wipe sweat from his brow.

"That's wonderful!" Liz's smile lit up her whole face.

"It's great," Michael agreed.

"I'm glad for your family and your mom." Liz broke eye contact. "Will she spend more time at the office now?"

"Don't know. Guess we'll find out on Sunday." Timothy clapped. "Double play. Go Twins!"

It went on like that. Short conversations during each inning. Timothy left, his brother, Stephen, took his seat.

Michael went up and chatted with his family and some of his staff. They'd seen him at the office enough that they didn't stare at him like he was dying.

But other employees avoided him like he had a fatal disease. Death by drunkenness. He went to the bathroom, and someone turned with a full beer in his hand and spilled it on his shirt.

"Fuck."

"Sorry. Sorry." The guy was half-lit.

Michael tried to wash out the spill, but the smell stuck with him. He couldn't wear this all day. He headed for a shirt concession and bought a jersey. In the bathroom he changed and shoved his beer soaked shirt into the bag, rolling it down so he wouldn't smell the appealing aroma of hops.

"You weren't wearing a jersey when you left," Liz said with a smile, a dimple at the corner of her mouth.

"Just my luck, an idiot spilled his beer on me."

Liz faced him. "Your luck's not too good today."

Stephen poked him in the back. "You're on the kiss-cam, man."

"What?" Michael asked.

He glanced over Liz's shoulder and their faces filled the video screen. The camera looked like it was eavesdropping on an intimate moment between him and Liz.

The MacBain section clapped and chanted, "Kiss, kiss, kiss."

He raised his eyebrows.

She shrugged.

This was stupid.

They leaned in.

Their lips met.

In the background applause broke out through the stadium.

He put his arms around her and tipped her lower, playing up the drama.

She laughed and tapped his back.

He pulled her up and set her back in her seat.

Her eyes flashed open and she looked up at the screen and laughed.

On the screen another couple in their sixties were on camera.

"I'm sorry," he mumbled. His fingers were tangled in her hair. Her clip was half off. "I'm really sorry."

She faced the field. "It's fine. Just part of the … game atmosphere."

She dug in her bag and retrieved a small brush. Then she pulled out her clip and ran the brush through her hair. Her fingers flew as she whipped her hair back into the claw.

Hair in place, she looked at him. Her apricot-flavored mouth creased into a smile.

"You two looked good up there." Stephen's knee nudged his back.

Michael ignored his brother and stared at the field as the players returned to the field. That was a mistake.

Pick up EDGE OF FRIENDSHIP now.

ABOUT THE AUTHOR

Best-selling author of the DESIGNER CHILDREN, THE MACBAINS, BIG SKY DREAMERS and FITZGERALD HOUSE series, Nan Dixon spent her formative years as an actress, singer, dancer and competitive golfer, but the need to eat had her studying accounting in college. Unfortunately, being a successful financial executive didn't feed her passion to perform. When the pharmaceutical company she worked for was purchased, Nan got the chance of a lifetime—the opportunity to pursue a writing career. She's a five-time Golden Heart[(R)] finalist and lives in the Midwest. She has five fabulous children, three wonderful son-in-laws, three granddaughters (one more on the way!), two grandsons and one neurotic cat.

Nan loves to hear from her readers so contact her through the following social media.

Printed in Great Britain
by Amazon

49798720R00192